Butterflies

by

Lynne Stone

2

Marie

The day had started full of promise; Marie had been expecting a long-awaited promotion. Breezing into her boss, Ben Grangers, office without knocking. Completely ignoring his secretary's attempt at stopping her. Thrown of guard she realised Ben was alone. Marie had wrongly thought the meeting was with all the directors of the company. Not just her immediate boss Ben, her friend and superior for ten years.

Ben had gestured for her to sit in the empty chair in front of him, Marie was suddenly unusually for her nervous, unsure of what was happening.

Ben cleared his throat and shuffled the papers on his untidy desk in front of him, looked up at her saying 'Thank you for coming in today, Marie, I am sure you know why you're here.'

'I've been waiting for this,' she paused 'it's all really exciting.'

Ben was momentarily bemused, but he went on, 'Exciting? I don't think there is anything about redundancy that could be called exciting.'

Marie sat in embarrassed silence, feeling her world tumbling around her. Certain, that she had misheard, Ben couldn't have said redundancy.

Redundancy was for secretaries and administrators not Account Executives like her.

Ben spoke first, 'I'm so sorry Marie, I assumed you were expecting redundancy along with the closure of your department.'

She hesitated and said slowly, 'Yes of course but I thought,' she faltered 'I thought I would be made a director and move into another department.

Ben looked embarrassed, 'I know that was what we originally discussed as the next step.' he paused and went on, ' but as you know too well, we have had two really bad years. These cuts are essential to keep the company afloat.'

Marie didn't speak, trying to make sense of what she was hearing,

Ben went on 'We or rather l, really appreciate all the hard work you have put in over the years. If I could find you another position I truly would. You do know that don't you Marie?'

Marie couldn't speak her face turned ashen under her spray tan and Ben seeing that she was struggling to hold back the tears went on, 'In view of your loyal service we have added six months' salary to your redundancy package, and you can keep your car for six months along with your gym membership.' With shaking hands, she took the envelope from him, without responding. She turned to leave, Ben said, 'Shall I come with you while you clear your desk, or would you prefer security?' Before she could answer, he added 'Marie I'm genuinely sorry that I have to do this, I should have realised you hadn't seen this day coming.'

Marie turned and straightening her back she said 'I know it's not personal, it's just a bit of a shock. I would rather it was you please, don't call security.' She could see the sympathy in his eyes, and instinctively she knew that it had been difficult for him to tell her she was finished today.

After all she had joined the company as a junior working her way up to where she was now. Accounts Executive, but times were tough, and cuts had to be made. Ben went down to her office where he closed the door behind them. Conscious of the tongues wagging in the outer office he watched as Marie sorted through her desk and put her few personal belongings into the box, which had been placed on her chair in readiness. She wished fervently that she had noticed it before she had gone upstairs for her meeting. Her office walls were bare apart from a photo of herself winning an award. Another of the award itself no family pictures, no pets just the one business memory. Ben took them down and placed them in the box and put his arm round her shoulder and said 'I'm sorry Marie; I wish you lots of luck and remember we are friends, aren't we? You've got my number ring me anytime. We must stay in touch.'

Marie nodded and still holding back the tears she said 'Can I go now? I will keep in touch for old time's sake, I'll speak soon,' she said unconvincingly.

Understanding how she felt Ben walked out in front of her, his presence in the general office ensured that all the remaining staff had their heads down, letting Marie leave without too much embarrassment.

Wordlessly she got into her car and drove off, reluctantly Ben watched her go, they had been a great team for ten years. He mentally resolved to stand by his promise to contact her in the near future and take her out for lunch.

Marie drove home in a daze, this couldn't be happening to her this was certainly becoming as she had predicted a day to remember, but for all the wrong reasons. As she pulled up outside her mews cottage, she switched off the engine. Sighing with relief and she finally let the tears flow. Tears held back only by her determination, not to let anyone see her cry. Slamming the car door, she walked slowly up the path. Looking down the street she

realised her front door was the only one not
displaying an extravagant Christmas wreath.
 Letting herself in she kicked of her heels and still
in her business suit grabbed a bottle of wine from
the wine cooler. Sighing with relief, she said a silent
prayer. Grateful that she had taken the time to have
her shopping, delivered by Waitrose. Now she
didn't need to leave her home until Christmas was
over. The fridge and wine cooler were full she
would draw the blinds until the festivities had
passed, all she wanted now was to be alone in her
misery.
Pouring herself a large glass of Chablis she sank
into her favourite armchair and went over the events
of the morning in her head.
   She had visualised it for months, Marie Halshaw
Director of Advertising at Jones- Macintosh.
Brushing aside the memory of when her name first
went on her office door, they got it wrong that time.
She winced as she remembered the sniggers in the
office when she had screamed at her then manager
because the sign writers had put her full name on
the door.
'Marion Halshaw I'm not. Marie I am. I don't
answer to Marion.' she had yelled.
 He had merely commented as he walked away 'it's
the name on your contract and your pay slips, I

don't hear you complaining about that do I?' She had vowed that wouldn't happen again, she had been determined to oversee the sign writers this time. But it wasn't to be.

As she drank her way down the bottle her situation hit her hard, how had it come to this? No job, no friends, huge mortgage, everything seemed bleak and for now she couldn't see a way forward.

Christmas went by unnoticed cards remained on the doormat unopened. Marie unplugged her landline, switched off her mobile and stayed in her pyjamas almost until New year. Eating very little but drinking every last drop of alcohol she had to hand just laying on her bed. She was completely unaware of anything else going on in the world. Just wallowing in her own misery. Scared of facing anything outside her front door. A big part of it fear of her neighbours realising she was unemployed, oh the shame of it.

Reality came in the shape of her eighty-year-old mother ringing at the doorbell for twenty minutes. For two weeks, Violet Branning had tried phoning, to no avail. She wasn't going to be ignored any longer, she would ring at the doorbell until Marie answered.

'Oh, it's you Mother.' Marie had said as she peered round the door.

'Don't just stand there, Marion let me in its cold out here,' demanded Violet.

'It's Marie and now is not a good time,' Marie moaned.

Violet pulled herself up to her full five foot and pushed passed Marie and walked into the kitchen and proceeded to make a cup of coffee. Marie pushed the mug away 'I don't want it.'

'Drink it, it looks like you've drunk everything else around here.'

Marie looked around her and felt ashamed there were so many empty bottles, what had she been thinking? She drank her coffee while her mother bustled around clearing up the mess.

'I'm not stopping, I just popped in to make sure you were still alive and talk some sense into you.'

'How did you know I was here?' asked Marie.

'When I didn't hear from you for two weeks, I phoned your office than Ben said you were no longer working there. What went wrong? What are you going to do? Talk to me, tell me what happened?' Violet asked.

Marie sat down at the small kitchen table cuddling her coffee mug, sighing deeply looked at her mother and spoke. 'So many questions Mother. Being made redundant was the last thing I was expecting. Sadly, I'm only just realising that it was my whole life all I did was work. How bad is that I have no idea what I'm going to do now? I've forgotten how to have fun. I'm finished I won't ever get another job at my age.

'Of course, you won't if you stick with that attitude, for goodness' sake stop feeling sorry for yourself. Fifty-eight is no age at all these days, you'll just have to look a bit harder for an opportunity that's all.' Violet stopped to draw breath and went on, 'shame you didn't hang on to that husband of yours, you wouldn't have to work at all now.'

She turned to face Marie who was staring at her mother completely aghast. Her mother wasn't giving up and went on, 'what about friends? Weren't you chummy with that office manager of yours, you know that Betty.'

'No mother she was just a work colleague not my type at all.'

'I'm off now, things to do I only came round to make sure you were alive so be a good girl and switch your phones on and do what you do best.'

'Exactly what do you mean?' asked Marie who was reeling from her mother's caustic comments.

'Plan Marion PLAN.' Said Violet firmly as she swept out of the kitchen. Marie shut the door behind her mother and shuddered as she caught sight of her reflection in the ornate mirror by the front door, a mirror that had cost her almost a week's salary, bought on a whim, at a time when money had been no object. A time when her future had been mapped out in front of her.

Now she stood and looked at herself for the first time since that day. Her hair was lank around her sallow face. Gone was the lustrous hair and clear skin. That was enough for Marie, her reflection shocked and frightened her, she looked sixty-eight not fifty-eight and if the truth were known she had always lied about her age and had always prided herself she could get away with forty-five. The worst thought was that at eighty her mother looked amazing, and her visit had shaken her.

With her mother's words ringing in her ears Marie realised it was time to get back in to shape and she would start by going for her usual early morning swim- tomorrow. After all she still had her gym membership which wasn't due to finish for another six months, it made sense to use it while she didn't have to pay for it.

Betty

Betty sat on the bench in her garden drinking a coffee, a plate of biscuits by her side. Braving the cold to stay out of Derek's way. Sitting huddled in a heavy coat she sighed as her phone rang. Pulling it out of her pocket she answered, not recognising the number. 'Hello Betty speaking.' she said tentatively.
'Oh, Betty its Junie from Jones Macintosh,'
'Nice to hear from you how's it going, you still there?'
'Yes just, guess who got the five o'clock walk before Christmas?' asked Junie.
Betty sighed she was not in the mood to care today, 'Who now?'
'That stuck up Marie Halshaw!'
At this Betty spirits lifted, 'Oh that's a surprise wonder what she thought about that?'
'Well, she didn't look happy when Ben Grainger walked her out.'
Betty quickly finished the conversation and picking up her mug and untouched biscuits went into the bungalow.
'Derek, I'm not feeling so good today, how about you do the shopping for a change?'
Derek was sat in front of the TV, his usual place these days. She thought he might help out for once, as he no longer had a job to go to.

He merely grunted, 'I am too busy.' And turned
away to watch yet another episode of Jeremy Kyle.'
'What about this afternoon then?' asked Betty?
'No going to the Dolphin.'

 Trying to ignore the hurt she felt at his attitude she
dragged a comb through her greying hair. Still
wearing the same tight grubby tracksuit that she had
worn for the past week she picked up her car keys
and shut the door. All the while resenting Derek's
worsening attitude toward her. Through the door
she could still hear the television. It was one of
those shows that even shut in another room you
could hear the misery and feel the pain.

 Once in her car she reversed put of the drive and
tried to give herself a talking to, after all she had
taken early retirement voluntarily from Jones
Macintosh. Derek hadn't dissuaded her from giving
up. Her intentions had been to help him in his
business and then sell it to fund their retirement and
travel.

 Things had not gone to plan, the business failed
only six months later. Betty was angry because
Derek had encouraged her to give up her precious
job. Knowing all the time that his business was in
trouble. Plus, he hadn't taken the time to warn her
how difficult things were.

14

It was finding themselves both without employment in the same year that was the end really, but they were both too apathetic to realise it.

Dull Derek retreated into a couch potato and Betty was lost. She tried all sorts of hobbies all of which she was good at, but really all she really wanted was to feel needed. A purpose to get up in the morning. It was at this time being childless and consequently having no grandchildren seemed a lot more difficult to cope with than she had ever imagined. Some days when she was feeling down, just to get out of the house, she would sit in the park watching grandparents and parents with their precious charges.

She started going to bed early and getting up late to try and shorten the days her positive attitude was becoming ever more negative. If she had seen the problems early retirement was to bring, she may have been able to plan. She hadn't foreseen anything; she simply did what she could to help. Now she was quite frankly lacking any motivation. It was tough knowing she had been a fair office manager. With secretarial skills beyond compare, how do you put that on a CV? She was fifty-nine last birthday, with the big six O looming and not only felt unemployable but seemed to have nothing in common with Derek anymore. Betty spent many long hours wondering how they had drifted so far apart. What happened to their sex life? These were all questions that fluttered through Betty's head on an almost daily basis. She pretended that she was happy with Derek sleeping in the spare room but then he stopped visiting her occasionally for sex. It was almost too depressing to think about. So just like everything else in her life she put off sorting it out until another day.

Betty knew he was devastated when his business went into receivership, only a few months after she was made redundant. They were lucky because they had no children, plus there was no longer a mortgage. Fortunately, she had been careful with money and used some of the savings she had carefully put away over the years to fund her retirement. This way they had paid off Derek's creditors. However, she had been astute enough to stash her retirement money away in a separate account for the future. Which Derek was unaware of. Running away money, she called it.

As she parked her car, she spotted a woman struggling to hold a crying baby and trying to pack her shopping into the boot at the same time.

'Here let me help you,' she said.

'Thank you. Here take her she is really grumpy this morning. I think she's fed up being out with granny.

I was going to take her to see Father Christmas today, but she won't stop crying,'
Betty awkwardly took the little girl, who immediately stopped crying and beamed at her.
'You have a way with children; she won't smile for me.
'I love children, but I'm not lucky enough to be a grandmother, unfortunately I wasn't able to have any children,' said Betty ruefully as she handed the child back. The woman smiled sympathetically and thanked Betty as she strapped the baby into the car seat.

As she walked to the supermarket entrance all could think about was the cuddly little girl she had just held. It was moments like this that brought to the fore the longing for a child of her own. How different her life might have been now.

It was as she was doing her reluctant weekly shop that she spotted Marie walking around the place dressed as if she were running the store. Really? Why wear a business suit shopping for bargains? It was at this moment she remembered what a good businesswoman Marie was and how she must be hurting at this moment. Betty did her best to avoid her, but Marie decided to treat herself to coffee, Betty was in front of her in the queue. Betty took

her coffee and sat down praying she hadn't been
seen.

'Betty, hope you don't mind if I join you?' Marie
asked as she stood in front of Betty.

Betty hesitated before she answered her feeling of
dislike was overshadowed by curiosity but worst of
all she knew she didn't look great; she tried to hide
the stains on her old tracksuit.

She looked hard at Marie and wondered could this
woman offer her anything? She had become
increasingly disappointed in life over the past fcw
weeks. It seemed no-one wanted to employ her. She
was just a washed-up almost pensioner with a
lifetime of dull Derek to look forward to. It was not
what she had expected or wanted, but right now she
had no direction in her life. Taking a deep breath
Betty reluctantly said, 'Of course sit down.'

Marie cleared her throat and said, 'How nice to see a
friendly face, what are you doing these days.'

'I'm retired Marion' she hesitated and went on 'I
hear you got made redundant,' she said bitchily.

'Betty its Marie you know I don't answer to
Marion.' Marie answered acidly.

'Sorry you were Marion when I first employed you.'

'Yes, I know that but that was twenty years ago you
know I only answer to Marie.'

Realising that the conversation had got off to a bad start Betty stood up and said, 'Sorry I have to be somewhere,' leaving Marie sitting with a cup of coffee in front of her, wondering what on earth she had said or done to upset Betty.

Betty drifted on but she was finding it was more and more difficult to get out of the house every day. Then one morning as she walked naked to the shower instead of avoiding the mirror in the hall, she looked at herself. She was horrified all she could see was white flab. This kick started her to go swimming. She went that day and joined the local health centre resolving to go every day for a couple of months. She didn't realise how much she would enjoy it. She began to feel more relaxed finding she could almost cope with Dull Derek and his inane chatter. But ultimately it was not enough to make her feel as fulfilled as she had been when working full time.

Chrissie

Chrissie woke up feeling her age, she was going to be sixty in a few weeks and reluctantly she had to admit she felt every minute of fifty-nine. Surely it was only five minutes ago that she had met Zack at the Isle of Wight Festival. Sadly, it was forty years ago. The world had moved on since then, but Zack was still touring with his band and not around much. While she was sitting alone waiting for his call. Still dressing as she had in her hippy days with wild curly blonde hair often tied back with a ribbon. Her maudlin thoughts were interrupted by her phone ringing. Picking it up she heard his familiar voice 'Hi, Chrissie, it's me I'm flying in this afternoon I should be with you at about three o'clock.'

'Good to hear from you will you be here for long?' Chrissie asked with her fingers crossed hoping this would be the Christmas that she wouldn't have to spend alone.

'Just flying visit, see you later.'

Chrissie switched off her phone her spirits now lifted by the sound of his voice. Quickly tidying away her latest project. Chrissie dragged a comb through her mass of wayward curly hair.

It was only a couple of hours later that Zack was dropped off by his chauffeur and Chrissie fell gratefully into his arms.

Later that day Chrissie carefully rolled a joint, lit it taking a drag before passing it to Zack, lying beside her on the sofa he took it from her and sighed.

'Hey that's a big sigh, that's not like you, what's up had a bad tour?'

'Nothing really Chrissie, it's just tough at my age being on the road all the time, I'm tired but I love to be here with you, this is my real world. It would be good to have had Xmas here but I've to be off again tomorrow. We are back on the road again in a couple of days.'

'It's only Christmas I'm used to being on my own, anyway you spend more than three days here and you get bored.'

'I know Chrissie you are my bit of sanity besides I was hoping to see our daughter I've got her a Xmas present. Is she coming home?'

'No, Summer is loving India and won't be back until next year sometime. I have spoken to her to keep up to date with her life.'

'Shame I'll ring her and have a chat, I did think she would enjoy India, you must miss her though.'

'I do Zack, it would have been good if she had settled down and got married near here.'

Zack laughed, 'You never settled down so she's just following your lead.'

Chrissie grinned and walked over to the window and gazed out at her garden, which was a constant source of joy to her. This time of year, the lawn was littered with falling leaves, bare trees. No sign of the honeysuckle after which the cottage was named.

Turning to Zack she sat down on the chintzy sofa beside him and asked. 'Do you think we should have done things differently?'

Zack looked at Chrissie and said, 'Truthfully I think we should have got married when we first met, but you turned me down every time.'

'I could never have coped with you always on the road all the time.' If she was honest with herself, she would have loved to be married, in a solid relationship. Zack had given her financial security but without the vodka and the pot there was very little point to her life.

'I should have married you forty years ago.'

'God forbid Zack how boring that would have been.' Chrissie passed the joint to Zack

'This is good. I have been all over the world and this stuff grown in your greenhouse is just the best. I don't know how you get away with it round here' he said.

'Same way as I get away with you staying here no-one knows anything about me or that I even know you.'

'I don't care that you are famous, you have always looked after us all be it from afar. The arrangement always worked. I suppose I just got used to being here on my own.

'I just think we may have got it wrong.'

'Zack you are freaking me out, what's with this conversation?'

'Chrissie doesn't it worry you that we are both going to be sixty this year?'

'No, it doesn't. I still feel and act twenty and you're still rocking so what more could we ask for?'

'It's tough being a bloke at sixty.'

'There's always Viagra.'

'I don't need Viagra when I am with you.'

'I'm flattered but I know you still go out with younger women' Chrissie sniggered as he winced.

'It's just part of being a famous rock god, it's all show you know that.'

Chrissie threw a cushion at him and said, 'I have my admirers too you know.'

If only he knew she didn't go out with anyone. In fact, when was the last time? Chrissie couldn't remember a quick vision of Paolo in Sardinia flashed through her mind but that was ten years ago.

It hadn't hurt to let Zack think she wasn't sitting at
home waiting for him.

'Charming' he laughed and went on 'The first time I
saw you, you were stripped naked running into the
sea, your hair down to your waist, with flowers in
your hair.'

 Chrissie laughed, 'Oh the Isle of Wight Festival
that was fun –there's a bit more of me these days,
but you you're still thin.'

 'Take your clothes off let me look at your lovely
body,' said Zack.

 Chrissie stood up slowly and dropped her long
floral skirt to the floor revealing a sensible pair of
white cotton knickers. Zack laughed 'The only
woman I have ever met who wears big pants.'
Chrissie turned and tried to run to the bedroom, but
Zack caught her hand, 'No Chrissie here in front of
the fire'

 A few minutes later it was obvious that Zack
wasn't able to rise to the occasion, Chrissie sat up
and looked down at him.

'I'm sorry Chrissie, that's never happened to me
before. I must be feeling more tired than I thought.'
said Zack rolling away from her and pulling on his
jeans he said, 'It will be fine I just need some sleep.'

'Don't worry I don't think the floor was a good idea anyway I don't think I can get up off this floor, my bones are really aching,' said Chrissie.

Zack leapt to his feet and pulled Chrissie to her feet, grabbing a daisy from the vase he tucked it gently behind her ear. Then laughed and said, 'you may have aching bones, but you are still my beautiful Chrissie why can't I come here and live with you permanently?'

'Don't beg Zack you know I love you, but our lives are poles apart I live in your cottage, in a very small, minded village and you travel the world, and everyone knows you wherever you go. When you come here, we can't even leave the cottage or you would be mobbed and my life would change. Neither of us want that why can't we leave things as they have been for the last forty years?'

'I don't know Chrissie I think it's the idea of being sixty this year and having so much money but no roots. You and Summer are the only stable thing in my life.

'Believe me Zack I couldn't live with you full time, it's perfect as it is. You come here and hide three or four times a year. Besides what would the neighbours think if they found out I have been the mistress of an old rocker like you all these years.'

'Do you really care about the neighbours?'
'No, I don't, I hardly ever see anyone. I think I'm
known as the mad hippy.'
 Zack laughed, 'Have we any food for supper?'
Chrissie wandered through to the kitchen and
opened the fridge door.
'Vodka?'
'Thanks yes.'
'Don't you have any food to wash it down with?'
'You turn up unannounced and you want feeding?'
'But you must eat sometimes?'
'Sure, I eat but food is not important to me, I'm
usually so busy I forget to eat.'
Zack went into the kitchen and opened the fridge
door and roared with laughter all there was inside,
one egg, some out of date yoghourt and a lump of
mouldy cheese.
'Why don't you order your shopping online?'
'I can't its's such a hassle I hate computers.'
'I bought you that state of the art computer, don't
you use it?'
'No, it's far too complicated.' answered Chrissie.
 Zack sighed, 'It will have to be Pizza then shall I
order it?'
'No, I can do it.'
 'Bet they would come quicker for me than you.'
'No remember you're not here Zack.'

Chrissie turned her back, made the call and sat down and poured another drink.

'Steady on girl that's a lot of vodka in a short space of time don't forget I'm the wild rocker not you.'

'Zack you're my part time lover, if you want to stay tonight then stop counting how many drinks I'm having.'

'I'm only thinking of you Chrissie.'

'Yeah, but you're the one feeling his age not me.'

'True here's the money for the pizza I'm going for a shower.'

Zack threw a bundle of notes and Chrissie grinned as she picked them up. Zack poked his head back round the door and said, 'You had better put some clothes on before you open the door.'

He was gone before the cushion Chrissie threw reached the door.

Zack was quiet after the pizza and even declined another drink,

Before they went up to bed, he asked Chrissie if she would let him sleep till lunchtime. Then give him a lift to the airport.

'I'm sorry Zack, if you need a lift to the airport it will have to be in the morning. Not the afternoon.'

'Oh, come on Chrissie I don't need to leave until 3pm. The rest of the band won't be there till midnight.'

'What sort of flight leaves after midnight?' asked
Chrissie.
'Don't wind me up we go on a private jet; we don't
go cattle class.'
'Scuse me Mr Famous you had better get a car to
pick you up. I'm not a bloody chauffeur.'
'Chrissie please, in fact come with me for a change.
We're only on tour for six weeks this time it could
be fun.'
'Precisely how do you expect to explain me away?'
'I'll think of something.'
'No Zack, sort it out for yourself I have stuff to do.'
'What stuff?'
'Well tomorrow afternoon I am going to the WI.'
'WI you're having a laugh, aren't you?
'It's not what you think.'
Zack laughed and she went on 'You simply forget
I'm a person I have a life. To you I'm just five
times a year shag.'
'Is it money you want?'
'No Zack it is not about money. You've always
looked after me it's about respect.'
'I do respect you Chrissie. Christ I love you I want
to be with you.'
'No, we leave it as it is, or we leave it? It's up to
you Zack.'

'No choice then. We leave it as it is. We could grow old together Chrissie; I could give up touring and you could move into my little pile in Surrey.'
'Absolutely not as I said my life is here. Just because you are having a late life crisis I won't change my mind. Your infrequent visits have had to be enough for me, for so many years. Now that's all you get, take it or leave it.'
'You've become a tough cookie Chrissie, what are you doing that you won't leave here?'
'Don't laugh at me Zack but I have been to college, I now have diplomas in Reiki and massage. I'm also into Tarot cards. I want to give talks to pass on my knowledge.'
Zack stifled a laugh as he looked at Chrissies serious face' 'What happened to the garden room I had built for my music studio? You turned it into a pottery studio? Now not used for anything.'
Chrissie blanched, 'I may use that for a beauty studio.'
 'Until you get bored with that,'he hesitated.
'Come on tour we can use you there, I'll pay you oodles to massage me every day.'
'You don't understand, do you? I want to do this by myself. I'm going to the WI I'm thinking of starting a business and l need somewhere to promote it.'

Zack looked at her and roared with laughter 'What a daft idea.

Looking at her crestfallen face he realised he had gone one step too far.

The next morning, they were barely speaking and Chrissie got up early and was standing in the kitchen drinking coffee when Zack loped in and helped himself to a cup.

Chrissie looked pointedly at her watch and said 'Right now I need to go, and I have to use the car today so can I drop you somewhere? Anywhere except the airport of course I won't drive that far anymore.'

'Yeah, sure drop me in the next town outside the bus garage I'll get a limo to pick me up.'

'Great be ready in ten.' Said Chrissie firmly.

'We are alright aren't we Chrissie babe?'

'Course we are Zack. Course we are.

Marie

It took Marie some weeks before she began to function normally. Today she sat looking at the bills in front of her. It had been extremely difficult not having a purpose to the day. Losing the job she had loved, had upset her deeply and she had spent too much time brooding on the past. Now it was time to let it go and move on. Not that she had had any luck with job hunting, just one interview, which had led to nothing. Hence the urgent evaluation of her finances. She had never been careful with money. Meaning that she still had a large mortgage on her luxury mews house and credit cards which should have been paid off years ago.

Then there was the worry that she needed to buy a car as the company car was due to be collected in three months. Plus, her expensive membership of the health club would also need renewing in June. She had to find a way. Signing on was not an option, she would not queue up with a load of down and outs or the great unwashed.

Marie had learnt one thing in the last few weeks and that was she was lonely. Up until now she hadn't needed anyone. She had spent too many hours wondering what it would be like to hear the phone ring and it be anyone else but her mother. Her career had taken over her life, what few friends

she once had, disappeared, only through her neglect.
She had to get back on track and part of that was
going swimming or to the gym early in the morning,
like she used to while she was working to give her a
purpose to her day.

In the sauna one morning a few days later, Marie
was half listening to the conversations going on
around her, her ears pricked up as an older
gentleman she knew only as John said, 'If I could
only find someone to come in and sort out the office
for me, I would be okay, I'm so sick of temps. They
come in late then won't do a stroke until they've
had breakfast. Then they disappear to the ladies, put
on full make up and chat on my phone until
lunchtime. It really is so frustrating'.

Marie kept quiet but her brain was buzzing, this
was an opportunity that she really had to pursue.
What a shame that she had been on nodding terms
with this man for several years. Never taken the
time to get to know him. She showered and dressed
and walked determinedly out to the busy coffee
shop. It didn't take her long to spot John, taking a
deep breath, she asked, 'Do you mind if I join you,
John?'

He gestured for her to sit down and over coffee and
croissants Marie slowly got into a proper
conversation with him.

It turned out that John owned a successful clothing factory. His wife had been keeping the office under control. Unfortunately, on a recent holiday she had fallen and broken her ankle. Now was reluctant to return to work having discovered the delights of getting up late and visiting the grandchildren. John had persuaded her to come back part time, she had agreed but only if the office was sorted out and re-organised before her return.

Marie set out her stall to John and offered her services, John was suitably impressed and took her on immediately. She took the job, spent two weeks filing, paying invoices and completely re-organising all the systems in the busy office. John Mason paid her handsomely and she saved the money. It was during this time she realised that life hadn't been so enjoyable for a very long time, not only that now she had someone to chat to at the Health Club. It had only taken ten years. She had to admit to herself that she was sorry when John's wife was fit enough to come back to work.

One morning a week later, this time in the Jacuzzi, John said 'Marie, how do you feel about helping out a friend of mine for a week or two? It's just answering the telephone and manning the reception desk. Nothing too onerous, Bill like me has an aversion to temps and his right-hand lady has got family problems and is taking extended leave. I told him about you and how you helped me out. He asked if I could give him your phone number. I hope you don't mind?'

'No not at all thank you, by all means give him my number.' Answered Marie happily.

 This went on for the next month- one job led to another and one Monday morning Marie looked in her diary and she was double booked for the following week, she needed help, her brain started to tick over and a plan began to form, she needed someone reliable and quickly to help her. Then it hit her, this could be the beginning of something good.

 Only last week Marie had been at the health club and had seen Betty Parker, she had shuddered as Betty l had wobbled towards her, it was that moment that she knew she had to put all personal feelings behind her and befriend her. Like it or not she was going to need someone with Betty's skills to help her form her Plan. Betty had been her office manager at the Agency. Marie had never tried to get on with her, mainly because she knew Betty disliked her.

 Feelings apart Marie knew she was very good at her job. However, she was shrewd enough to know that she had to put her these thoughts behind her. As she could see she was going to need reliable help in the future.

First, she had to go to the supermarket and shop then she would plot the way forward at the very smart coffee shop in the precinct.

As she drove the plan began to form in her mind, Marie pulled into the supermarket car park, her heart lighter than it had felt for a long time. Parked her car, walking in Marie knew she needed to swallow her pride if she wanted Betty to work with her. With ideas buzzing round her head, she went into the supermarket. Under normal circumstances Marie would never have shopped in this particular supermarket but needs must. As she collected her trolley, she rather hoped she would bump into Betty again, she did her weekly shop but of Betty there was no sign.

Betty

One day Betty was relaxing in the Jacuzzi when
Marie walked past. Betty had wanted to hide but
there was no way of avoiding her. When Marie got
in beside her she said, 'Marie how nice to see you
again I didn't know you came here?' Betty said
careful not to upset her again.

Marie looked at her and said, 'I've been coming
here for years I normally just use the gym or do and
exercise class, but today I fancied a swim.'

'I'm new to this, to be honest I find life a bit boring
now I'm retire,' answered Betty. 'What are you
doing with yourself these days?'

It was at this precise moment that Betty regretted
being rude to Marie the last time they met.

Marie thought for a moment and seizing the
opportunity replied. 'Well, I'm thinking of opening
my own employment agency. An agency with a
difference.'

Betty just looked at her for a moment and quickly
dismissed the wicked thoughts that were buzzing
through her brain. She knew Marie was capable, but
she would certainly be needing help.

With that Marie glanced up at the clock which said
nine o'clock and she almost leapt out of the Jacuzzi
saying, 'Betty, I really have to dash, I've an
appointment at ten o'clock but before I go, I need to

talk to you, I have an idea brewing, you might be interested in, can we meet sometime this week?' There it was the hook, Betty looked her directly in the eye and said, 'I am a bit busy Marie, at a push could fit you in on Thursday,' she answered despite knowing that every day was free.

'Fine' she said 'Meet me at eleven in the coffee shop on the High St.'

With that she waltzed off leaving Betty pondering over what to buy for dinner, still not really thinking her future lay with Marie Halshaw, Betty was left soaking in the bubbles thinking about the past. Maybe she hadn't liked her, but she had to admit Marie had done really well at the agency. Betty had been surprised when Marie was promoted to Accounts Manager but to be honest her hard work had kept everyone employed. When Betty took early retirement, she had a feeling that redundancies were looming in the future.

But she had always known that she didn't really like her. This meeting got to Betty and as she got dressed the reality hit her. She was jealous of Marion or bloody Marie as she called herself these days. Jealous of her because she lived alone and was known to be a workaholic.

Always expensively dressed and made up. Despite this Betty was pretty sure she didn't have much of a social life and never had she spoken of a man sharing her home. There it was she didn't have a Derek to go home to every night she had her own space. This made Betty envious especially now. Somehow, she had a strong feeling that knew she hadn't seen the last of Marie Halshaw and the possible opportunity she might offer.

Marie

Marie was tapping her pencil on the table, her cappuccino beside her getting cold. Not quite as cold as the dreadful March wind outside. Betty strolled nonchalantly up to the counter as if she hadn't a care in the world. She ordered a coffee and because she suspected it would irritate Marie, a doughnut to go with it. As she sat down Marie pointedly looked at her watch, 'I did say eleven Betty it's now nearly half past.'

Betty smirked 'Sorry I thought I was early.'

Marie sighed inwardly and bit her tongue, not wanting to get off on the wrong foot again, knowing how difficult Betty could be if she was so inclined. 'Never mind, can I just talk you through my ideas first and then we can if you are interested discuss where you could fit in.'

Marie picked up her briefcase and took out her carefully prepared story boards, all the while trying not to watch Betty eating her doughnut. She flinched as a splodge of jam just missed one of her boards. Betty blushed; Marie was annoyed that she was behaving so childishly while she was trying to do her small presentation. Betty moved her plate across to the next table and Marie continued. 'The idea for this came to me over a period of time, I went to help a local business sort out the office and

accounts while the office manager went in to
hospital for a few weeks.

Strangely enough I really enjoyed doing it. This job
led to another and another. I am now in the position
that in the next few weeks I'm double booked, with
enquiries are coming in all the time. I need help and
you are the best qualified person I know to help me.'

Betty hesitated before she spoke trying not to grin
at Marie's very formal speech, knowing full well
that Marie had struggled to admit she actually
needed anyone let alone her Betty.

'What you are saying is, you are going to open a
temp agency?' asked Betty.

'Well originally yes but over the last few weeks I
have spoken to a lot of people who want help in all
sorts of areas. There are a lot of skilled people who
would welcome a few hours or more employment a
week doing something they love.'

'What exactly are you selling?' asked Betty.

Marie put the first board in front of Betty, 'I think
this sums up what I am trying to do.'

'Marie and Me the specialist agency for all those
jobs you never get round to,' read Betty 'It's a
beautiful board Marie but it doesn't tell me what
skills you are offering.'

Marie placed the second board in front of her 'I
think this sums up what I am trying to do.

'Marie and Me a one-off shop, tap into the skills of the most highly trained and experienced people in a wide range of fields and offering them one off projects and part time work to suit.' read out Betty. Looking at Marie she replied without hesitation, 'I think your idea is brilliant but not quite different enough, and I don't like the name.'

Marie visibly bristled and asked, 'How do you mean not different enough?'

'Well one thing I've noticed since I've not been working is how many artistic and creative people there are around who have so much to offer.'

'I'm not sure what you mean?'

'I joined the WI. at first it was to get out of the house, but I'm amazed at the women who go there, a mix of very creative and talented people. They make cakes design gardens, redecorate, there are beauticians, card makers, dressmakers and curtain makers. You remember Chrissie Matthews? she was at school with us she's giving a talk on Reiki and its benefits soon. I could go on, but you do see what I am saying don't you?'

Marie went quiet, 'Yes, yes, I think I do. We could be a one stop place to get help with that task that you can't get round to or can't do. The possibilities are endless. Now you have really got me thinking.'

She turned one of the boards over and started to list all the skills that Betty had outlined, then she said, 'There's always ironing, dog walking, catering for dinner parties, oh and wedding stationery and even scrapbooking.'

Betty looked at Marie and said, 'are you trying to tell me that anyone will pay to have someone else put photographs in an album?'

Marie looked sheepish 'That's exactly what I'm saying. Most people have drawer full of memories that they can't throw away but never get around to sorting; or the memoirs that they never get around to writing and typing.

Imagine being able to pay someone, who is professional to do that job you have never got around too' she hesitated and laughed 'I actually paid someone to do a photo scrapbook for me, for my mother's eightieth birthday. What do you think Betty do you think we could work together? Would you be interested?'

Betty thought she had never really liked her, but she had been a great employee. Had Marie ever had a day off sick? Not that she could remember. Marie had lived for that company. Always first to arrive and last to leave. But she took everything far too seriously.

Slowly she said, 'Yes Marie I think we can.'

'Well, if you are interested, I already have a client who needs someone to sort his office out. Bill Hargreaves has a small building company. Apparently, his wife has just had a baby and can't cope with the job at the moment. It's only two days a week. If you are interested in the business, we can spend some time working out the advertising. Then a priority must be to find some willing hands to fill the jobs which I feel sure are going to come in soon. How would you feel about joining me?'

'Marie, I have to admit I do need to do something I think we could make it work.'

'I have to dash now but can we meet up tomorrow and go through things in more detail, I want to do this properly and will give us both time to think?' said Marie standing up.

Okay so it was only a small white lie, she had thought about opening an employment agency with a twist. Just hadn't formalised the plan to the extent that it now appeared to be growing thanks to Betty's input.

Marie didn't like Betty very much probably because she was one of the most popular women in the office. With her business head on Marie knew that Betty would do any job with the best of her ability, so when Bill Hargreaves had phoned needing help to organise his office. He ran a

building firm, but his wife had a very fractious baby
and needed to take time off, leaving the office in a
mess.

Marie immediately thought of Betty. Knowing she
would be perfect for the job, remembering how
desperate Betty had always been for money,
constantly bailing out her husband and trying to
keep her home life together.

Little did Marie know that Betty had her own
agenda and that was to live life to the full and travel
and if the truth were known it would not be with her
husband.

Shame she had let herself go though, thought
Marie, fancy going to a coffee shop in too tight
polyester trousers and then stuffing her face with a
jam doughnut. Marie shuddered, she never ate in
public unless she was out to dinner and then she ate
like a rabbit. It was all about self-control.
Marie considered anyone over a size ten to be obese
and out of control and she herself never went
anywhere without full make-up. Even her mother
never left the house without lipstick. At fifty-nine it
was a struggle but after all everything was about
appearances.
The new business was born over a cup of coffee and
a doughnut.

Marie

Marie listened to Bill Hargreaves with growing
excitement. He was praising Betty Parker to the hilt
he was over the moon with Betty's input.
What a stroke of luck it had been bumping into her
in the supermarket. On the very day the plan had
begun to form in her brain.

Something about what Betty had said in the coffee
bar, kept niggling at Marie. Even though work was
trickling in. Marie was working intermittently, and
Betty had spent two weeks sorting out the building
office. However, she was unsure what her next
move should be. Conscious that it was advice she
needed, about the ideas they had been discussing,
Marie had asked Betty about the WI, but she had
seemed strangely reluctant to take Marie along.

Marie turned to her mother who was probably the
only other person she knew well enough to ask.
Marie invited Violet over for Sunday lunch. Which
was extremely unusual, as Marie did not generally
cook on Sunday or any other day of the week. Over
lunch Marie spoke to her.
'Mother, you go to the WI and Church social clubs,
don't you?' asked Marie.
'Yes, Marion you know I do,'
'Could I perhaps come with you?' asked Marie
ignoring her mother's use of her hated real name.

Slight pause as Violet hurriedly gathered her thoughts.

'Marion are you alright dear, you've always scoffed at my social life before what's happened to you?' Violet asked almost laughing.

Marie was a little taken aback by her mother's reaction but ploughed on regardless.

'I do have a reason I need to talk to women and find out what skills they have. Skills that they take for granted hobbies that someone else would willingly pay for. Then promote and sell them on.'

'What on earth for.' asked Violet?

'I had this idea about an agency. A one stop place to get help with some annoying tasks that you just can't get round too. I've contacts for more office work. But what about someone who can make the curtains? Alter that dress? Maybe someone who is willing to do the ironing or babysit or walk the dog. If you have loads of photographs someone who would put them in the scrap book for you.' Marie answered feeling slightly guilty for almost repeating word for word the new presentation that she had put together after her initial meeting with Betty. Marie hesitated, waiting for mother's reaction. If she were really honest, she was seeking her approval and support

Violet didn't answer immediately and looked thoughtfully at her daughter.

'Well, I think the idea is different but worth a go. I certainly think the WI could be useful. Let me think, I know we have cake makers. I have just ordered a year's worth of birthday and Christmas cards from Jenny; you remember her, you went to school to the same school, her husband died not so long ago. Dropped dead in the street. She makes beautiful cards'

'Do you mean Jenny Moore? I haven't seen her in twenty years.' Answered Marie.

'Seems to me you have missed a lot working at that place all that time, you should have made time for friends.'

'Don't lecture me Mother I do know, so do you think it is worth me coming along then?

'Do you want to just come along or have you something else in mind?' asked Violet knowing her daughter would have more than one plan ready.

'I rather thought I could give a short presentation and then talk to the members' afterwards.' said Marie. 'What do you think?'

'I think I can organise that, probably next week. Just keep it short and please no Death by PowerPoint. That hippie Chrissie Mathews will be giving a talk that day.' Said Violet checking in her diary.

Marie laughed 'No problem and thanks Mum'.
'Mum? you never call me Mum Marion?'
'No, I know but then you never call me Marie, I just
felt flippant for a moment, and it's been good to talk
over my idea with someone, it's been whirring
around my head for a couple of weeks now.'
 Marie went through to her kitchen and began to
load her dishwasher, while her mother used the
cloakroom. She found herself humming as she
wiped over the marble surfaces.
'I will speak to the WI next week and let you know.
Meanwhile you get some little cards printed ready
to hand out. I must dash darling thanks for lunch but
I'm playing bridge tonight and at my age I need a
nap before I go out.'
Marie sighed as she shut the door behind her
mother,
 Maybe Betty was going to be a bigger asset than
she had originally realised, she needed to have a
chat with her soon. Marie picked up the phone no
time like the present.
'Hi Betty, its Marie,'
'Hi Marie, hope you are not phoning to say Bill
Hargreaves isn't happy with the job I'm doing.'
'No Betty quite the opposite he is raving about you,
he has recommended you to several of his friends
two who have already responded, I just wondered if

we could meet for lunch, there are a few things I
would like to talk to you about.'

Betty hesitated, 'Sure Marie, where shall we meet?'
'How about the Wine Bar in the High Street can you
make 1pm today?'

'No, I can't, I take my lunch break at 12'oclock.'
'Twelve is good, see you then.'

Marie sat down and reflected, first thing she needed
to do was to design a flier, then talk to the bank. Her
business plan wasn't ready and if she were to be
brutally honest with herself, she was out of her
depth and needed someone grounded to lead her.
Betty could be just that person. There was so much
to organise first the business had to be called
something, the vanity in Marie meant only one
thing – she wanted her name in the company title,
she pondered and scribbled on the pad in front of
her 'Marie Halshaw @ Marie & Me.' The list went
on and Marie decided she would tentatively brooch
the subject with Betty, but it was definitely not
going to be Marie and Betty. She wanted to call it
'Marie and Me' but she somehow thought Betty
would be difficult with that.

The phone shrilled interrupting her scribbles and
without thinking Marie said, 'good morning, Marie
and.' she hesitated and went on laughing 'Me how
can I help you?'

49

'Hi Marie, I hope you can, you come highly recommended. I'm Tom Sherman, I play golf with John Mason. He tells me that you are the one person can help me out.

Marie smiled to herself good old John he had certainly come up trumps again.

'Certainly, what is it you need Mr Sherman?' she asked.

'Call me Tom please. I need my block of flats cleaned quickly, I've been let down by my contractor and I have tenants moving in.'

'Ok can you give me a few more details?' Marie asked tentatively, inwardly worrying that she didn't know any cleaners.

'I have just completed a block of sixteen flats just off the High St. But they need a good clean and I need it done in two weeks.'

'Certainly, Tom, I will get back to you tomorrow with a quote, can I first take a few details. First thing I need know is how many rooms we are talking about altogether and the timescale.

'There are one hundred rooms altogether and they need cleaning ready for renting out. You have two weeks.'

'No problem just let me take all the details so I can prepare an estimate I will need to have a quick look first though can we meet up soon.'

Marie took a note of the address, with a pounding heart, this was big. Just one problem she didn't have one cleaner let alone a team to clean such a large number of rooms.

Betty she would know someone, hopefully. For the first time in her life Marie began to wish she had made a life for herself. Instead of giving it away for a salary. Having lived in the small town for thirty years she only knew a few people by name. No-one to talk to.

Switching her phone to voicemail decided to walk into the village to meet Betty in the wine bar. On the way back she was calling in to meet Tom Sherman and look over the flats, life was looking up all she had to hope was that Betty could pull a rabbit out of the hat in the form of a team of cleaners.

Twenty minutes later Marie breezed into the wine bar and spotted her in the corner waiting for her 'Betty so nice to see you,'

'Marie, I have an hour so can we cut the crap and get to the point.'

Marie tried not to show her disappointment at Betty's hostile attitude.

'Yes of course, would you like a glass of wine?'

'Certainly not Marie is that a trick question?'

'No of course not why would it be?'

'Because I am working for you at Hargreaves this week and it is unprofessional to drink whilst working.'

Marie had the grace to blush and whilst apologising thought of all the boozy lunches she had at the advertising agency. The realisation that she had a lot to learn swept over her like a tidal wave.

Betty looked at Marie and could almost read her mind but instead of gloating she began to feel sorry for her and said. 'Apology accepted, but I am sorry too I was rude. Shall we start again?'

'Thanks Betty, I'll order coffee and sandwiches, then I will tell you what I have in mind.'

While Marie went up to the bar to place their order thinking, I will not grovel to Betty, she mustn't know how much I need her. Waiting patiently, she looked around her, the bar was small, cosy and felt welcoming. Marie wished she had known about this place before. It seemed a good place to come in alone and have a glass of wine occasionally.

She sat down beside Betty in a comfortable armchair and began to speak, 'I won't beat about the bush, the agency has taken off quicker than I expected, I'm not really ready, I haven't finished my business plan, I don't know enough skilled people yet.' Marie was aware she was gabbling but Betty as always seemed so in control.

'I wondered if you would come and help me, I seem to be good at getting the business in but....' Marie struggled to get her words out, worrying at this point in case Betty wasn't as keen as her.

'But I don't know nearly as many people as you, I was hoping to do a presentation at the WI next week, but I have only got a five-minute slot, so what do you think?'

'I think we are good Marie, the business to my mind is a brilliant concept and we have worked alongside each other before, but I will insist we are equal partners. You aren't going to be my boss.'

Marie went white, her heart hammering in her chest. The bitch had turned the tables on her and had backed her into a corner. Her first instinct was to get up and walk out but she knew the business would fail without help. She took a deep breath and shook Betty's hand 'You're on.' Secretly hoping she hadn't just made the biggest mistake of her life.

'I know you have to get back to Hargreaves, but I need a team of reliable cleaners to start a job next week. It is a big contract, but I don't have any one to do the work.

'You could always do the job yourself Marie' said Betty looking at Marie's immaculate nails.

'Don't think I hadn't thought of that.' Retorted Marie 'but I thought it was somewhat

unprofessional but if push comes to shove, we will
have to do it together.' Betty blanched at that
suggestion.

Marie outlined what detail she had and said, 'I'm
going round there after lunch to have a look, I need
to know by the end of the day whether or not we
have a team we can call on. Can I leave that with
you? I know it's a tall order but if anyone can do it
it's you.' She said with her fingers crossed.
Betty answered positively, 'Give me till five o'clock
and I'll bring cleaners round for an interview at
your flat.' She wasn't going to admit that finding
cleaners was a tough call even for her, at such short
notice.

Marie breathed a sigh of relief what and Betty
dashed off back to Hargreaves with a huge grin on
her face. It had been so easy; she had won Marie
over without a fight.

Meanwhile Marie ordered another coffee got out
her notebook and started to make notes. The day
had started so well, unfortunately she felt that this
meeting had given Betty the upper hand. This was a
lot tougher than she imagined. Part of her longed for
the security of working for a large company, she
had never had to rely on anyone before now she was
stuck with Betty of all people and she wasn't going

to come cheap. Marie had almost been able to see the dollar signs in her eyes

Marie went home and despite Betty getting the better of her she had begun to feel more optimistic since their lunch. Her spirits lifted even more when she listened to her messages. One from Tom Sherman asking her to delay the estimate for a couple of days as he had to fly to Ireland on family business another from Betty saying she had found some cleaners, they would all be round at five o'clock.

Marie

Marie spent the rest of the afternoon polishing her business plan and trying to design business cards and leaflets, she was now going to have to include Betty's name on everything. That was more difficult because she didn't yet have a name for the company. Her mind was whirling with questions worried what she would do if Betty didn't come up trumps this afternoon. If she didn't what would she be able do about it? It was becoming apparent that she needed Betty much more than she had anticipated.

Sure, enough sharp at five, the doorbell rang.

'Hi Marie hope we're not late.' Said Betty.

'No spot on please all come in and sit down.' Marie stood in the doorway watching her new business colleague, her face was a picture as she looked at the trio Betty had brought with her.

Marie sat down and was reasonably controlled as she spoke, 'I'm Marie, I know Betty has told you all about the large cleaning job we are quoting for,' she paused then went on 'perhaps you could tell me a little bit about yourselves and what have you been up to recently?' although it did come out a trifle garbled.

The oldest of the three women spoke up 'I'm Stacey, and these are my daughters Tiffany and Chelsea, known as Tiff she's the one with the pink hair the other ones known as Chels.'

Marie looked from one to the other unable to speak for a moment her eyes taking in the extraordinary sight of so much bare tattooed flesh and if she wasn't mistaken, they were wearing Primark clothes.

Betty said quickly. 'Stacey comes highly recommended Marie; her references are impeccable.'

'Thanks but let Stacey speak for herself.' Said Marie bristling at Betty for butting in, for a moment she didn't feel in full control of the situation.

'Yes, that's right, I've got some references here, bin doing a bit for Lady Soames up at the Big House and we do the big office block at the other end of the village. Said Stacey.

Marie took the references from Stacy and turned to her new partner, 'They look to be in order, so how about we give you a trial run. I know Betty has already explained how important this is for us as a new business.'

Marie stumbled over the words we and us, causing Betty to grin.

'Thanks, you won't regret it.' Said Stacy 'Now what about money we prefer to be paid cash where possible.'

'I'm paying cash, just for this job, but it's up to you to declare it to the taxman and to pay your own stamp.'

'Taxman you got to be joking.' Laughed Stacy.

'That is entirely up to you what you do.' Spluttered Marie trying not to look at Betty. 'What we have is one hundred empty rooms to be done in two weeks, they have just been decorated, everything is brand new, but they have to be spotless.'

'No problem are you paying by room or by the hour?'

Marie hesitated, she had briefly discussed money with Tom, he had indicated that he would pay in the region of ten thousand pounds for the job which worked out at £100 a room and from that she had to take her cut of £1000.

'The twenty flats are all in one block and do need a deep clean. The builders have moved out and have taken all of the debris and rubble just left mountains of dust. I have looked them over and it is a tall order.'

Stacy took Marie's hesitation as uncertainty and said, 'Look we can't hang about we got another job to quote tonight; we'll charge you £60 per room you pay me, and we share the money out.'

Not trying to look as if she was about to bite her hand off Marie answered quickly, 'That'll be fine, is that okay with all of you?' She looked at Tiff and Chels who so far hadn't uttered a word.

'Yeah' they answered in unison. 'Mum knows what she's doin.'

'Betty, are you happy with that?' Betty merely nodded in response.

'Right, we really have got to go, give us a ring, and let us know when you want us to start.' With that they trooped out.

Betty looked at Marie and laughed 'Oh Marie your face was a picture.'

'I don't think I have ever seen pink hair up close before and those tattoos are something else.'

'Trust me Marie they look strange, but they are demon workers, and I bet they went out of here thinking they conned you by asking for £60 per room.'

'I was going to pay £90' Marie said.

'Well, how much profit are we making on this then?' asked Betty.

'We? Oh yes, we make four thousand pounds if Tom Sherman agrees the price.' 'Word of advice Marie, I heard the man is desperate and he'd made a deal with another company for more than ten thousand pounds, but they backed out because they couldn't do the job for the money. Don't undersell us this early in the game.'

'What do you reckon we should quote?' asked Marie.

'I think you start at £15k and if he doesn't go for it meet in the middle and then when the cleaners have done a good job, we give them a fat bonus and a bundle of business cards to give out and we are all happy.'

'Betty you are a treasure I think we deserve a drink, glass of wine?'

'Good idea Marie.'

Marie walked through to the kitchen and grabbed a bottle of wine. Thinking what a breakthrough that weird meeting had been. There was no way could she have got this far without Betty. Feeling very satisfied she almost danced back to the lounge and as she handed a glass to Betty, she raised hers and said, 'Thank you Partner!

Betty

Betty watched as Marie went into the kitchen, if her maths were right, she had just made herself at least £2000. Thank goodness she had joined the health club at that particular time. Brilliant. New York was in the bag. Maybe she could save up to start a new adventure. Maybe she would be able to see Las Vegas as well. Plans she had talked about with Derek years ago, the likelihood now was she would be going alone. Despite her previous misgivings she was going to enjoy working with Marie. Today had certainly been a breakthrough and she had taken a huge risk promising cleaners, but she knew somehow that the future of the business depended on this. She did feel just a little guilty about pushing Marie into this partnership, but now thinking about it, together they could be a force to be reckoned with.

When Marie came back and said, 'thank you partner.' Betty struggled not to jump up and kiss her but gratefully accepted the drink. Right now, the only fly in the ointment was Derek. Not only had he not noticed she wasn't in the house much, but he also hadn't realised she'd been working. Somehow, she was going to sit down and talk to Derek and tell him what she was getting in to.

Betty decided that she would soften him up tonight and took a taxi home and practised what she was going to say when she got home.

'Derek, its Easter next week how about we go away for a few days, it would be a nice change?'

Betty waited for his response, but as expected he laughed and said, 'In case you hadn't noticed Bet we are skint.'

Wincing at this response and feeling ever so guilty at knowing her running away fund was growing she said. 'What about we swap Easter eggs instead and perhaps book lunch out.'

'Now you are talking daft, Easter eggs are for kids.'

'Funny last time I looked we never had any of those.' replied Betty mournfully.

Derek growled and said, 'Don't start on that again, you are like a stuck record next, you'll be moaning about not having a holiday last year.

Betty stormed off into the kitchen, it was pointless trying to shift Derek off the sofa, what she wouldn't give to even walk to the park and watch children playing, something she found herself doing when she was really down. Just to pretend for a few moments that they were her grandchildren playing. But not today it was windy and cold outside.

Instead, she sat at the kitchen table and scribbled a few notes. Somehow, she was going to have to find the time to talk to Derek and tell him about Marie and their new venture. The mood he was in at the moment was not the right time and he would either not care or take it badly. For now, it was going to remain her secret.

Marie

Marie was surprised at how uncomfortable she felt at walking into the village hall alone. All her life she had lived in the area but somehow, she had never ventured into anywhere like it before.

Looking around drab room, Marie was disconcerted to notice that she was overdressed, she definitely shouldn't have worn a smart business suit. All the women were casual, smart but not as formal as she was. This immediately threw her off guard, there was so much to learn, and struggling to see any friendly or recognisable face Marie almost turned and walked away. She was contemplating what to do when she spotted Violet her mother waving across the room at her.

'Mother am I glad to see you?'

'Marion, I managed to get you a five-minute slot, the rest is down to you.'

'Mother its Marie and thank you I'm grateful. When is this Chrissie on?'

Violet sighed and said 'Now, we need to sit down, watch and learn Marion, talks are very popular here.'

'Yes mother,' sighed Marie as she sat down fiddling with her notes.

She turned to her mother and asked. 'Where's Jenny? I thought she was coming along to this meeting?'

'She was but she had a hot date, or so I am told.

'A hot date at her age shocking.' Retorted Marie, causing her mother to raise her eyebrows.

'Shush Chrissie is about to start.' Muttered a grumpy voice from the row behind as Chrissie walked out onto the small stage to a round of applause.

'Oh, got it now Chrissie, she's that weird hippie from Honeysuckle Cottage I couldn't quite remember who you meant.' Whispered Marie.

'Shush, Marion,' said Violet. Marie sat back and tried to concentrate on Chrissie's talk but missed the first few sentences as she was taking in her outfit of choice. The ankle length faded patchwork skirt was topped with white blouse. Finished off with a black velvet embroidered waistcoat. Her wild curly blonde hair clipped back from her face with a large artificial daisy. Such a contrast to her own dull style. Marie felt a pang of envy Chrissie appeared so comfortable in her own skin and didn't care what people thought of her. If only she could feel like that

Chrissie held the room mesmerised. Talking about the benefits of Reiki. Marie fidgeted in her seat, waiting for her turn. It soon became obvious that

Chrissie hadn't been told that she had to finish
early, because she paused and asked if anyone had
any questions and half a dozen hands shot
Marie slumped back in her seat, this was not going
to plan, and she listened to Chrissie and tried to
work out how she could salvage the situation to her
advantage. Already she could hear the sound of
rattling cups, the smell of coffee was pervading the
room.

Chrissie left the small stage to a round of applause.
Before Marie could be introduced, chairs began to
be scraped back as the members wafted over
towards the coffee.

Marie jumped up and abandoning her speech she
grabbed a handful of leaflets she had hastily
prepared the night before. She stationed herself by
the biscuits and pasting a smile on her face, she
handed them out. As she reached the end of the
queue a wave of despair wafted over her, not one of
the women had even acknowledged her, she had
failed.

A tap on the shoulder, had her spinning round to
face her mother. 'Not giving up are you, Marion?'
Marie sighed, 'I haven't got much choice, have I?'
'You have come on get chatting, promote yourself
show me what your made of.' Said Violet brusquely

with that she walked away leaving Marie open mouthed.

Violet's words hit home; this must not be a missed opportunity. There was no way was she going to fail. Straightening her shoulders, she flicked her auburn hair behind her ears and approached a group of women standing chatting in the corner, they appeared not to notice her. The old Marie came to the fore just in the nick of time.

'Excuse me ladies I would like to introduce myself, I'm Marie Halshaw of 'Marie and Me' the agency.' Marie had faltered as she said the name as Betty had been very sniffy about it, and they had agreed to discuss it further later, but a determined Marie had forged ahead and printed a few temporary leaflets anyway.

'What sort of agency?' asked a tall skinny brunette. Marie explained and managed to hold their attention long enough for them to start taking the leaflets she printed out earlier.

Encouraged by the lack of hostility, just genuine interest, Marie regained enough confidence to network the entire hall. She had a couple of very positive conversations, one with a mother, looking for personalised stationery and accessories for her daughter's wedding. Marie took her phone number and promised to call her the next day. Another woman asked about costumes for the local amateur dramatics group. Marie arranged to go to the theatre in a weeks' time.

All in all, Marie was pleased with the feedback and interest she had generated. Making the decision she stayed to have a coffee and while making notes, she was interrupted by Chrissie Mathews.

'It's Marie, isn't it?' she asked.

'Yes, yes, it is.' answered Marie.

'I want to apologise; I've just been told I over-ran and you missed your slot. No-one prompted me so I just rambled on.' Said Chrissie, her words tumbling out. 'I really am sorry.'

'It's not a problem; this is all a bit new to me. I don't know many people here. I knew I was only going to have a few minutes; besides I found your talk very interesting.' Replied Marie diplomatically. 'While you're here, please tell me all about this new venture, I've lived in the village for all my life, I think you were in the year below me in school, sure I can help you meet people if that's what you want.

Marie started to explain, her enthusiasm shining through and Chrissie said, 'what a brilliant concept, how interesting I am surprised no- one has thought of it before.'

'Chrissie, could we meet up another day, I think we could be of use to one another,'

'I don't see how I can be of use to you Marie I'm embarrassed to say I have never worked before.'
'Quite simply first of all you know a lot of people, secondly your skills are really saleable.'
'I only do everything for pleasure; I am not interested in money.' Laughed Chrissie.
'Even so think about it.' Said Marie.
Chrissie thought for a moment, 'Okay why not come to my cottage soon for coffee and we'll have a chat.'
'Yes, I will, is it Honeysuckle Cottage at the end of Barley Road?' Asked Marie.
'That's the one ring me,' with that Chrissie handed Marie her number and drifted off buoyed up with a quick shot from her hip flask.
Marie sat for a few moments more and scribbled a few more notes, time to go she had a lot of planning to do.

Chrissie

Chrissie walked into her cottage, slamming the door behind her, what on earth was she thinking about? She hated the WI; all those stuck-up women, all pretending to be interested in her. Thankfully she couldn't really remember what she had talked about; the couple of large vodkas she had swallowed before she left home had helped. Chrissie always fell into a depression after a visit to the W.I. she kidded herself that it was because she was different. Deep down it was unsettling to be among so many women who appeared to be really happy with their lives and their families. Not realising it was her they envied. She sank onto her sofa, heart pounding, wondering what she was doing with her life. From the moment Zack had pointed out so emotionally that they were both sixty this year Chrissie had felt her life go into freefall. Sixty how could she be that old, where had her life gone? Too much time spent sitting here in the cottage waiting for Zack and for what. Admittedly she had lived an extremely comfortable life, never having to pay a bill, Zack had paid everything for forty years. Now it all seemed so pointless and so shallow.

Chrissie knew she always felt like this after going to the WI but this time she felt it deeper, everything in her life seemed so dull. Summer was in India and Zack well he was always on tour. She was alone.

Whatever made her apologise to that Marie? If honest she didn't really care, whether the daft woman spoke or not. Truth was she was embarrassed because she spotted Marie's vulnerability and did nothing about it. Chrissie now couldn't work out why she had invited Marie round for coffee.

Chrissie reached out for the vodka bottle and poured herself a large one, taking a sip, she tried to work out where her life was going. She was feeling unhappy but at this moment didn't have any idea how to change or solve her feelings.

Truth, was she had met Zack fallen head over heels in love at twenty and since then just occasional one-night stands, nothing she was proud of. Zack was also getting restless, after forty years he wanted commitment. But Chrissie didn't know what she wanted want. One day she wanted marriage and other days she wanted freedom. Life was so confusing.

Leaning over she picked up the bottle and poured a very large measure into her glass. Today had struck her like a lightning bolt she was lonely; she had no close friends, no direction in her life. She didn't want to sit here waiting for Zack any longer, but without his money she had very little.

True the deeds to the cottage were in her name but she had no income and had never worked. She needed to decide what to do next. To finish with Zack meant she had to earn some money, how she had no idea. She couldn't rely on him to support her; to survive alone, she might have to sell the cottage.

That couldn't happen, the cottage was her life, her only home, she had moved here from living with her parents. Both long dead, but sell the cottage, not an option. Where would she go? What would she do? Then there was Zack, he had been part of her life forever, despite his touring he had been a brilliant father to Summer.

Chrissie sighed nothing to do but have another drink, regardless to the fact that she had drunk far more than was healthy for her but one way and another she had to sort her life out. Most people had done this years ago. Not Chrissie though, she had hung on to Zack, or had he hung on to her. Her thoughts became clouded, and she reached for the phone.

She dialled Zack's number. He answered quickly but he was distant and slightly offhand with her. In her maudlin and alcohol induced state, she felt sure she could hear a female giggling in the background. She hung up on him and sunk down on the sofa.

Betty

Betty didn't have long to dwell on her problems at
home as she had an urgent office job come up.
 Another recommendation from John Mason. She
left the house early thinking that surely Derek
would wonder why she was out all day again
This job was in a local double-glazing company,
just a short drive from her home.
Jim the proprietor was waiting for her and he led
her through the showroom.
'My daughter Melissa will be back in by the end of
April. I do hope you can sort us out in that time. I'm
so busy fitting the windows, there's no time for
paperwork.' He hesitated Melissa hasn't been too
good since her baby was born; she just needs to find
a reliable child minder then hopefully she will be
back.'
'Jim don't worry I'll just get on with it, just tell me
what your priorities are.'
 'Well, there are bills to pay and invoices to type up,
I think there may be some cheques need paying in,
best come through and see what you have let
yourself in for.'
 He led her through to a tiny office at the back of his
house, as he pushed open the door, Betty gasped
and Jim had the good grace to look embarrassed,

'sorry I did say it was a mess. Can I get you a coffee?'

'Yes please, I think I may well need some black sacks as well if you have some.'

There was soon a pile of estimates which should have been typed up and sent out, cheques which should have been paid into the bank, unpaid invoices and overdue payments which should have been paid on completion of jobs. Receipts and endless junk mail and catalogues.

Betty knew the key to running a successful business as a self-employed person was keeping on top of the paperwork. Knowing that from day one clear and accurate records of everything that happens to the business, especially financial transactions had to be kept. But she also knew that there was no way that Jim or his daughter had ever set aside enough time each week to keep paperwork up to date.

No wonder they were willing to hire her, not many people would be able to face the piles of paper, she thought even without the extra responsibility of a new baby. There's nothing more demotivating than having a large box with months' worth of paperwork to dredge through come VAT and tax time. Whereas filed organised paperwork would have made it a quick and easy process.

75

Betty worked methodically and the sorting alone
took three days of the first week, and without asking
she managed to dispose of three sacks of junk mail
envelopes and newspapers.

On the fourth day she was about to start typing
when there was a knock on her office door, it was a
young woman.

'Betty, can I come in, I'm Mel?' she said timidly.
'Of course, it's your office; you don't have to ask
me for permission.' Betty said but was surprised to
see a man behind her.

'This is Michael he's our sort of accountant.' Mel
said, as she pressed herself to the wall the home
office wasn't really big enough for three people.

'A sort of accountant, I don't think I've heard of
one of them before. I'm Betty a sort of Woman
Friday.' She said laughingly proffering her hand
and enjoying the feel of his firm grip.

The baby made its strange little squeal from across
the hall, where she was laying in her bouncy chair.
Betty thought of it as an early warning that she was
going to cry. Mel completely ignored the sound.
Resisting the urge to comfort the baby, Betty turned
her attention Michael, she liked men who took care
of themselves. He looked around the same age as
her own husband. But unlike Derek who was happy
pottering around in cheap slip-on shoes or wearing,

two for fifteen pounds polo shirts. Derek liked comfort, where this Michael was smart and smelt divine.

'Well, he's my dad's accountant. He said he would come and help us with the VAT, but when he saw the mess, he asked us to sort it out first.'

She could see him staring at the almost paper free room in amazement. The baby let out a loud wail, with intermittent sobs that everyone in the room knew would not stop until she'd been fed.

'Oh, I'd better just go …. Michael hopefully now you will be able to let Betty know what you need' Mel said.

'You go and look after your baby.' Betty said and smiled as Mel made a dash for the squawking infant.

'Was this office always as bad as this?' Asked Betty.

'I don't know what you mean?' Michael answered smiling.

'Well, I haven't ever seen such a mess before.'

Michael laughed; Betty noticed how warm his voice sounded. She didn't feel guilty at her shameless ogling, on the contrary, it was enjoyable, and she adored flirting when given a chance.

Wishing she had taken a bit more care with her appearance that morning, leaving the house without even bothering to put on her make- up.

Her mother use to say that it was a good job that Derek didn't have a jealous bone in his body. But her father used to say there no harm in looking at the menu, even if you aren't going to sit down to dinner.

'I wish I could say it's the fact that she's just had a baby, but alas no. Her father is the same, he starts with good intentions and then drifts off. You must tell me what you've done to this room – I didn't even know there was a chair here last time I called.'

'It was nothing really, I just sorted it out. All it need was a bit of organising' Betty said coquettishly.

Michael looked momentarily uncomfortable; Betty was flirting with him, so he quickly said 'look how about I come back next week when you have had a chance to sort through'?

As he was about to leave, he turned and asked, 'have you done VAT and wages before?'

Betty bristled and replied, 'Of course I have everything will be ready for you, come back Wednesday I should be done by then.'

Michael agreed and left Betty feeling unusually flustered, running her fingers through her greasy hair she decided to take a break, get some fresh air. Walking down the road she made towards the coffee shop where she intended to buy a doughnut or two to go with her sandwich. Passing the local hairdressers, she caught a glimpse of herself in the window, not liking what she saw, shuddering with the realisation that she had flirted with Michael looking unkempt. Time to take control, she walked in and was delighted when the receptionist said they had a space for a cut and blow dry immediately. Betty was really pleased with the results and vowed that if Marie could look the part, then she could to.

After a busy afternoon at her makeshift desk, it was time to go home as he picked up her bag her heart sinking, another evening in front of the tv with dull Derek. It sank even lower when she realised, he had asked for liver for dinner. She had quite forgotten that was what she went out for at lunchtime. What was wrong with her? Even the butcher seemed attractive as he slipped the liver into a bag for her. It was only a short ride home; she swung out of the car park and drove home to Derek who was still sitting on the couch in exactly the same position she had left him eight hours earlier. Not even looking up to notice her new hairdo.

This was a major turning point for Betty, all of a sudden, she was faced with decisions for her future and scaringly it was beginning to look as if she would be alone. Everything was uncertain with disinterested Derek. It was scary only a couple of years ago her future was mapped out. Everything was planned, the future looked rosy. What she really wanted was to go ahead with the plans they had made together, mini breaks, travel to places far away. Right now, it was not likely to happen. If that was what she wanted she was going to have to do it alone.

The next day Betty was driving through the village singing loudly as her favourite record had just come on the radio. Outside the sun was shining, and she was feeling much better today. The last argument had made her think the only way she was going to get a break was to go away on her own. Betty knew she couldn't live with Dull Derek much longer unless things changed radically. The prospect of divorce was a terrifying thought. When she had taken early retirement, life had looked so good Derek had been as keen as she was to travel. Losing his business had taken its toll and now he couldn't always be bothered to walk to the local pub.

Betty loved her little Clio; loud music always gave her a lift. Today she had heard three of her favourite songs in a row, she was certain it was a good omen. She slowed for the red light and glanced across and hooted with laughter. There in complete power suit was Marie studying a bus timetable as if it was ancient Greek. She pulled up and wound down the

window 'Marie what on earth are you doing where's
your car?'

'Marie reddened and said 'Oh am I glad to see you; I
quite forgot my company car was being collected
last night, I haven't yet sorted out a replacement.
'Where are you going? I can drop you.'

Marie looked sheepish' I was just going to the
BMW garage to see if I could lease a car.' Marie got
into the car, 'thank you.'

 Betty looked into the rear-view mirror, checked
there was no traffic and pulled out, she leaned
forward and switched the radio off.

 Marie said. 'Stupid of me, I got so carried away
with business I forgot to organise another car.' she
was silent for a moment then went on. 'I do
appreciate you stopping to give me a lift. I wasn't
looking forward to the bus.'

'Marie, don't you think a small hatchback would be
better to start with after all we are going to be
partners aren't we?'

She watched as Marie shifted uncomfortably in her
seat.

'I hadn't given it much thought as to what car, I
have always had BMW's.'

'Yes, but someone else had always paid for them,
this time you are paying or rather the company will

be.' Betty hesitated for a moment and then said, 'Did you manage to sort out an accountant yet?'

'Well sort of.' she tailed off.

'Who is it?' asked Betty?

'Well, I overheard two women at the WI praising a guy called Michael Lambert he has a place in town near the market square.'

'I met him he's the accountant for Jim at the double-glazing company. He seems competent, certainly looks great! Have you phoned him?' asked Betty.

'No but I will, and what do you mean he looks great? I'm more interested in whether he can do the job. I'm not interested in anything about him, just that he knows his stuff.

'Look why don't we drop in there now I'm not working today. Let's get this business started properly when we finish there we will go and lease you a car but nothing fancy.' Suggested Betty.

Marie winced 'I had forgotten what a bully you are Betty. You're right. I guess I'm so used to having people doing stuff for me I'm forgetting the basics all I'm interested in is an accountant doing a good job for us, not his looks.'

'That's why we are going to be a good team I'm good at the basics. Just thought it worth mentioning that he is an attractive man. She paused 'well then first stop Michael Lambert accountants.'

Marie visibly relaxed in her seat, smiling she said, 'Thank you so much.'

Betty swung her aging Clio into a space directly outside Michael Lambert's Accountancy offices. Which were in a new building on a small industrial estate, reasonably smart but tastefully landscaped the trees softening the view of warehouses opposite the office building.

Marie began to get out of the car Betty said, 'I hear he's seeing Jenny Moore.'

'I was expecting to see her at the WI last week, my mother said she had a hot date, must have been him. Let's see whether he's up too much.' Replied Marie, 'actually mother says Jenny is looking for work, she designs cards and dabbles in all sorts though she wasn't sure exactly what that meant. She did say her cards were beautiful, she buys all of hers from her.'

Betty laughed and together they walked into the offices.

Looking at the name plates Marie said, 'That's a bit of luck he's on the ground floor.'

Inside she took control, explaining to the bored receptionist that they wanted to see Michael Lambert urgently. Putting down her magazine the blonde buzzed through to Michael 'There's a couple of women here need to see you urgently can you spare ten minutes Michael?'

After a brief silence during which Michael was
obviously asking the receptionist what they wanted.
Marie said, 'We need business advice please,' the
response was quietly relayed to Michael.
 The bespectacled receptionist replaced the receiver
asking the two women to follow her. They went into
a large office at the back overlooking the village
green. Michael stood up and shook their hands. 'Sit
down ladies, how can I help you today?'
Betty beamed at Michael and watched Marie stiffen
as she looked round the messy room.
 Looking directly at Marie Michael said 'I'm sorry
about the mess. I've just moved into this office as
I've taken on a new partner hence the chaos. If you
need office space ladies, I'm your man, we have
offices to rent.'
'Marie laughed, 'It is a bit premature, hopefully we
will need an office soon. First, we need to set up the
business we have started officially plus we need
advice on our accounts.'
 'I can do all of that for you, just not today, first I
need you go through this?' He handed over a printed
list of requirements. ' I will also need your business
plan,' he hesitated while he checked his diary, 'How
about Friday will you have everything available by
then?'

Betty answered, 'I'm working until twelve Marie can you manage the afternoon?'

'Yes, I can, is that okay with you Michael? I can call you Michael, can't I?'

'Yes of course one thing, have you sorted out a business account yet?'

Marie winced 'It's on my list but no.'

'Well, there's no time like the present are you free for the rest of the day ladies?'

'More or less,' said Marie.

Michael dialled the number of the local bank and said, 'I do a lot of business with this Bank and they are very supportive of New Businesses.'

Marie and Betty sat and listened as Michael Lambert spoke, he turned to them and asked, 'is three o'clock good for you?'

They both nodded and when he confirmed the time he hung up and Betty thanked him profusely.

He stood up and said, 'Right ladies till Friday then.'

As they left the office Marie said, 'We had better get back to mine and pick up my business plan, and yes Betty I have managed to finish it.'

Betty laughed 'I didn't doubt you for a minute Marie, but seriously we can't go to the bank without a name.'

Marie sighed 'I know we need to decide, there is so much to think about, I am forever flitting from one thing to another.'

'What, like a butterfly?'

They looked at each other 'What do you think? Butterflies seems an appropriate name?' Asked Betty tentatively.

'Brilliant let's shake on it.' Said Marie delighted that one problem had been solved at least.

The meeting with the Bank went better than they had both expected, mainly because Betty had at the last moment decided to match the ten thousand pounds Marie was putting into Butterflies. The last-minute choice of the name Butterflies certainly swayed Betty's decision.

Once the account was set up the pair walked out into the street and Betty said 'This had better work Marie. That's a good portion of my life savings and was to be my ticket out of my crumbling marriage.' Marie whose adrenalin was firing on all cylinders replied, 'I think we can do this Betty. I really do; I need the money to be safe as much as you do. But I can't advise on saving your marriage, not with my track record.'

'Next we have to sort out a car for you,' said Betty deliberately ignoring Marie's comment.

'Okay, I suppose I could lease one, for now. We can
share it when necessary. The company will pay for
yours, something we will sort out on Friday.'
'What did you think of Michael Lambert Marie?'
'Honestly I thought he was arrogant and a tad
boring.' Marie replied.
'Hmmm but you must have found him attractive,'
responded Betty.
'Absolutely not. Not my type at all.'
'I wouldn't kick him out of bed.' Betty smiled as
she looked at Maries shocked face.
Getting a car sorted out was a lot more complicated
than Marie expected and they walked away from the
garage in the village feeling despondent. Then Betty
said 'Tell you what Derek has got a Focus in the
garage he doesn't use but refuses to sell it – just in
case. I'm sure he will let us use it'
'Just in case of what?'
'Haven't got a clue, he's always reluctant to get rid
of anything. I'll talk to him tonight.'
'A Focus that's a bit small, isn't it?'
'Not really it's a bit bigger than this but not as flash
as you are used to, but it will do until we are
earning proper money.'
Marie sighed and said, 'Thank you I didn't mean to
sound ungrateful, it's just that there is so much to
get used to.'

Betty dropped Marie off outside her flat and drove home to face Derek, he was sprawled across the sofa, same as every night dirty plates and mugs surrounding him. Sighing she removed them and went into the kitchen and prepared dinner. Only after Derek had wolfed down his dinner did she broach the subject of the car. She was apprehensive about asking, as she still didn't feel ready to tell him about Butterflies or her part in it. Especially the fact that she had put money into a new venture. He merely grunted and said disinterestedly 'Do what you like with it.'

Without even asking why she wanted the car; it had sat in the garage unused for the best part of a year. If he needed to go out, he used his old van. Lately that hadn't moved much either.

Marie

Marie's hand hovered over the telephone, she couldn't believe how nervous she was, after all it was only a business phone call, thousands of which she had made before at Jones Macintosh. This time it was different sure it was business but more important, it was her business, meaning it was far more important personally. She took a deep breath and dialled.

'Good morning, Mrs Smythe Browne, Marie Halshaw here, just a follow up call to your enquiry about the wedding accessory package for your daughter.' At this point Marie crossed her slender fingers and prayed, she didn't have a clue what exactly constituted a wedding package. Up until now she hadn't even worked out which one of her limited team would orchestrate it.

 The businesswoman inside her smelled old money, and she determined to give this opportunity her best shot.

'Marie so glad you called; I told Sophie you were going to phone. Please, you must call me Hattie everyone does.'

'Well Hattie, can we meet up? I need to sit with you and your daughter to work out exactly what you need. Then we can talk samples and Butterflies can

quote accordingly. Have you already had some
quotes?' Marie asked with her fingers crossed. After
all, if she could just take a peek at the quotes and
the samples, she would be home and dry, hopefully.
'Certainly, Marie I have a couple of quotes, I can
call you Marie, can't I?' asked Hattie.
'Of course, so when can we meet?'
'Well, my daughter is leaving soon for three months
in Australia. She's left me with detailed
instructions. We are paying for the entire wedding
all final decisions are down to us. Or rather me,
Henry is just writing the cheques for his little girl. I
suppose the sooner the better, Sophie wants to come
home and just get married, leaving me to sort
everything out for her meaning I've only a few
months to arrange the whole event.'
Marie hesitated, this was all sounding too good to
be true, 'Hattie can I come round tomorrow? I have
a free slot between two and five.'
'That will be fine.' Answered Hattie.
' I don't have your address.'
'No problem it's The Great Hall at the end of the
village,' said Hattie,
'I know it, see you at two if that suits you,' said
Marie.
 'Look forward to it,' with that Hattie had hung up
leaving Marie almost speechless. This could be

serious money. She could check up on Stacey and
her crew at the same time. After all their references
said they had worked there.

Marie looked at the list of phone calls and made an
entry into her diary for tomorrow, adding a call to
Jenny. To see if she was up to doing invitations.
Mother had recommended her for cards, as she had
been buying cards for all occasions from Jenny for
years. Meanwhile she googled wedding accessories
and was astounded at how far she could take this
opportunity. Jenny responded positively when
Marie roughly outlined her plans. Hoping she as
good as everyone said. Fingers crossed that she
Marie was capable of assessing Jenny's work. This
was her moving into completely unknown territory.
Next on the list Diane Goodson manageress of the
local theatre. The amateur dramatic company had
got a licence to perform 'Joseph and his
Technicolour Dream Coat.' Diane had approached
her about making costumes for the entire
production. This was worrying Marie as the only
seamstress she knew of was Nancy. While
supposedly being brilliant at what she did, could she
cope with the volume of work involved here?
Nancy was unknown to her just a name that Betty
had casually mentioned. What the hell this was
definitely challenging. If the worst came to the

worst, Marie had got her GCE in Needlework, okay it was forty years ago but needs must.

With all this in mind Marie picked up the telephone again and dialled the number Diane Goodson had given her. 'Hi Diane, its Marie of Butterflies.' It felt strange using the new name, so she went on to say, 'We met at the W.I I'm ringing about the costumes you mentioned.'

'Marie I'm so glad you rang, I have to say I'm desperate, oh no I'm not supposed to say that, but truth is I am. The costumes were going to be organised by the last manager. We thought it all under control, but he has gone to live in Los Angeles, and it appears we now have no costumes. Opening night is in two months,' gabbled Diane.

Marie paused before saying, 'That's a tall order, but before we can commit, we need to understand exactly what is involved.'

'I absolutely agree, can you get round to the theatre tomorrow morning?' asked Diane.

Marie hesitated, she was due at the gym with her personal trainer at ten, but instinct told her business should come first. 'I can meet you there about ten' she said quickly making a note to ring Justin and cancel her session.

So far Marie hadn't left her home and business was looking up, she was scared, so much emphasis was going to be placed on people who had been recommended to her. How capable and reliable were Jenny and Nancy going to be? Then there was Stacey, Betty had sworn she and her daughters were hardworking and were good at what they did. Marie was suspicious and determined to check them out. Suddenly it hit her, Butterflies was definitely going to take off. The paperwork was threatening to drown her and worryingly all these unknown people, she was going to have to depend on.

Marie rang Betty to tell her about the appointments she had made for the following day, with her fingers crossed she asked her if she was free to come with her. Betty had news of her own, 'I can't make it Marie, Michael has asked me to go in and sort his office out,' she hesitated and went on 'He was so impressed with what I did at the last place.'
'That's good news why don't you pop round later then we can go over everything.'
'Good idea, I'll drop in at home first and pick up the car for you.

<u>Betty</u>

Betty finished work around five and went home to
pick up the car. Stopping only to speak briefly to
Derek. Thinking he would be curious to know why
she was going out again. Had he shown any interest
Betty was determined to tell him about Butterflies.
He merely grunted as she handed him a plate of fish
and chips. Not even taking his eyes off the
television. So having missed yet another chance to
talk to him, she backed the car out of the garage. It
started first time and was as clean as when Derek
had abandoned it all those months ago. Feeling
despondent Betty drove over to Marie's house,
parked the car in Marie's now empty parking space.
Her spirits did lift a little as she rang the bell, Marie
answered immediately and for the first time Betty
went into her immaculate mews house. Marie was
looking very casual in a navy track suit- obviously
designer, but casual for Marie.
'Sit down, I've a takeaway for later,' she said
handing her a glass of wine.
'Thank you I need this.' Said Betty.
'I take it you will get a taxi back or is Derek
collecting you?'
Betty spluttered, 'You must be joking! I don't think
he has even realised I'm not there.'

94

'Oh dear, 'said Marie.
Betty handed her the keys to the car and said, 'I parked in your bay as you said.'
'Thank you did your husband make a fuss about us using the car for business?'
 Betty looked sheepish, 'I haven't got round to telling him about Butterflies yet. Derek didn't even ask what I was going to do with the car, so I have taxed and insured it for us and there is an Mot on it.'
'That's great put in docket for petty cash, but I am worried that you haven't told Derek.'
 Betty sighed, 'It's been such a miserable year, and Derek has turned from a fun-loving hard-working husband to a couch potato with no interest in anything. I fear we are heading for divorce. Retirement hasn't turned out well for me I'm afraid.'
Marie looked shocked and said, 'I'm divorced but I'm a firm believer that divorce is not always the answer. I was a lot younger than you and we weren't together long. That didn't stop it being tough. If I'm honest it's still painful.'
'It seems my only option at the moment.'
'You have to talk to him.'
'That's easier said than done, I've tried but it's just like talking to a brick wall.'

'You do need to tell him about the business soon.'
said Marie.
'I know I just haven't found the right moment.'
'I'm not the best person to advise you but the longer
you leave it the harder it will be, you need to tell
him. You have put serious money into this business;
Derek should be aware of that.'
'It was my money; he had no idea I had saved so
much it was my running away money.'
'Rest assured we will make money and then you can
run away if that's really what you want.'
 Betty took a deep breath and said, 'Do you ever
wish you'd had children Marie?' she said this
looking directly at her. Marie looked flustered just
for a moment and said, 'no not at all what about
you?'
Betty sighed, 'I think that lack of children is part of
my problem, I couldn't get pregnant, so I worked
and seemed to get over it. We were busy and happy
and eventually it didn't matter, but now.'
'Now?' asked Marie.
'Now I look at grandmothers with their
grandchildren and my heart aches all over again.'
'I think you need to get busy again and talk to Derek
about everything and then that won't be so
important again.'
'I'm sure you're right sorry to be so maudlin.'

'We need to eat.' Said Marie walking through to the kitchen leaving Betty deep in thought. She looked around the room, it was light and airy with large grey leather sofas that looked like they had never been sat in and adorned with beautiful cushions that had obviously cost a fortune and certainly not bought from Matalan. Nothing out of place even the plants on the windowsill looked like they were designed to be immaculate. The thought struck her that she liked Marie but was envious, she was single, had a very smart home and now Butterflies. No one to wait on hand foot and finger.

Marie said 'we are going to have to eat on our laps as there is too much paper on the table' she handed Betty a dish of lasagne and salad.

After they had eaten Marie said, 'We need to go through a few things tonight, but I have a really busy day tomorrow are you free to come with me?'

'No, I promised Michael another day's work.'

'I hope you are charging him full price.'

'Yes of course.'

Despite both needing an early night it was after eleven when Betty called a cab to go home to Derek. Feeling more optimistic that Butterflies was becoming an exciting business.

Marie

Early the next morning Marie was awake early up making lists, today was going to be a big day, she had two major potential customers.

Now she needed to check that Butterflies been paid for everything they had done already. Roughly draw up a list for wedding stationery package. More worryingly was not knowing how many costumes were needed for Joseph. Marie's brain was whirling so fast, her thoughts were coming out all in a jumble. Deep breath she chided herself. Slow down. Swinging her legs out of bed she padded barefoot into the kitchen. Coffee that was what she needed, she set her percolator up and raising the hand painted roller blind in her kitchen. She looked across the road to the gated gardens. One of her neighbours, who she was only on nodding terms was already sitting on a bench reading his daily newspaper.

Marie loved this time of day; dawn had just broken, and her creative juices always flowed better early. She poured a strong black coffee cursing as she splashed her cream satin pyjama top. As the coffee hit the spot she sat on the stool, spreading her lists on the breakfast bar, she needed more space, this business was taking over her tiny house.

Who would ever imagine she Marie would have a whiteboard in her bedroom, where one of her expensive mirrors used to be. Now she was making lists of her lists. This had to stop she forced herself just to concentrate on the day ahead. Remembering what her mother had always told her 'One step at a time Marie one step at a time.'

As she poured another coffee the telephone rang, and Marie glanced at her Rolex eight o'clock already. 'Good morning, Marie speaking.'

'Ah Marie Tom Sherman here, just want to thank you for the sterling job your cleaners did on my flats.'

'Gosh, you've checked them already, I was going to pop in today I didn't realise they had finished so quickly '

'No need Marie they did a great job, though I have to say I was very dubious when I first saw them. I bet they'll want paying soon.' Said Tom.

Marie suppressed a giggle and answered, 'Yes they are a strange bunch, even so they came well recommended.'

'I'm round your way today, I'll put the cheque through your office door, I've added a bonus for you as well.'

Marie interrupted. 'There was no need for that Tom.'

'On the contrary, time is money, those girls finished inside a week, now I can put the flats up for sale a week earlier. Cash flow Marie, cash flow that's what it's all about.'

'Thank you.' Said Marie gratefully.

'Now while you are on the phone what about curtains?' asked Harry.

'Curtains? how do you mean?

'Any of your ladies make curtains? I have four flats on the other side of town, which have just been refurbished. I let these out as well, also they give the wife something to do looking after them, but she can't sew so I need some curtains making.'

Marie paused she didn't want to turn down a job but there was a lot of sewing needed at the moment, with limited number of machinists available.

'Fine, I'll sort out someone to come round and measure up in the next few days and ring you as soon as I can organise that. Is that going to be alright?'

'That will be grand lass.'

Marie put the phone down; she did a little jig that was a huge cheque coming in without chasing and more work on the horizon. It did cross her mind that she could always use readymade curtains to hang at the windows if she didn't have machinists. Plus, more jobs to add to her to her lists- find machinists, pay the cleaners, tell Betty the cheque was coming in and so it went on. Marie was really buzzing as she got into the shower. Focus, Marie's first meeting this morning was for the Joseph costumes. Once she knew how many were needed, the next problem was who was going to make them.

The Victorian theatre was way outside the village on the outskirts of the next town, very popular with the locals. Known as the Box because of its size but officially called The Show House. Marie had done her research and was nervous, this was way too vague, she had googled Joseph and despite being in a production at school she was scared at the number of cast members. Surely, she wasn't expected to make for the entire cast in such a short space of time.

The front door of the theatre was locked, Marie walked round to the side, bingo it was open, she pushed open the heavy door, walked in smelling the years of greasepaint and make-up, mixed with damp and sweat. There didn't seem to be anyone around she shivered as the dim lights flickered. Oh God the ghosts of shows gone by. The hairs bristled on the back of her neck and then out of the shadows drifted a figure dressed all in black.

'Oh, you made me jump, I thought there was ...'
Marie stopped herself as she realised how ridiculous
she was sounding.

'You must be Marie I'm Diane; come through I
have a pot of coffee on.'

Marie followed Diane into a room which at first
glance seemed full of old clothes and junk. As her
eyes became adjusted to the dim light it became
obvious that she wasn't in a charity shop, these
were costumes. The musty smell was almost
overpowering a bit like Diane. A tall intimidating
figure of a woman, hair drawn back in a bun
accentuating her long thin nose. Marie smiled to
herself; the woman apparently needed her long nose
to support the huge tortoiseshell rimmed glasses
through which she was peering at Marie.

'I asked how do you like your coffee? Marie are
you listening?' asked Diane.

'Oh, sorry I er haven't ever been backstage in a
theatre before- just black please.'

Marie shook herself what was wrong with her this
morning? Truth, was she felt spooked the moment
she walked in, now faced with Diane, she felt like
running out of the door.

'Sit down,' said Diane 'and I'll tell you what we
want.'

Marie who had just about gathered her composure got out her notebook. Determined not to let Diane railroad her into anything. Her gut instinct was to turn down the job down and walk away, but when Diane said Butterflies would get full credit for the costumes on the programmes and the posters she was drawn in. After all any advertising was good especially free advertising. 'We do have some costumes already, but we are short of around a dozen including Joseph's coat of many colours.'

'What about fabrics and patterns?' asked Marie.
'No problem they're all in the basement ready I can get them delivered as soon as you want. You do want this job, don't you?' asked Diane looking down at the white-faced Marie.

'How long have we got?' asked Marie desperate to get away, her heart was beating faster by the minute, she felt suffocated with her oppressive attitude.

Diane's eyes glittered behind her glasses, as she answered Dress rehearsal is in four weeks.'
'Four weeks?'
'You'll do it then?' Diane put out her hand to shake Marie's in agreement.
'I didn't say that I think four weeks is a bit tight you said two months on the phone.'

'Don't worry about that, it's only a dress rehearsal, doesn't matter if there are a few pins left in First performance is four week later.' Said Diane airily. 'I'll let you know, 'stammered Marie pushing away Diane's clammy hand, she stood up to go and Diane said 'I take it you mean you will let me know where to deliver the fabric, the sooner the better don't you think? With that she left Marie standing open mouthed, surely, she was coming back. But no, she called back to Marie 'See yourself out.' And she was gone. Gone back into the shadows where she had come out from only a quarter of an hour earlier.

Marie stood still for a moment she had been railroaded, that had never happened to her before, she was always in control, this spooky theatre had got to her. She took a deep breath and walked back the way she had come in, her back stiff with tension, hands clutching her handbag and notebook. She reached the door and made a dash for the daylight. Her car was parked just around the corner, and she sank into her seat and swiftly locked the door. She looked at her notes. All she had written was twelve costumes to be ready, four weeks, get the fabric delivered next week. Marie stared at the words in front of her, not only did she not remember writing anything it did not look like her handwriting. The words she had written didn't make any sense. What had happened to her in the theatre?

Marie just had time to go home and change, she would forfeit lunch to take a shower and try and get rid of the musty theatre smell on her clothes, then on to visit Hattie Smyth Brown. She fervently hoped this encounter would go a little more smoothly than this morning.

Marie parked on the drive of the Great Hall looked around, the gardens were immaculate, obviously a gardener was employed to keep them in such fine order. The house was on first sight deserving of its name, and impressive building the date stone embedded in the wall next to the large oak door said 1898.

Suitably calm now and prepared Marie knocked on the door of the Great Hall, a voice boomed out 'Coming, coming.' The huge door creaked open and Hattie said, 'come in Marie so nice to see you again.'

Marie followed Hattie through to the kitchen where she had spread pictures and swatches over the huge pine table, she smiled to herself it was always a pleasure to work with someone like her who had an organised mind. Hattie's heels clacked over the stone floors, Marie watched as Hattie walked into an enormous pantry and put her head round the door

waving a bottle said 'Sherry Marie? Sorry it's not
decanted'.

'Oh gosh no bit early for me,' answered Marie.

'Rubbish, never too early for a sherry,'

 While Hattie busied herself, Marie looked around
the kitchen. It wasn't to her taste, but it was large
and dominated not by a modern glossy island but by
an old well-worn pine table. No fancy kitchen
equipment in this kitchen, plenty of copper pots
hanging above an ancient aga.

 Hattie poured two large schooners and placed them
on the table.

Marie sighed and vowed to herself to not drink the
sherry; she would pour it down the sink at the first
opportunity. Getting out her notebook she waited
for Hattie to take her seat and asked her to give as
much detail as possible.

Hattie was organised, she downed her sherry in one
and poured another, 'I have a list here and some
samples of what Sophie likes.'

She handed the list to Marie, who studied it and
said. 'Before we go any further Hattie this is a very
comprehensive list, I've looked at prices on the
internet and for the large quantity you want I have
to say it is going to be expensive. Everything is
going to be handmade.'

'I'm perfectly aware of that Marie,' Hattie hesitated and went on 'Sophie is our only daughter and there is no expense spared. What I want you to do is to take away these mock-up's, she's had done then come back with some samples and a price. All I'm interested in is that my Sophie is happy.'

'That's fine I'll get back to you in the next week, can I take these samples? Asked Marie.

'Of course, just let me know when you want to come back, and don't worry Sophie has left everything to me.'

'Before I go Hattie, this is nothing to do with the wedding package- Stacey O' Neill she says she works for you.'

'Stacey has worked for me for the last ten years, but recently she brought her daughters along, I have to say they are not like their mother, in fact I had to tell Stacey they weren't welcome anymore.'

'Why Hattie?' asked Marie.

'Well as I said Stacey is honest and reliable, but her daughters are lazy and light fingered, I had to do this as, a couple of bits and bobs had gone missing. Nothing valuable but it hadn't happened until those two came along. But Stacey is a diamond. Just don't get too involved with her family or perhaps be careful where you send them.'

'Thank you, Hattie that is really helpful, I'll ring
you next week and at our next meeting I'll bring
Jenny along, who will be covering this project.' she
said with her fingers crossed.
'I'll look forward to that and thank you.' Said Hattie.
 Marie drove home with mixed emotions it seems
Stacey could be trusted but her daughters couldn't,
going forward she was going to have to be very
careful which jobs she allocated to them. This last
meeting had relaxed her. She opened the car
window and let the May sunshine lift her spirits a
little higher.
 Marie felt totally drained and exhausted, once
inside her flat she kicked off her shoes and went to
the kitchen, to wound up to eat. She would have one
glass of wine then ring Betty, she needed to talk to
her before they met later.
Slumping down on to the sofa Marie took a large
sip of wine and promptly fell asleep. An hour later
she woke with a start her heart racing, she hadn't
priced the theatre job. The atmosphere in the theatre
and Diane had really spooked her, she shuddered;
not used to being so unprofessional. She had to get
a grip too much was resting on this. Just as she was
about to get into the shower to liven herself up,
Betty rang her, she was stuck in the Michaels office

with still more to do. They decided to meet early the
next morning.

 The shower had given her a new lease of life and
after putting on her pyjamas she made herself a
quick ham sandwich. Pouring herself a strong black
coffee got out her laptop. Decision time, she sent an
e-mail to Diane at the theatre saying she would get
back to her within the week with a price for the
costumes. Then went on to tell Betty where they
were after her meetings of the day. Omitting to say
about the theatre pricing. Emphasising that at
tomorrow's meeting they needed to discuss the way
forward. Butterflies still had to price up the curtains,
so much to be done in such a small space of time.
Could Jenny do Hattie's wedding package? Strike
while the iron is hot, she thought and fired of an e-
mail to Jenny. Outlining Hattie's requirements and
arranging for her to be there for the next meeting
First Marie had to drop off the samples. Add this to
the list.

 The costumes and the curtains were a major
problem as Nancy was Butterflies only seamstress
at the moment. Even though she had shown interest
in working for them. She was heavily committed to
a patchwork quilt for a private client for the next
couple of weeks. Marie had been told Nancy needed
the money, but then so did Butterflies. The

question was would she cope with all of this? Did
she have anyone else who could help? There must
be people out there. It was late she wished she had
someone she could call, but there was no-one, what
a depressing thought, ten o'clock at night and she
was alone. No-one to talk to no-one to e-mail. She
walked through to the lounge where her laptop was
flashing 'you have mail'.

 Betty, thank goodness someone was checking their
mail at this late hour. Marie sat down to read. Betty
had plenty of ideas to solve the problems that Marie
had outlined; she was looking forward to meeting
up as planned tomorrow. That's all she said, no
clues as to what she had in mind. Marie was
frustrated she looked at the clock was it too late to
ring her? Eleven o'clock probably best not to. After
all she had a husband and might not welcome an
intrusion to her evening. She sighed and sat down
time enough to worry about that, she wouldn't sleep
until she had written up her notes to print off for
Betty. Then to the whiteboard that was rapidly
filling up with a long list of work. With the
exception of Stacey all her girls were busy for what
looked like six weeks. The business was short in
both the office areas and the sewing. She was going
to have to take on some of the office work herself
and talk again to Chrissie Mathews. They had

chatted briefly a few weeks earlier, now she needed to talk further with her as she said she knew loads of people in the area. Chrissie had offered her coffee. Unfortunately, she had been too busy to take her up on the offer. Marie finally shut her laptop and went to bed praying that she could handle the next few weeks without crumbling. Oh, and ring Mother another one who knows everybody, this was the last thought that raced through her brain as she fell asleep as the church clock struck one.

The following morning Marie woke up feeling completely refreshed and ready for action, after a quick breakfast and plenty of black coffee she switched on her laptop twenty-four e-mails, she waded through them but there was a lot of administration that needed doing, when was she ever going to get time to do that? She made another list, just things to organise from the messages. Then making a late dash she drove to meet Betty in the local coffee shop.

Betty

Betty was already seated at a table in the corner of what was fast becoming their favourite coffee shop. She waved to Marie as she walked through the door. Grinning to herself when she spotted her obviously new jeans, shame she had pressed a crease in them. Marie sat down opposite her and said, 'Am I glad to see you, there's so much work coming in we really need to work closer together, when do you finish the job at Michaels?'

Betty laughed at Marie nervously gabbling without taking a breath and replied.

'I finished this morning I managed a couple of hours after he went home last night, how about you get the coffee? I may have stumbled on a solution to some of your problems.'

To Betty's utter surprise Marie jumped up without further ado and got a tray of coffee and biscuits. Betty smirked, Marie must be desperate she had bought biscuits, everyone knew she would not allow a single crumb to pass her lips. One up to me she thought.

'What's your idea, you saw how much work is coming in I sent you the forward plan, have you had enough time to look at it?' Marie asked.

'Yes, I did,' she paused. 'To be honest we are going to be stretched far too thin, so yesterday I was talking to Michael, he wants me to do just a few hours a week for him on a permanent basis, but he can't afford to pay me.'

'That's no good to us we can't do freebies Betty we are in this to make a profit.' Said Marie frostily.

'So what profit are we making out of Diane Goodson then?' asked Betty bitchily.

'What do you mean, we are still negotiating?'

'Negotiating my arse,' laughed Betty, 'That old witch has never paid for a costume to be made, I bet she promised free advertising for the company on the posters and programmes.'

'Well yes she did, but we are still talking money.' Said Marie testily.

'Face it partner you have been screwed, Diane won't pay you a penny best work out a way to turn this round to our benefit.'

'Trust me I'm working on it I know we can't afford to lose any money at this stage. What about Michael?' asked Marie hastily changing the subject?

'Well, you'll like this I work a maximum of twelve hours a week and we can have use of his spare office in exchange, 'she went on 'It's big enough for at least two desks and has everything we need.' Said Betty with her fingers crossed behind her back, praying Marie would go for this, knowing she had already agreed it with Michael.

 There was a moments silence as Marie thought it through.

'I must say it sounds good to me you sure there is no catch?' she asked.

'No, he's straight and reliable plus you can walk there from your house, unfortunately the parking outside is restricted to two hours, all allocated spaces are taken and there's no all-day parking near, what do you think?'

'I'm not sure.'

'I quite like him; he seems to be easy going I am sure we can work together.' Said Betty crossing her fingers.

'Anything else?' asked Marie.

'Nothing really. Except he's seeing Jenny.'

'Our Jenny?'

'Yes, that's the one, shouldn't be a problem though.'

'When can we go and see this place then? Asked Marie.

'I said we would be there at two.' Said Betty grinning.

'Come on partner what are we waiting for.? Asked Marie grabbing her briefcase. She picked up the unopened biscuits and thrust them at Betty. Here you had better have these I paid for them on expenses' Betty grinned to herself was this another breakthrough?

Betty drove the short way to Michael's offices, with Marie beside her busy sending messages on her phone. She parked up in the short-term car park and they walked across the green to the office block. Betty pressed the buzzer and Michael himself came to let them in.

'Hi Marie, nice to see you again I take it Betty has told you what I am offering.'

'Yes' Marie replied waspishly.

'To be honest Betty has been a godsend to me and my business can't stretch to anther salary since I have taken on a new partner, so this seems a reasonable solution.' Said Michael.

'Yes, so she said.'

'What do you think about using the office and its facilities?' Michael asked

'Obviously I need to see what you are offering first Michael.' She answered frostily.

Betty frowned this was not going as well as she had hoped, Marie seemed even more hostile with Michael at this meeting than at the last one, her body language was offensive her shoulders stiff she was really on the defensive. This attitude really bothered Betty as she was really keen to work close to Michael, she really fancied him, but she was

already married and dull as her marriage had turned
out she was at least faithful. Why couldn't Marie
soften up and try a bit of light-hearted flirting it
might at least get a better deal, but no Marie was
concentrating on playing the part of a tough nosed
businesswoman.

Betty looked at Michel, she could sense he was not
impressed at Marie's attitude after all he was doing
her a favour. This was a two-way deal and as he led
them across to the empty office, she was hoping he
wasn't having serious doubts about this offer.

The office was a large light space next to his office
and although it was empty it was easy to see that the
space would accommodate at least three desks, not
the two that Betty had previously said and the space
was perfect for their needs.

Marie remained silent Betty clapped her hands in
excitement and said, 'It's great, isn't it?'

Marie glared at her and replied, 'Adequate Betty
merely adequate.'

Looking directly at Michael she asked, 'So what's
the deal Michael?'

Michael frowned but aware that this was important
to him, he really needed Betty and couldn't afford
to hire anyone else of her calibre so he swallowed
his pride and instead of telling Marie to get the hell
out of his office he smiled and said 'I am happy to

let Butterflies have use of this space rent free in exchange for twelve hours a week of Betty's precious time.' He leant against the wall waiting for a response, Marie remained silent so he ploughed on 'I have two desks you can have immediately, you can use the photocopier, but you will have to supply all your other equipment.'

'Twelve hours is unacceptable, I am willing to offer ten hours at our current rate that equates to £250 a week, I'm not sure this is office is worth that much,' she paused and went on 'Throw in internet and a phone line and you have got a deal.'

Both Michael and Betty drew in their breath at the same time and Michael held out his hand and Marie grudgingly shook it. Betty winked at Michael and he said. 'I'll draw up a contract and you can move in at the beginning of the month.'

Betty looked at Michael in surprise he seemed to be impressed by Marie not angry at her attitude not at all what she expected

'I am sure Betty will sort everything out.'

With that she turned to leave and beckoned to Betty to follow who did at least have the grace to mouth thank you before they reached the door to the street, Outside Betty turned to her partner and said 'Was that necessary, you were a bit tough on him, he didn't deserve that?'

'I don't like him, and he obviously needs us a lot more than we need him.' said Marie firmly

'Admit it we really need that office and it is a bloody good deal.'

'I'm just worried we are moving on too fast,' she hesitated as she saw the look on Betty's face and softened her tone, she could see she was walking on thin ice with her.' And thanks to you Betty we now have a business address so will you manage the office?'

'I will do my ten hours with Michael and a couple of days for Butterflies just doing admin, but we both need to use it as a base.'

'Good because I intend to come in every morning and check we are covered everywhere and we need at least half an hour with each other so as we don't miss anything.' she paused you do realise this is going to be seven days a week for a while, don't you?'

'Yes, I do and I don't mind as long as you pay me for the time, I put in.' said Betty with her fingers crossed tight behind her back.

'We won't be drawing wages for seven days a week yet, but I promise it will happen eventually. Meanwhile until we move into the office we need to sit down and talk about resource to me at the moment that is our biggest problem I am concerned

that we are not going to be able to cope.' Marie
responded cautiously.

'Let's sort it out now.'

'Don't you have to get home? If you don't, we could
do it over a glass of wine?'

Looking at Marie's face Betty softened, 'Sure but a
glass is not enough better make it a bottle. Then I'll
know how much you care after all we've still got
problems to sort out.'

They walked into the wine bar and sat at a table in
the corner Marie was surprised when the waiter
recognised Betty and said 'Bottle of your usual
Betty?'

'Sure, make sure it's chilled Mark.'

Marie looked at her and said, 'You are a dark horse
I didn't know you came in here.'

'I'll be frank with you Marie everyone from the
office used to come in here nearly every night after
work- when you stayed on working all hours, we
had a life after work, you chose not to.'

Marie surprised her by saying 'I'm fast beginning to
realise what a waste it was giving my time to the
company.'

'Well, it's not too late this business will be great if
you can just loosen up and trust us all.'

'I know, it's not easy, this is all new for me,' she paused looking across the room 'Is that Chrissie Matthews sitting over there?'

'Yep, that's her she's in here most days, bit of a lost soul, but very talented and she could be a great asset for Butterflies you know.' Said Betty.

'Ask her over I have been meaning to catch up with her since I saw her at the WI.' Said Marie.

'Good idea, but I warn you Chrissie is not a wine drinker, her tipple is vodka on the rocks and plenty of it' she replied, standing up and walking over to Chrissie.

Chrissie didn't hesitate when Betty approached her, she stood up and grabbing her purple velvet shoulder bag she plonked herself down beside Marie.

'It's good to see a friendly face,' said Chrissie.

Betty smiled to herself, Marie a friendly face, things were changing.

Chrissie asked 'how's your new business going Marie?

'Chrissie I am glad we bumped into you, I've been thinking we all ought to get together. Betty and I are partners now and we are getting in more work than we think we can cope with. We are looking for skilled help, at the moment we are desperate for machinists and administrators'

Betty interrupted and said 'We have just shaken hands on a new office, we move in next month but we don't think we can wait till then, we want to get everyone together there is just a question of a venue, there will be six of us and it would be good if we could all sit around a table and plan our timetables. But first can the three of us meet and share information?' I know Marie is going to insist everyone checks in to the office on a Friday afternoon for a briefing but meanwhile we need a meeting place.'

Chrissie looked thoughtful and she paused and said 'Look since we met up last time I have done a lot of thinking, I know I said I wasn't interested but your idea has grown on me, I really would like to get involved in some way. So how about my cottage?' 'That sounds perfect, can you manage tomorrow does that give you time to sort out any contacts and ideas?

'Yes, no problem I'm free all day in fact I'm free everyday lately.' Said Chrissie wistfully.

'Great, so do either of you fancy a sandwich, I'm starving.' Said Marie.

Betty stared at her in amazement; Marie was hungry that had got to be a good sign. They ordered sandwiches and while they were waiting Marie got out her notebook. 'First problem we have Chrissie;

is we seem to have more enquiries for sewing than
we have machinists available and to make things
worse Diane at the theatre is expecting us to make
the costumes for Joseph for nothing. Just free
publicity.'
Chrissie thought for a moment 'I think there may be
something I can do; I'll talk to a few people this
afternoon and let you know tomorrow.'
'Well, what I want from tomorrow is names of
anyone you know looking for employment and their
availability and skills, to let me know their
specialist areas. It doesn't matter how bizarre their
talents maybe; we are getting very mixed enquiries,
it would be great to fulfil them all.' She paused and
went on 'Also I am concerned that Jenny and Nancy
are overcommitted and that we don't have enough
work for Stacey.'
'Kind of a brainstorming session then,' said Betty
'That will be it,' said Marie, and went on 'In a
nutshell we need experienced machinists and
efficient administrators. Quickly.'
'I have a few more contacts as well,' said Betty.
'Soon as we finish here, I'll get on to it. How about
we make it tomorrow? '
'Fine by me is it ok with you Chrissie?' asked Marie.

'Sure, no problem with me, in fact I need to get off now as I need to hook up with some of my old cronies and see what I can sort out for tomorrow.'
'Thanks Chrissie that will be a great help.' See you about eleven, we can sort out how you can help then we will decide when we can all get together ahead of our new office.'

Chrissie made her way up to the bar, Marie declined another drink but before she left the wine bar said to Betty, 'So how do you feel about the way things are going so far?'

'I reckon we've made a great headway today and after tomorrow we are going to have to really put the hours in, to keep up the momentum.'

'Great so we both feel the same, do we? Let's toast to it then I'm off to ring the others and draw up a forward plan.'

'Cheers here's to Butterflies.'

'Cheers and Betty thank you.'

'My pleasure Marie, my pleasure' answered Betty thinking of her travel plans not just New York and Las Vegas but the World.

Zack

Los Angeles, last day of another grueling tour Zack glanced to the wings, the chair was there as always and as ever it was empty. Ten years had passed. Still no sign. His son had disappeared from his life along with his wife. Joe was eight, sitting in the chair watching his dad on stage one minute, then he was gone snatched by his estranged wife. Zack never gave up hope, each performance he insisted on putting the chair in the wings, just in case Joe turned up. He never did but he never gave up hope. He finished the encore and ran off the stage to his dressing room closing the door firmly behind him, the rest of the band knew him well enough that if the door was closed then, it stayed closed, and they would leave Zack to it.

Sinking into the chair he felt every minute of his age, picking up the letter he had left on the side - Chrissie his lovely Chrissie she always wrote to him never used modern technology. Despite the state-of-the-art phone he had bought her she still chose to write, complaining that she couldn't work out how to use a mobile to text. He sighed, what a mess his life was, this tour was going to be his last. He had more money than he could ever spend, more houses than he could ever live in and a wife he couldn't find to divorce and Joe his lovely son, now approaching manhood would he ever see him again?

Re reading the letter from Chrissie, after all these years she wanted to settle down with him the letter written a month ago taken time to track him down whilst he was on tour. This was a complication he hadn't anticipated when he fell in love with her at the Isle of Wight Festival in 1970, Summer their daughter born nine months later, he had asked her for years to marry him and she had always refused, preferring to live alone in the cottage he had set her up in. He was happy to go and stay with her half a dozen times a year and watched Summer grow in to the fine woman she was today. It wasn't enough for Zack he had married Suzy quietly on beach in the Caribbean, lucky for him the Paparazzi never discovered this and if Chrissie knew she never let on. She had no idea that Summer had a half-brother. More importantly she never knew Joe had gone missing. On top of that he was still married to Suzy. That was a stumbling block, not because he hoped Suzy would come back but because she had Joe. Never a day went past that he didn't think about his son, but he hadn't a clue where they were. The rest of the band and his entourage had humored him, no-one had ever dared sit in that seat. Without question it was loaded on the truck and a roadie always ensured that the blue director's chair with the word JOE written boldly on the back was in place before Zack went on stage.

Chrissie, she must be feeling her age. She wouldn't want to settle down if there was any other motive. He looked at his reflection in the huge mirror. He hadn't an ounce of fat on him, but the papers were right he certainly was a wrinkly rocker, too many years of debauchery showed in his lined face and through it all there had been Chrissie had always been there for him, never complaining.

Zack poured himself a large shot of bourbon and paced up and down the dressing room, decision time the tour was over, he could go home, but home was where Joe had been born and there were too many memories there. No home was with Chrissie where he should have settled years ago, he would sell everything and move into the cottage with her, right that was what he would do, in fact he would ring her now and tell her. Without thinking he picked up his mobile and pressed her number. As he sank back into the chair the phone rang and rang, no reply, Zack got more and more agitated as it rang on, where was she? He left a message 'Chrissie, sorry I missed you; we need to talk I've decided to cut the tour short will be back soon.'

Unable to wait he opened the door and shouted out for his driver what he needed now was sleep.

'Dan, please bring the car round I want to go back to my hotel.' Dan wasn't happy he was heavily involved in a game of poker and had fully expected Zack to party all night with the others. He took one look at his boss's face and the reality hit; this truly was the last tour. Zack looked every one of his sixty years and more than that he looked totally worn out.

Back at his hotel, Zack stood looking out on to the beach, the sea glistening in the moonlight, he shivered, he was so lonely, he looked at his schedule, he was booked to stay here for another three days. He didn't care about the others; they had all been paid he would go in the morning. He rang the desk and said, 'Do me a favour darling book me a first-class flight back to London in the morning.' The receptionist giggled 'Of course Zack just one seat?'

'Yes, just one and don't tell anyone else, they need to think I'm just resting so keep the do not disturb sign on my door until the end of the week when the others check out.'

'Of course, I understand.'

'There's $100 dollars in it for you, can you please order me a car to go to the airport.'

The next morning the wakeup call roused him from a deep sleep; he had already packed taking only his regular clothes. The rest could follow with the crew. He went unseen downstairs and walked over to the reception desk.

'Good morning. Zack, your taxi is outside, I've printed off your flight details and ticket.' She handed the documents over to him.

As promised, he handed her a $100 bill. 'Thank you, could you sign this please?'

Zack smiled as he signed a program from last night's concert, his smile faded as she said, 'Great my grandma will be over the moon with that.'

He left LA quietly and almost un-noticed. Once when he was at the height of his career he was as famous as John Lennon then there would have been fans everywhere. This time Zack felt almost normal as he checked in his own luggage and walked in to the First-Class lounge for a late breakfast. He rang Chrissie's number again, this time she picked up, 'Do you know what time it is here Zack?'

'Sorry forgot I did call last night.'

'Yes, I got the message are you back at the weekend?'

'No honey I'll be back tomorrow, I'm at the airport now.' Zack answered, 'I can't wait to see you Chrissie.'

'It's difficult tomorrow Zack I've got plans.'
'Whatever do you mean, you don't do anything.'
 He tensed as it hit him his Chrissie was busy, she
replied slowly, 'It's too late I can't change my plans
now.'
'But Chrissie I'm coming home early because of
you?' there was a silence and Chrissie hesitated,
Zack could hear her intake of breath as she said
'Zack I am sorry ring me in a couple of days I will
be free then.' and to his astonishment she hung up.
Now he was really stressed, just about to get on a
plane back to where? Sod Chrissie he was going
straight there he had a key; he owned the cottage
she had better be there they needed to talk.

Chrissie

Chrissie stared at the handset, wondering why on
earth she had done that. Never in forty years had
she put the phone down on Zack. What on earth was
happening to her? She hadn't put anyone or
anything before him. Until now, she immediately
felt agitated, Zack would be furious with her, NO-
ONE BUT NO-ONE hung up on him.

 He was going to turn up she knew him well enough
for that she was just praying he did not appear when
Marie and Betty were there. Her better self- told her
to ring them and cancel but it was far too early.
Curiosity about Butterflies and boredom won,
hopefully Zack would take the hint but secretly she
doubted it. Nothing for it but to go back to
bed.Chrissie woke up and groaned as she saw the
time. Ten o'clock, it hurt to lift her head, what on
earth had she done this time. Spotting the empty
Vodka bottle she was mortified this had to stop,
every time she tried to sort out her feelings, she
turned to alcohol.

 She rolled over and pulled the pillow over her
head, trying desperately to recall the events of
yesterday that had led her to this sorry state. She
moaned as the recollection of speaking to that stuck
up bitch with the red hair, without a clue what they

had talked about. Searching her mind and there it was she had apologised to Marie and invited her round this morning at eleven. Chrissie sat bolt upright, eleven she had just an hour to get her hangover under control and try and look presentable. She struggled to remember why she had invited Marie. Slowly it dawned on her, Marie was offering her work. That was what triggered of all her thoughts of dumping Zack. In the cold light of day and with the hangover from hell, Chrissie knew that Zack was part of her life which was going to be difficult to change, if she was going to straighten herself out, she needed something positive to do.

Maybe this Marie could have the answer. She stood up, stripped of her clothes and walked into the kitchen switched on the kettle, opening the fridge no milk! Carefully opening the front door, she peered round looking for milk. No milk just a bottle of Vodka. Good Old Fred never failed to deliver, without thinking Chrissie picked it up and unscrewed the cap and pouring a large measure into her coffee mug then she took a quick shower.

Half an hour later the hair of the dog had kicked in, Chrissie emerged from the bedroom feeling calm and in control, a quick tidy round her cottage and she was ready. This time she poured vodka into a

glass of orange juice and put on a percolator of
fresh coffee. If the bitch took milk tough.
Barely glancing in the mirror, she rushed around her
huge living room hiding last night's bottles and
generally tidying.

Marie

Marie woke up the next morning feeling totally re-
vitalised. This was all new to her so used to
wearing business suits she was uncertain what to
wear. she settled for a pair of pressed jeans, tee shirt
with blazer, not too business-like she felt, but
certainly smart enough to impress Chrissie
Matthews. Little did she know that Chrissie
Matthews would laugh at a woman of her age in
jeans, especially with sharp creases down the front.
  Marie strode up the path to the front door of
Honeysuckle Cottage, before she could knock the
door flew open and Chrissie came flying out empty
bottles in hand.
'Oh! you're early' squeaked Chrissie 'go in I'm just
going to the dustbin,'
Marie walked into the hallway and sucked in her
breath and as Chrissie came back in, she resisted
making any comment about bottles at eleven
o'clock in the morning. Instead, she said 'What a
lovely place you have here, it's so much bigger than
it looks from the outside.'
'I have been here for forty years; I moved here when
I was pregnant with Summer and been here ever
since.' Realising she was gabbling Chrissie said
'Coffee Marie?'

'Yes please, black no sugar.' She replied patting her skinny frame, 'got to watch my weight.'

Chrissie said as she went out to the kitchen 'that's good I'm out of milk.' Marie took time the poke around the lounge, she looked out into the garden, it was beautifully kept, not manicured but borders of cottage plants all in various colours and stages of flower. Outside the kitchen window was a large herb garden and Marie felt a pang of envy, how on earth had this woman got so much when she had obviously never done a day's work in her life? She moved away from the window and turned to the photos on the mantelpiece.

 Chrissie came in with the coffee and apologised for the lack of milk.

'Isn't that Zack??' asked Marie, holding a photo of Chrissie with Zack and presumably her daughter apparently taken in the very garden she was looking out at now.

 Ignoring Marie Chrissie said quickly 'Come into the dining room we can sit at the table.'

Marie realised Chrissie wasn't going to admit anything, but Marie was clever enough to know that she could file the information away and use it at another time.

'Now what was it you wanted to see me about?
Asked Chrissie swiftly moving the conversation on
to safer ground.

Marie stopped to answer her phone, 'Sure Betty see
you later and oh you had better bring some milk.'
Without giving Betty, the opportunity to question
the request, she hung up and turned to Chrissie who
was looking uncomfortable.

Chrissie

'I am not sure exactly what you want from me,' said Chrissie trying to divert Marie's attention away from the photograph of Zack. She silently cursed herself again, if she hadn't drunk herself in to a stupor last night that wouldn't have happened. She was always very careful to hide any evidence of Zack away, he was her secret and she wanted it to stay that way. She slipped the photo into a drawer when Marie wasn't looking turned to her and said 'I can't think how I can be of help to you

'Let me tell you a bit more about Butterflies and then you can tell me if you are interested.' Said Marie.

'I am curious about the name Butterflies why choose that?'

Marie bristled 'Well I wanted 'Marie and Me' but Betty in all her wisdom said it was unfair as her name should be up there too. As we were at the time flitting from one job to another Butterflies seemed apt. Also, we decided to keep it light as we are covering so many different skills.'

She looked at Chrissie, who was sitting very quietly obviously deep in thought. Chrissie was thinking, this was interesting, she had felt so unsettled these last few weeks, her life lacking direction and an overwhelming feeling of loneliness since Summer had taken off for India. Determined not to show too much interest to Marie she said, 'I think your idea is good but I'm not sure where I fit into it, I'm not particularly good at anything.'

'But you are, the ladies at the WI were raving about your massages, they kept telling me you had healing hands.'

'I haven't ever charged for anything before, I did once think about starting a business myself, I even had a name for it,' she hesitated and then went on 'Chrissies Magic Fingers but someone I know laughed at the idea so I shelved it' answered Chrissie.

'Seems a waste all that learning, and you should never be put off by one person not liking a name.' said Marie, thinking of Betty not liking the name Marie and me.

'I suppose I never thought about, it everything I have ever done has just been a hobby, not a business.'

'First thing we will do is make a list of all your 'hobbies and which ones you have qualifications for- you do have qualifications don't you?'

'Yes, yes I went to college practically every year to study one thing or another- nothing academic, more just stuff I was interested in, I've loads of certificates, hang on they are in the drawer.'

Chrissie walked over to the bureau in the corner of the dining room and pulled out a large floral file stuffed full of papers and said 'There should be some stuff in here, see what you think.' She handed the file to Marie who took it eagerly.

Marie took a few minutes to sort through the papers and Chrissie went out to the kitchen to fetch more coffee, and as she came back in Marie looked at her and said 'You do have a lot to offer, she waved a pile of papers at her. Marie started to make a list, we have massage, Reiki, Indian head massage, yoga, aromatherapy, reflexology. And colour therapy.'

'I may have diplomas for all of that Marie, but I never use any of it,' sighed Chrissie.

'You spoke well about it; the WI were really enthusiastic about your talk on the benefits of Reiki.'

Chrissie hesitated; her brain was whirling was this could be the answer to her problems. For years she had been going to college every term, it started as a way to pass the time while Summer it was at school and then it had become a habit and truth was, she didn't need the money so all she had done was file the diplomas and move on to the next course. Now dissatisfied with her life Marie was offering her a way out. She wasn't going to let her know she was keen. She wasn't going to let the bitch think she was going to grab this without a lot of thinking.

'What do you say Chrissie are you interested?' Chrissie wavered, the devil on her shoulder saying let her sweat. But her head took over and she said 'Yes, I am, I haven't got a clue what to charge though.'

'Fantastic, leave the costing to me, can I take these Diplomas away and I'll copy them and do some research on pricing and get back to you.' She paused 'you do have a computer, don't you?'

'Yes, but I hate modern technology,' answered Chrissie. Thinking of the expensive computer sat untouched in the dining room. Another gift from Zack.

'Well, you need to go over the courses and do a bit of revision.' Said Marie.

'That's no problem I've got all my files and coursework in my workroom. There must be three bookshelves of it.'

'Workshop, why have you got a workshop Chrissie?' Asked Marie.

'Ah one of my projects' she giggled, I thought I would try pottery, I bought a wheel and got bored.'

'Shall I add it to your CV?' asked Marie with a huge smirk on her face.

Marie made Chrissie feel really stupid and so she quickly said, 'Do you want my contacts now or shall we wait for Betty?'

'I think Betty will be here in a moment, save going over the same thing twice, meanwhile I would love another coffee please.

With that the doorbell rang and Betty rushed in looking flustered and somewhat dishevelled.

'So sorry, I got caught by Jenny Moore, apparently she has been round to your flat looking for you.'

'Oh, damn I meant to ring her, mother has been mithering on about how clever she is and I do have the samples for her to cost for Hattie Smythe Browne.'

'Well, she is definitely keen looking for work, where are we I'm dying for a coffee,' she giggled and produced a carton of milk from behind her back. 'Here you are Chrissie, two sugars please.'

Chrissie bustled out to the kitchen and Betty looked questionably at Marie, 'How's it going?' she mouthed.

'Not sure she seems a bit hostile; I think it's me; she really doesn't seem to like me.'

'Okay let me do the talking and see where we get too.'

Chrissie came back in, they all sat around the huge table she handed out the mugs and apologised for the lack of biscuits.

Marie said, 'Don't worry about biscuits, we don't need biscuits, do we?' She looked directly at Betty who glared back at her.

'Chrissie have you had time to think about people you know who may be able to help'

Before she could answer Betty Marie piped up 'A little bird tells me you make beautiful cakes as well as your Reiki and all your other talents.'

Chrissie hesitated before she answered. 'I have got contacts and ideas but haven't had time to speak too anyone yet, but I'm happy to pass over their details. If you could possibly outline what you need, I will see where I can help personally. As for cakes I don't bake anymore. I well yeah can do all sorts of stuff but not seriously as I just told Marie.'

'I'm sure we can use your skills please don't underestimate yourself.' Replied Betty

'Why on earth not?' asked Marie.

Marie took the diplomas from her briefcase and handed them to Betty, who took a few minutes to sort through the papers and Chrissie went out to the kitchen to fetch more coffee, and as she came back in Betty looked at her and said 'You have a lot to offer' and she waved the pile of papers at her.

Chrissie wavered, the devil on her shoulder saying let her sweat. But her head took over and she said 'I just try to keep busy I suppose.'

Marie made Chrissie feel uncomfortable and anxious to bring the meeting to a close, she quickly said, 'I have to be somewhere, can we carry this on another day give me a chance to talk to some people I need to think about all of this.'

Marie was not happy, but she took a deep breath and pasted a smile on her face. 'If you want to join us Chrissie we don't have too much time.'

'Look why don't I ring you tonight with an update.' With that Marie and Betty picked up their belongings and left. Once outside Betty looked at Marie and said, 'I haven't a clue whether she is going to be able to help us, but one thing I think is clear is she doesn't like you very much.

Marie laughed and said, 'I felt that too.'

Chrissie shut the door after them unsure whether this was what she really wanted, feeling very confused and uncertain as to what she had let herself

She took the photo from the drawer and put it back on the shelf 'Zack' she said 'Oh Zack where are you when I need you?'

Little did she know that Zack was back in the UK and holed up in a hotel and cooling his heels before he plucked up courage to visit her and tell her he was married. For years he had hidden this from her, but still offering her marriage knowing full well she would refuse. Now in her letter she had changed her mind, he didn't know how to break this news to her.

Marie

Marie got home after coffee with Betty and Chrissie and sat at her kitchen table. For the first time since she had started Butterflies, she began to feel very positive, from Monday she had an office all be it she had to put up with that creep Michael Lambert. That was a small price to pay for office space, after all she was used to dealing with smart arses like him. Just because he was good looking didn't mean, he could win her over. He was only a man, she was sure she was doing him a favour not the other way round. Betty didn't come cheap.

Marie checked her voicemail, three enquiries, she winced as the first one was for someone who wanted flat pack Ikea furniture put together. She duly returned the call and said she would get back in two days with a price. She wrote down the details, thinking putting together flat pack furniture couldn't be that difficult, could it? She would do it herself if necessary. She made a further note to find the Ikea catalogue and check out what they charged to assemble furniture.

The landline rang, before Marie could speak a voice said. 'Marion, at last I've been trying to get you.'

'Mother it's you.' Said Marie.

'Of course, it's me I have rung you six times,
you've been out each time.'
'Mother, I have voicemail, I also have a mobile, so
it can't have been that urgent can it?'
'You know I can't stand those voice thingummies
Marion.' Said Violet.
'Well now you've got me what do you want?'
'Oh, too busy to ask how I am then!!' asked Violet.
'Sorry Mother how are you?' without waiting for
Violet to answer Marie went on 'Once again Mother
its Marie, not Marion.'
'You were born Marion, I'm too old to change now.'
Said Violet frostily.
'Anyway, thanks for asking but yes I am busy, was
there anything in particular you wanted?' asked
Marie tetchily.
'Yes, there was as a matter of fact, can you come to
the next WI meeting there are a couple of women
who need your services.'
'What are they looking for? Can I not contact them
before hand?' asked Marie.
'Well yes I suppose, hold on while I get their
numbers.' Said Violet as she left Marie hanging on
to find the phone numbers. 'Here we are, first is
Mavis Fordham, her mother has broken her hip and
needs someone to go in everyday and clean, do her

shopping and walk her dog, her number is 06789
345892. Did you get that Marion?'
'Yes Mother, is that it?'
'No there's June Davies- you know her who owns
the tea shop in the village, she needs someone to
make speciality cakes to order. She has been doing
it herself up until now, but it has really taken off
and she can no longer cope. You could just pop in
and see her.'
'Thanks Mother I'll get on to them both this
afternoon, then I will drop some business cards in to
you, so you can hand them out save you passing on
messages.'
'Marion, I don't mind passing on messages and I
don't expect a commission.' Said Violet.
Marie laughed 'Thanks Mother I do appreciate it, let
me take you out for Sunday lunch then we can have
a proper chat.'
'That will be lovely.'
'I'll pick you up at 1 and I will book us a table at the
Plough and Barleycorn.'
'See you then'
Marie put the phone down and contemplated the
ever-growing list and made herself a jug of coffee
and cracked on with the phone calls and began to
lay out a plan of action ready for the next get

together at Chrissies. Thinking about the meeting
she rang Betty.

'Betty did you see the workshop at the end of
Chrissies Garden?'

'I seem to remember hearing that it was enormous.'

'I did try looking out of the window but there are
conifers in the way. I guess it must be behind there.'
answered Marie,

'She is a bit of a dark horse that one all those
certificates and no obvious income. How on earth
does she live? Those courses don't come cheap.'

'I wondered about that mind you; it was odd when I
went round there, she had a huge photo of herself
with Zack.'

'Not the Zack?'

'Yes, it was definitely him.'

'Well did you ask her?'

'I did, but she just fielded the question and when I
next looked the photo was gone.'

'It was probably at a festival or something she's
always been a hippy,' said Betty.

'No I'm pretty sure it was her back garden, and what
a garden.'

'They say she grows marijuana in her greenhouse.'

'Nothing wrong with a bit of pot Marie perhaps you
should try some.'

'I don't think so.'

'However, I do think she will be an asset to the business, but we may just have to deal with some of her issues.' said Marie

'She's all right I think she is lonely, that's why she goes into the wine bar, strange thing is she used to be a brilliant cake maker but when the WI asked her to make some cakes, she point blank said she couldn't bake.' Answered Betty

'Perhaps she just didn't want seems to me she has tried her hand at everything she flits from one thing to another.' as she said that she laughed 'Chrissie Mathews will be an ideal Butterfly associate then!!'

'Now what is our biggest immediate problem, Marie?' asked Betty.

Marie had to end the conversation at this point as the doorbell was ringing, promising to call Betty back later.

148

Jenny

No-one was more surprised than Jenny when she
was approached by Marie Halshaw's mother Violet
at last week's W. I. Meeting. It had been years since
she had had any contact with Marie and the thought
of getting involved with that snobby woman was
not an attractive proposition. Jenny put the business
card Violet had given her behind the photo of her
late husband. Sighing she sat down staring at the
picture, there was no doubt her life was a mess.
Peter had died suddenly and left her alone with two
teenage boys at university, in a rambling house with
a huge mortgage and very little life insurance. What
money she had was fast diminishing and Jenny
knew she was going to have to get a job of some
description, but with Marie? She shuddered at the
thought. They had been in the same year at school
and Marie had been a lot brighter than her and far
more popular. Jenny had been the dumpy girl with
acne, always on the side-lines, wishing she was part
of the popular gang.

They had been happy her and Peter, when you are
young, old age seems so far away. Peter had been a
dreamer and lived for the moment. Who would have
ever imagined he would die at forty-eight? Leaving
her with a huge hole in her life and all of her dreams

of a retirement spent running dog boarding kennels,
gone.

Jenny spent her time making cards and painting
portraits, mainly of dogs. If she were brutally
honest, she preferred dogs to people any day.
Selling what she could at the W. I. was not going
particularly well, and she was fast realising that she
needed more if she was going to be able to stay in
her house.

Violet had indicated that Marie had fallen on hard
times but was trying to get her new business off the
ground. Jenny wasn't really keen to catch up with
Marie, they hadn't been good friends at school and
after school they just drifted apart. She had always
been jealous of Marie, her with her high-flying job
and posh house, while she had been a mere
housewife.

Having reluctantly told Violet she would contact
Marie she reached for the phone, then hesitated that
could wait until morning. She would go round after
walking the dogs.

Tonight, she was going out with Michael Lambert.
It was only their second date but despite the first
date being almost a disaster, Jenny had high hopes
for Michael. An accountant, she loved the thought
of a man organised, with money, rumour had it he
was loaded and best of all he was divorced. Jenny

had big plans for a future together, the first problem
she had to overcome was his fear of dogs. He swore
he wasn't scared of dogs, just didn't like them he
much preferred cats. That couldn't be right, surely
everyone loved dogs,

There was a sharp knock on the door. Jenny
answered it, 'Michael, you are early come in come
in.'

Michael didn't move, 'Why don't I wait in the car?'
'I'll shut the dogs in the kitchen.'

He hesitated and pressing the button on his key fob
to lock his beloved jaguar he reluctantly followed
Jenny in.

'Sit down I will only be a few minutes.' She said and
left him standing in the middle of the room.

He stood looking out into the neglected back
garden, an overgrown tangle of weeds and shrubs,
lawn littered with dog mess. He shuddered and at
this moment Jenny came back into the room, still
wearing grubby jeans, although she had changed her
sweatshirt.

'I thought we were going out?'

'No, I can't leave the dogs for too long, so I've
made us a lovely tea.' said Jenny, as she spoke, she
saw Michael's expression change and she watched
as he sat down and immediately brushed off a dog
hair from his immaculate trousers. He did sit

through tea and with great difficulty ate his way
through cucumber sandwiches and chocolate eclairs
not what he had on his mind to eat that evening. He
was expecting a huge steak, it was difficult not to
show his disappointment at the food that Jenny put
in front of him. Luckily his phone buzzed, with that
he made his excuses and left on the pretext of an
urgent issue with a client.

 Jenny was upset, she knew it was her fault of
course she should have made more effort, but
moments later Michel was forgotten as she went out
to walk her beloved dogs.

 The next morning Marie answered the ringing
doorbell and on seeing Jenny standing there said
'Oh Jenny I was going to ring you later; sorry I
missed you yesterday. Betty told me you had called
round. Come in come in.'

 Jenny hesitated and being confronted by an
immaculate Marie confused her slightly, not what
she was expecting, she mumbled foolishly 'your
mother said you wanted to see me about a wedding
package.'

'Come in, coffee is on sit down and I will tell you
all about it.'

 Jenny looked around the immaculate room and
anxiously brushed the dog hairs off her grubby
jogging pants. What was she thinking expecting no

hoping to see Marie in a mess. Even the piles of paper were straight oh why had she not gone home and changed after walking her dogs?

Marie came back into the room carrying a tray of coffee and biscuits, placing the tray down on the coffee table, she picked up the file from the top of the pile and handed it to Jenny saying 'This is for Hattie Smythe Browne's daughter, she is getting married next year sometime, yet to fix a date. Do you know the Smythe-Browne's?'

'Yes, I do.'

Jenny took the file and spread the samples in front of her and looking at the detailed list she said, 'They are beautiful, and the quantities they are huge!'

'What she wants is designs similar to this in this shade of peach and the paper must be top quality grade, better than the samples.'

'I have a very good source of supply, which I love to use but it is often too expensive so this will be a joy.' Jenny looked at the list again and asked, 'What's the time scale?'

Marie held her breath, seemed like Jenny was interested, 'We have two months to submit samples and agree prices, from there we will agree a delivery schedule. If we get this order the rest will be up to you. What do you think?'

Jenny looked down again at the list in her lap and said, 'I would love the opportunity Marie, it's a great challenge, just what I need right now.'
'It's yours if you think you are up to it.'
'I am, absolutely, thank you Marie, I won't let you down.'
'In that case take this file away- I have a copy. 'If you could do me some samples and costings, will two weeks be enough time?'
'Yes, no problem I am so excited I can't wait to get started; I have been at a bit of a loose end lately.'
'I'm sorry, I forgot your husband died, didn't he?'
'Yes, it was three years ago now, in the meantime I have been doing very little' She tailed off and went on quietly 'Plus I am not too ashamed to admit I do need to earn some money. Things are a bit tight at the moment.'
Marie tried to look sympathetic 'Hopefully this will be just the beginning, do you have any other hobbies or skills that we may be able to use?'
Jenny thought for a moment and replied 'I do pet portraits and scrapbooks and of course I do cards and calendars, mostly I sell at the W. I. But I'm not very good at promoting myself though.'
'Sounds good to me, I'm planning a brochure of everything Butterflies has to offer, once I have all

samples available, I'll include everything of yours along with it.'

'Lovely, just give me a few days to get together some samples of my work.'

Marie said 'We are arranging a coffee morning at Chrissie Mathews place, basically to talk through where we are, what we need and where we are going. I will let you know which day next week; it would be good if you could be there.'

'I thought you were taking office space in Michael's building?' Jenny asked blushing.

'He told you, did he? News travels fast. We will have an office there, but it won't be ready for a couple of weeks.' She paused 'Are you two an item then'

Jenny giggled girlishly, 'we have been out a couple of times, but he doesn't like dogs, or children come to that.'

'How many dogs have you got?'

'Only four'

'Four sounds like a nightmare to me!'

Jenny spotted Marie looking at her watch, obviously bored by the mention of dogs. Sensing she was in danger of overstaying her welcome she stood up and said 'better go dogs need feeding. I take it Chrissie still lives in Honeysuckle Cottage?'

'Yes, I'll give you a ring as soon as I have a firm date and time.'

Once Jenny had gone Marie rang Betty back and said,' That was Jenny and good news she is very keen, so I think she can handle the wedding stationery package.'

'I hope so Hattie wotsit is a big noise in the village. If we get this right who knows what will follow.'

'Smythe Browne.'

'What?'

'Hattie Smythe Browne, that's her name.'

Betty bristled, trust Marie to be pedantic, but went on to say, 'that may be sorted but one of our pressing problems is the theatre costumes and those curtains.'

'I know the costumes are bothering me, we are going to make nothing out of this but we need positive promotion so to me the priority is to get them out of the way.'

'I know the woman who runs Stitch and Bitch, I'm sure they will help out.'

'Stitch and Bitch? What the hell is that?' asked Marie.

'A group of women, or at least I think it is just women. They meet in the local community centre every week just to sew but I'm not sure how much stitching goes on.'

'Ok can you pop in and see if they are interested then we need a representative to come to our meeting,'

'No problem have we got a firm date yet?'

'Yes, if we can all make it, Friday at ten.'

'Great I will get on it, I will leave sorting everyone else to you.' She thought for a moment and said, 'While I'm out I will drop into the sewing machine shop, I know the manageress Jane and see who she knows. She was in a year below us at school, she's had the shop for years, and there is nothing she doesn't know about sewing.'

'Good sounds encouraging, speak to you tomorrow Betty and thank you.'

Marie sat back on the sofa, her brain whirring, first she made a list of enquiries and once she had transferred all the enquiries to a white board, she felt confident that the meeting would tie up some of the loose ends at least, if not all.

Betty

Betty was tired it had been a long day, trying to get Michael's office sorted out. This was only supposed to take the morning, but she had stayed on to get it to a manageable level. Followed by her weekly supermarket shop which had to sit in the boot of her car while she had a quick wash and blow dry.

With a heavy heart opened the door to find Derek fast asleep in the chair TV blaring out, empty beer bottles at his side. What had happened to them? When he had his business, he was a real fun guy and Betty had looked forward to cooking dinner while he poured them a glass of wine chatting about his day. Maybe Butterflies was going to be her salvation. Admittedly at the moment it was a bit disjointed, but Marie was really focused and between them they were going to bc a great team. She still fantasised about leaving Derek and travelling, that was not the future she had imagine she would have preferred them to be making plans together.

After unloading the shopping, while Derek snored on, she shut herself into the kitchen, Betty laid all her notes out on the table and made a list of everything she had promised Marie she would do.

First call was to Jane, 'Hi Jane its Betty Parker, how are you keeping?'

'Lovely to hear from you Betty what are you up to these days?'

Betty briefly explained Butterflies and what she could do for them. Jane was enthusiastic in her response, 'Firstly Stitch and Bitch is still running, the organiser is Sue Brown she has a dozen women who regularly attend her meetings. But she is struggling for premises, as it happens tomorrow, they are using the back room of my shop. Why don't you come along and meet the team?'

'That would be great, thank you. But first Nancy Bolton? ' Asked Betty.

'What about her?'

'She showed interest when I spoke to her a couple of weeks ago but said she was busy on a project, since then we have been unable to contact her.' Betty replied.

Jane hesitated, 'It may be just gossip but I heard she had left her husband and moved up to Scotland to be with her daughter.'

'I'd better cross her off my list then, no point in waiting on one person when there is so much at stake. What time will be convenient to drop in?'

'Anytime tomorrow after ten, and I also have a list of dressmakers who I recommend to customers for

alterations and help with special projects. We can
go through that together if you like.'
'Perfect thank you Jane see you tomorrow.' she
ended the call

Betty poured another coffee and looked at a pile of
dirty breakfast dishes, Derek hadn't even bothered
to load the dishwasher. Had he even had dinner? It
was difficult to determine, normally she would have
rustled a meal for him whatever time she got in.
She decided if he was hungry then he could get
something for himself. Today had been good so far
and Betty was running on adrenalin so leaving the
messy kitchen she went upstairs, time to soak in the
bath with some music and an early night – alone.
This was not a day to be spoilt by waking Derek
and nagging him to clear up and although she
wanted to talk to him about Butterflies, clearly there
was no point tonight. She poured the last of her
Molton Brown bath oil into the bath and ran the
taps. With Neil Diamond playing on her cd player,
she wrapped her aged towelling dressing gown
round her, before stepping into the bath dashed
downstairs, seeing Derek still sprawled in the chair,
she poured herself a large glass of Pinot Grigio to
be enjoyed while soaking. Then on impulse she
fished around and found a Jo Malone candle one
she had carefully stashed away. It had been part of

her leaving present from Jones Macintosh not the sort of extravagant thing she would ever have bought for herself. She placed it at the end of the bath.

Laying back in the fragrant water, holding her glass, she watched the flickering flame and all she could think was her marriage was like the flame and somehow, she had to stop it going out completely. It had to be kept alive somehow, but how?

Stacey

Stacey picked up the phone, fully expecting the call to be from someone wanting money. Putting on her poshest voice she said, 'Stacey O Neill here.'

'Oh, hi Stacey, Marie Halshaw.'

Stacey's heart sank; her first thought was that something had gone wrong with the flat cleaning job. Had her two daughters from hell ruined everything? She was dependant on Marie paying her for cleaning that block of flats they can't have been stealing the flats were empty. She took a deep breath and said, 'Nice to hear from you Marie.'

'You too Stacey, I have your money, you did a really good job. Thank you. I take it you want cash?'

'Please.'

'That's fine this time but going forward if you want more work it will have to be paid into a bank account. We will leave it to you to pay your tax.'

Stacey laughed 'Yeah of course is there anything else coming up?'

'Yes, there is, are you free tomorrow?'

'Sure am,' said Stacey. 'Don't have much work at the moment.'

'Do you know Chrissie Mathews cottage?'

'Yeah, why does she need it cleaning?' asked Stacey.

Marie laughed 'No we want to get everyone who
wants to be associated or work for Butterflies to get
together and sort out everyone's schedules.'
'I'll be there, what time?'
'Eleven for coffee and biscuits.'
'I ain't eating biscuits in her house.'
'Why ever not?' asked Marie.
'Cos, I heard she cooks with that marijuana stuff.'
'I don't think so Stacey, that's just gossip,'
'It's not gossip she grows the stuff herself in her
greenhouse- pretends its tobacco plants.'
'Well alright if it makes you feel better, I'll bring
you a packet of custard creams. See you then.
  With that Stacey switched off her phone and
danced around the room and let out a whoop. What
could be better than a huge pay day tomorrow and
more work promised. She could put up with that
snotty Marie if she continued to pay well, besides
her escape fund was growing. She walked through
to her tiny kitchen and filled the kettle all the time
thinking about the six thousand pounds coming her
way. All it had taken was two weeks really hard
work. And how she had grafted and her lazy good
for nothing daughters hadn't bothered to get out of
bed until almost lunchtime, where she had got up
religiously at five every morning, gone to the flats
and cleaned.

Then gone back home for lunch dragging Tracy
and Chelsea back with her she had made them work
till tea time, then the pair of them had gone out
drinking while Stacey had made Pats dinner and left
it on the side in case he came home as usual, falling
in bone tired around midnight. She had told no-one
how much money this job was worth, luckily Trace
and Chels were stupid and completely unable to do
basic maths, so when the job was first up for offer,
they had not a clue how much money was involved,
typically they hadn't paid attention to the
conversation, too busy checking their phones, so
were only interested in what she said she would pay
them. They were happy with that and had no idea
they were being ripped off. As for Pat he wasn't
interested as long as he had money to go to the
betting office.
  Still Stacey was worried, Marie would be giving
her a huge amount of cash to hide in the house. She
had a secret stash, kept in a tin in the wardrobe
inside her suitcase. It was risky but she relied on the
fact that Pat was too lazy to open a suitcase let
alone lift it from the top of the wardrobe. To her
this was a shed load of money to leave laying
around. Not a good idea with gambler of a husband.
Tomorrow afternoon she would take some of the
cash to a bank in the village. It was time she got

herself a bank account as Marie had suggested. Then when it was safe, she would be somebody, no longer poor Stacey, Pat O'Neill's long-suffering wife. But she wasn't his wife, they had never got round to marrying. Time had passed and they had muddled along, it hadn't taken Stacey long to realise that the only way she could cope with his useless ways was to immerse herself in work. The only work she could get was cleaning since the factory where she had worked for years as a machinist had closed down.

The girls were a huge disappointment, they were like their father, all hated work, they had the morals of alley cats, would sleep with any man providing he had a pulse, for a couple of drinks.

Stacey sat down to drink her tea; a warm feeling swept over her- this was as near to happiness as she had felt for years. Pat was down the pub; the girls were sleeping of the booze from last night and her escape money was growing faster than she had dared believe.

On the spur of the moment, she looked at her watch and picked up the phone, 'Hi Terri, hope I'm not ringing too early for you.'

'Stace lovely to hear from you how's it going sis?'

'Better than I thought, I've got myself a nice little job with a promise of plenty of work at last.'

'Great so are you still going to come out to LA?'
'That's the plan, I reckon by the end of next year I will be packing my case.'
'Perfect, I will start decorating a couple of rooms for you.'
'I can't wait Terri, I really believe it's going to happen now.'
'Speak soon Stace got to go now taxi has just hooted I'm off to town shopping.'
The plan had formed over the years and she knew now it was going to work. Her sister lived on the outskirts of Los Angeles and had been recently widowed and was begging Stacey to go and live with her. Stacey had dismissed it at first but as the girls had got older, her situation got worse and America her dream. Pat would never find her, not that he would bother. That was the sad part twenty-two years wasted with him, not an iota of affection since day one, Stacey had simply taken over from his mother. She had borne him two children, both conceived when he had come home drunk after a tidy win at the bookies.

Now at forty-two, she was mourning her wasted youth, and yearning for affection. She looked in the mirror. Hard work had kept her slim and fit but the hard life and smoking too much had taken its toll. Her face was lined and there were constant bags under her eyes, her blonde hair was cropped but neglected, dark roots showing through, but hey that was fashionable now. Nothing was impossible she would re-invent herself and become Staci Kemp of L.A.

Betty

Feeling refreshed after her early night Betty drove down to meet up with Jane at her shop in the High St.

'I love coming into this place,' she said as she stroked a roll of purple velvet.

'What happened to you Betty you were always popping in for wool or fabric for one project or another? I haven't seen you for ages.'

'Life happened to me Jane, you know how it is? I thought retirement would be the answer, but it turned out to be the complete opposite I've lost my mojo!'

'I know how you feel, business isn't so good and I'm struggling myself, now come out the back and meet the Stitch and Bitch team!'

As Betty followed Jane through the shop, she looked longingly at the rainbow-coloured embroidery threads, her eyes lit up as she spotted a rack of wools in every colour under the sun. Sighing she promised herself to get out her knitting, it would be satisfying to hear the gentle clacking of needles again.

The team were sitting at a round table, plenty of coffee cups around, very little sewing visible.

Jane introduced Betty to Sue and the girls and Betty sat down and explained what she wanted.

Sue spoke first, 'I know we are capable but the problem we have is that we have to work from our homes as we don't have any where we can all work together. These meetings are just for advice and any hand sewing.' As an afterthought she said, 'With plenty of gossip in between coffee and cake!'
Betty smiled and thought for a moment, and answered 'I am catching up with my partner and the rest of the team tomorrow and it would be good if you could come along Sue and we can discuss things in more detail, also if you could talk to all your girls and see who will be interested.'
'Sure, sounds interesting, I trust we will be paid not just volunteers.'
'Of course we will be paying,' she scribbled down the address and handed the paper to Sue.
 Before they went back into the shop, Betty said, 'could you bring a list with you tomorrow of all those who are interested in joining us and what their speciality skills are. It would also help if you could list what machines they have.'
'That shouldn't be a problem, though we may be short of an overlocking machine, I know that Carole had one and it has been playing up.'
'List everything and we will talk about the detail tomorrow.'

They walked back through to the shop and Jane invited her to sit down and have a coffee, as she poured the steaming drink into the mugs, she said, 'I have spoken to my dressmaking contacts and I've come up with a list of six which added to the Stitch and Bitch girls will make a fair mix. I can vouch for all of them, they've given me the go ahead to give you, their details.' She handed a typewritten list to Betty.

Betty looked at the sheet of paper, 'Thank you Jane, I'll make contact with all of them, but we won't be in a position to use them just yet.'

'Don't worry about that, they are all very busy at the moment.'

'The other thing is supply of trimmings threads etc Jane, how can you help us in the future?'

'I'm not sure, it depends, what are you thinking?'

Betty thought for a moment and said, 'It occurred to me that we are going to need help with the purchasing of all the materials and accessories?'

'I could certainly help but business is not brilliant at the moment so there would have to be something in it for me and the shop of course. I certainly have the contacts,'

'Plus, you have the knowledge, which will be invaluable to us. Like I said before its early days yet but I am sure we can work something out which will be to all of our advantages. Can you get someone to look after the shop tomorrow and come to our meeting?'

'Yes, I can no problem, I'll come with Sue she has the details I assume.'

'I gave them to her earlier. Look I must dash and thank you so much Jane you have been more than helpful.'

Jane waved Betty off and as she drove away, she realised that she had sorted one problem but by doing that she had a possible twelve machinists with plenty of skills and loads of work to give them. The downside was it was going to be a huge logistic problem with them all working from their back bedrooms at home. If this was going to work at all they need a driver who was also a mechanic, to look after the machines and collect and deliver the work.

Derek would be ideal, if only she could talk to him, he had the experience but unless she could pluck up the courage to talk to him. The problem would grow. At the moment his indifference was increasing rather than decreasing she was finding it extremely difficult to bring up the subject of Butterflies, so he still remained in dark about the venture.

Chrissie

Chrissie tumbled out of bed a lot earlier than her normal ten o'clock, half of her was looking forward to Marie's get together pep talk or briefing whatever she wanted to call it, the other half was desperately anxious that Zack hadn't answered her calls. Chrissie checked her voicemail again, nothing, not a word. Perhaps he was going to surprise her, whatever she was uneasy she hadn't heard from him since she had put the phone down on him. Maybe that hadn't been a good move on her part. She had never done that before, she was sure Zack was going to be really angry with her.

Chrissie shrugged her shoulders, today she had to put Zack and marriage out of her head and concentrate on getting sorted out for Marie's meeting.

Luckily, she had stayed sober enough last night to tidy up and this time she had carefully removed every trace of Zack from downstairs and boxed everything up and stacked it well out of sight, she showered and dressed and cycled down to the bakers to pick up pastries and croissants. She'd show that Marie, she wasn't the dumb hippy that she always made her feel. Back at the cottage she put a large pot of coffee on her Aga and waited for Marie to arrive. True to form Marie was early and laden down with, whiteboards and planners.

Chrissie took a deep breath and said, 'Hi Marie, so glad to see you come in go through to the dining room, sort out what you want to do.'

Marie said, 'Thanks Chrissie, for helping us out today.'

'I'm glad to have something to do Marie, coffees on and I picked up croissants and pastries.'

'I didn't think about food just a couple of packets of custard creams!' said Marie.

'No, I don't imagine food is very high on your agenda,' she laughed as she looked at Marie's skinny frame.

'Sorry, let me pay for those, they look divine.' Said Marie.

'No, I'm happy to do it I picked them up from the village bakery, just let's get on with the morning. You set up what you need, I'll go and sort out everything else.'

'I do appreciate it Chrissie, thank you.' Said Marie.

Chrissie left Marie to it and went out into the garden to pick some flowers, glancing at the phone to see if she had missed a call from Zack. Nothing, she shrugged and went on to collect roses as she walked back through the French doors she flicked on the stereo. The sound of music lifted her spirits.

Marie

Marie had only been to Chrissies once before, it was a beautiful cottage, very comfortable if not her style. It felt welcoming and Marie felt a pang of envy; it was a lovely place to be.

Once she was set up, she went into the kitchen to find Chrissie, who was leaning against the kitchen sink, gazing out into the garden, singing softly to herself.

Marie watched her for wishing just for a moment that she could be so relaxed. Marie cleared her throat and Chrissie jumped.

'Sorry Chrissie just wondered if I could have a coffee before the others arrive.'

'Yes, silly me of course.'

She poured a mug for Marie.

Marie held the mug up, 'Oh my goodness what a lovely mug.'

'I made them, I dabbled briefly in pottery.'

Marie looked around and on the tray were a dozen at least hand painted mugs. A spray of honeysuckle on each all signed by Chrissie. Just then the doorbell rang, Chrissie let Betty in.

'Sorry I am a bit late I stopped off to buy pastries.'

Marie giggled which surprised Betty, as she spotted the array of food Chrissie had laid out on the table she began to laugh as well.

'Now, now girls,' said Chrissie as the doorbell rang
again. As she disappeared into the hall Marie
looked at Betty, 'Are you ready for this partner?'
'Sure am,' she pulled out her notes, 'worked on this
last night.'

 As she said that the doorbell rang, Chrissie opened
the door to Jenny who had bumped into Sue
outside.'

'Lovely grab a coffee and take a seat.' Said Betty.
Marie said, 'Welcome ladies we just need Stacey
and Jane then we can get started.' Said Marie.

 Chrissie called out 'Stacey's here and closely
followed by Jane, we're ready to start.'

 They all took their seats round the long table,
where Marie had carefully laid out agendas and
notepads and pencils for everyone. Chrissie poured
them all coffee and before Marie started the
meeting, they tucked into the huge feast of food laid
out in front of them.

 Marie started to speak. 'Before we start, I would
like to say don't expect all this food every time or
not until we make our first million! Thank you,
Chrissie, for letting us use this lovely cottage as our
meeting room.'

 They all laughed, and Marie went on 'anyway
thank you all for coming, you will see I have put an
agenda in front of you all, I would appreciate it if

we could stick to it. Betty and I have left plenty of time for questions at the end of the morning. We welcome all your comments, suggestions and ideas.' Marie stopped as the door was flung open. Chrissie went white and dropped her coffee cup all over the highly polished table and said 'Zack?'

'What the fuck is going on here Chrissie?' he asked angrily.

Chrissie stood up quickly and ushered Zack out of the room saying, 'Just give me a few moments' girls.' She closed the door behind her.

Stacey stood up and calmly grabbed a handful of serviettes to mop up the coffee and squeaked 'Ain't that the Zack?'

Betty asked, 'Sure looks like him to me, what on earth is he doing here?'

The others looked blankly at each other, but all so bemused at the scene that had unravelled in front of them. Marie having spotted Zack's picture on a previous visit said. 'I don't think it is any of our business, I'm sure Chrissie will tell us if she wants. Let's press on I can fill Chrissie in later we don't have that much time.

Chrissie

 Meanwhile Chrissie went into the lounge with Zack, she was beaming from ear to ear. Hoping that the fact he had turned up meant he had changed his mind and that they were getting married after all.

'You look tired Zack.' she said quietly.

'Yeah, got in from the States first thing this morning, picked up your messages and here I am. Didn't expect that lot in there though. Thought we had an agreement, no getting involved with the locals. This is my hideaway or bloody was.'

 'I'll sort them out, don't worry, has your driver gone?'

'Yeah, he'll be back tomorrow.'

'Go on go upstairs, have a bath and sleep. When you wake up, they will have long gone I promise.'

'Chrissie, I don't expect to walk in and find a load of old busybodies sitting round my table. What the hell are you thinking? The whole bloody world will know about me now.'

'I've kept your secret for forty years; you might own this cottage but remember you don't own me.'

'We had an agreement girl.'

'Yes, we did but as I have already told you I'm bored sitting here waiting for the moment you deign to fly in. Only to spend a couple of measly days with me in secret, then fly off again.'

'It's been good enough for years I don't know why you've changed now.' With that Zack loped off down the hall and upstairs to the master bedroom as he went Chrissie realised, he hadn't even kissed her. Shaking off the feeling of impending disaster she had no choice but to carry on. Deep down she couldn't decide which was more important Zack or Butterflies. She collected the coffee pot and went back into the lounge as if nothing had happened and said, 'Sorry about that now, where are we?'

It was all quiet round the table when she walked back in. Chrissie knew she had to say something more, then they could move on. Before she could speak Stacey piped up 'Ain't that Zack the old rocker, I see him about thirty years ago he was bloody good in them days. What's he up to now? How dya know im?'

Marie interrupted, 'I don't think it's any of our business Staccy.'

Chrissie blushed and said 'Yes, it is Zack, he's an old friend and comes here sometimes to get away from his celebrity life. Now shall we get on with the meeting? She took her place at the table and sat looking ahead, clasping her shaking hands in her lap, wondering what she was going to do to sort out this mess.

Betty

Betty was almost unable to contain herself. She just witnessed that scene that had unfolded in front of them, Zack in this house, he had been one of her heroes ever since her teens. Seeing him had made her feel sixteen again plus he had been standing just a few feet away from her. The nearest she had ever been to a superstar or used to be superstar. She guessed he was closer to Chrissie than she was letting on. Not a relative and certainly not just the friend she had claimed him to be. Her face had been radiant, her eyes shining when he had stormed in, and now he was apparently upstairs in her bed. This was really interesting, how could she have lived in this village all these years and not known that Zack was a frequent visitor here. This unexpected revelation certainly explained the beautiful cottage and why Chrissie had never done a day's work in her life.

Betty turned her attention back to the meeting, looking around it appeared she wasn't the only one to be confused at Zack's sudden appearance.

Marie said 'Right ladies, the purpose of this meeting is to establish whether you all want to work for Butterflies.' Trying to get the meeting back on track said, 'I know that Betty sent you all an outline of where we are plus what work we have available.

Are we all happy to carry on and be a real team of
Butterflies?'
 Betty said 'could we have a show of hands please?
Everyone raised their hands enthusiastically.
'Good,' said Marie, 'That's all of us.'
'First on the agenda, is admin Betty needs these
forms filled in as soon as possible after all we will
need to pay you.'
 Marie handed out the forms and went on to say,
'You will all be responsible for your tax and
national insurances, Butterflies will cover public
and private liability insurance. Of course, not all of
you have to pay tax etc. but we are running a
business now and we will be disclosing all income
for our company accounts. It is important you all
understand these implications now, not twelve
months down the road.'
She looked round the table only Stacey looked
uncomfortable, but it was Chrissie who spoke first,
'Marie, I'm embarrassed to admit, I haven't ever
worked so never paid tax and I'm not sure what my
national insurance number is.'
'I'm sure our accountant Michael will help you.' She
said looking at Betty quizzically.
'I don't see a problem with that Chrissie.'
 Sensing Chrissies discomfort Marie said. 'You are
extremely fortunate to be in that position Chrissie;

you have so many talents I'm sure you will be a great asset to us.'

'The more I think about it the less sure I am that I will be useful, though,' she paused, 'I was thinking maybe you could use my workshop.'

'Workshop, you have a workshop? Where is it?' asked Marie pretending not to know that she had already been made aware of it.

'At the end of the garden,' Chrissie stood up and walked to the French doors, ' It was built a summerhouse, but I call it my workshop, as i use it for all my hobbies. It is a bit hidden now behind the conifers, I don't use it anymore. Come on take a look and see what you think.'

The team followed Chrissie whose patchwork skirt swished along the path; she led them to end of her beautiful garden.

Jenny sighed 'What a lovely garden, who on earth looks after it? She asked. 'I just love these amazing herbaceous borders.'

'I do it all myself, that's how I spend my days, I can lose myself out here, behind the workshop is a vegetable patch which I have rather neglected, really I just love flowers.'

'It's a lovely space.' Said Marie.

Chrissie smiled and pushed open the door and said, 'Welcome to my workshop though it was originally supposed to be summer house.'

As they all stepped inside Stacey gasped 'Bleedin hell it's bigger than my house.'

Marie shot her a look, but Stacey carried on 'Is that Zack really only a friend. Or does he pay for all this?'

Chrissie smiled but chose to ignore Stacey and said, 'Sorry for the mess, it won't take long to sort out, I once fancied myself as a potter, but I got bored with it.'

Chrissie walked over to the far end of the cabin and drew back a purple velvet curtain, to reveal two shelves neatly stashed with brightly coloured vase and pots and more honeysuckle painted mugs.

Betty ran her hands over them and sighed 'Chrissie they are lovely, haven't you ever tried to sell any?'

'No like I said I got bored and sold the kiln they have been covered up in here ever since.'

'Well, I think they are amazing, I could see them in my house.' Said Jenny.

Marie interrupted, 'I have an idea for them but right now what did you have in mind for this space?'

Chrissie said, 'I was thinking there's enough space for about six sewing machines I thought it would make a great sewing room.'

'That would be fantastic what do you think Sue?
Could you use this space?'

Sue said, 'It's perfect.'

'All that remains then is to work out how much you
are going to charge for the space, then we can start
to get organised.

'No charge Marie, I don't need the money I'm just
glad to help any way I can.' She led the way back to
the house conscious that she had made yet another
decision that would upset Zack. All the while
thinking of him waiting upstairs in her bed.

Chrissie

Betty picked up where they left off and said, 'I know we said we were going to stick to the agenda, but I was passing a factory in Bushberry the other day and they had machines for sale. I suggest we first ask Sue what machines we need as a priority and then put a bid in for them. Now that we have somewhere to set them up.'

'Good idea Betty we will go over there as soon as we finish here. Meanwhile if you've got a number for them ring them and tell them we are interested. We can go over this afternoon, perhaps Sue could meet us there. She can advise us.' Said Marie.

Betty went out of the room to make the call, while Marie moved onto the next item on the agenda.

The costumes for the theatre,' This is a loss leader for Butterflies, but we will get free publicity for this. I would like to get them made and delivered as soon as possible. First, we need to arrange storage space for the fabric, it's currently at the theatre but they are threatening to deliver to my house. I certainly don't have room for it.'

'Simple get it delivered here,' said Chrissie crossing her fingers, Zack was not going to like this. She was willing to risk it, if she was honest despite her earlier concerns this project was beginning to make her feel interested in life again.

'Good that's settled then,'

 Betty walked in grinning, 'Seems they are desperate to get rid of the machines as they have sold of part of the factory, so we could possibly get them for a song.'

'Then on that positive note we need machinists, I take it your team are up for it Sue?'

'Yes, please Marie we are really in need of a new project. We have spent too much time just chatting lately.'

'And me please,' said Stacey, 'I used to be a sample machinist at that factory a few years ago but got made redundant, so I took up cleaning. '

 Betty took deep breath and said,' I haven't asked him yet, but Derek used to be a mechanic in a clothing factory, I'm sure I could persuade him to step in. I for one would be glad to find him something to do. Thinking it about it he's a dab hand at flat pack furniture to so pencil him in for that as well.' Betty crossed her fingers at this point knowing she was going to have to work hard and super quickly to get Derek on her side.

 Marie ticked off the next item on her list and collected all the forms and put them into her briefcase. Betty went on to explain that she would oversee their new office and would be allocating job sheets on a Friday. It was her intention to be in the office every morning. Also going to be her job was to pay the wages. She would only be able to do so if everyone submitted a time sheet on time. Payment would be agreed when the jobs were allocated. Marie would be in the office most afternoons, but her primary job was to keep existing customers happy and to build new business. Seeing everyone seemed happy with that she handed the chair back to Marie.

'Betty will issue work sheets during the course of next week. To sum up Sue you can be in charge of all sewing, we will sort out machines and costumes fabric delivery, you will need to arrange threads and anything else needed for the workroom. Of course we will give you petty cash for that.'

'I'm happy with that but if the fabric for the curtains is ready before we finish the costumes, we are going to be seriously short of space. I may need to delay the delivery can you give me phone numbers measurements etc.'

'Will do, mind you I am far from an expert but looking at the measurements and remember it is a block of flats I reckon it will be a lot of fabric; space could be an issue.' Answered Marie.

Jenny turned to Sue and offered space in her garage, which she assured everyone was dry and secure. After checking that Jenny was happy with her workload and the rest of the team were fired up and chatting animatedly between each other. Marie announced that she had arranged to take a stall at the W.I. Autumn Fayre. The idea being to promote the new business and show all the skills on offer, Betty asked them to drop samples of their work into the new office then Marie turned to Chrissie who blushed as she was caught looking at her watch, obviously got Zack on her mind. 'I thought it would be a good draw if we could offer an Indian Head Massage as a prize in our raffle. Could you do that Chrissie?'

Chrissie mumbled a reply agreeing reluctantly but hoping that Marie would end this meeting and as an afterthought she offered a couple of her pots as prizes. Pleased with this response Marie thanked them all and told them she would send out minutes of the meeting and all other details in the next twenty-four hours. This did not amuse Betty who knew that it would be up to her to do all the admin later that afternoon plus she had promised Derek's services and she had yet to tell him exactly what she was involved in. It was going to have to be sooner rather than later as Butterflies needed his help and important that she sweet talk him urgently.

Chrissie shut the door and sighed a huge sigh of relief, what a strain, listening to Marie waffle on

and on and on. Butterflies had all those jobs lined
up for her, but Chrissie didn't want them. All she
wanted was Zack and he was here upstairs in their
bed, this time when he asked her to marry him, she
would say yes .It had been madness to have turned
him down so many times. She should never have
waited so long.

 Still feeling uneasy that Zack had walked in with
all the new Butterflies team sitting round his table.
His table, thereby lies the problem the reality of the
situation flooded over her.

 Forty years she had been with Zack, forty years he
had kept her, if she was honest, she had nothing of
her own. Sixty this year and nothing really to show
for it.

Wearily she hand-washed all her precious mugs.
Grabbing a bottle of vodka and a couple of glasses
she went upstairs. To wake Zack in the way only
she knew how. Determined now to marry him. It
was time, she would propose this time, not give him
a chance to say no.

Zack

It had been with extremely mixed feelings that Zack had turned up at Chrissies door, without letting her know he was coming. Then to be faced with a room full of women whom he didn't know, worst of all it had been clear from their faces they knew exactly who he was. All these years he had managed to stay in the background of Chrissies life, he sensed that when he had told her what he should have told her years ago, she was going to be furious with him. despite dreading facing her, he did fall asleep, a long deep sleep. When he woke up, she was leaning over him, her long curly hair brushing across his chest and the smell of patchouli oil, a perfume that would always remind him of his Chrissie. Before he could speak, she handed him a drink and said, 'I'm sorry I won't have those women round again.' She paused to take a large gulp of her vodka 'I don't know how to say this, but I think it's time.'

Zack sat up, 'Time for what?'

'Time, we got married Zack, time for us to live together properly.'

This was the last thing he'd been expecting, for years he had been asking her to marry him. All the time knowing he was still married to Suzy. Chrissie had been hinting at marriage lately. That's why he had turned up today, not just to surprise her but to tell the truth. Aware that Chrissie was looking directly at him waiting for his response he took a deep breath and not thinking straight he said, 'I was going to tell you, there's someone else.' He stopped and decided to not tell her the real truth, the look on her face said it all.

 Chrissie laughed nervously and poured another drink and went and sat on the window seat, legs curled up under her. She said,' I knew it, bad timing I've left it too late again. Story of my life.'

 Zack sighed, he really had messed this up somehow, he had to retrieve this situation, the lie was out there, his mother had always told him to tell the truth. Which if he had done years ago, would have meant he wouldn't be in this situation now. Crossing his fingers, he said quietly, 'I don't want this to change us in any way Chrissie, this is your home, I'm still your man I just have a complication now. It's never bothered you before.'

'I was younger then, and you never stayed long with any one you always came back to me.'

'You had lovers too Chrissie don't forget that.'

'We were both younger then, nothing mattered.'

'You are saying it matters now?'

'Oddly Zack, I think it does!'

'I have to re-join the band tomorrow,'

Chrissie interrupted 'will she be there?'
'No, this is so weird Chrissie, you've never
questioned me before.'
'It's my age, I just want some normality, security I
suppose.'
'You have security Chrissie, the cottage is in your
name all the bills come to me, you have a generous
allowance.' He walked over to her and stroked her
face 'I won't ever let you down, I promise. It's just a
bad time for me at the moment. I want to stop
touring; I've a lot of stuff to clear up.'
 Chrissie looked at him and said 'come to bed I want
to remember how it feels to sleep in your arms, just
leave early in the morning, don't wake me. I don't
want to hear you go.'
 Zack helped her down from the seat and gently
lifted her on to the bed. He lay down beside her and
she curled up in his arms. Despite the turmoil going
on in both their heads, they fell asleep, Zack crept
out quietly the next morning.

191

Chrissie

Chrissie wandered into the hall; it was late she hadn't felt like getting up this morning. Zack had gone leaving her devastated. Before he left, he made her a coffee but refused to tell her any more about his current beau, so her imagination was left to run riot.

It was all becoming clear to her; Zack had used her. Sure, he had looked after her well all this time, but she now felt that she had only been somewhere for him to escape to. This left her feeling very naïve and somewhat stupid.

The mail was on the mat, Chrissie picked it up, mostly junk, just one bill her off licence bill. The only bill she had ever had to pay in her life Zack had covered everything else. It was then it struck her, she had been a kept woman for so long she had lost sight of her real self.

Among the junk a postcard, her heart missed a beat, she sat down, hands shaking, every year for ten years the same message. 'We would have been so good together miss you. Paolo xxx'
Chrissie looked at the picture on the front, the same every year. Message was always the same, picture always the same and always she had ignored it.

However, it didn't mean she hadn't thought about it. Time for a coffee and thinking time, holding the postcard close to her chest she went into her den and sat, mug in hand. Paolo she should never have let him go, Zack that was reason, she had prided herself on being a free spirit, but Zack had trapped her and now she was lost.

Sipping her coffee, she studied the picture and as always, the memories poured over her she was back there. Sardinia, it was supposed to be a break away together but at the last-minute Zack had to be somewhere else and Chrissie had gone on her own.

Nerves had taken over and she had spent most of the trip alone, in the hotel or on the beach, but the temptation of Sunday lunch in the sunshine eased her out of her hotel room and on to a coach with other holidaymakers- her worst nightmare. Chrissie had paid her money and gone on the trip, it could have been a disaster, but the sun had been shining and there was lunch, the tour rep had promised that she would enjoy herself, but she had doubted it.

Once off the coach she followed the other tourists into a beautiful walled garden finding a seat, feeling very alone. Chrissie once again cursed Zack for letting her down. She relaxed in the seat, her eyes closed, face towards the hot sun. A hand touched her shoulder; she opened her eyes and there he was the man of every woman's fantasy.

'Is it ok if I seet here pleeze?' he had asked. Chrissie
had nodded unable to speak as she looked into his
chocolate brown eyes.

Paolo waved his hand and spoke in Italian to the
waiter, who promptly brought over a bottle of red
wine and poured out two glasses. Chrissie was too
embarrassed to say she didn't drink wine.

He sat uncomfortably close to Chrissie, she turned
away and picked up her wine glass at the same time
as him, somehow their hands had touched, and
Chrissie spilt her wine as an electric shock jolted up
her arm. He had leant over her and grabbing a
napkin from the table he poured water on to it and
began to rub the stain. He spoke softly, 'Eet looks
like blood in ze snow.' He said as he stroked away
the stain. His hand so close to Chrissie's breast she
couldn't breathe. 'There it ees better.' He paused and
held out his hand, 'I'm Paolo'.

Chrissie went to speak but her mouth was dry,
Paolo handed her a glass of water, she took a sip
'Chrissie.' She whispered.

They spent the rest of the week together and both
cried when Chrissie had to fly home.

Reality for her was Zack waiting at the cottage full
of remorse and a few hours in his arms and Paolo
was just a fantasy. A fantasy that over the next few
years Chrissie remembered as each postcard

arrived. Each treasured but today it was different, time maybe to move on. The phone number as always was clearly written on the back of the postcard. A number that Chrissie had never until now bothered to ring. Seizing the moment, Chrissie dialled the number, Paolo answered on the third ring. 'Chrissie, eez it reelly you?'

'Yes, it's me where are you?'

'I'm in London on business.'

'Are you here for long?'

'Just as long as you want, cara come and meet me. How about next Wednesday?'

Chrissie hesitated just for a moment and said, 'I would love to let me get a pen.'

With a shaking hand she wrote down the name of his hotel and said 'I will ring you when my train gets into London'

'Chrissie am so pleezed ciao.'

Chrissie sat for a while with the phone in her hand, what had she done? Was this a wise move? Whatever the outcome of the meeting it could only add to the complications in her life that she could not see a solution to. Nevertheless, she was determined to go and face the consequences whatever the outcome.

Marie

'Mother what's up? Not like you to ring so early on a Sunday morning?'

'I'm not feeling too great can we do lunch another Sunday?'

'Of course, what's up can I do anything?'

'I'm just overtired and didn't sleep well last night.'

'Promise me you will ring if you need anything.'

'I will, bye.'

Marie replaced he receiver and frowned, it was quite unlike her mother to turn down lunch in fact she couldn't even remember her mother being tired, she had always had boundless energy for her age. In a way it was a relief Marie had the keys to the office and she was meeting Betty there to move in as much as they could, while no-one else was around. To have a whole day instead of half was a bonus. The phone call was causing a niggling worry that Marie found difficult to put to the back of her mind.

It took a full to bursting carload to move all the files and office equipment from her house. As she put the last box in the boot, she felt a shiver of excitement run through her. Her dream was finally coming together it was going to be hard work, but after the meeting at Chrissies it felt like a jigsaw puzzle where all the pieces were beginning to slot nicely into place.

Betty was already unloading her car when Marie
pulled up, being a Sunday, they were safe to leave
their cars outside without fear of dreaded parking
tickets. They carried box after box into the office.
Betty had taken charge of stationary and had
collected the headed paper, business cards and
promotional leaflets from the printers only
yesterday and neither of them had seen the finished
goods.
'First things first put the kettle on,' said Betty.
'You do that, I want to look at our stationery.' She
said as she started to rip open the packages.
'Betty, they are beautiful didn't we do well.'
'Don't forget Jenny had an input we used her
drawings for the logo.'
'That's a point we need to pay her.' Marie grabbed a
whiteboard and stood it up against the wall and
quickly wrote 1. Pay Jenny.
'Bet that board will be filled up before we go home.'
Said Betty laughing as she handed Marie a coffee.
Marie looked at the mug and said, 'Betty you are a
genius, these are fabulous mugs.' This said as she
ran her fingers over the bone china mug adorned
with colourful butterflies. 'The detail always the
detail that's what's important, you might not be so
happy when I put the petty cash docket in!'

'Better do it soon while I'm happy!' answered
Marie.

Marie lifted a box on to the corner of one of the
desks as she pulled out a new printer saying, 'I hope
you are better at setting this stuff up than me.'

'Shouldn't be too difficult are we going to link our
laptops to it?'

'I reckon so, then we have to get the web site sorted,
don't suppose you can do that can you?'

'No haven't a clue but Michael has just done his, I
think he paid someone to do it but it will be worth
it. I'll ask him in the morning.'

It was the middle of the afternoon by the time they
finished and with the planners on the wall and all
files labelled and standing neatly on the shelves that
Michael had thoughtfully installed. After testing the
printer and packing up all the rubbish, Betty said, 'I
think we're done here I have to be home to cook
dinner, what are your plans?'

'Me I need to check on mother and to be honest I
am going to soak in the bath and try and switch off
Butterflies for a couple of hours. From tomorrow it
is going to be full on.'

'See you in the morning I am loving this, Marie.'

'Me too Betty me too.'

Betty

Betty went home only stopping to buy a bottle of wine. Somehow it seemed right that she should talk to Derek. It was time to tell him about Butterflies. An idea was forming in her head as to how she could gently nudge him back to being the man she married.

While they had been making plans for a sewing room in Chrissies back garden Betty had been thinking deeply about Derek. He was a brilliant mechanic and was once DIY fanatic if only she could reignite his enthusiasm and then just maybe it could be a new beginning.

Determined to make the evening go in the right direction, Betty set the table and defrosted Derek's favourite lasagne and tossed a green salad and garlic bread to go with it. She even had serviettes not paper ones but the linen ones she normally saved for special occasions. Drawing the line at candles she softened the lights in the dining room and went into the living room and grabbing the remote control, switched off the tv and said. 'Dinner is on the table ready now.' Leaving Derek open mouthed looking at her back as she went through to the dining room, normally meals were eaten on their laps in front of the tv.

Derek followed her meekly and as he surveyed the set table he said, 'Bloody hell girl what's going on now?'

Betty quickly realised she had wrong footed him and said, 'Sit down and eat and after we need to talk.'

'Right but there's footy on tele I'm missing the match.' This said as he tucked into his food.

'No Derek this is important TV can wait for once.'

'Pass the wine then.'

Betty relaxed she had his attention at last determined not to mess it up she had brandy and glasses ready to soften him even more when they had finished the meal.

'That was good so what do you want to talk about?'

Betty took a deep breath, 'Well it's like this Derek, you know I've not been happy since taking early retirement.'

'That's my fault, is it?'

'Not at all it was an unexpectedly bad time for both of us and I've managed to move on as it were.'

'You leaving me then?'

'Oh, don't think I haven't thought about it Derek, but no I may have something you would be interested in.'

'Doubt it Bet.'

Betty went on to tell him about Butterflies omitting only the ten-thousand-pound investment and explaining the need for an experienced handyman and mechanic.

'You expect me to run around after a load of daft old women and not get paid?'

'I never said that Derek, its early stages but we have already got some good well-paid contracts and we need someone with your experience to help us move this on.'

'Sounds dodgy to me.'

'Will you not just give it a chance Derek we will pay above the national wage to start, but each contract where you would be involved would be negotiable.'

'No too busy,' he said stroppily.

'Derek would you please think about it, I need you to be involved, there's so much riding on this for me.'

'It's only another job Bet,' he paused 'I'll think about it, can I watch the footy now?' this said as he poured a large brandy and went to sit in front of the tv. Leaving Betty to clear up, thinking she had been stupid to have even thought that Derek would be interested.

Marie

When Marie left the office, she drove to her mother's flat to check up on her. She pressed the buzzer, no response, she phoned, nothing it just rang on to voicemail. Marie left a message quite annoyed that her mother had gone out after all but hadn't thought to let her know.

Feeling satisfied that the day had gone well, and that tomorrow was going to be the first day in the new office. They had left it all looking professional, she wasn't sure about the two colourful butterflies that Betty put on the door at the last minute, but she had to admit Betty was right it was the detail that counted.

One niggling worry was that Betty hadn't yet told Derek, but she had promised her that she would do it tonight. Marie was praying that Betty would come in in the morning saying that Derek would come on board, if not Butterflies was going to need a handyman very soon.

Tonight, though was to be a self-indulgent evening, no work a takeaway and a long soak in the bath and then maybe a couple of episodes of Friends.

Just as she started to run the bath the telephone rang a quick glance at the clock it was nine o'clock. No-one rang her land line at this time it had to be her mother.

Picking up the receiver she said, 'Hello Mum you went out after all today?'

'I'm not your mother I was rather hoping you would be able to tell me where she is.'

'I'm sorry who's speaking?' asked Marie not recognising the deep masculine voice.

'Yes of course, I'm a friend of your mothers Maurice surely she has mentioned me?'

'No, she hasn't' Marie answered sharply. 'Hang on if you're a so-called friend why are you ringing me have you been round to her flat, do you know where she lives?'

'Of course, I have, we play Bridge together every Sunday evening but tonight she didn't turn up, she's not answering the door or her phone.' He said with a tremor in his voice.

Marie replied, 'She did call me this morning saying she felt unwell,' she paused, 'Look I have a key I can be there in twenty minutes, where are you?'

'Sitting outside the building in my car, thank you Marie, I would appreciate it.'

Marie hung up and looked longingly at her bath, no way could she ignore this call. But who on earth was Maurice? How strange that her mother had never mentioned him. Fancy her mother having a gentleman friend at eighty. Life was full of surprises.

 Dragging on a pair of jeans and a sweatshirt she hurried down to her car and drove quickly to her mother's apartment. Sure enough, outside was parked a very smart Jaguar and as she pulled up beside it. A tall, distinguished gentleman jumped out and hurried towards her. He shook her hand and apologised for disturbing her and offered to go into the flat with her.

 Marie said, 'I would appreciate that, though knowing mother she has taken a sleeping pill and we will find her tucked up in bed. Stay a bit behind me I don't want to scare her.'

She unlocked the door, and went into the narrow hallway, it was in darkness, so she switched on the light and called out, 'Mother it's me Marie, just wondered how you were feeling?'

 Nothing just silence, Marie was beginning to feel extremely agitated, turning left into the lounge, no sign of her mother. Spotting her handbag on the mahogany coffee table Marie said, 'She must be here she would never leave the flat without her precious bag. Let me go through to the bedroom, wait here.'

 Cautiously she pushed open the door and relief washed over her when she saw her mother sitting by

the window in her favourite armchair. Marie called
out to Maurice it's okay she's here asleep. Maurice
hurried in, went over to Violet and took her hand
his mouth dropped, he turned to Marie and said, 'I
don't think she's asleep dear,'
Marie saw the tears in his eyes and froze on the
spot, 'No, no, you must be mistaken.'
Maurice told Marie to sit down as she was
obviously in shock. He went through and got her a
drink of water, when he came back Marie was sat
on the dressing table stool staring at her mother.
 When she was finally to speak, she asked quietly
'What do we do now?'
Maurice replied, 'I've called the Doctor Marie.'
'She doesn't need a doctor she's dead,' she said
bluntly.
'Look trust me you need a certificate from the
doctor and your mother will have to be taken away.
You can't leave her here.' He paused and looking at
her stricken face said, 'Come into the kitchen I'll
make some tea.'
 Marie followed him, still trembling and watched as
he made a pot of tea, as she did so she realised that
Maurice was more than an acquaintance of her
mother, he knew his way around her kitchen. He
was obviously a remarkably close friend, closer to
Violet than she had ever been. Marie didn't even

know where the tea or coffee was kept in her own mothers flat. This fact was now disturbing her more than the thought of her mother being dead in the bedroom.

'Thank you, Maurice, this is all a bit of a shock, Mum has always been so fit, this is so sudden.'

'I know you have been really busy lately, but Violet- your mother has been undergoing tests for her heart, she didn't want to worry you.'

Marie sighed, 'We were never that close, both too independent I suppose but she looks so peaceful just sitting in the corner in her favourite chair.'

'She was very happy, and I'm proud to have been her friend.' He wiped away a tear and was interrupted by the doorbell. Marie opened the door and was relieved to see that it was her mother's long-term GP who had come out immediately. He signed the medical certificate giving the cause of death as result of an existing heart condition. For which he had been treating her. Once the undertaker had taken Violet away, Marie sank into an armchair and said, 'I don't have a clue what to do now.' Looking round the room she said, 'I don't even know if there's a will.'

Maurice looked a bit uncomfortable and said, 'I know where everything is Marie, your mum left everything in order the files are all with her solicitor and copies in the bottom drawer of her desk she told me a few months ago when she first started having pains.'

'I can't face anything tonight its late and I have a really busy day tomorrow can we meet here tomorrow evening?'

'Yes, that's fine, I can help you sort everything out,' he hesitated and went on 'I will be a bit lost myself now, we've been bridge partners for so long.'

'Thank you again, I will get here about seven is that ok?'

'Of course, I should tell you I do have a key, but I had a feeling something was really wrong, and I didn't want to be the one to come in. I really thought you knew about me so that was the right decision to ring you.'

Marie pulled on her jacket and went out and got into her car driving slowly home she was able to keep her composure until she got inside her flat only then did, she breakdown.

How could she not have known her mother was ill? How did she not know her mother had a gentleman friend? It left her wondering how many more secrets her mother had kept from her.

Betty

Betty got into the new Butterflies office early only to find Michael was already in and had left a large vase of flowers outside the door for them. She went through to thank him, he blushed and said, 'Just to welcome you I didn't go in but would love to see what
feminine touches you have made to the space.'
'Come on then, I'll even make you a coffee in our new coffee maker.'

She almost skipped through and as she unlocked the door Michael smiled and said, 'Lovely job, butterflies everywhere!'
Betty looked at her watch, 'That's odd Marie is late, not like her she's never late.'

Michael took his coffee and went back to his desk, while Betty busied herself getting ready for the team meeting scheduled for eleven o'clock. When nine o'clock came and went and there was still no sign of Marie. Betty was about to dial her number but before she could a text came through 'Sorry Betty I am just leaving been up most of the night explain when I get there.'

Marie came in half an hour later, looking very pale and tired and said 'Oh Betty I need a coffee please.'
Betty busied herself making a fresh pot of coffee and Marie slowly told her about her mother and

Maurice and said, 'I'm not sure which the bigger
shock was, mum dying suddenly, or Maurice being
her long-time companion. It's all a bit weird. I'm
finding it difficult to understand why she never told
me about him. He knew she was ill, and he knew
where her will, and personal papers were. Which is
more than I did. I didn't even know where the coffee
was kept.'
'What is he like can you trust him?' asked Betty.
'I was apprehensive of course but he seems kind and
a real gentleman, he wants to help with all the
arrangements,' she paused. 'I hope I've made the
right decision; I said I would meet him in the flat
tonight to go through everything with him.'
'You have to trust your instincts Marie just take
care; he's not a con man maybe do a search online.'
'I'll be careful don't worry. That hit the spot.' She
said draining her coffee. 'Now we must focus on the
day ahead' she said opening her briefcase.
'If you're sure, you are up to it Marie?'
'I am, it was a shock, but Mother and I were never
best friends, and she was eighty, besides Butterflies
must come first we have too much riding on it.'
Betty took a deep breath and said 'Business it is
then; I spoke to Derek last night and he was a bit
offhand and said he would think about helping us
out and then went off and watched tv. However, this

morning he went out early which was unusual, but he left a note saying he was going to get his van cleaned and serviced as it looked like he would need it!'

'You think it's a yes then?'

'Pretty much, pretty much,' she said with more conviction than she felt.

'That's good news so are we ready for this meeting?'

'We are, the others will be here at eleven. Michael has half a dozen fold up chairs we can use.'

'Perfect, have we managed to print off the agenda?'

'Yes,' Betty pointed to the pile of papers, 'Time sheets are ready, coffee is on and we have biscuits. The only thing we haven't got right yet are employment contracts, but Michael knows someone who can advise us so we can say they are in hand.'

Marie asked, 'Has everyone given over their bank details yet.'

'No, we are still waiting on Stacey.'

'She could be a problem, but we need her so we could, if we have to pay her cash until she sorts out a bank account.' 'Right let's just sit down we have half an hour before they arrive.' Marie sank down into her chair and said, 'I feel like I haven't slept for a week, but at the time am fired up ready to go does that make sense Betty 'I think it does and there is the buzzer someone's keen and early.'

Chrissie

For the first time in weeks Chrissie was up early and ready to go to Butterflies new office. Having cleared out her garden room making it all ready for the sewing machines to be delivered. The fabric for the costumes and patterns were safely stored.

It had taken around a week to make the space ready and for a couple of days she hadn't given Zack a thought, hadn't been constantly checking her phone for messages, this was surely a breakthrough. Plus, she was going to meet up with Paolo next week. Chrissie had high hopes for this date and was already planning on what to wear which was quite out of character for her.

Despite being up and ready early she wasn't the first to get to the meeting in fact she was the last. Stacey Sue and Jenny were already seated studying the agenda. Chrissie apologised and took her seat and Betty handed her a coffee. 'Oh, what a beautiful mug,' she said. Betty smiled. Chrissie thought Marie looked ill, but she started the meeting and did manage to brighten up when she started to enthuse about the company's current work commitments.

First up was Jenny's wedding stationery. She was on schedule to bring her samples and costings into the next meeting. Betty asked that she provided a detailed worksheet so the price to Hattie Smythe

Browne could be calculated accurately. Ensuring they made a good profit.

 Sue was to go and measure up for the curtains, at this point Marie interrupted and said, 'If we can buy ready- made curtains that may need adjusting that would give us a breathing space as there is the problem of the costumes for the theatre to be sorted first.'

Betty said, 'We might have to revisit that as I think Tom Carter has purchased the fabric already.'

'Okay so I'll measure up and come back next week with both options once I have seen the windows.' Said Sue.

'Next are the costumes, we need to sort these as quickly as possible, we need to get them out of the way quickly, as we are regrettably not going to make any money on them. As we said before all we are going to get out of this is free publicity.' Said Betty.

 Chrissie said 'I had an idea about the costumes, as the fabric and patterns are already in my workshop why don't we ask Stitch and Bitch to make them for us as a trial run. We can give them publicity and if they can pull it off then it will give us confidence to use them going forward.'

'Hmm that's a good idea, after all we don't know how good they are yet.' Answered Marie.

'What about the machines?' asked Chrissie?

'We have bought them, and they will be ready for collection by the end of the week.'

'Collection? How will we manage that? Asked Chrissie.

'It's all in hand' answered Betty crossing her fingers, Marie grinned at this point.

'Moving on there are a couple of cleaning contracts for you Stacey, we have priced them and providing all goes well they will be regular customers.' She handed the contracts over to Stacey and said, 'Both want a certain number of hours a week but times are negotiable all details are there. Just up to you to arrange hours to suit you and your girls.'

'Thank you I should be able to fit them in with my other regulars, oh and eres me bank account details.'

'Great, now Betty and I will cover the admin jobs although we may need to take on someone else in the next few weeks.' Marie looked down her list all I have outstanding is a cake maker to help out June Davis her regular girl has had an operation and will be out of action for a few weeks. Any ideas ladies?' she looked around.

Chrissie blushed and said, 'I'll do it I know June I've made cakes for her over the years as long as its's temporary.'

Marie looked surprised and Chrissie was quick to explain, she would only do them for 'Junies Cakes' as long as it was short term and only for June as June was a good mate. Plus, she knew exactly what she wants.'

'That's good perhaps you could pop in and see what she needs now, give me a ring when you know, and we will give her a price obviously we will need your costs first.' said Betty.

'That's no problem, I have all my recipes and notes from before, I can drop them in tomorrow. I'll nip into see her on my way home see exactly what she wants.

'Thank you, Chrissie, that's brilliant,' she paused and went on 'I think that's all for today, same time next week and don't forget to bring your time sheets and anything else we have discussed this morning. Thank you, ladies, and have a good week.'

With that they all left leaving Marie and Betty sitting in their new office.

Marie

'I thought that went well, very positive, didn't you?' asked Betty.

'It was better than I thought especially Chrissie, it feels really like a business now.'

'Will you be all right this afternoon?' she paused?

'Only I need to do my four hours with Michael.'

'No problem I have a list of calls to make,' she broke off as there was a knock on the door and Michael's receptionist put her head round and said, 'there's a gentleman here to see you, he wouldn't give me his name says its business?'

Marie said 'you can go through to Michaels office now, if he's genuine send him in.'

Betty followed the receptionist out and was astounded to see Derek standing there. Not only had he had a haircut he was clean shaven and for him smartly dressed.

Before she could speak Derek said, 'Thought I had better come and see what you are up to and meet my new employers!'

'I don't know what to say,' seizing the moment she grabbed his arm and pulled him into the Butterflies office and said excitedly 'Marie meet our newest member of the team Derek.'

Marie smiled, 'Sit down Derek I am so pleased to meet you.' All the while thinking that this man was

not in the slightest bit like Betty's description of
him or the man she imagined married to Betty.

 To give herself time to gather her thoughts she
stood up and poured a coffee, when offered a cup
Derek declined, she sat at her desk and handed a
Butterflies advertising flier and quickly scribbled a
few notes while Derek read the text.

'I know that Betty has told you a bit about us and I
am really pleased that you want to become one of
the team.'

'I didn't know what Betty had been up to, so it was
a surprise I did a lot of thinking after she told me
last night, I didn't sleep much and woke up this
morning and thought why not. Think I have been
drifting too long. So, what can I do for you Marie?'

 Marie outlined what she needed, which was him to
collect the sewing machines they had bought from
the factory in the next village. Then deliver them to
Chrissie's workshop. Then to set them up and in full
working order for the next week. They agreed terms
and Marie gave him petty cash to purchase threads
and parts which could be needed to achieve this.
Once this was done, he would be required to be on
call to fix any problems for the sewing team. There
was also an urgent request to build some Ikea
furniture for a customer who needed a whole

bedroom full of furniture to be built whilst she was on holiday.

Derek was quiet just taking a few notes while Marie spoke, 'so what do you think Derek are you in?' she went on grinning 'are you ready to be a Butterfly?'

Derek laughed and said 'I think I may still be a chrysalis! But yes, I'm in.'

'Terrific then here's all the information you need, just make sure we have receipts for the petty cash and keep a record of your mileage.'

'Thanks, I'll crack on then.'

With that he walked out of the office leaving Marie sitting stunned at her desk did that really just happen? Was that really the same Derek that Betty had been moaning about? At the same time extremely grateful that Betty had finally been persuaded to tell him about the new company. Looking at the bigger picture Marie did wonder how much Betty was at fault with the supposed cracks in their marriage. Betty was a complex character one she had locked horns with many times when they had worked together at Jones Macintosh.

Chrissie

It was a surprise when Chrissie answered her door the next day to find a strange man with a white van parked on her drive. He held out his hand and said, 'Derek,' he paused 'I have the first of the machines for your workshop'.

Chrissie smiled 'Oh how exciting I'll open the gate round the side.'

Derek went to open up his van and using a trolley that had been gathering dust in the garage for a few years, proceeded to unload the first machine and wheeled it through the gate, stopping to admire the garden, which was a breath-taking sight, herbaceous borders all in full bloom, not a weed in sight, just the kind of space that you could sit and dream away the day in.

Chrissie led him down the path to the workshop which unbeknown to anyone she had painted the inside yellow and white. Outside the door she had hung a huge butterfly, positioned to catch the light.

'Wow,' said Derek as Chrissie led him in, what an amazing space and newly decorated nice job who did this?'

Chrissie blushed, 'All my own work just don't look too close, I'm so grateful that it is going to be used, I must confess I'm excited about how all this is working out.'

Derek spent the rest of the afternoon taking machines down to the workshop and Chrissie stayed out of the way, talking to June Davis, agreeing prices and delivery. Now all she had to do was buy all the ingredients and bake the cakes. She was writing her shopping list when Derek came to the back door looking hot and tired. 'Sit down I have some lemonade in the fridge you need to cool down.'

'This is delicious where do you buy this?'

'I make it, usually stick a very large vodka in it.'

'Sounds good to me but no vodka today?'

'No,' she laughed thinking it was odd for her, but she hadn't had any vodka for a couple of days, and she felt good.

Derek stood up and said, 'I have got all the machines in but there is a few days' work setting them up, so ok if I just let myself in the gate in the morning, I'll try not to disturb you.'

'No problem, look could I ask a huge favour from you?'

'Yes whatever.'

'Could I cadge a lift into town I need to go to the supermarket, your amazing wife has got me cake making and I don't have enough ingredients.'

Derek looked at her and said 'Is there no end to your talents cake making, eh? A lift is not a problem, but

I might want cake in return tomorrow. Come on get in the van I'm going that way.'

 Chrissie climbed into the van and looking at Derek as he drove her the short distance into town she felt a pang of envy, he seemed a lovely easy-going man she was jealous of Betty who obviously had no idea how lucky she was. Derek insisted on waiting outside while Chrissie shopped and drove her back to the cottage, carrying her groceries into the kitchen. Then he went home to Betty happier than he had been for a long time.

Betty

That evening Betty had gone to a lot of trouble
preparing a meal for Derek. It had been a shock all
be it a good one when he had turned up at the office
that morning. Marie had praised him to the hilt and
to give Marie her due congratulated her on
persuading Derek to join them.

Despite all Marie's problems she had laughed and
asked Betty if she had seduced him did, she have to
don a basque and stockings to gain his attention?

Betty looked embarrassed but said 'No a big lasagne
and a bottle of red, that's all it took.'

'Well done Betty he's going to be a great help.'

Betty gulped and said, 'Oh I hope so Marie I hope
so.'

It was a turning point, possibly only a small one but
positive, Derek came in and was more animated
than Betty could remember. Even smiling when she
asked what he had been up to.

Filling her in on the afternoon spent delivering the
machines to Chrissie. Then driving her to the
supermarket. Betty felt stirrings of jealousy when he
said, 'that Chrissie is one lovely woman.'

Betty snorted and said bitchily 'things aren't always
what they seem; she is a kept woman.'

'Lucky how did she manage that?' Who is the lucky
fella?'

'That's just it he's famous.'
'Famous how come in this small town we didn't
know? Who is it do you know?'
Betty hesitated and went on 'Zack.'
'Zack the Zack omg how long?'
 'She doesn't talk about him. I heard they have a
daughter Summer. She's forty and living in India so
figure it out.'
'Zack and Chrissie and no one knew. This is bizarre
surely, someone has seen him around here before?'
'Apparently not they seem to have kept the secret
for all these years.'
 'I'm amazed that no one ever wondered how she
managed to live in that beautiful place without ever
working for a living.'
'I'm not really bothered Betty, she's a really nice
easy-going woman, I don't care if she has some
aging rock star paying her bills.'
'You think she's attractive then, she's just an old
hippy?'
'I never said that Bet, she is uncomplicated and has
a good heart.'
'What are you saying? I don't?'
'Don't put words in my mouth Bet all I am saying is
she is a likeable lady, we got on. Now we've been
married a very long time, I have never strayed so

don't even think that just because I admire someone
that I am going do anything now.'

Betty sighed and said, 'Sorry it's been a tough time
and well it's not been great between us has it?'

'No but we can build it back we do need to talk to
each other no more secrets.'

'Is that a dig at me because I didn't tell you about
Butterflies?'

'No not really but I have to admit it was all a bit of a
shock when you told me, I had no idea, I suppose
the revelation kick-started me. When I got up this
morning, I thought we do need to get back to where
we were a couple of years ago. It's not the money
Bet but you and me we've always been mates.'

Betty took his hand and said, 'We still are Derek we
still are.'

Long after Derek had gone to bed, Betty sat in the
dark thinking, perhaps it was time to surprise Derek
and creep into his room and snuggle up. It used to
be so good between them, Betty had had such a
huge hole in her heart when they found they
couldn't have children but lately the hole had
developed into a huge chasm. When she saw
women her age with their grandchildren there was
nothing that could repair that, so she went to bed
alone again.

Marie

After such a good first official day in the office Butterflies was truly becoming a reality. Tonight was another bridge to cross she was meeting Maurice at her mother's flat, feeling decidedly uneasy about the whole thing. Her biggest worry was that he would see through her and realise that she wasn't a loving daughter at all, just a cold-hearted bitch who to be honest was not too upset about her mother's death. More than a little put out at the timing of it, was nearer the truth.

When she got there Maurice was already inside and had put the coffee maker on, this rattled Marie from the start. The man not only had a key he knew how to use the coffee machine an art which she had never been instructed in. Taking a look around she realised he hadn't moved anything, everything seemed to be as she had left it. Gratefully she took a coffee and sat down at the kitchen table and got out her notepad and quickly wrote TO DO LIST-MUM at the top.

Maurice sat down opposite her and said, 'I was a close friend of your mother for almost ten years, and I insist on paying for her funeral.'

'Ten years I can't believe she never mentioned you. I know we weren't close, but you would have thought she....' Marie tailed off and made a mental note to do that internet search on this man just to put her mind at rest that he hadn't been ripping her mother off.

'As for the funeral let's first concentrate on registering her death.' She said firmly. 'I suppose I had better go and get the files.'

'Well, that's where we'll start then, do you want to get them while I pour another coffee? You know which drawer they are in.'

'Of course,' Marie went reluctantly through to her mother's bedroom. She stood for a moment just holding tightly on to the door handle, staring at the chair where she had found her mother, that had been a shock, but it was Maurice's appearance that had made her feel far more discombobulated than her mother's death.

She walked across the pale green carpet and towards the desk, mentally noting that the orchids on the windowsill would need to be moved sooner rather than later. The drawer slid open, to reveal half a dozen files all labelled. Marie lifted them out and took them back to the kitchen and placed them on the table, she sat looking at them for a moment without attempting to open any of them.

Maurice spoke, 'Look if you would rather do this on your own, I can go,'

'No no please stay.' Gingerly she opened the first one marked Personal in bold black felt tip pen.

'This is a good place to start here is her birth certificate, and all her NHS card, along with her pension details.'

'You already have the medical certificate, so that's all you need I think to register the death.'

Marie went quiet, 'Silly question I know but where do I do that?'

'Registry office in the next town, but I could do that for you Marie.'

'It should be me, shouldn't it?'

'I really don't think it matters who does it. I have all the time in the world you have a lot of pressure on you at the moment. Let me help you, with Violet gone I am going to be at a loose end.' This said with a trembling voice and a tear in his eye.

Marie thought for a moment and said softly 'that would be a great help, but I want us to go to the funeral parlour together if that is okay with you.'

Maurice took her hand and said 'look why don't you take the files home with you and go through them when you feel like it. There's no rush not untill I have the death certificate.'

'Thank you, Maurice I think, I will do that, ring me once you have the certificate and we'll go to the funeral parlour and sort all of that out.'

Maurice let himself out, Marie watched as he walked dejectedly to his car, the Jaguar she had seen the first time they met. So at least it was his and not borrowed she found herself rather hoping that when she ran the check on him it wouldn't show up anything untoward. After the initial shock of discovering he was a close friend of her mother's she rather quite liked him. He was she thought how she imagined her father would have been if she had known him. Sadly, he had died when she was only nine months old and her mother had never remarried, she knew absolutely nothing about her real father. She made a mental note to do some research on him when she had more time. It was ridiculous but until now she hadn't been the slightest bit curious about that missing part of her family.

227

Chrissie

Chrissie went down to the workshop early the next
morning only to find Derek already working on the
machines. Whistling as he worked. She smiled to
herself, thinking Betty has a gem in him, little
knowing the difficulties that their marriage had
been going through.

She coughed politely and Derek turned round
quickly and said, 'Morning Chrissie I thought I
would make an early start, didn't want to disturb
you.'

'I was up early baking for Junie's Cakes, they have
just collected them. I've made coffee if you want.'

'Thanks, I could murder one.'

'Come up to the kitchen, I might even have some
biscuits.'

He smiled as he followed her into the kitchen
which was full of the smell of fresh coffee and
baking.

'I'm leaving in a moment to catch the train to
London, Sue will be popping round later to see if
there is anything you need.' Said Chrissie.

'London, eh? Going shopping?' he asked.

Chrissie blushed 'No meeting an old friend for a
spot of lunch.'

'Do you need a lift to the station?'

'No thank you I have booked a taxi.' She looked at her watch and said, 'Oops better get myself sorted, finish your coffee and I'll leave the back door open if you need anything.'

'Do you want me to lock up when I finish?'

'No need no-one ever comes round here, just shut the back gate please.'

With that Chrissie almost ran upstairs, needing to tidy herself up, it was a long time since she had felt so excited. Lunch with Paolo an actual date at her age. Opening her wardrobe, she was almost ashamed to realise that most of the skirts hanging there were the same ones she wore all those years ago in Sardinia. She pulled out her favourite, blue and green patchwork, one that Paolo had had said the blue matched her eyes, teamed with an off the shoulder white blouse and her statement beads and she was ready. The summer sun had helped bleach her blond hair, which helped cover the grey roots that she had meant to go to get coloured. This had got forgotten with her involvement with Butterflies. As she looked at her reflection, the taxi hooted, Chrissie shrugged that would have to do and dashed to the door.

The train journey took just over the hour, she sat staring out of the window, seeing nothing, just daydreaming anticipating the meeting ahead of her.

Her stomach doing flip flops as she thought of Paolo. Remembering his kisses, his tanned firm body lying beside her. Part of her excited the rest nervous, wondering why she had ever thought this a good idea.

Once at Waterloo she rummaged into her bag for her phone, she had arranged to phone Paolo as soon as she reached the station. No phone and then she remembered she had left it in the kitchen charging. Now what she looked around her, he must be here somewhere, what was the most obvious place to wait? Under the clock, she remembered hearing that's where people often met. Nervously she made her way to the meeting place. All she could do now was wait there; she was earlier than she expected by ten minutes. There were a few people standing around the area, she scanned their faces. If only she had thought to write down his number, not just put it into her phone. The minutes ticked by, people came and went. She watched as loved ones exchanged kisses and bouquets of flowers and still, she stood alone. This was a mistake, why on earth had she agreed to this, she was so out of her comfort zone, here on this busy station.

'Chrissie, Chrissie I'm so sorry I'm late.' A deep voice called out.

She looked around panicking she couldn't see
Paolo. Then he was in front of her. It was not the
Paolo she remembered. This man was balding and
wearing a business suit all be it that his shirt collar
was open, revealing his now grey curly chest hair.
Not the long-haired beach bum of her memory.
Chrissie took the flowers he was offering and took
the time to sniff them giving her time to think.
Forcing a smile she said, 'You don't look any
different Paolo.'
'And you Chrissie haven't changed a bit still
beautiful.' he kissed her on both cheeks. She smiled
broadly of course she had changed, but so had he,
she was far too polite to say so. He took her hand
and said, 'I've booked at table a short walk away
from here on the Embankment, I hope you are
hungry.'
'I'm always hungry Paolo.' She replied.
They chatted amiably as they walked the short
distance to the restaurant. Chrissie was feeling
quite disorientated. The man walking beside her
was nothing like the bronzed Greek god she had
met in Sardinia all those years ago. Her heart sank
when they stopped outside the restaurant. It was one
of a popular chain, overpriced over hyped dismal
food. Not the intimate bistro she had seen in her
dreams of today. She shuddered when they went

inside, bright lights, loud music plastic bench seats, but before she could give her opinion Paolo said 'I come here a lot.'

Before Chrissie could respond the receptionist said, 'Hello Paul I've got your usual table.'

'Paul? Usual table, perhaps you could explain. This is all very confusing.'

'Have a glass of wine and I'll tell you my story and I want to hear yours.'

Chrissie gingerly took a sip of the wine, He obviously had forgotten that she didn't drink wine, her tipple being vodka. 'You go first; I don't have much to tell.'

Paolo slowly explained that shortly after Chrissie had left Sardinia his father had demanded he get a proper job and he was going to cut off his allowance if he didn't smarten up. Then a friend of his father offered him a job here in London. Leaving him no choice but to accept the respectable position in a bank.

'Do you mean you have been in London a long time?' asked Chrissie wondering why he had never told her that before. 'But your postcards always came from Sardinia and why Paul?'

Paolo answered 'I have been here nine years and called myself Paul for an easy life. I just thought working in the City I would be better as Paul.'

Chrissie thought for a moment and asked, 'Your accent you sound English now how why?'

He had the grace to blush and replied, 'I actually went to school in London and my accent may have been over exaggerated when I met you. I found as a teenager that tourists love an Italian accent especially the girls.'

'So, this is who you really are? Not the hunk I met on the beach.'

'Fraid so Chrissie I hate to disappoint you.'

Chrissie sat quietly for a moment, while she gathered her thoughts, picked up the menu pretending to read it. Thinking that she somehow had to get through this meal with a man she had nothing in common with anymore.

'I recommend the Chicken and ham pie,' he said.

'Not for me just a Caesar salad,' she said noting his waistline was considerably wider than she remembered.

Paul ordered the food and said, 'So tell me about you Chrissie are you still with that man who let you down when we met in Sardinia?'

Unwilling to give too much of her private life Chrissie lied and said 'we actually live together properly now, he took early retirement and moved in.' This was said with her fingers crossed under the

table, well it was only a white lie, all be it a very big white lie. 'What about you are you still single?'
'Not exactly,' he replied.
'Well, what does that mean?' She asked.
Paul sighed 'It means yes I have a partner.'
'How long have you been together?'
'A few years,' he muttered.
'So why keep sending me the postcards?'
'Habit, I suppose, I never thought you would respond so I sent one each time I went home to visit my family.'
'Your partner what does she think about you meeting me have you got a photo of her?'
Paul fished into his jacket pocket and pulled out a photo. Handing it to her he waited while she studied the picture in front of her.
'Look Chrissie,' he hesitated and went on taking her hand he stroked it gently saying, 'I know I should have told you before.'
Chrissie pulled her hand away and took a moment to digest this information. All she could say was 'It is all coming clear now,' she took a deep breath and said 'he looks nice. Look I can't deal with this without a proper drink. I hate wine she held out her glass to Paul saying, 'I really feel like throwing this over you- you'd better take it away from me.'

Chrissie called the waiter over and ordered a treble vodka on the rocks and once it was in front of her, she asked 'What was I an experiment?'

Taking a deep breath, he said, 'You were the only girl I have ever been with, so yes an experiment I suppose.'

'I'm sorry but I have to go,' she stood up and said, 'all I can say is you fooled me completely, I don't care that you are gay, what I do care about is the fact that you used me and kept up the pretence all these years.' Before she left, she downed her drink and throwing £20 on to the table and said, 'Keep the change.'

Head held high she left the restaurant and walked to the station; she didn't cry she was shaking with anger the silly fantasy she had carried around in her head destroyed in an hour.

On the train as the buffet cart came past, she gave in and ordered a couple of mini bottles of Vodka that would dull the pain.

Marie

Marie was having mixed feelings about her mother's death, she put off going through the paperwork and locked the file into her desk drawer. Thinking that she would deal with it once the funeral was over meanwhile her focus was going to stay on Butterflies and progressing the business. Maurice rang in the evening, he had managed to obtain the death certificate, had arranged an appointment the following day, with the local funeral directors for eleven o'clock. Marie checked her diary and agreed to meet him there.

Picking up the phone she rang Betty and said, 'Hi Betty, I want to go to the WI tomorrow afternoon, will you come along? I have to go and sort out the funeral in the morning so shall we say three o'clock?'

Betty hesitated, 'I don't see why not, any reason for going?'

'Two things really, I need to tell them about mother, after all she was a member there for years and I don't know who exactly to talk to.'

'I understand and the second thing?'

'Oh yes it was to talk about taking a stall at the Autumn Fair, we talked about it briefly before.'

'Great idea, shall I meet you there?'

'Thanks Betty see you at three then.'

Marie sighed wrote the two appointments into her
diary, she still preferred to carry a diary, finding
electronic devices far too impersonal. Next on her
list she called Chrissie.

'Hi Chrissie, just a quick call to see how things are
going with the workshop?'

'I've been out all day and just got in,' Chrissie
replied. 'But Derek left a note to say all was
finished.'

'Look its only six o'clock could I come round and
have a look with you? I must admit I am fretting
about these costumes for the theatre.'

Chrissie hesitated and went on, 'Fine I'm here
come anytime.'

Marie switched off her phone, thinking Chrissie
didn't sound her normal bright self, she hoped
nothing had upset her, the workshop was becoming
a vital part of their business going forward. A lot
was resting on it. Especially the speedy delivery of
the costumes to the theatre, this was a definite loss
leader, they needed to move on with other sewing
jobs which were coming in almost daily.

Half an hour later she pulled up outside Chrissie's
cottage, once again she felt a tug of envy, it was
such an idyllic place. Even walking up the pathway
it seemed welcoming. The path was curved and
surrounded by a fragrant herbaceous border, she

touched the lavender and rubbed it thoughtfully in her fingers, another idea buzzed into her brain. Chrissie was watching from the window and said as she opened the door. 'My favourite lavender so restful.'

Marie looked at her thinking she looked tired and drawn and asked, 'You ok Chrissie?'

'Yeah, just had a really crap day.'

'Nothing to do with us I hope?'

'No, I made a stupid mistake, went to meet someone in London and it turned out to be a waste of time.'

'Do you want to talk about it?'

'Not really, I can deal with it. Anyway, come and look what Derek has done, you'll be over the moon.'

Marie followed Chrissie down the garden, Chrissie unlocked the door of the summerhouse and said, 'Da da look what he's achieved!'

'That is amazing is it ready to go?'

'I think so Derek left me a note shall we go in and phone him? I think Sue was here this afternoon so we should call her too.'

Marie looked around the new sewing room. Derek had built a cutting table at one end, with a rack for all the fabric. Which he had carefully stacked by colour ready for use. Eight machines were all set up with white thread and sample fabrics showing their stitches at the side.

'I can't believe he has achieved all this in a week.' said Marie, 'What a star he is.'

Chrissie laughed, 'Not quite the useless lump Betty made him out to be.'

'Indeed, he is a surprise. I only hope she appreciates him.'

Chrissie switched off the light and locked the door and as they walked through the garden Marie picked another small bunch of lavender and said, 'Can I just take this I have an idea what we can do with it, just need a bit of thinking time.'

'Sure, it is always so beautiful, but I never do anything with it.'

Once inside Marie dialled Betty's number and she answered promptly. Marie thought she was a bit frosty when she asked to speak to Derek. She did hand the phone over to him without any further comment.

'Derek, its Marie I'm so pleased with our sewing room, is there anything we need to know?'

'No, I think it's ready to run, Sue came round this afternoon, and she went through everything and went away to buy threads and trims to match the patterns and fabrics. I don't think there is anything more for me to do at the moment. I think you should

give it a week and then I'll come back, and we can
iron out any problems that come up.'

'Sounds good to me, thank you again, would you
please put your time sheet in, we have another job
for you next week.'

'Thanks Marie.' He said and hung up.

'Now for Sue, Derek seems happy hope that cheers
Betty up!' said Chrissie.

Sue answered the phone quickly, 'Oh Marie so glad
you called, I'm so excited about the sewing room
Derek has done an amazing job.'

'I've just had a look round it and I have to say it's
perfect, now did you get everything you need from
Jane's shop today?'

'Yes, I think so and she gave us a very nice discount
and will put a promotional poster in her window if
you could sort one out.'

'Well done, Sue, now the tricky part, the costumes
are a freebie, and we can't afford to pay much for
them.'

'I know that and Stitch and Bitch are happy to work
for nothing for a week they are all keen to be
involved with Butterflies.'

'Thank them for that I'm confident that there's
plenty of sewing in the pipeline. We just need to get
these costumes out of the way. When do you plan
on starting?'

'We have agreed Monday, Chrissie will cut the
costumes out over the weekend, we reckon they will
take six of us a week they aren't very complicated
styles.'
'Perfect, that will work well with everything else.
Please let Chrissie know if there is anything else
you need and thank you Sue.'
'Pleasure speak soon.'
 Marie turned to Chrissie and said, 'It's fabulous I
am so grateful for everything, don't forget I want
your electricity bills when they come in and you
need to fill in your hours just like everyone else.'
Chrissie waved her hand and said, 'there's no need.'
'I'm not arguing with you Chrissie, but you are
going to be paid like it or not.' Marie replied
forcibly.
Chrissie smiled, and said, 'Ok boss.'
Marie drove home feeling satisfied that everything
in the business was coming together nicely, which
was more than could be said about her personal life.

Betty

Betty watched as Derek came off the phone and
went out into the garden whistling as he went,
unable to restrain herself she followed him and said,
'I really think we need to talk.'

'Yes, if you want just going to water the garden.' He
replied.

Betty sighed and went inside and put the kettle on
and she sat down and waited and waited. When she
got fed up, she popped her head round the door, he
was sitting outside his shed reading the paper,
completely oblivious to the fact that she expected
him inside.

This was not going to plan, all Betty wanted was to
sit in the late evening sun with a glass of wine and
start to make plans. In her mind the plans had
changed slightly since Butterflies had come into
their lives, but still plans needed to be made
together. So why had she spoken to him like a
school mistress? Sighing she went and switched on
her laptop, work would take her mind off her
relationship problems she couldn't help wondering
why she was suddenly conscious that Derek had
begun to smarten himself up. He was shaving every
day and yesterday after he had left the house she
caught a whiff of aftershave. A familiar smell but it
had been a long time since he had used it. The bottle

had sat on the side for so long. Chrissie it could
only be her, surely, he couldn't fancy her, this
thought troubled Betty, she pushed it away
resolving to not talk about it tonight after all, but
just maybe she could ask Marie what she thought,
she always saw problems clearly from both sides.
 With this thought she decided to leave Derek
outside and go and soak in the bath. She stood for a
long time looking at her naked self in the mirror and
was less than happy with what she could see. How
did she let this happen? Apathy that's what a voice
in her head said apathy. Slowly it dawned on her,
she didn't need to talk to Marie. The solutions or at
least some of them were really down to her.
Admittedly she had taken the time to get a decent
haircut but that had been the extent of it. After a
bath she decided to write herself a private to do list
and tick at least one off the list every week. This
list terrified her when she read it back to herself. At
this rate it was going to take six months with all the
waxing, manicures pedicures and exercise classes
involved. At what point in her life had her face
decided to grow more hair than her pubic area.
Well, if Marie could manage it then so could she
then just maybe Derek might move out of the spare
room and back into their bed.

As she pulled on her grubby towelling robe Derek called out 'where are you Bet, thought we were going to have a chat?'

'Be down in a minute pour the wine please' answered Betty hurriedly tying her belt. As she walked downstairs looking a right mess she decided to change the planned discussion, after all she now realised that there had to be a certain amount of effort on both sides.

'Sorry about that Bet must have dozed off in the garden?' he handed her a glass and went on 'Whaddya wanna talk about?'

Thinking quickly Betty said, 'Butterflies, Marie tells me you have done a great job at Chrissies. I just don't want you to carry on unless you really want to. There seems to be a lot of work for you in the next few weeks.'

'What's the problem?' he asked.

'The problem is we didn't really talk about whether you wanted to carry on or if you did this as a one off?'

'I told Marie I am more than happy to work as and when you need me.'

'Really I was just worried you might think I pushed you into it.' Said Betty.

'No, it was the kick start I needed, I wasn't sure when you asked but as you have said many times, we all need a reason to get up in the morning,' he paused and went on 'I enjoyed setting up those machines, took me back.'

'I am so relieved; you seem so much happier.' She stood up and kissed him on the forehead.

'Steady on girl steady on.' He said smiling at her sudden show of affection.

'Do you want another drink or are you off to bed?' asked Betty.

'No, I have to be up early in the morning, got to go into the office and get my instructions for next week.' With that he winked at Betty and went up to have a shower before going to bed.

Leaving Betty feeling a lot more contented than she had for years. Tomorrow she would make a start on her list. One step at a time.

<u>Marie</u>

 After a very brief visit to the funeral parlour, where Maurice had taken the lead on the arrangements. Marie hadn't argued when he settled the bill in advance, she did promise to repay him once her mother's estate was finally settled. Maurice just dismissed her saying, 'we'll talk about it later.'

'Are you sure you don't want say a final goodbye to your mother Marie?' asked Maurice.

'No, you go ahead, I saw her dead in her flat that's enough for me.'

'Well wait here I won't be long.' He was then led through to the viewing room.

Marie gratefully accepted a cup of coffee and sat back to think, feeling really grateful that Maurice had been such a support at this difficult time. After all he was probably suffering more than she was. When he came back, he looked distraught, she took his hand and said, 'come on let's go and get a drink, you look like you could use one.'

'But it's only just lunchtime.' He protested.

'Maurice its five o'clock somewhere one drink won't hurt.'

'But haven't you got to get back to the office?'

'No Betty has everything under control; I'll go and relieve her later. Right now, we still have a few things to sort out.'

'Okay lets go to the Dolphin near your office, I'll
follow you to your house and drop your car off and
then I'll leave mine in the pub car park. I can walk
home from there.'

'Will your car be all right there?' asked Marie.

'Yes, the landlord is a good friend your mother and I
were regulars there.'

'Something else I didn't know,' said Marie
frowning.

'Stop beating yourself up Marie, how you chose to
live your life was right for both of you. If it is any
consolation your mother was really proud of what
you have achieved.'

Marie brushed away a tear and said 'Sorry I don't
usually cry I just feel guilty I seem to have missed
so much. All for a bloody job which dumped me
without hesitation.'

'Stop! Don't look back you have Butterflies now
and your strength and determination will make that
a success.'

'I hope you are right.'

Half an hour later they found a quiet table in the
Dolphin and Marie was quite composed and had her
pad and pencil ready in front of her. Maurice came
back with the drinks and a menu.

'I don't want to eat,' said Marie with a look of panic
on her face.

'When was the last time you had a meal?' asked
Maurice quietly.
Marie hesitated, 'I can't remember,'
'We still have a few things to sort out and I need to
eat so perhaps this menu will tempt you.' He handed
her the menu; she opened it not caring that Maurice
was going to eat alone. Maurice went for steak and
ale pie and mash, she asked for a bowl of soup.
While they waited for their food, Maurice asked 'the
wake where do you want to hold it, Marie?'
'I haven't a clue I don't even know who to invite,
we have no family living as far as I know.'
Maurice reached into his pocket and pulled out a
sheet of paper, a handwritten list of friends and
acquaintances of Violet.
'I think we should invite these people and just notify
the W.I in case any of them want to come. But keep
the wake small, could be here if you like.'
'That sounds good to me. Do they have a private
room here?' asked Marie.
'Yes, we can look at it after we have eaten.' He
hesitated and went on 'Violet liked it here; the food
is good, not too expensive.'
'We only need a finger buffet, don't we?'
'Of course, once we get an idea of numbers then we
can organise that. We should book the room today
and sort the food out next week.' Said Maurice.

Before they could talk any more their lunch arrived and as Marie started to eat, she realised that she wasn't hungry after all, only managing a few mouthfuls she pushed the soup around her bowl. 'Thank you, Maurice, I really appreciate your help and support over this, I'm just stressing a bit about the service, should I speak?'

'You are as far as I am concerned her only family, so yes you should.'

Marie pulled a face, 'I guessed you would say that I don't mind standing up and doing presentations, this is different it's more personal.'

'I'll stand up as well if you want, and the rest of the service Violet has already planned it so we don't have to worry about that.' Said Maurice.

'That's good I did see that she had tucked it in with the will. I haven't had time to go through any of the other paperwork though, I must do that this weekend, hopefully it will be straightforward I've made an appointment with her solicitor for Monday so I will do that beforehand.' She looked at her watch and said 'Can we look at the room now? I must get back to the office and meet Betty we're going to the WI this afternoon.'

Maurice got the bill and paid before Marie could even get her credit card out and the Manager led them through to the back room of the pub. Marie looked round the beamed room, it was cosy and bright with double doors that led out to a garden with more seating. Views down to the river and said 'it's perfect. A lovely space.'

'Good that's settled, do you want a taxi to the office Marie?'

'No, I can walk from here it's not far; I need to think about a few things on the way.'

Impulsively she leant up and kissed Maurice on the cheek and said, 'I am so glad you were in my mother's life Maurice.' With that she walked quickly out of the pub and went outside and into the autumn sunshine and made her way back to the office deep in thought.

Michael

Michael came out of his office to find Marie
looking around, obviously looking for Betty.
'Can I help you, Marie? I sent Betty out to pick up
some accounts from a client. Anything I can do?'
Marie hesitated and said, ' Betty left me this card
and a message to ring this number. I really wanted
to know if she knew him or if he said what he
wanted. The card says he is a solicitor, local.'
'Let me have a look, I know most of the solicitors
round here.'
'Marie fished around in her pocket and pulled out
the card and replied, 'David Finnegan.'
'Yes, I know him, went to school with him a good
chap. Why?'
'I'm not sure the card was left on my desk with a
note to call him.'
'Is he your mother's solicitor?'
'No, I don't think so, I haven't been through her file
yet, but I feel sure she used old Frank Simmons in
the High St. I'll give this David a call.' She turned
to go and looked back and said, 'Thank you
Michael.'
Michael watched her go and wished fervently he
could break through the barrier that Marie always
put up around her. He was obviously going to have
to work on that, but first he had to sort out Jenny.

He wasn't sure how he was going to let her down
gently, but he was going to have to do it soon. They
had been out together a couple of times; each date
had in his eyes been a total disaster. Jenny however
had seen everything differently, she had taken to
ringing him three or four times a day, leaving
messages, asking him to go over for a meal.
 Michael wasn't sure whether he was being
unreasonable, the first date was just a drink in the
local pub, but Jenny had brought her dogs with her.
Luckily it was a dog friendly establishment, but
Michael loathed dogs, not only had he been bitten
as a child he was also allergic to dog hair. Jenny's
four dogs were Labradors, big fat and quite frankly
smelly and unlikeable. As is always the way, dogs
know when they are not liked and these four would
not leave him alone. He suffered for three days after
that. It was with great reluctance that he accepted an
invitation to tea. If it had been left to him, he
wouldn't have made a second date, but Jenny was
nothing if not persistent. This tea was even worse,
Jenny had promised to shut the dogs in the garden,
but it was raining, and Michael couldn't relax
knowing they were in the kitchen. He came away
then covered in black dog hair on his cream chinos
vowing never to go back there and never wanting to

have to sit in a house that smelt so badly of dogs again.

His mobile rang, 'Michael Lambert.'

'Michael its Betty, I've been held up, the accounts I was supposed to collect weren't ready, I am just helping her finish them off I may not be back until tomorrow, then I should be going to meet Marie at the W.I.'

'Don't worry we need to work on those accounts tomorrow, so that's fine Betty.'

Michael leant back in his chair he had to deal with Jenny tonight; she had talked him into that third date. Only because she promised to leave all the dogs and all talk of them at home. Sure enough, she had left them at home, but she spent the evening talking about her sons and their families, even bringing along photos of grubby looking grandchildren and worst of all her late husband. His photo she left by her wine glass throughout the meal. Not exactly inspiring him to make conversation. He had made it clear from the start that his marriage had failed because he did not want to be a father, he had been happily single for fifteen years and wanted to stay that way, but Jenny seemed only focused on his single status and was a little too curious about his financial situation.

There was no point waiting any longer he would call her now, he punched in her number and waited it rang on but just as he was about to hang up, she answered breathlessly 'Yes hello?'

'Jenny its Michael, have you got a minute to chat?'

'Always got time for you Michael,' she gushed.

He took a deep breath and thinking it was now or never he said, 'Jenny I'm so sorry I can't make tonight; something has come up that I can't get out of.'

Jenny went quiet for a few seconds and then said, 'How about tomorrow then?'

'Look, I don't think this is working, I'm really busy and don't want to mess you about.'

'Why don't you just come out and say it?'

'Say what?'

'You don't want to see me at all.'

'Okay.' Before he could finish his sentence Jenny hung up on him. Leaving him feeling like a heartless bastard.

He looked at the clock and seeing it was past six he decided to see if Marie was still at her desk, he would ask her what she thought and to warn her that he might have upset Jenny. After all he knew Jenny was working on a couple of projects for Butterflies. He knocked on Marie's door there was a shuffling of papers, a muffled voice said 'come in.'

Michael stared at Marie, she had obviously been
crying, 'I came for a shoulder to lean on' he said,
'but it looks like you could use the shoulder to cry
on.'
 Marie hesitated, and said, 'I could do with someone
to talk to, and I need a drink a strong one.'
'Grab your bag we will go to the pub and have a bite
to eat.'
'Marie said, 'Give me a minute I'll only be a couple
of minutes.'
 Michael watched as she began to scoop up some
papers from her desk and carefully put them back in
the envelope, which she then put into her bag. He
then went and closed his office and waited by the
front door until Marie came out, hair brushed, and
fresh lipstick applied, no sign of the tears of earlier.
After setting the alarm they walked the short
distance to the pub.

Marie

Marie's first instinct had been to dismiss Michael when he knocked on her office door, but one look at his face, she could tell he was upset, and she also desperately needed someone to talk to. Going through her mother's file had upset her, more secrets had come to light, and she probably shouldn't have read through the papers in the office. She agreed to go thinking that maybe they could help each other. Betty had been held up at the accountants where she was working, so the WI meeting had been postponed, she found herself more than happy to go with Michael.

Without asking and before Marie could object Michael ordered a bottle of wine.

Marie almost smiled and said, 'I had never been in this pub until lunchtime today and twice in one day is a record for me.'

'Don't you use any of the pubs in the village?'

'No until Betty and I got together I hadn't been in any, she introduced me to the delights of the wine bar.'

'I prefer this place it's less pretentious.' As he poured the wine he said, 'You looked upset when I came into your office earlier do you want to talk about it?'

'Perhaps you could go first I am still sorting things in my mind, after a glass of this I should be able to talk.'

'Right, all I wanted to do is to warn you that I may have upset Jenny.' Michael said.

'Oh really, I wouldn't worry, Jenny is desperate for money and if you two have fallen out it won't affect her working for me.'

Michael sighed, 'Not exactly fallen out finished more like. It didn't really even start at least from my side.'

'Have you finished with her?'

'Yes, she was too clingy, plus I hate dogs. I just feel bad about it. I shouldn't have finished it by telephone. It's not my style.'

'It's far worse to carry on any kind of one-sided relationship, sometimes you have to cruel to be kind.'

'I wasn't cruel, I tried to let her down gently, but she didn't listen didn't give me a chance to explain. I feel bad that I knew from the first date that it wasn't right.'

'Don't feel bad Michael, Jenny will get over it, you may have had a lucky escape, she's looking for a man with a big bank balance to keep her and her dogs. If it's any consolation, I hate dogs too especially big ones and when I went round there, I came away covered in dog hair.'

'Thanks Marie, that puts it in perspective, but I do feel bad. What do I say when Jenny comes into the office?'

'Don't worry about that she will be as embarrassed as you. Just acknowledge her as if nothing happened.'

'Enough about me, lets order another bottle and food and you can tell me what's bugging you.'

Michael handed Marie the menu and said, 'The Beef Wellington here is to die for.'

'I normally have salad, but what with everything going on I can't remember when I last ate a proper meal. Make that two. I couldn't eat at lunchtime I was far to wound up.'

Michael ordered and poured the last of the first bottle into Marie's glass, she looked at him properly for the first time. Maybe it was the wine, but he was good company not the arrogant bastard she first thought.

'What put that sad look on your face tonight?' he asked tactfully.

Marie fiddled with the stem of her glass and taking a deep breath said, 'I just feel totally overwhelmed, with my mother dying.'

'That's understandable.'

'We weren't close, but I didn't know she had a gentleman friend, nor did I know she had a heart condition. Then I find out she had sold her apartment to an equity release company. I only found that out this afternoon.'

'That is a lot to deal with let's break it down. The gentleman friend first?'

'Maurice he is a lovely man, I just feel cheated I suppose. Mother has been friends with him for years and I didn't know. He has been a great help to me he's even paid for the funeral.'

'What is the problem here?'

'I like him and wish I had known them as a couple, I never knew my father so a few years with a substitute, as kind as him would have been good. I don't even know why mother kept him a secret.'

'I didn't know your mother so I can't answer that but my advice to you would be to take him into your life. If he is a good man, he may want to be a friend or even a father figure to you all, be it a bit late.'

'I suppose you're right; I am a bit concerned that a lot of this is because I was so wrapped up in my job that I saw nothing around me.'

Just as Marie was about to go on the waitress placed two steaming dishes of beef wellington in front of them. She looked at the plate in front of her and said, 'Do you know all of a sudden I'm starving.' Michael smiled as he watched her tuck in this was not the Marie, he thought he knew.

After they both cleared their plates Marie sighed and said, 'You were right that was to die for.' Michael smiled and said as he poured another glass 'Let's address problem number two.'

'The heart condition,'

'Yes that, answer me honestly would you tell anyone if you had a health problem?'

'No of course not, I would deal with it.'

'There's your answer you are more like your mother than you think.'

'I never thought of it like that.'

'Lastly we have the equity release, what is your problem with that?' Michael asked quietly.

'It's not the money it's the fact that I had no idea, I suppose I am upset that I was always so preoccupied that she never confided in me. I only found out about it when I was going through the papers last night.'

'Your mother needed money and all she did was take it out of the property she owned, she was proud of you and probably thought you did'nt need the money.'

'It was never about the money.'

'No, I am sure it wasn't.' said Michael.

Marie said, 'There was one more thing, David Finnegan, I rang him, he just said he had important papers for me to see.'

'Is he dealing with the will and apartment sale?'

'No nothing to do with that he just said it was personal, I needed to go in and see him.'

'Are you worried about this?'

'Not worried terrified maybe.'

'Have you any idea what it can be?'

'Not a clue.'

'Would it help if I came with you Marie?'

She thought for a moment and said, 'I think it would Michael, I think it would.'

Chrissie

It was late but Chrissie had spent most of the evening tidying the workshop and putting final touches to the costumes. They were ready early and hanging on the rail ready to be delivered. Chrissie was really proud, it was a sense of achievement for her, she had interpreted the patterns and worked out the easiest and most economical way to make them. She was feeling grateful to her needlework teacher who had kept her interest during one of her courses a few years ago. Butterflies might not have made any money out of this project, but Chrissie's confidence had grown immeasurably and with the workshop tidy she was looking forward to the next project.

She was humming to herself as she walked up the path to her back door. Her landline was ringing; her first thought was to ignore it as she had done many times before but with her new business head on, she hurried in and picked up the call.

'Butterflies.' She said with a smile on her face.

'Butterflies what the bloody hell Chrissie.'

'Oh Zack.'

'Don't sound so excited girl.'

'I wasn't expecting you.'

'What the fuck is Butterflies?'

'It's a business that I am involved in.' Chrissie
answered quietly.

'How many times have I told you, I don't want you
to work?'

'Look Zack I need to work for my sanity. Anyway, I
was just going to have a bath what did you want?'

'I want to see you, I'm round the corner, can I come
round please? He asked.

 Chrissie thought for a moment and thought it
would be safer if he came round now rather than the
morning. It would give her a chance to explain her
involvement in Butterflies, so she agreed. Before
she could tidy herself up Zack was at the door. She
laughed when she saw that his car was boldly
parked outside. The first time that he had ever
driven himself as his number plate ZAC1 would
have given away their secret relationship. 'This is a
first Zack don't you care what the neighbours think
anymore?'

'Bit late now that lot you had in last time, I was here
would have spread the word by now.'

'I did warn you; you just took no notice.'

'Yeah, okay how about a drink?'

 Chrissie looked around as she realised, she couldn't
remember where the vodka was, she had been so
busy the last couple of weeks she hadn't needed a
drink. When it was clear there was none in the

cottage, she remembered that she hadn't cancelled her weekly delivery with Fred, merely asked him to put it into the garage.

Zack looked at her quizzically as she dashed out of the door, when she came back clutching two bottles of Grey Goose vodka he asked, 'what on earth Chrissie, there's normally nothing in your fridge except vodka, what has happened to you?'

Chrissie poured him a drink added some ice and said sit down and let me tell you what I have been doing.

Zack sat down on the floral sofa and sank into the cushions and listened while Chrissie told him all about her involvement with Marie and Betty. Her enthusiasm was obvious as she went into great detail about the sewing room she now had at the bottom of the garden. She smiled to herself as she saw Zack wince when she told him what she had done with the Summerhouse.

'This is permanent then, what about me?'

'Last time I saw you, I put myself in the ridiculous position of being rejected. You've been proposing to me regularly for forty odd years and when I finally feel the time is right, you calmly tell me there is someone else. This opportunity came up for me and I am beginning to realise that I want more than just being a kept woman.'

He sighed, 'I'm sorry Chrissie, I came here today to tell you the whole truth.'

'I do think it might be too late, but I am listening.'

Zack proceeded to explain about his marriage, previously he had omitted to tell Chrissie that he had a son and hadn't seen either his wife or Joe for ten years merely told her there was someone else. He stammered a bit when she asked how old his son was. And he had to admit that he hadn't been married for ten years as he had told her on his last visit but eighteen.

Chrissie needed time to digest this information, this made her feel even worse but to discover it had been eighteen years was a huge blow. Plus, Summer had a half-brother somewhere. Feeling very confused she went out into the garden and sat on the bench underneath the apple tree still clutching her untouched drink. Zack gave her a few moments and followed sitting beside her and taking her hand said, 'I know I should have told you before, but you were always such a free spirit, you turned me down so many times.'

'Married for eighteen years, that's just too difficult to digest.'

Zack went on 'She left me ten years ago, taking Joe with her and I have never seen either of them since.'

'Ten years? Have you tried to find them?'

'Of course, I wanted to support Joe, but no-one has
been able to find them.' He hesitated, 'I have been to
a solicitor and because I can prove that I have paid
out thousands to private detectives trying to find
them, I have started divorce proceedings. I should
be free in three months.'

'What about Joe?'

'I have set up a trust fund for him, he will be
eighteen next month and the money will just sit
there in case he ever turns up.'

'Have you no idea at all where they went?'

'Not a clue it's a complete mystery, I am so sorry
Chrissie I should have told you earlier, but I never
found the right time.'

'When exactly did you get married? How come I
never suspected was it in the papers?'

'We got married when I was supposed to go to
Sardinia with you.'

Chrissie blushed at the memory of the fling she had
entered into on that idyllic island.

'Were you happy with her?' she asked tentatively.

'No, we only got married because she was expecting
Joe. In fact, I hardly saw her over the years we
rarely spoke although I was close to Joe his Nanny
used to bring him to concerts whenever she could,
he even had his own chair.'

'What about Summer, you never gave her your name.'

'That's unfair and you know it, you never wanted to get married, I have lost count of how many times I asked you. I love Summer and I have always been there for her.'

'My turn to be sorry I suppose,' she took his hand and led him inside he looked at her and asked, 'Where do we go from here?'

'I don't know Zack I really don't there is a lot to think about. I have changed Butterflies has been a change of direction for me and I love it.'

'I understand we both need to sort out what we want but right now I think we should …'

Chrissie grinned and said, 'Zack you are such a randy old goat.' She turned and he followed her up the stairs.

Betty

Monday morning and Betty was first in the office
wearing a smart new outfit. The first step in her new
regime had been to go shopping on Saturday. Derek
was in a good mood which in itself had been a
bonus. He looked at her purchase of a navy blue
slim fit trousers and pale blue shirt, while admiring
them, did say, 'I hope you haven't spent too much
money. We aren't out of the woods yet.'

This was the reception that she had anticipated,
carefully she had hidden the dress and shoes bought
at the same time, to the back of the wardrobe.
Perhaps it was a bit over the top to buy two outfits
and expect him not to moan. She wasn't going to
admit to Derek how much she had actually spent,
but more to the point she had never told him how
much money she had tucked away. Hopefully, he
wouldn't notice when she wore them anyway.
'Morning Betty, oh you look nice' said Michael
popping his head round the door.
'Oh, thank you Michael,' responded Betty coyly.
'When Marie gets in could you ask her to pop
through and see me for a minute, please.'
'Sure,' she answered turning away to try and hide
her blushes. She was still feeling pleased with
herself when the phone rang, looking at her watch
she realised it was only eight fifteen and the office

wasn't due to open until eight thirty. Nevertheless, Betty picked up and grabbed her notebook.

'Good morning, Butterflies.'

'Morning, is that Betty.'

'Yes, that's me, how can I help?'

'Thank goodness, its John Mason, Marie told me you would be in the office early. I've an emergency situation my wife has had to go away to look after her elderly aunt, I need help, especially as wages have to be done for month end.'

Betty thought quickly and said, 'Give me your number and I will get back to you in half an hour but first how many hours do you need this week?'

'My wife usually only does mornings; I suppose about twenty should do it.' He replied.

She wrote down the details and then was writing down a note for Marie when she walked in.

'Was that John Mason? He rang me at home last night, he only had my mobile number from when I worked there.'

'Do you want me to take this job, I can fit it in with Michael's hours if you like, it just means you will have to be in the office most of the week.'

'That's fine I have a lot to do so yes, but Betty we do need to recruit office/admin staff.'

'I was just about to write that on your list, oh and Michael wants to speak to you.' She hesitated 'Will you be ok to be in the office? Don't you have arrangements to make?'

'Everything is under control and Butterflies comes first and I do need to catch up so ring John back and fit his hours in for a week at least.'

Betty went to the board and filled in her hours for the week and as Marie went through to talk to Michael she turned to Betty and said, 'don't worry I'll cover the meeting this morning and take notes for you.'

Betty laughed and said, 'I'm sure you can, I'll just sort the post and be off then.'

She watched as Marie walked out, she thought that at least she looked more relaxed this morning than she had done all of last week.

Marie

 After speaking to Michael, Marie was feeling less stressed than yesterday, he had arranged for them to see David Finnegan after work that night.

Thankfully, Michael was keeping his promise and going to be with her. She wasn't sure why she was so nervous, surely there couldn't be any more surprises to come.

Marie looked at her diary and seeing she had a full day ahead, made a pot of coffee and settled down at her desk and waited for her first meeting. Jenny was scheduled for ten o'clock but turned up late and flustered. Marie had been concerned that she wouldn't turn up at all, but she didn't seem to be worried about bumping into Michael and Marie didn't broach the subject.

'Jenny these samples are great, are we ready to present to Hattie Smythe Brown?'

'Yes, but I'm a little worried my prices are too high,' she handed over her list to Marie who looked at it and said, 'I will add our profit to this and email you a price list and estimate on Butterflies headed paper later today. As long as you are happy that you are making money out of these prices then don't worry about Hattie. If she likes what you show her, she will pay, but don't be surprised if she makes a few minor changes.'

'I won't mind that, what do you think?'
Marie fingered the 'save the date cards' and
invitations. All beautifully handwritten in gold on
pale peach vellum paper. 'These are exactly what
she wants classy, and smart though personally I
would have preferred cream. I like the menus,
orders of service and table plans, just make sure you
have allowed enough space for wording when the
menu is finalised.'
'Yes, I'm sure they will be right, if anything I over
costed them. I also have some samples of table
favours, serviettes, and hen party paraphernalia.
Which I haven't costed yet.'
Jenny handed over the new samples to Marie who
said, 'I love them, and I feel sure Hattie will too.
How do you feel about going to Hattie on your
own?'
Jenny hesitated and then said, 'I'm fine with that,
I'm more confident now that you have seen them
and approved them.'
Marie handed over Hattie's phone number and said
'I have a couple of other jobs for you, first Chrissie
has a lot of fabric left over from the Joseph
costumes which Diane Goodson doesn't want.
Could you pop round to Chrissies and have a look,
we need some patterns drawn up. I know Chrissie
has some ideas, but we need some lines we can sell

from our new web site and at the upcoming WI.
Fair.'

'That's sounds good.'

'Also, could you design a small leaflet using our
logo we need to do a leaflet drop locally, we need
part time workers to join us.' She handed over a
rough draft. 'Obviously this one is urgent as it needs
to go to the printers sooner rather than later.'

Jenny carefully put all the information into her bag
along with the samples and stood up to go. 'Thank
you, Marie, I'm so enjoying these challenges.' This
said as Chrissie burst through the door. 'Good Jenny
I want to show this.' She rummaged around in her
huge, embroidered shoulder bag and pulled out a
sketch she had made of a Butterfly.

Jenny looked at it and said, 'That's a good drawing
what do you want from me?'

'I had this idea,' she looked at Marie and went on, 'I
saw Marie rubbing the lavender between her
fingers.'

Marie interrupted 'I was thinking we should use it,
you have so much of it, and it would be a shame to
let it go to waste, but I hadn't quite worked out
how.'

'I thought Jenny could make us a pattern for a
butterfly lavender 'bag' well I say bag, but the shape

would be a butterfly, just to hang in wardrobes or lay in drawers.'

'Can you do that Jenny?' asked Marie.

'I don't see why not; do we have the right sort of satins Chrissie?'

'Yes, that's the whole point there are about three rolls left over from the Joseph costumes.'

Marie winced at the mention of these, still reeling from the fact that they had made a loss from making them. 'What about Maggie are we certain she isn't expecting the fabric back? Only I have asked Jenny to come and look at what you have got left.'

'No, she doesn't want it, apparently it was mostly donated from John Mason's factory. Anyway, Derek and I are going to deliver the costumes this afternoon, and I'll get her to sign for them and that will be the end of that problem.'

'Good, that will be a relief , I said earlier to Jenny, we can sell anything we make on our website and at the upcoming WI fair. Have you taken photos of the costumes, who knows we may need them for promotional reasons?' Said Marie.

'Yes, Derek did that. I was also thinking that we could approach the local hotels and see if they would be interested.' Said Chrissie enthusiastically wandering from one subject to another.

'Not sure why they would be interested?' asked
Marie curiously her mind still on the costumes.
'I thought tiny butterflies filled with lavender, to be
put on pillows, you know instead of chocolates.'
She looked at Marie waiting for a response.
'Now that is a good idea, but we need to think about
labelling, everything you make should have a
Butterflies label on. We need to establish the brand.
I'll get on with sorting that.'
Marie stopped to make a note and asked,'what
about the costumes Chrissie did we put any labels in
them?'
'Yes, we did, Sue machine embroidered some tape
we had,' she rummaged in her bag again and pulled
out an envelope with a sample and handed it to
Marie.
'Perfect well done.'
Jenny stood up and said, 'I must dash, looks like I
have a lot to do, thanks both of you, will pop over to
you in the morning Chrissie and look at the fabrics.'
'Lovely see you then.'
Marie poured more coffee , 'Thank you Chrissie you
have done a great job, how is having the sewing
room in your garden working out for you?'
'Actually, a lot better than I thought it would, I
didn't realise how much I needed a reason to get up
in the mornings.'

'What about work going forward?' asked Marie?
'Tomorrow, I have the curtain fabric coming and so
Sue and I will cut them out, that's quite a big job as
all the windows are different shapes and sizes. What
we thought is we would get them ready this week
and the team will come back Monday to stitch
them.'
'Tom Carter has come back to me, and he is looking
at bedspreads and roman blinds then he has more
flats he's renovating so providing I get the costings
right you are going to be busy for the next few
weeks.'
'Perfect, the posters have gone up in Jane's shop
and I put the office phone number on them, so all
enquiries will come through to you.'
'Excellent Chrissie what about the cakes?'
'You should get payment through in the next few
days I invoiced each delivery with the prices we
agreed. I filled in for the two weeks by getting up
early and they collected them before the shop
opened. Long term I don't think I can do too much
since the sewing workshop has taken off, don't take
it off our offers I might know someone else. Plus,
Sue seems happy to take on more responsibility in
the workshop.' She replied.
'I imagine she is pleased to be paid for something
that has been a hobby for so long.'

'True, if that's all I'll get off as Derek will be round soon to drive me to the theatre.'
'Just your time sheets please.' Said Marie.
Chrissie handed them over and said her goodbyes and cycled back to her cottage singing at the top of her voice.

Betty

Betty finished her shift at John Mason's factory and drove home hoping against hope that Derek was home and had her dinner ready. After all he was only driving to the next village, and he only had to unload the costumes. She was extremely disappointed to see his van wasn't parked outside, then there was a voicemail message on the landline. Her sister asking if they would look after her two grandchildren for the day on Sunday as they had to go to a wedding and children weren't invited. Betty quickly returned the call and said she would be delighted to have the two girls and as she made dinner for Derek, she planned a whole lot of activities they could do, such a shame they were only coming for a few hours.

When Derek came home, she decided against questioning him as to why he was late. Instead she poured him a drink and announced, 'We've got Amy and Sophie on Sunday.'

Derek didn't respond immediately he took a sip of his wine 'You didn't think to ask me first?'

'I didn't think you would mind; you love the girls.'

'Of course I love the girls.'

'What's the problem then?'

'Come on Betty you will be hell to live with for at least ten days when they go home.'

'I promise it will be different this time Derek.'

'You have been saying that for years and nothing ever changes. First it was your sisters' children, now her grandchildren how long is this going to go on?'

'I am sorry you of all people know how difficult I've found it not having children.'

'That's hardly fair, it hasn't been easy for me either I would love to have been a dad and a grandad, but it never happened. We should be making plans to enjoy our latter years don't keep harping on about being childless.'

They finished their meal in silence. Once she had cleared away the dishes and loaded the dishwasher Betty took the remains of the wine through, pouring Derek a glass said, 'It's a warm evening let's sit outside for a while, I don't want to row with you about Saturday.'

Derek followed Betty out into the garden, pausing to deadhead a rose on the way, 'Betty, you know I won't stop the girls coming, I wouldn't do that.'

'I do know, I'm feeling good about everything now. Butterflies is doing well, plus I can see that you are happy helping out. You are, aren't you?'

Derek replied smiling, 'Surprisingly I'm enjoying it, not only that, I'm earning again and so far, the work is varied and interesting.'

'You don't mind working for women then?'

Derek grinned and said, 'I know what I used to say about women bosses but you lot seem to be alright.'

Betty slapped his arm playfully and said 'I never thought I would work with Marie, but I have to say we are becoming really good friends, I love what we are doing.

'As long as we are looking forward now not backwards.' Replied Derek softly.

Betty was quiet for a moment and then said, 'I will try Derek, I will I promise.'

'We both need to Betty we both need to, but we have to forget that we are never going to be grandparents. Now's the time to start planning our future, we only have a few years left to work.'

He took Betty's hand and went on, 'I know it has been a tough five years, I'm sure a lot of it is my fault. We've lost our way but it's not the end it's a new beginning.'

'So do you think you will be moving out of the spare room any time soon?'

'Let's see what happens after the weekend, all being well I will.'

Betty sighed and sat back she only had to get
through this weekend and then her focus had to shift
from lack of children to getting her body and most
important her marriage back into shape.

Marie

The evening for Marie was quite different, Michael
had arranged an out of office hours appointment
with David Finnegan she was nervous as to what
this solicitor had to give her or tell her. It was only a
short walk from Butterflies; David had a suite of
offices just a few doors away from the Dolphin
where they had eaten just a day ago.

'Marie smile, it can't be that bad.'

'I just don't have a clue what else there can be?
Mother had a long-term partner, sold her flat to an
equity release company. Had a serious heart
condition, what on earth am I going to find out
next.'

'Relax we're here now. Do you want me to come in
with you?'

Marie thought for a moment she was becoming
comfortable with Michael. If she was honest apart
from her new 'stepfather' she didn't have anyone to
talk to so she said, 'That would be good, I know if
it's bad I will need a shoulder to lean on or cry on
even.'

'That's good cos I've got a pair of them, who knows
you might not need them though.'

Michael rapped on the solid oak door and David
opened the door, 'Michael good to see you again,
you must be Marie?'

Marie looked at the man in front of her, another good-looking older man, beautifully dressed a full head of hair all be it a lovely shade of grey. What was she thinking looking for the inevitable gold band on his finger? Yes married. Still, he looked good, and his office was expensively furnished with antique and leather chairs and desk. The pictures on the wall were all originals, blending in with the décor very tasteful.

Marie spoke, 'I'm nervous about this, it is the worry about the unknown, honestly I just want to find out what else my mother has hidden from me please?'

David looked at Michael and said, 'This is really difficult for me, I do know what's in the envelope. Your mother brought it to me a couple of months ago' He reached into the desk drawer and put a large envelope onto the desk, 'However I would advise that you open it with someone close to you. Your mother insisted that I just hand it to you after her death.'

Marie took the envelope and stood up and said, 'is that it?'

'Yes, that's all Violet asked me to do, and Marie, I wish you well.'

With that Marie walked out clutching the envelope to her chest, Michael hovered behind and said to

David 'Should I worry about is in that? Is Marie
going to be upset by its revelations?'

'Yes mate, yes you should worry, she's going to
need someone to be there for her. I hope you're up
to it.'

'Right, thank you I'm on it.'

He joined Marie who was standing outside still
clutching the envelope she looked at Michael and
said, 'I'm scared what do you think if I just set light
to this would anything to change?'

'No nothing would change; you will just spend the
rest of your life wondering what its contents were
and wishing you hadn't burnt it.'

'So where am I going to open it?'

'I think we should go back to your house, then if it's
bad I can tuck you up in bed.'

Marie grinned and agreed, surprisingly this was not
the most un- agreeable ending to the evening that
she had anticipated.

'Walk or taxi?' he asked.

Marie anxious to eke out the inevitable moment
said, 'Walk if you don't mind.'

The evening was balmy for September, and they
walked quietly to Marie's, once inside she placed
the envelope on the coffee table and went into the
kitchen and put the kettle on. Leaving Michael to
look round the immaculate room. He was studying

the painting hanging on the wall when she came in carrying a fresh pot of coffee and two mugs.

'I love this picture, it reminds me of my childhood, beach holidays in Cornwall.'

'It is Cornwall, St Ives, I picked it up one day when I was on holiday down there, I fell in love with the place and every time I look at it, I am reminded of that holiday.'

'Did you never go back?'

'No that was the only real break I had in twenty years.'

'What no other holidays?' he asked.

'No, I never got round to it.' She said quietly then went on, 'I suppose I never had anyone to go with. Work kept me so busy; I did take my two weeks off every year, but I just slept for two weeks and then went back to work.'

Michael took his coffee and looked at her and said, 'That's terrible you should always make time to get away, just to recharge your batteries, even if it's just for a couple of days.'

'I know, and I think having Betty and Butterflies is helping me. I am beginning to realise how much I gave up for a career. A job that dumped me in the end anyway.'

Michael picked up the envelope and handed it to Marie, 'I think you should open this now.'

Marie sighed, 'You're right I need to get this over with.'

Carefully she opened the envelope and pulled out three pages, she recognised her mother's handwriting immediately. Michael watched as she read the first page her already pale face became paler with every line she read. Without saying a word, she handed the letter to Michael and put the other two sheets back on to the table. While he read it, she sat clasping her shaking hands and biting her lip desperately trying to hold back the tears.

Michael stood up, 'Wow I think you need a brandy that is some revelation.'

Marie lifted her hand and pointed him in the direction of the drink's cabinet. He poured two large drinks and handed one to Marie. He put his arm around her, to comfort her, she leaned back against his strong body and said, 'It is so much worse than I could have ever imagined, it's terrible, how could she?'

Marie picked up the letter from the table and began to read it again.

Marion,

There is no easy way to tell you this, and I should have taken the time to talk to you years ago, but as time went on, I simply could not find the right words. You must understand that this has been an incredibly difficult burden for me to carry alone, I told no-one.

When you came to me at fifteen, claiming you had been raped by my brother, I refused to believe you and did nothing about it. I am truly sorry; I found out later that it was true, which made my actions even more unforgiveable.

I couldn't admit to myself that you were a pregnant schoolgirl, that is why I sent you away, this is the hardest part, these words have never been spoken before. I'm struggling to write them now. Your baby didn't die at birth. I paid for him (yes it was a boy that much was the truth.) to be taken away for adoption. I told you that we held a quiet funeral before you came home. That was also untrue. The simple facts are that your son is alive and living in London. I have lived with this guilt for over forty years, and I know this will be a terrible shock to you at first. I 'm sure you will find the strength to deal with it, you are a very strong woman. I hope you can find it in yourself to forgive me, I couldn't go to my grave without telling you.

I have enclosed full details of your son and his family; I understand you are a grandmother a joy I never had due to my selfish actions.

I have been in touch with Brian (that's his name) His adoptive parents contacted me a couple of months ago to say he was starting to search for his birth mother while researching his family tree. The rest is up to you. I cannot put right this wrong or make up for lost time. I just hope you will seize the opportunity to meet Brian and his family.

Best wishes

Mother

Michael took the letter from Marie's still shaking hand and sat down opposite her, 'That is some revelation, Marie.'

'I can't think straight, I had no idea, I buried the memory of that pregnancy so long ago. I never told a soul about it.' She sobbed gently as the tears began to flow.

'Not even your husband?'

'No not even him. I just told him I didn't ever want children. I was afraid that if I had another baby it would die at birth. It was easier to pretend I didn't want children.'

'What about the rape?' he paused 'Did you have counselling for that?'

'I had years of it, I never knew whether it worked or not, but I went anyway. I suppose I just buried myself in work, distancing myself from the horror. Don't forget I was a teenager, and I didn't pay too much attention, just got on with being a teenager.'

Michael glanced at this watch, 'Do you want me to
stay tonight.'
'Thank you but I need to think about this, and I
really don't want to talk about it anymore until I
have digested it.' She took his hand and said, 'I do
so appreciate you being here, you are so kind.'
She began to cry again, 'So many wasted years,
things should have been so different. My mother
was always aloof, even in telling me this, there is no
word of love nothing. Best wishes from mother
what kind of person signs a letter like that? I'll be
fine Michael, you go home, I'll see you tomorrow.'
'It's Saturday tomorrow I'll call you, try and get
some sleep.'
Michael let himself out, leaving Marie staring at the
letter not even noticing he had gone. She sat for a
long time trying to process all she had learnt that
day and in the previous weeks. How different her
life could have been if she had only, she had known
her baby had not died at birth.

Michael

Michael walked home, deep in thought, the events of the evening had disturbed him. Coming from a close family he could not imagine how a mother could treat a child in the way that Marie had been. It was tantamount to abuse. There was a small part of him that was happy to see the hard shell she had shown him, was now being stripped away showing her vulnerability, her true self.

Letting himself into his house, he poured a glass of water and went and sat outside. The terrace was small and filled with pots of red geraniums the only plant he cared for, these reminding him of happy holidays in Spain with his parents. His better self was telling him to help Marie, but having been hurt so many times before he was wary of what he should do next. Decision made he pulled out his mobile and pressed the number. 'Hello, Sis, have you got a minute?'

'For you Mikey of course what's up?'

Michael sighed at his sister's use of his childhood name

'Long story but I feel a bit out of my depth.'

'Wow and you think your baby sister can help?'

'Yes, I think you can.'

'Tell me.'

Michael went on to tell his sister Liz, Marie's story, she was quiet for a while and said, 'I suppose you want my honest opinion and not what you want to hear?'

'Yup that's why I rang you just tell me what you think.'

'Well, my first reaction is walk away Mikey it's not your problem, but I reckon you are more involved than you think. You usually just turn your back if there is a problem in a relationship.'

'That's my point I'm not in a relationship with Marie, in fact when I first met her, I found her totally obnoxious.'

'What's changed?'

'Liz, I don't know, I just feel I need to help her, she is just so vulnerable.'

'All I would say is follow your heart, but she is going to be in a bad place for a while, she doesn't need someone like you being there and then walking away.' She paused for a moment and went on 'I'm surprised it's not like you to be thinking so deeply about a woman.'

'This is so different to anything I have been involved in before; we haven't even kissed I just feel scared I suppose.'

'Ask me and I only have one thing to say, from what you have just told me, if you take that road then

please don't break her heart she has enough to deal
with.'
'Thanks Liz I know what I am going to do just
wanted to talk about it.'
'Should I get a hat?'
'Ha ha watch this space.'
Michael checked his watch, bit late to ring Marie
so he sent her an email inviting her to lunch
tomorrow and feeling better after the short
conversation with his ever-sensible younger sister
he went to bed determined to be the only shoulder
that Marie leant on. His life suddenly feeling that it
was taking a most unexpected turn.

Betty

Walking into the office on Monday morning Betty was feeling extremely blue. Sunday had been wonderful. The girls had been so much fun, they went to the zoo and then finished off in MacDonald's. Even Derek had to admit it had been a brilliant day, the sun had shone, Amy and Sophie had giggled their way round taking photos of themselves by all of their favourite animals. Sophie wanted to take a penguin home with her but in the end had settled for a stuffed one.

It had been hard talking to him over breakfast, but she had promised not to be miserable, but it was so difficult. Children should have been such a big part of her life. She had to stop blaming him. It wasn't his fault they couldn't afford IVF all those years ago, Derek was able to enjoy these snatches of family life and carry on as normal, but oh how she struggled. As she unlocked the door Michael came through and said, 'Marie has had some bad news and is having to stay at home today and wants to know if you will take the meeting this morning?'

Betty bristled what on earth was Marie doing talking to Michael and not her? However, she answered 'Of course.' All the time thinking it odd Marie talking to Michael.

First things first a fresh pot of coffee and then check the messages and Marie of course had left a list. However many worries she had, she still left a list every night. Betty sat down and downloaded all the emails then recorded all the voicemail messages. Her spirits lifted as she made three interviews for admin staff, responded to several enquiries for help, in the home, gardens and best of all so many sewing enquiries.

Marie did ring she seeming surprised that Michael had taken control by saying she was staying home, 'It's just a hiccup Betty, I've had something come up which I didn't expect. I will be in tomorrow.'
'Yes, so Michael said.' she replied frostily.

'I'm sorry I didn't ask him to call you, he was just there last night when I had some bad news, he is just trying to help. I'm ringing you now.'
'Sorry Marie that was insensitive of me do you need to talk?' asked Betty sensing the tremor in Marie's voice.
'Possibly, I just need a few hours to sort my head out, I'll check in later, thank you Betty you are a star.' With that she hung up leaving Betty feeling more confused than ever, and why did Michael seem to know what was going on and she didn't. Chrissie came in and Betty didn't stay agitated for very long, Chrissie's enthusiasm was infectious, her

bubbly personality soon brought a smile to Betty's face and she forgot all about her concern for Marie.

Marie

It was unheard of for Marie not to go into work, so this was an exception, so many issues to deal with at one time. Marie did what she did best, perhaps it was her way of coping when life got too difficult. For her the simple act of writing everything down somehow eased the pain.

Funeral and wake

Clear mothers flat.

Sell flat.

Contact her son Brian her son??

Number four, definitely one to think about later, first numbers one to three had to be dealt with once the funeral was over, she wouldn't feel too bothered about clearing out her mother's things. The revelations she had left behind had formed ice around Marie's heart and she felt she could deal with everything. Her son that was going to take some time to adjust to.

'Hi Maurice, I wondered if you were free this morning?'

'For you Marie of course, shall I come to you?'

'Would you I am working from home today. Have you got details of the funeral and everything.'

'Certainly, everything sorted have you got your eulogy written?'

'Er sort of, see you later.'

Marie hastily added write eulogy to the top of her list.

Maurice arrived clutching a bunch of lilies, Marie took them and said, 'Thank you, very fitting.'
The funeral was for Friday and Maurice had printed out the order of service and said 'Just you and I to speak. Your mother had many acquaintances but few close friends so it will be a short service.'
'The shorter the better really, are we expecting many?'
'Not sure but I have just ordered a buffet, and I doubt whether many from the W. I. will come and as you know there is no family that I know of. Do you think I have missed anyone?'
Marie drew in her breath and asked 'What about mother's brother, my uncle? Does he know?'
'Violet hadn't spoken to him for years and last time she mentioned him he was living in Australia; do you know anything more about him?' Maurice asked.
'No and I don't want to know where he is, and I certainly don't want him at the funeral.'
Maurice took one look at her face and changed the subject without further comment.
Marie asked, 'Do you want me to settle the funeral bills now?'

'No certainly not, it can wait until your mother's estate is sorted out.'

'Thank you I appreciate that Maurice, one other thing, next week I am going to start clearing the flat, is there anything you want or perhaps something you have left there?'

'No Marie I don't think so but if you want help, I'm more than willing to come with you?'

'I'm not sure at the moment but I'll let you know.' Maurice looked at his watch, 'Look I must dash I'm playing bridge later and I need to do some errands first.'

'Of course, I'll see you at the crematorium.'

Marie was very thoughtful after Maurice had left, it was odd that he knew of her uncle, to her knowledge Violet hadn't had had any contact with him since the rape. She shook her head; this was a memory that if she was to stay sane, she had to forget. These latest revelations had brought the sordid memories back to the forefront of her mind, they had to be buried along with her mother. Marie hoped that the fact that Maurice knew of her uncle didn't mean that Violet had confided in Maurice before her. However, she was determined not to give Maurice any indication that she was upset or that her mother had left her any bad news.

The sun was shining outside, she decided to drive over to her mother's flat and start to sort through her things today rather than wait until next week. Under normal circumstances this would have been a depressing thing to do, but the letter had finally killed off the few feelings that Marie had for her mother. Now it was just a simple act of clearing out a flat she had rarely been in.

Marie pushed open the door of her mother's apartment and picked up the post from the doormat. Glancing through it was mainly bills, she sighed deciding to take them all along to the solicitor, let him sort out the chaos of her mother's financial affairs. The flat already felt musty and the dark skies outside made the whole place gloomy and oppressive. Making it easier to clear out her mother's personal effects.

The first thing Marie wanted to do was to speak to an estate agent, she called one near to her new office. 'Good morning, I would like to make an appointment for a valuation on my late mothers flat.'

'Certainly, can I take a few details please?' asked a friendly female voice.

Marie relaxed slightly and gave over the relevant details, then said 'Look I know its short notice, but I don't suppose there is anyone available this afternoon? It would be a great help as it's not my flat and there is a lot for me to do'

'Just a moment I will check I think Barry Jones is in that area at the moment, can I call you back?'

'Thank you.'

Shortly after there was a knock on the door and Barry introduced himself, 'I was literally at the end of the road and as Shelley told me it was urgent, I came straight along I hope you don't mind?'

'No thank its fine in fact more than fine.'

Marie let him in and sighed, he looked about twelve making her feel ancient she said 'I've no idea what these properties are worth or how long they take to sell.'

Barry said, 'Prices vary, generally these apartments are in demand and sell quickly, first thing I need to know is there a chain involved?'

'No, it's my late mother's apartment so it will be vacant possession. Does it need to be completely empty before you show people around?'

'That's not necessary, but I would remove anything personal unless you are going to be here for the viewings.'

'I won't be here, just want to get this place sold and out of the way. I'll probably just get a house clearance firm in.'

'Don't be too hasty some of this furniture may be worth good money.' He said looking round the room.

Marie didn't answer immediately all she could focus on was getting a valuation and getting away from the oppressive atmosphere in the place that had never been her home. 'Could you please just give me a valuation and let me worry about the contents.' She said a little too sharply.

'It won't take me long I'll just quickly measure up and I'll be out of your hair in no time.'

Marie sat down by her mother's bureau; it seemed as good a place to start as any. She sifted through the neatly piled papers, then sorted them into, shredding, needing attention, and keeping for the solicitor. She found a few old photos of her mother as a young woman and a man who was more than likely her father. It was odd looking at the picture, her mother had never talked about her father, and as far as she could remember she had never seen a photograph of him. So many complications to come in her life so late, she had always imagined retiring at sixty and living a comfortable life. Now she had a son out there with his own family. A sudden urge to find out exactly what had happened to her father, a fleeting thought flashed through her mind who was he? Was he the man in the photograph or someone else? Another mystery to solve another mystery to keep her awake at night.

Her thoughts were interrupted by Barry walking back into the room he coughed to get her attention. 'I think we could put this property up for £200,000 but if you want a quick sale £175,000.' He waited for Marie to answer and shuffled his papers as she looked at him coldly 'Put it up for 195 and no offers what percentage are you charging?'

'We charge 2.5%.'

Marie now had her business head on and said, '1.5% and if it doesn't sell in six weeks, I'll put it out to every agent in the area.'

He hesitated and realising Marie wasn't going to budge he put out his hand, she shook it, 'How quick can you get it on to your website?'

'It can go on today if I can just take a few photos.'

'That's fine, I have a spare key here, I will get the place cleaned and tidied up tomorrow, I would appreciate you letting me know by email when you are showing people round. I don't want to be here.'

Marie handed him her business card.

'I understand,' He went out to his car to collect his camera, after only ten minutes he left saying he would send all the details over that evening.

The bureau papers were soon boxed up ready to be moved into her car. Marie went through to her

mother's bedroom, which was exactly as she had
left it the night her mother died. It felt weird, only
the third time she had ever been in this room, the
only familiar thing in it was the chair, she
remembered it from growing up. Now a bit battered
and tired looking but still comfortable. Feeling
uncharacteristically nostalgic Marie decided to keep
the chair, making a mental note to get Derek to
collect it. Though quite where she was going to put
it at this moment, she wasn't sure. Before she could
change her mind, she stuck a post it note on it and
opened the wardrobe. Clothes all neatly hanging, all
beautifully colour coordinated, shoes all boxed with
photos on the front of the boxes, exactly as Marie
now kept her wardrobe, so there was something of
her mother in her after all. She opened the top
drawer of the ornate dressing table and as she did,
she caught a whiff of Violets signature perfume,
Chanel No. 5. There was a cream leather jewellery
box, old and slightly battered. Without opening it
Marie took it through to the lounge and put it beside
the box of papers. Glancing at her watch she
realised she had already spent longer than she
intended there, and she wanted to check in with
Betty before she went home, after all business had
to come first.

Betty

After a busy day on her own in the office, Betty was pleased to see Marie turn up looking brighter than she had done of late.

'So glad to see you Marie, it's not like you to stay at home, missed you here.'

'Do you know what Betty I had to sort my head out,' she paused, 'I always thought of myself as strong, but it turns out my mother was the tough one. I have been manipulated all my life.'

Betty walked over and gave her a hug and turned away quickly embarrassed at her impetuous action poured the coffee and said, 'Do you want to talk about it? We don't have any appointments until eleven tomorrow.'

'What's happening at eleven?' asked Marie ignoring Betty's original question.

'A woman looking for part time admin work, after that we are supposed to be at the WI.'

'Oh yes, good.' she answered distractedly. 'Is Michael in?'

'He was with a client earlier. Do you want me to check for you?'

'No, I'll just pop my head round and see.' With that Marie went in search of Michael leaving Betty even more confused than before.

Michael had gone out to see a client, Marie came
back and sat down at her desk, glancing at her list of
messages asked, 'Would Derek be up for clearing
my mother's apartment do you think?'
Betty gulped, 'I'm sure he would as long as he gets
paid.'
'He will need a bigger van and someone to help him
and we can put it through the books, but I'll cover
that cost.'
'What about personal stuff?' asked Betty?
Marie thought for a moment and said, 'There's not
much left I have all the paperwork and jewellery,
biggest problem is the clothes and shoes, she has
more pairs than me. I don't think she has ever got
rid of anything I havent a clue what to do with them
all.'
Betty thought for a moment, 'Is there nothing you
want, you know a memento, reminder something?'
'No, as I said I have the jewellery, the photos and all
the other crap she's left me, that's enough.'
Betty was desperate to know more but thought it
prudent to now wait until Marie was ready to talk.
'Why not ask that Sadie who runs the vintage shop
in the village to have a look, she's bound to take
some of it, and she pays good money.'
'Good idea, some of it is or rather was expensive
and goes back to the fifties. In fact, I'll try and pop

in there on my way home. Better get it done sooner
rather than later.'
'What about the furniture? Do you want to get the
value checked?'
'To be honest my first instinct is to just get shot of it
all. Might as well donate it to charity'
'Don't you think you owe it to your mother to see
what it's worth?'
'I don't owe my mother anything. She owes me big
time.'
Betty was shocked at Marie's tone but didn't think
the time to be right to question her any further, so
she tried to stay bright, 'Are you selling the
apartment?'
'Yes, I've already instructed the agents so the
sooner I get it clear the better. Could you ask Stacey
to go in and give it a clean once Derek has finished.
Bill that to me as well.'
'Are you sure you are not rushing things Marie,
after all you haven't had the funeral yet.'
 Marie sighed and ran her hands through her hair,
'Betty I never thought about mother dying, and I'm
just so shocked at my own reaction. I didn't expect
to feel like this.'
'What do you mean your reaction?'
'I don't feel anything just relief, surely I should be
weeping buckets.'

'Not necessarily, we all react differently to death.
And you two weren't ever close, were you?'
'No but she was my mother surely I should be more
upset?' she went quiet for a moment and before
Betty could respond she said, 'I've found out so
many secrets that have been buried for so long and I
now realise I didn't know her at all.'
'So, she had a man friend and sold her apartment to
an equity release company none of that is so
terrible, is it?'
'If it were only that Betty, but there is so much more
that I've found out.'
'Do you want to talk about it?'
 Marie looked at her watch and said, 'I think I do,
let's close up here and go to the wine bar or do you
have to get home for Derek?'
Betty said, 'I'll give him a ring, but I think he is
playing darts tonight anyway it will do him good to
get his own food for a change.'
 She rang Derek while Marie tidied her desk and
wrote a list ready to be actioned in the morning. It
was only a short stroll to the bar, they walked in
silence, both deep in thought. Betty wondering what
on earth was Marie stressing about and realising
that she really cared about her. The business had
really brought them closer, she now thought of her
as a friend not just a work colleague who certainly

did not deserve the 'bitch' label she had given her before the birth of Butterflies.

Marie

Marie spotted a table in the corner and Betty went
to the bar and ordered a bottle of wine, joining
Marie, who laughed nervously saying, 'I feel like
I'm becoming a regular, first the pub and now the
wine bar, who would have thought it?'
'It's called socialising, that's what people do.' Said
Betty. The waiter brought over the chilled Pinot
Grigio, and two glasses and the pair were silent as
he poured the wine.
'Between you and me I come in here just to look at
his arse.'
Marie was just about to take a sip of her wine and
burst out laughing 'That's what I like about you;
you tell it as it is… and you're right he is really
cute.'
As she said the words, reality hit her, he could be
her son, what was she thinking? Her son was out
there somewhere; she may even have unknowingly
spoken to him at some point.
She took a deep breath and said 'What I am going to
tell you has to be in confidence, at least for now.
Michael is the only other person that knows.'
'Michael?' Betty questioned.
'I know, I made a snap judgement when we first
met, you don't have to remind me, he has been very
supportive, and he was there when I got the news.'

Marie opened her handbag, pulled out the letter
from her mother and handed it to Betty. 'Read this it
is the easiest way to explain, I'm still struggling to
say the words let alone think about it.'

Betty read it through and was visibly pale when she
finished, she sat for a moment just looking at the
page. 'I don't know what to say Marie, it's a lot to
take in. What on earth was your mother doing
keeping this secret for so long?'

'I have no idea, to be honest I'm struggling to accept
it as true, but it must be. It's all so long ago, not for
a second did I ever think my baby lived. It is just so
cruel. How different would my life have been if I
had known or even been given a choice.'

'What are you going to do?'

'My first thought was do nothing, what good can
come of it after all these years?'

'You have to do something; there is a family out
there missing a grandmother.'

'Some grandmother, I never even had the chance to
be a mother.'

'Marie your mum did what she thought was right at
the time. You were only a child, you were raped by
her brother. Think how hard that was for her to deal
with.'

'I know, I've tried to look at it from her point of view, but it isn't easy. I buried the truth about the rape, all this time I never told a soul.'

'Weren't you married when you first came to Jones Macintosh? Didn't you tell your husband?'

'No, I couldn't tell him, truth was he left me because I wouldn't have children, I was scared that another baby would die on me, but he never died, did he? I think what hurts most is that mothers decision shaped my life, things could have been so different.'

Betty thought for a moment, 'Not being able to have children has been a huge problem in my marriage Marie, but lately Derek and I have decided that we have to make the best of these latter years. We both have regrets and wish things had been different. I see other women of our age out with their grandchildren, I'm so envious. All I can say to you is think carefully before you decide.' She paused for a moment 'I personally think you should make contact.'

'That's what Michael said, I suppose its fear of rejection that scares me most. But as the letter says he has been looking for me I'm just not sure how much contact mother had with him before she died.'

'If you do nothing it will be a burden that you'll carry around for years. If he rejects you at least you will know you tried. You aren't to blame here don't forget that.'

'I suppose you're right; the funeral is in two days' time; I will do something after that.'

'Whatever you do Marie don't rush into a decision, there is a lot to think about.'

'I know but I'm also scared that it's such a life changing decision.'

Betty said, 'Has it occurred to you that your mother might have given the family your address?'

'Yes, I did ask the solicitor that, but he didn't know anything, she just used him to deliver the letter to me. He wasn't her regular solicitor. Of course, there's always the possibility that she used yet another solicitor to pass on information. Right now, I wouldn't put anything past her.'

'It could be the decision will be taken out of your hands, had you thought that if she had sent another letter, to be delivered on her death, then your son might turn up at the funeral?'

'That would be too weird, but yes that thought had crossed my mind. I have asked Michael to come with me, he has been such a support.'

'What happened to he's a creep then?'

Marie laughed and leaning back in her chair and said, 'Okay, Betty you were right, guess I'm not such a good judge of character as you.'

Betty smiled and topped up their glasses.

Marie raised her glass and said, 'I could get so used to this, relaxing after work with a glass of wine and someone to talk to.' Aware that the wine was encouraging her to relax at last she giggled and said, 'We are supposed to be talking shop not about me.'

Betty replied 'Sometimes it is more important to talk about personal issues not bottle them up. You've got a tough road ahead and whatever you think and feel now it won't be easy.'

'I know, I suppose I feel like I'm on a moving rollercoaster which I'm not going to be able to get off until it stops.'

'Well, you know I'm here for you, just take everything one day at a time.'

'Thanks Betty you have no idea how much I appreciate that.'

Marie stood up and as she walked to the ladies she turned back and said, 'I am going to call a cab do you want to share?'

'There's no need Derek will be here in a few minutes he just messaged me he will drop you off. He's just finishing his game of darts.'

It was only a few minutes later that Derek appeared in the doorway of the wine bar and ushered the two women out into the night air. After dropping Marie home Betty turned to Derek and said, 'Sometimes it helps to listen to other people's problems to put your own into perspective.'

Derek looked at her quizzically, 'So what secrets have you learned today?'

'Nothing I can tell you yet, just be assured, I may not always show it but I do appreciate you.' She touched his hand and he squeezed it, they walked up the path to their bungalow. The closest they had been for years.

Meanwhile Marie went back to her empty house, sitting in her favourite armchair she did something she hadn't been able to do for years. She cried, not for the loss of her mother but the child she never knew. When she was all cried out, she resolved that she would get through this difficult situation trying not to dwell on might have been, just try and stay focused on the future.

Marie

Marie was up early, after drinking two large
expressos before six o'clock. It was still hours away
from the funeral, her nerves were beginning to get
the better of her. She desperately wanted to speak to
Michael, but it was far too early. She was surprised
to find she needed to hear his reassuring voice.

This was a new feeling for her, it had come as
something of a surprise. All it had been a long time
since she had felt so vulnerable, and all the recent
revelations had exposed part of her that had been
buried for so long. Opening her blinds she watched
the sunrise, wishing she could fast forward twenty-
four hours. The funeral would be over.

Her mobile beeped, she picked it up and to her
delight it was Michael.

'I hope I didn't wake you Marie, I know it's early.'

'No no I have been awake for hours, I just can't stop
turning everything over in my mind.'

'I guessed that, so how about I pick you up in an
hour and we go out for breakfast? You can talk over
all your fears; I'm a good listener.'

'I know you are Michael, I think that would be a
great help, though I can't promise to eat much.'

'No matter I will pick you up in an hour' before she
could answer Michael had hung up, she stood
looking at her phone for a moment and then walked

through to her bedroom to get ready. Hanging on
the wardrobe door ready for her to wear was a smart
black suit, without thinking Marie slipped it back
into the wardrobe,selected a navy dress with a
check jacket. Today for her was merely goodbye to
the woman she had known as her mother. Today
was time to move on. Although she wouldn't admit
it, she was dressing for Michael, not for her mother.
 True to his promise Michael rang her doorbell
exactly an hour later, Marie grabbed her bag and as
she opened the door, she had an overwhelming
desire to throw her arms around his neck, another
alien feeling for her. He smiled and took her hand,
'You look lovely Marie, what no black?'
'No, mother didn't believe in black for funerals,' she
replied hoping she could be forgiven the white lie
today of all days. Truth, was she had no idea what
her mother believed.
They walked in silence to his car and as she sat
back in the seat Michael leant over and buckled her
seat belt, saying quietly, 'Today will be fine Marie,
if she's up there watching you, she will know how
you are feeling, she would be proud of the way you
are dealing with all of this.'
'I hope so Michael, I really do.'
 Michael drove the short distance to a small café on
the outskirts of the town and parked outside. Marie

looked uncertain when she saw the building, which from the outside looked nothing more than a workman's café.

'Have you not eaten here before?' Michael asked as he looked at her bemused face.

'Can't say that I have. Aren't I a little overdressed for this?' she asked.

'No not at all I come here a lot before work, a lot of local businessmen use it, the food is excellent. It's important to start the day with a good breakfast.'

'I don't normally bother eating in the mornings.' She protested.

Michael pushed open the door and to her surprise the café was crowded, Michael led her to a small table in the corner, covered in a red and white gingham cloth, laid for two.

Marie looked around; sure, enough Michael was right, the clientele was not as suggested by the shabby exterior of the café. Michael said, 'Can I suggest Eggs Benedict, it really is the best I have ever eaten.'

Marie looked dubious but knowing that he had her best interest at heart agreed and opted for a pot of tea instead of risking another coffee giving her jitters. The waiter, who was wearing a surprisingly white apron over his uniform poured the tea, Marie

declined milk and took a sip, 'Earl Grey, my
favourite, this is a treat.'

 Michael smiled, 'Trust me the best is yet to come.'
Marie didn't like to ask if he meant the food or
something else, thinking about it for a moment, but
before she could speak her breakfast was in front of
her. Michael watched as she carefully took a
mouthful, she nodded approvingly and for the first
time in a long time she cleared her plate and said,
'Truly superb, you were right the best Eggs
Benedict ever.'

'I must say it's good to see you eating properly
Marie.'

'Eating has never been high on my favourite
pastimes, so it is unusual for me, now I need you to
read through my speech.' She fished around in her
bag and pulled out a beautifully handwritten sheet
of cream paper and handed it to Michael who
looking at it and said, 'not exactly what I was
expecting, lovely handwriting,' he read it through,
'That is a very thoughtful eulogy Marie, no-one will
ever know how you really feel, nor do they ever
need to know.'

'I did give it a lot of thought and decided to give her
the kind of send-off I would expect, I'll put all my
bad thoughts aside and deal with them another day.'

'We have about an hour before the service; do you want to do anything? We could walk for a bit and get some fresh air?

'What in these shoes?' she kicked out one foot to show a four-inch heel. 'If its ok with you I would like to sit here a bit longer, perhaps another pot of tea? I would like to be early at the crematorium; I want to meet everyone before the service if possible.'

'That's fine by me,' he got up, ordered more tea and as he sat back down, he asked,

'Are you worried that Brian might turn up?'

'In a way, but in some way, it might be easier if he does, I just don't know what I think, it feels like a huge mountain in front of me, and I'm going to have to climb it at some point.'

'I can understand that, drink your tea, do you want me to sit with you during the service, or should I loiter at the back?'

'No loitering Michael sit with me; the only other close person is Maurice; the front row will be sparse to say the least. In fact, if none of her WI cronies turn up it's going to be a quiet brief service.'

'You've done your best Marie, besides Betty will be there with Chrissie and some of the sewing team, Betty will make sure they are all there to support you'

They finished their tea, Michael paid the bill and
they walked outside into the sunshine.
'At least it's not raining that would have made it all
worse.' Said Marie quietly.
Outside the crematorium Marie was pleased to see a
few cars. Maurice was standing waiting, looking
very dapper dressed all in black. Marie felt
momentarily uncomfortable, maybe she should have
worn black after all. Michael sensing her discomfort
squeezed her hand reassuringly.
'Hello Maurice, how are you coping?' asked Marie.
'Hello Marie,' he turned to Michael and said, 'You
must be Michael, Marie has told me all about you.'
Michael shook his hand, 'I'm fine just always hate
this part. Seems more people have turned up than
you expected,' he said as Betty and Derek were
walking up the gravel path towards them.
 They walked through to the waiting area just as the
hearst carrying Violet arrived. Marie and Maurice
followed it into the small chapel, closely followed
by Michael. They took their seats at the front and
Marie was heartened as a few unfamiliar faces
began to trickle in filling some of the empty seats.
She was nervous when it came to her turn to speak
as she had to face the mourners, her heart was
pounding, what if Brian had chosen to turn up? She
glanced around her and satisfied there wasn't a forty

something male in the congregation she began her short eulogy. When finished, she sank back in her seat and began to breathe normally, Maurice said his few words and then service was over.

Michael was nudging her to stand up and she realised that she had switched off and missed the last part of the sermon. The coffin had gone, disappeared behind the curtain, they filed out to look at the flowers. Marie said to Michael 'Do you think I should take all the cards from the flowers; I feel I need to thank those who bothered?'

'I'll get them for you, let everyone pass by first, do you want to take any flowers home with you?'

'Not really, though it does seem a waste, they just move them and let them die don't they.'

'I believe that's right, but don't take them if you don't want or you could just ask for them to be taken to a care home.'

'Marie thought for a moment, and said 'I don't want, let's just go, leave the flowers, let the funeral company deal with them. I just want to get the wake over, once that's finished, I can concentrate on Butterflies.'

Michael looked at her, 'Whatever you want Marie business must come first.'

They both laughed and Michael carefully removed the cards and without reading them slipped them into his top pocket, to give to Marie later.

Chrissie

Chrissie found funerals of all descriptions depressing to say the least. Making her excuses she slipped away before the wake. She undid the padlock on her bicycle, which was chained to the gate outside the church. Feeling satisfied that she had made an appearance she cycled happily back towards her cottage. The sewing team had the large order of curtains to complete. Chrissie was anxious that they were finished and hung by the end of the week. If she delivered as promised, then there was the strong possibility of a lot more work in the near future.

As she pushed her way up the drive, she could see the front door was slightly open, thinking maybe one of the girls had gone in for something she put her bike away and went in.

'Hello Chrissie, hope you don't mind I let myself in.'

Chrissie went pale, 'Zack what the fuck are you doing here? I thought you were going to ring me if you were coming, and you left your key here how did you get in?'

'Your cleaning lady let me in. So many questions, aren't you pleased to see me?'

'Not really Zack, I'm very busy at the moment can't it wait?'

'Quite the businesswoman all of a sudden, aren't you? Tell you what I'm going to have a bath and a nap, and we can talk later.'

With that he left Chrissie standing open mouthed as he went upstairs humming as he went. She was furious with him, his sudden appearance after weeks of silence had completely thrown her, she just hoped that he hadn't been down to the workroom and disturbed the girls from their work. Closing the kitchen door behind her she walked through to the garden, her hand brushing against the prolific row of lavender as she went.

The workshop was as she had hoped a hive of activity, her mood lightened when she saw Sue waving her over. 'Chrissie how did it go?'

'Oh, you know just a funeral, I hadn't even met Marie's mother, I just went to support her.'

'Was she ok?'

'You know Marie she hides her emotions well, who knows what she was thinking or feeling?'

'Was she on her own?'

'No Michael our office landlord was with her.'

'He seems very nice, I met him when I went into the office last week, do you think they are an item?'

'I hadn't thought about it but yes I suppose it's possible, though don't expect me to be the one to ask her.'

Sue chuckled, 'Don't blame you, she would probably give you one of her stares, anyway the good news from here is the curtains are all finished. I'll be in tomorrow to give them a final press and Derek is going to collect them and hang them over the weekend.'

'Brilliant, if you ask the girls to come in on Tuesday, I'll have another couple of weeks work ready. The fabrics will be delivered over the weekend just thank everyone and tell them there will be cakes all round on Tuesday.

As she went into the cottage her phone was ringing, picking it up from the worktop where she had left it earlier that day, she saw she had six missed calls.

'Hi Chrissie, here.'

'Thank goodness I have been trying to get hold of you, oops sorry it's John Mason here.'

'Sorry John, I stupidly left my phone at home, I was at Marie mothers funeral,' she hesitated 'What can I do for you?'

'I seem to be in a difficult situation, I have a diminishing workforce and orders coming in that I can't cover.'

'So do you want Butterflies to help?'

'If you can, there is on order which I am desperate to get completed on time, it is a very good customer of mine.'

'What do you want us to do?'

'There are a thousand Cami tops, they are all cut out and bagged ready.'

'A thousand that's a lot we are only a workforce of eight.' Answered Chrissie.

'I have done the calculations, and if you deliver half in two weeks and the balance two weeks later it shouldn't be a problem. I can still meet my deadline.'

'I need to talk to Sue before she leaves, to check if she can fit them in. I'll ring you back.'

Chrissie hung up and went to leave the kitchen and Zack appeared wrapped only in one of her fluffy white bath towels. She looked at him and said, 'Not now Zack, not now, go and put some clothes on please.'

'She walked out on him knowing by the time she had time to talk to him he would be furious, but that didn't stop her almost running down the garden to speak to Sue. It was only later did it occur to her how much her priorities had changed over the last few months.

Sue was enthusiastic and said, 'I don't think that will be a problem, we can surely fit them in with the roman blinds,' she paused to think for a moment and went on 'Tell you what I am finishing now, I can call in and see John then I can find out what's involved.'

'Great I'll let him know you are on your way, call me later, we need to make sure we have the right machines and girls available. You might need to talk to Derek when you know what is needed.'

'No problem,' with that Sue pulled on her coat and after locking up the workroom drove off to meet up with John Mason, while Chrissie phoned him and let him know that Sue was on her way to sort out the finer details. Satisfied that everything was under control she switched her mind to a bigger personal problem, Zack what on earth was she going to do about Zack?

Zack

It had taken a great deal of money and emotional energy for Zack to be in a position to confront Chrissie. To convince her that he was now free to marry her, what had happened when he finally got to her cottage? She wasn't there, luckily her cleaner had let him in as Chrissie had taken back his key. The workshop in the garden was full of whirring sewing machines and giggling women. What on earth was Chrissie thinking? This was so completely out of character for her. His Chrissie had never needed to work, sure she had hobbies, numerous projects, nothing had lasted for long, now she appeared to have a business being run from his workshop.

He heard Chrissie speaking on the phone, it went quiet, he waited for Chrissie to come up and throw herself at him, apologising for being offhand. But when it was obvious she wasn't coming, he steeled himself and went down the stairs to find her standing staring out into the garden.

Nervously he cleared his throat and said, 'Look we got off on the wrong foot, can we start again?'
'Why, what is there to say Zack, it's over you left me, not a word since and I have had to get on with my life.'
'I've been on tour for months before and nothing

changed when I came back you were always pleased to see me, what's different now?'

'Oh, come on Zack, how can you say that? You told me you had a wife and a son and had been married for years and only decided to tell me when I decided finally to let you make an honest woman of me. How do you think that made me feel?'

Zack looked uncomfortable and shuffled his feet, 'I want to make this right Chrissie, but right now I need a drink. First time I've been in my house, and you haven't given me a drink.'

Realising immediately, he had said the wrong thing he laughed nervously. This was ridiculous he was Zack who never got nervous performing in front of hundreds of thousands of screaming fans. He was extremely agitated now he saw the look on Chrissie's face and in that moment, he knew it was going to be a long road back. He should never have called the cottage his house he may have paid for it, but it had always been one hundred percent Chrissies home.

Chrissie went to the fridge and took out a bottle of vodka, she stood for a moment just holding the bottle looking directly at him. Zack trembled inwardly surely; she wasn't going to hit him with it. Finally, she spoke, 'Let's just get one thing straight Zack, you might have kept me for all these years, but this cottage is mine, you signed it over to me. I bloody earnt it; you left me to bring up Summer on my own, years spent sitting waiting for you to drop in for sex, all the time reading all about your antics in the papers. Don't you ever say it's your house? Now go and get some glasses and sit down we need to talk properly.'

Zack meekly did as he was told, all the time inwardly seething, somehow, he had to retrieve this situation, he was finding it increasingly difficult to find the right words. Feeling very much as if he was no longer in control, a scenario he was not used to. Chrissie had changed grown stronger and from where he was now sitting, she appeared to hold all the cards. He watched as she poured the drinks, noticing that she gave herself a small measure when once hers would have matched the large one she poured him.

She sat down opposite him and picked up one of her favourite handmade cushions and clutching it to her chest said, 'Speak Zack you have obviously come here to say something so spit it out you might have noticed I'm a busy at the moment.'

Zack was visibly shaken by her tone and hand shaking took a large slug of his vodka and taking a deep breath, he said, 'I came here today just to tell you I'm now divorced and oh shit I've quit the band,' his voice wavered, and he looked at Chrissie who just sat there expressionless.

'What exactly do you want from me now? And just how did you get divorced so quickly when you supposedly didn't even know where your wife was.'

He hesitated and said 'I just want to say sorry I should have told you years ago, I didn't think you would care. You turned me down so many times. As for the divorce, my solicitor has searched for her for years and he pushed the divorce through.'

'Is that legal.'

'I assume so, but it didn't come cheap, doesn't change the fact that you never wanted to marry me before.'

'I turned you down Zack because I didn't want your lifestyle, thinking about it I now realise this is the most sober I have ever seen you.'

'You've changed Chrissie.'

'Yep, I have, I finally found something I enjoy doing, I have a reason to get out of bed every morning and do you know what, I am happy. I haven't found myself scouring the papers searching for gossip about you or sitting for hours willing the phone to ring.'

'I didn't realise, I always thought you were happy, you have always been the only stable thing in my life. To come here after a gruelling tour has always

been an escape from my other life and all those
other women, they meant nothing Chrissie nothing.'
He shook his head and looked despairingly at her.
'Yet you got married Zack, married and you have a
son, Summer has a half-brother somewhere.'
'We married in a moment of madness, too many
drugs I guess.'
'Don't make excuses it won't make things better.'
'What will Chrissie, what can I do to make things
better?'
'Right now, I really don't know.' She picked up her
glass and walked over to the window and stood in
silence looking into the garden, turning to Zack she
said, 'I think you had better go, you need to realise
that I have changed,' she paused and went on 'if you
really have left the band and divorced your wife. If
that is true, I don't want you here just because you
have nothing else. If and it is a big if you come back
then you come back on my terms, I am working
now and not intending to give it up for anyone, least
of all an aging rock star.'
 Zack replied carefully, 'I'll call a cab now but
believe me Chrissie I have never loved anyone but
you. I need to think but I promise you I will make
every effort to be with you.'
 Chrissie didn't respond, just let him make the call
and watched as he went upstairs and collected his

bag. She was still standing in the same place long after he had quietly closed the old oak door behind him. Uncertain as to whether she would ever see him again.

Betty

'I don't see why you can't help me today, Derek.'

'I already told you Betty I promised Chrissie I would set up her machines for this John Mason's order.'

'That job is not on the books, I checked, let Chrissie do it herself.'

'For goodness' sake woman, all you have to do is cover a stall at the W.I. this is far more important to the business.'

'Why do you always put Chrissie before me? What has she got that I haven't?'

'I'm not listening to any more of this, what is it with you? You got me this job is it just to keep tabs on me?'

'Don't be silly of course not.'

'Then let me get on with what I have agreed to do.'

With that Derek slammed out of the house.

Betty banged her fist on the table, she knew she was being irrational but yes, she was jealous of Chrissie. Her with the wild crazy hair, hippy clothes and that laugh, how come she was never miserable? It wasn't only the funeral yesterday that had upset her, not that it was a sad occasion, she had never met Marie's mother, it was seeing Marie and Michael together. They had seemed so comfortable with each other; he was being so protective towards

Marie. It wasn't fair she had introduced them, and
Marie had disliked Michael on sight now look at
them. That had made her angry, Betty thought he
was wonderful but now he didn't even give her a
second look. She was married, but she couldn't see
that these irrational thoughts were not helping her
already rocky marriage.

Her mobile buzzed, she picked it up Marie, that's
all she needed a pep talk from her this early, but she
answered it anyway.

'Morning Betty how are you this lovely morning?'
asked Marie.

Betty looked out of the window; she was ashamed
to admit that she hadn't even noticed the beautiful
autumn morning. 'Marie what can I do for you?'

'I was wondering do you need a hand setting up
today. I've only a couple of appointments and they
aren't till later.'

Before answering Betty took a deep breath and said
'Yes, I would please, I'll come by the office and
pick you up from there. See you about nine thirty.'
With that she hung up and banishing all her wicked
thoughts she loaded the dishwasher and went
upstairs to put on her make-up and brush her hair.
Despite all her good intentions she still had not lost
any weight and looking at her to body to do list she
was cross with herself that she had not been to the

gym or hairdressers for weeks. It was no wonder
Derek was so disinterested in her. Nothing to be
done but make the best of herself today and try
harder tomorrow.

 Derek had loaded her car the night before so within
half an hour of the phone call she was at the office
to collect Marie.

'I think as parking is difficult at the hall we'll take
my car, and we can drop yours home I've still got
plenty of room in my car. It was only a short drive
to the hall where the WI were holding their Autumn
fair, Betty let Marie chatter on about work quite
aware that she was trying to concentrate on
Butterflies. All the while avoiding the issues that
she still had to face. Betty desperately wanted to ask
questions about her personal life but decided against
it.

 The hall was busy, Butterflies had a large stall at
one corner by a window overlooking the car park
with a good view of how many people were coming
through the door. It didn't take long for the stall to
be laid out with stationery and pet portrait samples
from Jenny. Chrissie supplied her range of colourful
pots for sale and pictures of the curtains, blinds and
of the costumes they had made for the theatre. All
beautifully decorated with satin butterfly shaped
lavender bags which sold out long before the Fair

finished. Chrissie was delighted she had also taken a large order for cushions and had appointments for them to quote for curtains, the interest was almost overwhelming, but she was confident that the team could deal with it all.

Betty meanwhile was busy arranging interviews for skilled administrators; she found it so amazing that their small town held so many women with skills that were not being used but looking for employment mostly on a temporary basis. Perfect for Butterflies

All in all, despite putting the event together at the last minute due to so many personal issues interrupting the team, it was a huge success. They packed away their advertising material Betty said to Marie 'What a day can you believe the interest. Who would ever have thought it?'

Marie smiled and said, 'I always knew we would make a great team and Chrissie joining us was inspirational Betty so now it's onwards and upwards. Me I have a few personal mountains to climb but I do now feel I can deal with them all.'

'At least you have Michael to help you.' Smirked Betty.

'Yes, he has turned out to be a good friend.'

'Only a friend?' queried Betty.

'Well, a very good friend,' answered Marie
blushing.

 Before Betty could comment the door to the hall
opened and Michael walked in and waved cheerily
to them. 'Just thought I would see if you two needed
a hand packing up.'

'We have just about finished, not that we have a lot
left, the boxes are all ready, you could put them into
my boot then I can get Jenny and Chrissie to collect
them from the office tomorrow.' Said Marie.

'Are you going back to the office now Marie?' asked
Betty.

'No, I don't think so, if there are any messages, they
can wait until tomorrow. Do you need a lift?'

As she spoke Betty's phone rang, she answered it
and said, 'Derek is outside so no I am fine, I'll get
off now if you don't need me anymore.'

'No everything is done here, thanks a lot Betty see
you in the morning.'

Betty picked up her bag and went out of the hall to
face Derek aware that they hadn't parted on the best
of terms that morning. Derek appeared to have
forgotten the mornings spat and as she got into his
van he said 'Thought you would fancy fish and
chips tonight; I ordered them from Bert's earlier and
have got to just stop and pick them up as we go
past. Have you had a good day?'

338

Betty sighed, 'Yes yes it has been really good, even Marie seems happy, despite all she has got going on in her life. How was your day?' she added almost as an afterthought.

'Surprisingly good I spent a couple of hours with John Mason, and he put me in the picture about the machines and even gave me some fittings for our machines, so we are all set up ready to do his order.'

'I don't want to put a damper on this, but your Chrissie hasn't put this on to the books yet.'

'Firstly, she's not my Chrissie as you so bitchily put it, secondly she has spoken to Marie, because I heard her so do you want fish and chips or not?'

'Sorry, sorry yes please, no vinegar though.'

'Ha ha you certainly don't need vinegar.' Answered Derek almost laughing as he got out of the van.

Betty winced and watched as he strolled across the road, why oh why couldn't she just keep her mouth shut and keep her wicked thoughts to herself sometimes.

Marie

After Betty had gone Marie looked awkwardly at
Michael and said, 'Look I haven't got much in, but
would you like to come back for a bite to eat?'
'Yes, that'll be nice I just need to pop home first and
feed Benjie.'
Marie pulled a face, she wasn't used to anyone
putting a scruffy looking cat before her, animals
were not her thing at all but Michael loved his
ancient ginger tom.
 They got into their separate cars and set off in
different directions both pondering on the evening
ahead. Michael stopped off and bought flowers, a
bottle of wine and box of chocolates, looking
forward to some time with Marie. Marie however
stopped off and selected an expensive ready meal
from Marks and Spencer with every intention of
convincing Michael she could cook proper food.
Quite forgetting that Michael lived on ready meals
and was also an expert with the microwave.
Marie set the dining room table carefully, lighting a
candle and even getting out her best linen serviettes.
When Michael arrived, she smiled warmly as he
handed her a bunch of lilies.
'Very appropriate,' she said still smiling. Michael
blushed realising his gaff mumbled 'sorry didn't
think.'

'It's fine really, I love lilies they are my favourites.
Come through to the kitchen supper is almost
ready.'
'I thought we were just having a bite,' said Michael
as they passed the open dining room door.'
'Oh, it's nothing special just one of my signature
dishes,' lied Marie.
Michael grinned as he spotted the tell-tale M&S
empty carton on the side which Marie had in her
haste forgotten to hide.
 After they had eaten, Michael said 'I quite forgot to
give you the cards after the funeral, stupidly tucked
them in my pocket.'
'Have you looked at them?' she asked.
'No, I didn't,' he reached into his jacket pocket and
handed them to Marie. She took them and said
'There aren't many really for a woman of eighty, I
always thought she was a popular woman.'
'I think as you have already discovered she was a
very private woman; you take after her in that
respect.'
'What do you mean by that?' she asked testily.
'Don't take umbrage Marie I merely meant that you
are like her in some ways. You've admitted to me
that you never really knew her, even though she was
your mother' he hesitated and then said, 'I don't

really know you even though we have worked in adjacent offices for months now.'

'Well, I am what I am. What you see is what you get.'

Michael leant across the table and taking her hand he looked directly into her eyes and said, 'No Marie I want to get below your tough exterior. Get to know the real you, I rather suspect even you don't know who you really are.'

Marie snatched her hand away and said, 'I'll make coffee and bring it through to the lounge.'

As she rattled the coffee machine and banged the mugs, she wanted to kick herself what should have been a lovely moment, had been ruined by her own fault, why couldn't relax? She was getting fond of Michael, but it had been such a long time since she had felt close to any man. Deep down she wanted to keep this one in her life. Resolving to try harder she carried the tray of coffee through into the lounge. Forcing herself to breathe normally asked Michael to pour a couple of brandies. He protested at first but Marie suggested he leave his car and call a taxi, which Michael had intended to do all along, but had not mentioned this fact for fear of unsettling Marie. She obviously had no idea that he never touched a drop of alcohol before driving a car but hey they both still had a lot to learn about each other.

Marie kicked off her shoes and curled up on the
sofa and facing Michael who was sipping his
brandy waiting for her to speak. She picked up the
pile of cards and leafing through them she said, 'It is
so sad – I don't know any of these people, I feel so
guilty I didn't even know about Maurice.' She broke
off and held up a card, 'This is what I didn't want to
find.' Michael stood up and took the card from her
and read it out loud. 'Best wishes at this difficult
time Brian. Followed by his mobile number.'
'Now what should I do?' she asked.
Michael thought for a moment and said, 'It's a
gesture Marie, just proves what your mother said,
he is aware of you, and I think this proves he wants
to make contact.'
'I'm scared, I don't know how to deal with this, I
think I need another brandy, my brain is whirling.'
 Giving her a moment Michael poured another drink
and handing the glass to her he said, 'This is not
going to be as difficult as you are imagining, but if
you don't call him, I think you'll regret it for the
rest of your life.'
Marie did not respond so he went on, 'Look it's a
lifeline, after all, he is making it easy for you, he
must be aware that this is all new to you.'

'I know I just don't know how to approach this, to make that call, I don't think I have the strength to do it.'

'It might be a good idea to think about it before you decide but I'll help you. That's if you want me too.'

'Yes, Michael I would like that thank you.'

Michael looked at his watch and said 'Gosh I best call a cab I have a busy day tomorrow.'

Before he left Marie asked him if he would mind spending Saturday finishing clearing her mother's apartment. He agreed and to her surprise he leant over and kissed her as he left. Michael went home happy that Marie actually seemed to want to be with him and she hadn't rejected his kiss. Marie meanwhile stood for a moment facing the closed door with a huge smile on her face her fingers on her lips where she had been kissed. The first time in years and she found herself wondering just what would have happened if she had asked him to stay the night.

Chrissie

Derek had gone home, and Chrissie went down to
the workroom to chase Sue. It was late and she
should have gone home ages ago. She pushed open
the door grinning when she saw her, she was
singing along to the radio at the top her voice.
Ironically it was one of Zack and his group's
number one hits but she doubted very much if Sue
had got the connection between her and Zack. Yet
he never looked like a rock star when he was with
Chrissie, just lounged around in baggy tracksuits,
not very rock and roll at all.

'Sue, whatever you are doing leave it, go home you
need to spend some time with your family.'

'I should stay, this place needs cleaning before the
Masons order comes in.'

Chrissie thought for a moment and said. 'Not up to
you Sue, leave it I will get it done before Monday
morning I know just who can do it.'

Sue grinned, 'You don't have to tell me twice, I hate
cleaning, certainly not my favourite way of
spending an evening.' With that she picked up her
coat and bag and left Chrissie looking round. Derek
had done a good job at setting up all the machines,
but the room needed a good sweep and because the
machinists would be working on light-coloured
satin fabrics for the next few weeks, there should

not be any dust or traces of oil to mark the
garments.

Chrissie was about to ring Marie and ask if she
could use Stacey. Then decided if Marie didn't like
it she would add it to Derek's invoice, failing that
she would pay Stacey herself. She was already
using Stacey in the cottage. For the first time for as
long as she could remember she was too occupied
with the workshop and there had been no time to do
her own housework. Why not, after all she could
afford it. She locked up the workroom and walked
up the garden noting that her herbaceous borders
were in need of attention also suffering from her
neglect. Mind made up she would ask Derek, he had
told her once how he loved her garden, and it
seemed that Betty didn't like borders or lawns, so
he only had decking and pots to look after.

Once she had made the necessary phone calls,
Chrissie poured herself a cold lemonade she took
her mobile and went to sit in the garden. Her
favourite spot was under the apple tree where she
could see her cottage in all its beauty. She stretched
out on her wooden steamer chair and just closed her
eyes enjoying the early evening sunshine and quiet.
Within minutes, drink untouched she was asleep.
She felt rather than saw a shadow block out the sun

and she sat up abruptly, heart pounding, 'Zack, you
scared me what are you doing here?'
Zack thrust a bunch of red roses, from behind his
back at her. I just wanted to see you Chrissie.'
Chrissie went quiet for a moment and said, 'You
bought flowers, you've never bought flowers
before.'
Zack looked uncomfortable and said, 'There's lots
of things I haven't done which I should have, I have
done a lot of thinking, I just wanted to talk to you.'
'Sit down, we can talk now, or do you need a drink?'
'Sure do, you know me babe.'
 Chrissie got up saying, 'I'll put these in water- and
thank you, do you want your usual?'
'Please and you had better bring the bottle.'
Chrissie went indoors and went into the hall to put
the vase on the hall table. She glanced in the mirror
to check her hair and grinned to herself as she
spotted Zack's suitcase tucked in the corner.
Collecting the glasses and vodka from the freezer
she walked out towards Zack, knowing for once she
had the upper hand. The next couple of hours were
certainly going to be interesting. After pouring out a
large measure, Chrissie looked directly at him and
said, 'OK Zack what is this all about I thought we
had agreed it was all over?'

Zack took a large sip of his drink and began to speak slowly as if he had spent a long time rehearsing the speech to come. 'It's like this, I have never been alone before, and I left the band thinking I would be free of touring and for once I would be able to do all those things I missed out on.'

'Like what?'

'Go on holiday, theatre, cinema eat out in restaurants that sort of stuff.'

'What stopped you?'

'I was going to book a holiday, then realised that I couldn't face travelling alone. Then I realised there wasn't anywhere in the world I wanted to go.'

'What about the rest?' Chrissie asked.

Zack went quiet and taking a deep breath said, 'I realised that I really don't want to do anything without you.'

'Surely you have loads of friends who would be glad to partner you?'

'No, just loads of hangers on, seems I have neglected thinking of my future,' he paused and took her hand, 'You have always been there for me and now I need you, but you don't seem to want or need me.'

Chrissie sat quietly for a few minutes and gathered her thoughts, if she was honest with herself Zack had always been around, he had supported her and

Summer, but he was often away touring for months at a time, she was used to that. Always pleased to see him, never wanting to share his lifestyle. It was obvious that he hadn't thought out his sudden retirement properly. Now he was put out that she had found herself an interest which was taking up much of her time. Thinking he would not like what she was about to say she grabbed the bottle and poured out large measures into their glasses. Eventually she began to speak. 'I've had time to think as well, the way I see it is I don't want us to finish. You are part of my life, you were all of my life until recently, but I have found myself, a little late at my age I know, but I love what I'm doing now.'

'I was kinda thinking that you would get bored with the workroom.'

'You mean like everything else I have dabbled in?' Zack looked uncomfortable and answered 'Yeah that's what I meant.

Chrissie sighed, 'What you need to understand that this has become more of a job for me than a hobby.

Everything else has been a something to pass the time while you were on tour.'

'I don't see how you are going to fit me into this new life.'

'I wish you had made some sort of plan before just announcing to the world you were retiring.'

'You know me I never plan.'

'Exactly now the way forward has to be planning. First where do you want to live, that has got to be the first decision? 'Asked Chrissie.

'I thought I could come here, I've always thought of it as my home.'

'Really Zack what will you do with your other houses? What you have to remember this is my house and don't say you paid for it because I bloody earnt it. Forty years I have always been here for you.'

Zack opened his mouth to speak, 'No let me finish you need seriously think about what it will be like living in a village plus have you thought what you are going to do with your time.'

'I haven't thought about that I suppose, the trouble is I have always had a manager who has thought for me.'

'Well, you have got to think for yourself now.' Said Chrissie sharply, she stood up and following the example that Marie had set to them all, she collected a notebook and pen and put them down on the table. Before Zack could speak, she said 'I see you are planning on stopping over?'

'Yeah, kind of thought you wouldn't mind, you
haven't ever said no before.'
'Of course it's all right, but now we are going to
make some sort of plan to occupy yourself.'
 Zack began to look a little uncomfortable and he
mumbled 'since when did you get to be so bossy?'
Chrissie looked at her watch and said, 'Just need to
make a couple of calls then we will start our new
life together.'
 Zack perked up a bit expecting Chrissie to mean a
quick snack and off to bed which was their normal.
Seeing Zac's expression, she laughed, 'No not that
Zack go and wash and we are going to walk to the
pub and have a pint and perhaps supper.'
'A pint will it be safe?'
'What the hell do you mean safe? You are planning
to live in a village, most of these people know you
are my partner, thanks to you walking in
unannounced and guess what I doubt anyone gives a
dam who you are.'
'Sorry I'm so used to pretending I'm not here and
worrying about photographers.'
 Chrissie giggled, 'Don't worry there's no press
round here and the regulars in the pub won't even
recognise you besides, that's what couples do on a
Saturday night.'

Zack looked a bit affronted at the thought of not
being recognised but he went upstairs to change
while Chrissie organised the cleaning of the
workroom. Stacey was more than happy to work on
a Sunday and Chrissie decided to take the
opportunity to ask her to come in and clean the
workshop on a regular basis. Something else that
would annoy Zack, having agreed that he could
come back one thing was for sure this time it was
going to be on her terms and hers alone.

Marie

'Once I have cleared out the bedroom, I'm getting a house clearance company in to just take away all this furniture.' Said Marie decisively.

'I thought you were going to ask Derek to do it?' asked Michael.

'No, it's too much for one man and besides his van is too small for most of this heavy furniture, I don't suppose there is anything you need is there?'

'No, I have too much stuff, I kept far too many pieces from my marriage when my wife ran off to Australia and left it all behind.' Why don't you phone around and get one of the local charities to come and get it all?'

'Yes, l might just do that.'

Marie smiled, she hadn't yet been to Michael's house, but she rather suspected it would be a typical bachelor's pad, he had been divorced and lived alone for such a long time. He had been promising to cook for her for the last few weeks but so far, no real definite invitation. A plan had been forming in her mind, there was a stack of boxes ready to go but she had nowhere to stash them maybe if he would give her some space in his garage, she would get to see how he lived.

'Derek is going to pick up all the sacks of clothes and shoes and take them to the Age Concern charity shop, but he can't pick them up until Monday he has something on today and they aren't open tomorrow being Sunday. Shame really there are some really expensive pieces there, but I don't have the time or inclination to sort through them. To be honest I want to push this sale through and get on with my life.' She paused 'whatever way that is going to take me now, I really don't know just a few hurdles to face, I know.'

'Why don't you give them to The Vintage Shop? I know Geraldine she will take what she can sell and then she'll pass anything she doesn't want to Age Concern.' Said Michael.

'That's what Betty suggested, I suppose it's better than just giving them away.'

Michael said 'Of course. As far as your hurdles, I will be with you all the way, rest assured, but it might be bumpy ride.'

'I know that I just need to shut the door on this flat and then I will face everything else, but I am expecting it to be difficult, I just hope that learning what my mother did has made me strong enough to face whatever lies ahead.'

'It won't be easy; you really don't know how much truth is in her letter.'

'I know that she took my baby away said he was dead, now I learn that he is alive and well. I have not the slightest idea of how much he really knows, only that he sent flowers with his number.'

'As long as you are not expecting happy families ahead.'

'No certainly not but whatever the result I just want to know what really happened and I have had a lot of sleepless nights over this and once this apartment is gone, I will deal with Brian and whatever family that might involve.'

Michael looked at his watch, 'Time we went home there isn't much else we can do here, what about the boxes in the hall?'

'I do want to keep them, I need to sort through them, there might be some important information in there somewhere, and I'm just a bit stuck for space at the moment.'

'They can go in my garage if you like, it's a bit of a mess but room for this lot that's for sure.'

Marie smiled this was going well, just what she wanted to happen so with fingers crossed she said.

'Thank you, I'll take one for now and once I've gone through it, I'll shred it in the office.'

'We can take them now and' he hesitated 'perhaps I can cook us a late lunch.'

'You cook as well, do you?' asked Marie.

Michael laughed, 'It won't be cordon bleu but I've had to feed myself for a long time now, so I do know my way round the kitchen.'
'Listen I just exist on salad and takeaways I hate cooking so this will be a treat.'

They loaded the boxes and bags into his car and Michael suggested they stop off at Marie's flat and leave the things she wanted to keep there. He had a very nice bottle of wine chilling in the fridge, he was thinking she could get a taxi home later. Once at the flat Marie took time to change out of her jeans and with the thought of sitting outside in the sunshine, she put on a cotton dress over carefully chosen elegant silk underwear and as she grabbed her blazer in case she was late, she stopped and did something she had never done before, she put a clean pair of knickers and a toothbrush into the bottom of her large handbag.

Marie was pleasantly surprised when they drew up outside Michael's detached house, everything about its external appearance was pristine and surprisingly welcoming. Once the boxes were stashed into the garage he led the way into the house, downstairs was a huge modern kitchen diner with old antique pine furniture, which surprising worked really well.

Patio doors took up the back of the house and opened up on to a small but manicured garden.

Michael sat Marie down at the table facing the garden saying, 'Now sit there and watch me for a change.' She did as she was told, as he set about defrosting chilli con carne a batch of which he assured her he had prepared himself weeks earlier. The meal was ready in less than half an hour and was beautifully presented and served with a green salad and perfectly cooked rice. Marie said, 'This is so good Michael how on earth do you manage to do all this yourself?'

'Thank you but I confess I do have a cleaner and a gardener mind you my cleaner is finishing soon, but I do enjoy the cooking, plus I don't do much else at weekends except work, so cooking is my relaxation.'

'Still impressive, if you need a new cleaner, I have a lady called Stacey on my books if you are interested.'

'Always one eye on business Marie don't you ever relax?'

She thought for a moment and replied 'I think I'm getting better; I certainly still struggle with weekends. I worked so hard before Butterflies I never had time for a social life so I don't like weekends much.'

'Just as I thought, how about we make a weekend of it?'

Marie hesitated for a second and asked, 'What have you got in mind?'

'I think there's band on at the Dolphin tonight, usually is on a Saturday night.'

'Do you often watch live music?'

'No not often enough really, I suppose I don't like going on my own to the pub on a Saturday night. Its couple's night!'

Marie laughed so you think we are a couple then?'

Michael looked uncomfortable and answered carefully, 'I think we are good together, don't you?'

'Yes, to the pub, and yes we are good.'

Marie helped Michael clear away and load the dishwasher and they went into the garden to enjoy half an hour of late afternoon sun before walking across the green to the pub. Despite the fact that it was early the bar was crowded, they managed to find a table for two in the corner away from the speakers as the band were already setting up. Michael went off to get drinks. Marie thought it a bit odd that he hadn't bothered to ask her what she was drinking but sat back to look around her. Feeling out of place, she was sat in his local about to listen to live music. For the life of her she couldn't remember being out on a Saturday night with a date, let alone about to watch a band play. Michael put two pints down on the table and from

his pocket produced two bags of crisps. Seeing
Marie's bemused face, he laughed and said, 'Cider
and crisps best part of the evening try it.' Marie took
a sip and replied, 'It's good thank you.'
'Isn't that one of the women who works for you
Marie? Over by the door.'
 Marie looked over and saw Chrissie looking around
her for a seat, she waved to her and asked Michael
'Do you mind if she joins us?'
'Not at all will I pull up a chair?'
 Chrissie bounced over and Marie was surprised at
how heads turned to look at her, her hair was its
usual mass of tangled curls tied back with ribbons
and her face completely devoid of make-up but as
usual she looked stunning without any effort.
'Thanks, but I am here with a friend' she said
looking at the single chair Michael had found.
'That's ok Michael will get another if you want.'
 Another chair found 'Chrissie said 'I've not seen
you in here before Marie do you follow this band?'
Before she could answer Zack appeared he was
carrying two pints and although Marie knew who he
was he looked just like any other Saturday night
pub goer, blue faded jeans and black tee shirt. She
grinned to herself knowing that Michael hadn't a
clue who Zack was, it seemed no one else in the
room had either. She quickly took control and made

introductions noting that Michael looked puzzled when he heard the name Zack. Before they could get into any form of conversation the band started to play. Zack turned his seat round to watch the group. The next hour passed quickly as they all listened to the music. It was Chrissie that got up and replenished their drinks before the band stopped for a break and when they stopped playing Zack looked at Chrissie and asked, 'Do you mind if I?'
'No go on.'
Michael looked at Marie then at Chrissie and both the women laughed. Chrissie spoke and told Michael who Zack was. Although he was officially retired, he had music running through his bones and had to sing at every opportunity. They watched as Zack approached the four boys who were at the counter waiting on their drinks and it only took minutes before the four became five.
The boys came back on stage and the lead singer announced, 'We have a very special guest tonight who has agreed to do us the honour of singing for us.'
Zack walked on to the front of the small stage and took the mike and signalled to the group to start playing. It took a few bars of one of his hits before he was recognised and Chrissie stood up and pulled Michael and Marie onto the very small, crowded

dancefloor. Where everyone was just swaying to the
music and singing along to the words. Marie was
very self-conscious, that she seemed to be the only
one who didn't know the words of all of the songs.
Nevertheless, she hung on to Michael's arm and
swayed along with him.

Zack left the stage to tumultuous applause, they all
sat down again. Michael raised his glass saying,
'Sorry mate I had no idea who you were.'
'This is a first for me, all the years I have been
coming here I have never been in this pub.'
He looked at Chrissie and said, 'You minx you
knew I wouldn't be able to just sit there and not talk
to the boys, didn't you?'
'I don't know what you mean but I am sure you'll
be welcome here any time after tonight's
performance, old Tom the landlord has got a very
rare smile on his face.

Zack and Chrissie got up to leave and Marie
grabbed Chrissies hand and said, 'Thank you what a
great evening.' Chrissie just grinned and as they
walked through the pub Zack stopped a couple of
times to sign autographs.
Michael said, 'That was a surprising twist to the
evening, fancy Chrissie knowing Zack did you
know?'

'I had seen his photo in her cottage, but she was very secretive about it at the time but Betty got all the gossip from Derek who is as far as she's concerned a bit too friendly with Chrissie.'
'I don't see that Derek and Chrissie he's too.......'
he tailed off and Marie jumped in, 'Dull I think that's the word you're looking for.'
'Right, what's the rest of the story then? Do you want another drink?'
'No let's walk back now and I will tell you what I know on the way.'
 Despite it being nearly eleven o'clock it was warm and made a very pleasant walk, Marie didn't know the whole story about Chrissies relationship with Zack but told Michael that Betty thought he owned the cottage. Derek said he had turned up a couple of times and he obviously had a key. Derek had been in the workshop setting up the machines and Zack had gone in looking for Chrissie. Seemingly upset because she wasn't there. He had made it clear he knew nothing about the sewing room. But Derek hadn't seen him for a while so thought it was all over.
 Once back at Michael's house Marie felt uncomfortable and said nervously, 'Gosh it's gone eleven can you call me a cab please.'

Michael hesitated and putting his hands on her shoulder saying, 'Stay Marie stay, I don't want this evening to end.' Marie smiled she didn't need to think she leant towards him and whispered 'Yes.' He then led her into the lounge and poured them a night cap and Marie curled up beside him on the very masculine brown leather sofa, where they stayed for half an hour and then without speaking Michael stood up and took her hand and led her upstairs 'Your choice Marie, spare room or...' he pushed open the door to the master bedroom and without any hesitation Marie walked in and Michael followed her in, kicking the door shut behind them. Waking up in Michael's bed the next morning Marie realised exactly what she had been missing all those years. Michael had been gentle with her; it had been years since either of them had been in a serious relationship. They had spent time exploring each other's bodies. It was the best sex that Marie could remember. It occurred to her that Michael was the only man she had told about the rape. The first time she had been able to completely put it out of her mind while making love. She sat up and caught a glimpse of herself in the mirror, her hair was tousled and even though she hadn't removed her make-up she looked positively wanton.

The smell of fresh coffee wafted up the stairs and
Marie snuggled down under the duvet, unsure
whether to get up or wait. It was only seconds later
that Michael came in carrying a tray with two mugs
of coffee and a plate of warm croissants, which set
down on the bedside table. Drawing back the
curtains he revealed French doors which led out to a
small balcony. 'I thought we could eat out here as
it's such a lovely morning,' he hesitated as Marie
threw back the duvet and went to get out of bed.
'Best put some clothes on first' he said throwing his
towelling dressing gown at her, 'Don't want the
neighbours to see a naked woman coming out of my
bedroom, mustn't spoil my spotless reputation.' He
laughed as Marie made a rude gesture as she pulled
on Michael's robe, walked barefoot out onto the
balcony and took in the view of the garden, it was
beautifully laid out and very well cared for.
'Croissants my favourite.' she said taking a bite and
giggled as the flaky crumbs fell on to her partially
covered breasts. Michael leant over and gently
flicked the crumbs away his hand lingering just
above her nipple. Marie moved his hand and said,
'Mm there's a choice croissant or morning delight?'
Michael picked up a croissant and answered
grinning 'Not a choice I'll go for both, first warm
croissants. Though I've never heard of morning

delight, but I think I know what you mean though!'
he said with a glint in his eye.

'Morning delight just made that up sort of thought it
sounded good,' she said coyly.

Michael stood up and said, 'You really are a minx.'
And led her back to the bedroom.

 It was around eleven o'clock before Marie finally
tore herself away from Michael and went and had a
shower, once dressed in yesterday's clothes she
went downstairs to the kitchen where Michael was
loading the dishwasher. Beaming at her he asked,
'What would you like to do today my lovely?'

Marie hesitated, 'Sit down Michael we need to talk.'

Michael frowned and did as he was told saying,
'This sounds serious all of a sudden.'

'It is serious, but you haven't done anything, its
Brian.'

 'Of course I did promise to help you, have you
decided what you want to do first?'

'I have given it lots of thought and I admit it has
kept me awake at night, oh apart from last night of
course.' She answered blushing.

'I'm glad you added that! What do you want either
tell me what your thoughts are, or do you want my
view on it?'

'Truthfully I would rather follow my instinct.'

'And that is?'

'I need to speak to him and make initial contact that way.'

Michael stood for a few moments thinking, 'that would probably be my advice too I thought about using the solicitor who gave you the letter but then I tried to put myself in Brian's position and although he might be difficult, a solicitor might just antagonise him more.'

'Do you think he will be difficult with me?' asked Marie.

'Honestly yes of course he will, it has been a dreadful shock for him and whatever your mother said in that letter. You still don't know whether he was looking for you or if it was your mothers' guilty conscience that sought him out. Of course it's essential you need to establish this.'

'I'd already thought about it, but I need to move forward with this it will be difficult, I don't want to leave it too much longer. After all he did send flowers to mother's funeral. Putting the ball firmly in my court.'

'Okay sounds like you have thought it through, what if we go for a walk down by the canal and have a lunch in the pub, you can ring him from there,'

Before they could go for a walk, Marie needed to go home and change. Once she was in her jeans and trainers they set off for the river and sat for a while

watching the barges go by, waving to the holiday
makers as they chugged along in front of them. It
was only a short walk to the canal side pub and
without asking Michael sat Marie away from the
main outside seating area. Handing her a glass of
wine said, 'I've booked a table for 1.30 so you have
half an hour just take a deep breath and remember it
won't be easy first time.'

 Marie thanked him and sat for a few moments just
looking at her phone. Michael was sitting on a
bench a few feet away, drinking a pint of cider and
reading a newspaper that had been left on the seat.
Taking a deep breath, she dialled the number that
Brian had written on the memorial card. Waiting
nervously while it rang. It was picked up just as
Marie was about to hang up. A female voice asked
who it was, Marie asked to speak to Brian. The
female asked, 'He's on barbeque duty at the moment
can it wait?'

Marie answered softly, 'No it is important please it
won't take long.'

 There was silence for a while and then Brian came
on the line 'Yes who is this?'

Marie answered quietly, 'Its Marie.'

Silence followed by 'Oh not a good time we've got
all the family here.'

Marie swallowed hard and went on 'This is difficult
for me, I really do not want to have a conversation
over the phone, could we meet face to face?'
This was followed by another short silence, 'Yes
why not.'
Marie said, 'I'll text you my email and contact
details, then Brian, I will leave it to you, but I do
think we should meet at some point.'
   He merely muttered that it was okay and rang off.
After she had hung up, she quickly sent over her
details to Brian and draining her glass she walked
over to Michael. Sitting down she sighed and said,
'it wasn't as bad as it could have been. Now I just
have to wait and see, it's up to him now to contact
me.' She paused and went on 'what I'll do if he
doesn't get back to me, I don't know. At least he
didn't say no or hang up on me.'
'Have faith Marie, this is a shock for both of you,
just remember it's likely to take a lot of talking and
understanding before you will be able to see a way
forward.'
   Marie relaxed a little and managed to eat her lunch,
but the limited conversation with Brian unsettled
her. It wasn't long before she suggested they walk
back, telling Michael, she wanted to get back to her
flat to prepare for work the next day. 'I understand, I
also have work to do but thank you Marie it has

been a lovely weekend don't let this come between us.'

'I won't Michael I just need a bit of a space; it's such a lot to think about plus Butterflies needs my full attention.'

'It's okay Marie we have all the time in the world.' They parted shortly after and as he kissed her goodbye he whispered in her ear, 'I think I'm falling in love with you.' With that he turned and walked away leaving Marie standing open mouthed in her hallway.

Betty

It was late and the carefully prepared dinner was ruined. Betty reluctantly put Derek's meal back in the oven and went upstairs to run a bath. Pouring a large dollop of expensive bath oil in she sank into the now heavily perfumed water and began to reflect on her day. The turning point for her had been when she saw Marie and Michael coming into the office together, one glance and she knew they were now more than friends, but she still felt pangs of jealousy.

Totally irrational thoughts had been flitting through her brain, for a married woman of her age. The fantasy had grown until she had imagined her and Michael walking off into the sunset together. The reality was totally different to the dream, what she had was a husband who was completely disinterested in her and her friend Marie obviously becoming involved with Michael, who it had to be said had hardly ever given her Betty a second look.

She reached for a magazine that was laying on the stool beside the bath, as she did, she wished she had thought to bring a glass of wine up with her. The drink would have given her a lift. Idly flicking through the magazine came across an article 'How to save a dying marriage' The title made her giggle despite her feeling miserable, nevertheless she began to read and as she read, she began to feel more positive, and a plan began to form in her mind.

The door opened and Derek poked his head round and said, 'Oh there you are Bet, thought you were out tonight?'

Betty bit back a bitchy remark and instead said, 'No I changed my mind I came home early and cooked a special dinner for us.'

Derek looked uncomfortable and looked at his watch and said, 'Oops suppose it's too late for it now?'

'It's probably not much good now, but you could stick it in the microwave. 'What kept you anyway?'

'I bumped into George who I used to play darts with, and we went for a drink and just got chatting about old times.'

'Really you weren't with Chrissie then?'

'Betty what is wrong with you of course I wasn't with Chrissie, besides that boyfriend of hers seems to be back on the scene.'

'Zack, do you mean him?' Betty asked.

'Not sure of his name but he's a scruffy git, walks around like he owns the place.'

'He's a famous rock star, rumour has it he's the father of Chrissies daughter and I think he does actually own Honeysuckle cottage.'

'Chrissie has a daughter?' asked Derek.

'Yes, bit of a hippie like her mother gone abroad last I heard, saw a photo of the three of them once but Chrissie doesn't talk about herself much.'

Derek slapped his hand to his forehead. 'It all fits now!'

'What fits?'

'In the pub, they were all raving about a music night, on Sunday where a well-known singer got up and sang with the regular group. I wasn't paying too much attention, but it must have been him doncha think?'

'Sounds about right, now hand me a towel this water's getting cold.' Derek handed her a towel and went downstairs in search of food.

Betty dried herself quickly and feeling a little more confident that Chrissie was not the threat to her marriage that she had originally thought. With that in mind, wrapping herself in the towel she padded into the bedroom and was surprised to see that Derek had bought her up a glass of Prosecco. It was this unusually thoughtful act that almost stopped her in her tracks, Derek must have bought the wine home with him as she would never have bought that particular bottle. Fizzy wine was for celebrating wasn't it, what were they celebrating? She sat on the edge of the bed and sipping on her drink she

could hear Derek banging around in the kitchen and
he was whistling. A sound she hadn't heard for a
very long time. It was from this moment that Betty
realised that she had been so busy blaming Derek
for all that had been going wrong in their marriage.
She hadn't really looked at herself. Rummaging
around in the drawer she found an unused pot of
moisturiser and as she rubbed the cream into her
neglected body, she chided herself on looking for
problems that didn't exist. It was time to stop being
jealous of Chrissie with her hedonistic carefree life
and to curb her envy of Marie's growing closeness
to Michael. Time to concentrate on making the best
of the rest of their life together.

Listening at the top of the stairs she was satisfied
that Derek was now eating his supper while
watching football, she went through to their tiny
third bedroom which was now an office and
switched on her laptop. Time to surprise him, for all
the reasons in the world they had not been away for
years. Searching for Last Minute Breaks she soon
found just what she was looking for. A long
weekend in Venice, whilst on their honeymoon they
had stayed nearby but ran out of money and
couldn't afford the extra cost to make the short
journey to see the famous city. Venice had always
been on their bucket list, which with all their other

dreams had been put to one side. Betty decided it was now time and booked it, quickly printing off the details, receipt and itinerary. Pulling on a pair of silky pyjamas she went downstairs to talk to Derek. He was sitting on the sofa beer in hand empty plate on the floor beside him. As she walked in, he picked up the remote control and switched off the football. 'Betty sit down there is something I need to tell you.'

Without saying a word Betty sat down opposite Derek who she had to admit looked extremely pleased with himself. He went on, 'I had a call today from a solicitor in Norfolk.'

'We don't know anyone in Norfolk Derek.'

'I know, I thought it was a wind up at first but it turns out that my god father has died.'

'Your god father who the devil was he?'

'You met him a few times I called him Uncle Bertie you remember, dapper little man with a crazy moustache.'

'He must have been ancient; he was old when I last saw him and that was years ago.'

'He was ninety-four.'

'Why the phone call then?' asked Betty.

'This solicitor wants me to go and see him says Uncle Bertie has left me something in his will.'

'What has he left you tell me?'

'That's just it Bet he wouldn't tell me over the phone. He wants me to go up there and sit down with me and tell me.'

'Sounds fishy to me are you sure he's for real?'

'No, I'm not sure but I will go and find out.'

'It's a long way to go for a cracked teapot.' Said Betty.

'I hope it's more than that I want to go and check it out but you should come with me. Let's make a weekend of it, we can drive up Thursday do the business on Friday and spend a couple of days having a look around.'

Betty thought for a moment, 'Norfolk is not my idea of a weekend break, but if your hunch is right, we had better go. I've been busy too.' She handed him the freshly printed off papers and waited for his response. 'Looks good Bett so we are going to be away for two long weekends.'

Betty leant over and kissed him on the top of his head and said, 'Looks like it, Derek but not sure which one sounds best. But I know which one I fancy the most.

Chrissie

The morning after Zack had joined the local group
in the pub, a plan began to form in Chrissie's mind.
Last night had convinced her that Zack was never
going to be satisfied with staying in the cottage and
not singing. He had to have something to occupy his
time. One thing was for sure Chrissie had just
discovered the pleasure of working, a bit late in life
but Butterflies had given her a terrific boost and she
was not about to give it up for Zack. As if sensing
her mixed emotions Zack said, 'I was thinking could
we go to my house in Surrey today? There are a
few things I need to collect, and I guess it's time
you saw where I have been living, all be it part time
maybe you might want to move there.'

'Sure, I'll come with you I've always been curious
about your house, but let's get one thing straight, if
this is to try and lure me away from here then I can
assure you that's never going to happen.'

Zack laughed, 'Don't worry I just want you to see it,
plus I need to get my guitar and a few bits, nothing
sinister.'

'Ok that's good I'll just get changed and we can be
off.'

 Chrissie went upstairs and pulled on a pair of jeans
and tee shirt, which she had taken to wearing for
work rather than her trademark flowing skirts and

blouses. Zack drove which was in itself a novelty,
his driver had chosen to retire at the same time as
Zack and as a reward Zack had presented him with
his aging Rolls Royce and bought himself a sensible
Range Rover. At the time Chrissie had laughed at
the description sensible? Sensible would have been
a family saloon or similar but a large Range Rover
was extravagant. Zack had argued that it was totally
suitable for the country.

The journey to the house took just over an hour and
as they pulled up outside the elaborate wrought iron
gates Chrissie gasped 'Oh my god it's a bloody
mansion.'

'This is the smallest of my houses Chrissie but it's
not a home just a building.'

'You mean there are more,'

'Yes, there are a few but I haven't ever lived in any
of them, I've put them all up for sale, its time I
consolidated my assets.'

'Considering how long we have been together;
seems there's a lot I don't know about you.' Said
Chrissie quietly.

'Well, none of it has been a secret, you have never
asked or shown any interest, but it is all past I want
to share the future, no more touring just us.'

'What about Summer?'

'What do you mean? She's an independent forty-year-old woman.'

'You are her father, a part time father at that, but she will come home, and the cottage is her home.'

'I promise that's not a problem, but I've already bought a house nearby and it's in her name. I know you don't think I care about you, but the pair of you have always been the only stability in my life.'

'Does she know?'

'I told her I would always take care of her, she should just follow her dreams and live her life to the full, I didn't want to her to miss out on any opportunity in life. As for the house its rented out, just for a year.'

'You are a dark horse.'

'My life has been crazy, you know that, but I've always been useless with money so years ago I handed over management of my finances to an accountant. That was probably the best decision I ever made apart from hanging on to you that is.

Chrissie smiled and sat quietly as they drove slowly along an avenue of old oak trees, her thoughts were of all the years she had sat waiting for Zack to come home and give up touring. Now it was a reality but also terrifying, she had imagined his other life but just pulling up outside of this mansion was a real eye opener.

The large oak door opened, a voice said, 'Welcome home Mr Zack are you stopping?'

Zack responded, 'No Jones just come to pick up some bits, but we would love some lunch out on the terrace please.'

Jones bustled off to prepare lunch and giggling Chrissie said 'You have staff? And she called you Mr Zack this is unreal.'

Zack led her through the vast hall and out onto the terrace which overlooked a beautifully manicured garden. Chrissie sat down and looked around her and sighed, 'It's beautiful how long have you had this little place as you call it?'

'No idea donkey's years I think.'

'Have you ever really lived here; I mean spent more than a week here?'

'Good god no just a couple of days at a time.'

'Why keep it though such an expense.'

Zack went quiet and after a moment said, 'I suppose in my mind I wanted something to give to Summer.'

Chrissie gasped and then laughingly said, 'That's crazy Summer would no more live here than I would. Whatever made you think that? Besides, you have a son.'

'Whatever it is an investment and if Summer doesn't want it, I suppose as I've never really lived here, I should sell it. As for Joe he and my bitch of

an ex-wife have completely disappeared, I think I
just hung on to this for the staff. After all they have
lived here for so long it doesn't seem fair to make
them homeless.'
'It's not my business but surely you could come to
some arrangement, I really thought this was your
home.'
'No not home, the only place I have ever thought of
is Honeysuckle cottage. Home is with you Chrissie
always has been always will be,' he hesitated and
looked directly at her and went on, 'At least I hope
it will be.'
'But this place is huge the cottage would fit in here
at least a dozen times.'
'It's just a big house, never been a home, talking to
you I reckon it's time to let it go.'
'Yes, if you need the money sell it or…' she tailed
off.
'Or what?'
'Depends on your finances, we never talk about
money, do we?'
'Chrissie I've more money than I know what to do
with you only have to say if you need money.'
'Don't be daft, I don't need money, you have looked
after me so well over the years plus I'm working
now. If you don't need this place do something with
it?'

and Sue and the team did it really helped me out but now I have a much bigger problem which I need to sort quickly.'

Betty and Marie looked at one another and Betty said quickly 'We don't have any machine space for a couple of weeks I hope it's not that urgent.'

'It's not machine space I'm after its.' he hesitated for a moment and then said, 'My wife has cancer, and the prognosis is not good.'

'I am so sorry,' said Marie, Betty nodded in agreement.

'It's a difficult time for us both so reluctantly I have decided to sell up to spend as much time with her as I can. Therefore, I want to give you first refusal on the business. The order book is full for the next six months, I've drawn up a proposal and will leave it with you for a couple of days. Then when you have had time to think about it come and see me and we will talk further say ten days will that be ok with you? '

Marie answered, 'Wow a lot to take in for this time in the morning shall I say next Wednesday here at eleven?' John nodded and stood up and drew a file out of his briefcase and after handing it to a shocked Marie he turned and left the office.

'Well!' said Betty 'what a turn up for the books, what do we do now?'

'Just glancing at this proposal, I think we need
Chrissie and Michael to sit down with us and see
what we can come up with. I'll show this to
Michael and see what he thinks about finance, plus
then we need to talk to Chrissie.' She handed the
document to Betty who looking at the bottom line
said, 'OMG that's a lot of money, that's going to
take a lot of talking about.'

Marie was thoughtful for a moment and then said,
'One thing I have learnt over the years is that
everything is possible, and this will be a bit of a
diversion but good for all of us what do you think?'

'Me I'm up for it if we can sort out the money,
which reminds me I booked a weekend away,
thought it was time I took Derek away. It's not until
the weekend after next but I do need this Friday off
as well,we have to drive up to Norfolk to see some
solicitor. Derek's godfather died and has left him
something in his will. I think it is probably a waste
of petrol, but I told him if it's a cracked teapot I
might just chuck it at him.'

'No that's not a problem after I talk to Michael; I'll
pop round and see Chrissie and get her view on this.
Right now, we need to get on with the rest of the
business, Jenny is coming in later she is looking for
work.'

'Look you don't have to explain anything to me I just need to talk to you about something that has happened unexpectedly this morning,'
'Go on I'm all ears.'
Marie laid her file on the table but looked apprehensively at Zack, who had sat himself down in the armchair by the window.
 Chrissie laughed and said, 'Zack has been part of my life for forty years and seems to be living here permanently now so I guess we have no secrets.'
 Slowly Marie went through John Mason's proposal and became more animated as she sensed Chrissies enthusiasm. Marie said, 'We are a long way from reaching a financial agreement Chrissie it is just really important that you stay on board to manage the factory if we close the deal satisfactorily, we can't do it without you.' As she said this, she glanced at Zack who appeared to be listening intently to every word.
Chrissie stood up and without looking in Zack's direction she said, 'I'm so up for this just give me a couple of days, I'll look at my finances and see what I can do.'
'At this point I just need your commitment; Betty will get in touch as soon we have done a bit more research and arrange a meeting between the four of

us probably Monday or Tuesday next week.'

'Four of us?' queried Chrissie.

'Yes, we have to include Michael after all he is our accountant.'

Marie stood up and said, 'Anyway think about it Chrissie this is a really big deal for all of us, we do need each other to make this work.'

'I know and thank you Marie such an exciting project.'

'It is but not cut and dried yet, see you very soon, meanwhile you might need to work out a proposal?'

'Proposal what for?'

'Chrissie if we can pull this off you will be in a senior position and be salaried and be contracted to Butterflies. But one step at a time I have to get Michael on board first think about it and when we meet up next week let me have your thoughts.'

Chrissie

Chrissie closed the door behind Marie and without thinking went to the fridge and took out a bottle of vodka, pouring out two large glasses and sat down in the chair opposite Zack. Taking a huge gulp, she asked 'What do you think?'

'This is mad Chrissie do you really want all this responsibility and work? I thought we were...' he tailed off as she said,

'What sailing off into the sunset together?'

'Not quite but I didn't see myself sitting around idly while you worked.'

'At one time that might have been the plan but now Butterflies has so energised me I just feel it is now my time I really love my workshop, and the team are fantastic.'

'Do you think Butterflies can pull this off?'

'Not sure but I do have a bit stashed away I am happy to put all I can into this.'

'There is a lot to think about Chrissie, only you know if it is a viable proposition, I'll back you.'

'Back me?'

'Look I could buy that factory a hundred times over, but it has to be right for both of us, I can't see a life for both of us if you are working full time and I'm sat here waiting for you.'

'Zack, I agree this is a bolt from the blue and I have to say totally unexpected, but we just need to think about what we both want. You need to remember that I have sat here waiting for you years while you toured around the world. It is difficult for me as I have never really had a job or to be honest a purpose in life until now and I really don't want to choose between you and Butterflies.' '
'I have no desire to go back on the road, so we really have to think about this.'
'I agree but there must be a solution somewhere we just need to find it. Right now, I need to get down to the workshop and crack the whip.'
With that she put her glass in the dishwasher and looked at Zack who hadn't touched his drink, he grinned and said, 'it's weeks since I saw you touch the vodka bottle thought you had gone teetotal on me!'
Chrissie laughed and said, 'I've been far too busy to drink.'
She left Zack sitting at the kitchen table and hummed softly to herself as she made her way down to the busy workroom. There was really no need for Chrissie to crack the whip Sue was so organised and kept everything ticking over smoothly. What Chrissie wanted deep down was to expand but there was no capacity to increase

production here in such a short time they had outgrown the space. Marie's visit this morning had completely energised her and the plan that had started in her head yesterday was beginning today becoming a reality. As soon as Marie had outlined the offer to her, she knew that Zack would jump in but before she could put his offer to use, she would need to present him with an idea to keep him occupied and near her, because she now knew that they were better together than apart.

Betty

With Marie out of the office Betty got on with her everyday tasks, she could only admit to herself that she was feeling put out. Marie had gone rushing off to see Chrissie then no doubt she would sit and have cosy chats with Michael. It didn't matter to her that one of the most lucrative parts of Butterflies had proved to be the workshop it was just, she felt left out. Before she could let her resentment and jealousy overpower her Jenny turned up.

Looking very tired and miserable she slumped into the chair and said, 'I hope you've got some work for me I'm struggling for money at the moment.' Betty reassured her and went to the file as she turned away Jenny said, 'I hear on the grapevine that Marie is seeing that loser, Michael.'

'They are friends, yes but he is our accountant, and we don't think he is a loser.' She responded brusquely.

Jenny had the grace to blush and took the orders from Betty. 'Sorry,' she mumbled 'I shouldn't have said that.'

'Give me a ring when you have the samples for that wedding order ready so we can prepare a quote for the client. I gather they are in a hurry to get everything sorted.'

Jenny hesitated before asking, 'I'm owed some money from the last order I did, and could you tell me when I get paid?'

'No problem let me just check, I'm sure it's been processed.' Betty went into the accounts page on her system and told Jenny that the payment had in fact gone into her account the previous day. Jenny merely mumbled and left the office saying she would be in touch leaving Betty sitting worrying about Jenny's problems, Butterflies prided themselves on paying invoices promptly and on checking saw that Jenny had only sent the invoice in a week ago so they certainly hadn't kept her waiting for her money. Even more concerning was the payment was for quite a large amount and strange that someone who was worried about money hadn't noticed the money was already in her account. She made a mental note to ensure Jenny was paid promptly every time and to keep an eye on her expenses as she hadn't appeared to have been claiming anything, unlike most of the others on the books who claimed for absolutely everything.

The door buzzed again and smiled as she let Derek in, 'What have I done to deserve this? A visit from my husband don't tell me we owe you money?'

'No of course not I haven't anything on for the rest of the day so thought we could go for lunch.'

'That would be good, just let me tell Marie I will be out for a while.' She quickly phoned her and said she would be back by 2.30pm. Locking the door and switching on the answer phone she followed Derek out of the building.

 Over lunch Betty explained that she was worried about the possible direction that Butterflies was going in. The fact Chrissie's side of the business was really busy, and Marie seemed keen to expand, she felt like she was being side-lined.

'What you mean is you feel left out, I know you Bet.'

'Yes, I suppose I do.'

'I think you should see what happens, you know that Marie has a lot on her mind at the moment and I know she would be really upset if she knew what you were thinking.'

'I'm sure you're right, it's just that I saw the figures on that proposal, and they were pretty terrifying, I just don't want to go down the road of being in debt again.'

'Finish your lunch and let this take its course you know what I always say one day at a time.'

 Outside the café Derek left Betty to walk the short distance to the office where she found Marie sat at her desk munching on a sandwich. Betty poured herself a glass of water and waiting for Marie to

finish she listened to the messages that had come in
while she was out.

Marie went out to wash her hands and came back
and sat on the corner of Betty's desk and asked,
'Have you given any thought about John's
proposal?'

'Not really' she paused, 'I must admit the figures
terrified me what does Michael think.'

'I haven't spoken to him yet, I wanted to run it past
you and Chrissie first.'

'What did she say?'

'Obviously she is interested even said she would be
up for putting some money in.'

'Can she afford it?'

'I have no idea, but Zack was there, so I didn't ask
too many questions just left her to think about it.'

'Before you speak to Michael, I need to make it
clear I don't have any more money to put in, I have
already put in more than I've told Derek, 'She
answered sharply.

'Don't worry neither do I Betty It's going to be
some while before mums' estate is settled and I
don't think that is what Michael would advise
either. I will talk to him over the course of the
weekend then we can sit down on Monday and talk
further. Meanwhile here is a copy of the proposal
just for you to look at. Why don't you get off early

after all you've got a long journey in the morning
you know what motorway traffic is like.'
 Betty accepted Marie's offer thankfully and
quickly tidied her desk and set off for the short
drive home. Time to focus on her private life,
Butterflies could be put on a back burner for a
couple of days.

Marie

Marie was about to go into speak to Michael her
phone rang; it was a number she didn't recognise.
When she heard his voice, she had to sit back down
in her chair.

'Marie, is it all right to call you Marie,' slight pause
and he went on nervously 'Its Brian.'

'Oh yes of course, how are you?' She asked
awkwardly.

'Fine, look I'll be brief can we meet tomorrow I will
be in your area for a meeting.'

'Sure, I'm available.'

'Good I'll text you as soon as I finish my meeting.'
With that he hung up leaving Marie sitting looking
at her phone.

At the moment Michael walked in and taking one
look at her stricken face said, 'Come on you look
like you need a drink.'

Marie grabbed her bag and without saying a word
followed Michael locking the door behind her.

Once in the now familiar pub Michael said, 'Do you
want to talk about it? You look like you've had a
tough day.'

'Not tough Michael just unexpected, surprising
scary don't really know where to start.'

'I reckon you start with the scary get that out of the
way first.'

'It's Brian he wants to meet up tomorrow.'
'Why is that scary? You were hoping he was going
to eventually contact you and now he has.'
'I know but now I have to face up to telling him
everything all the stuff I've shut away for years and
all that my mother revealed.'
'Slow down, first of all you need to let him speak,
let him tell you what he knows he may know more
than you think.'
'Or less.'
'Only you can do this Marie, I'm sure it won't be
easy, but you must start on the right foot, be honest.'
'What if he walks away?'
'He may well walk away; it is a lot for anyone to
take on board, but I'm sure he'll come round
eventually.'
 Marie went quiet and fingered her now empty wine
glass Michael waited for her to speak and when she
stayed quiet, he stood up and went to the bar and
ordered another drink. Marie had composed herself
and took the glass from him and said, 'Thank you.'
Michael looked at her and said, 'Come on what else,
I can tell there's more.'
'There is but it's not bad just a surprise.'
She leant down to her handbag, taking out John
Mason's proposal, before showing Michael the
figures, she outlined her vision, which was

enhanced by the enthusiasm Chrissie had shown.
Michael glanced at the figures and said, 'I don't
really want to comment until I have looked at the
financial detail, after all I'm your accountant. What
I would say is that it will be a huge investment to
take on.'

'Money aside what do you think.'

'Marie it's not what I think I'm only advising on the
business finances. What do Betty and Chrissie
think. More to the point what do you think?'

'That's not easy to answer, initially I was excited
and so was Betty, but I think she has had second
thoughts which has thrown me a bit.'

'Maybe that's because she wouldn't really be as
involved in it as you and Chrissie. What did she
say?'

'You know Chrissie, she was really enthusiastic; her
partner Zack was there but I couldn't work out how
he felt. My instinct tells me that he resents her
working anyway.'

'It's a tough one Marie and my advice is leave it for
the weekend, let me look at the financial
implications and let the rest of the team chew it
over, we can all meet up on Monday morning. A lot
can happen over the weekend. Now you need to get
an early night and concentrate on meeting Brian.'

'You're right I suppose, can you drop me home? I walked in this morning as I needed to clear my head.'

Michael drove Marie home in relative silence both wondering what the next few days were going to reveal.

Betty

Betty got up early and was surprised to find Derek already drinking tea in the kitchen obviously raring to get on the road. It only took half an hour before Betty was ready their overnight cases packed. Derek loaded them into the car the journey was slower than they had anticipated, as always, the M25 was like a carpark and Betty found herself getting extremely agitated she would much rather have gone into work today. Feeling uneasy that Marie might be making plans for expansion without consulting her. To make matters worse she couldn't get excited or even interested in visiting a solicitor about an inheritance from someone she had only met once. Knowing her and Derek's luck it would end up with them owing money. Plus, having got up so early she hadn't had any breakfast and only one coffee and now they were stuck on the motorway with just queues of traffic to look at. Derek was his usual calm unflustered self and Betty wanted to punch him.

Eventually the traffic cleared, and they made it to Norfolk on time to get to the solicitors, time enough to park the car in the hotel and walk to the office. Not enough time to get a much needed shot of caffeine.

They were ushered into the office and sat down opposite Bill Crabtree who spoke quietly, his glasses perched on the end of his long-pointed nose, but it was his bony hands with unusually long fingernails, which mesmerised Betty. He started to speak, and Derek leant closer so as not to miss anything, but Betty zoned out looking at his claw like fingers.

'Well, what do you think Betty shall we take a look this afternoon.' Asked Derek disturbing Betty from her reverie. 'What? Oh, sorry yes of course.' She responded with some dismay as she realised that she had missed almost everything that had been said. All she could think was her vision was becoming blurred, she could feel a migraine coming on.

Derek took a file of papers from the solicitor arranging to return later that afternoon, they left the office.

'Look Derek before we do anything, I must have a coffee and some food please I don't feel great.'

'No problem Bet, we can have lunch at the hotel it's only five minutes away plenty of time. '

On arriving at the hotel Derek found them a table and ordered coffee and brandy and a menu.

'Brandy Derek? It's not like you.'

'It might seem a little premature, but I think this is cause for celebration.'

'It's a bit early to celebrate it might be a real dump.'
'Well, we'll see this afternoon, won't we?'
Betty took a sip of her coffe, deciding not to spoil
the moment by telling her husband she had hardly
heard a word the solicitor had said so she said, 'Can
I look at the file please I found it difficult to
understand everything Crabtree said.'
'I need to go to our room and change out of these
clothes, why don't you go through the papers and
order some sandwiches at the same time.' He replied
standing up and leaving Betty with the papers. She
smiled to herself this would give her time to catch
up and Derek to get out of his suit, back into his
everyday wear of jeans and sweatshirt.
The sandwiches arrived as Derek strolled into the
small restaurant and sat down opposite her, 'Gosh
they look good I didn't feel hungry till I saw that
plate full.'
They ate in silence and Betty said, 'I think I'm in
shock, this will is much more than the cracked
teapot I was expecting.'
'I don't know about that it's more like a whole
bloody dinner service. Anyway, let's go along and
see exactly what old Crabtree is talking about. Then
we can see whether it is as good as it looks on
paper.'
'What time is he picking us up?'

Derek looked at his watch, 'In about twenty minutes, enough time for you to go and freshen up if you want.'

Betty went upstairs slowly her heart sinking, now she had a grasp of what was in the will she fervently wished it had been a cracked teapot. That she could have disposed of quickly, but the contents of Uncle Bert's will were about to change everything and for Betty the timing could not have been worse. When she reached the room, her head was buzzing and after swallowing a couple of migraine pills, she lay down on the bed and closed her eyes.

Derek came up a few minutes later only to find her fast asleep. Spotting her migraine tablets beside her decided to go and look at his inheritance without her.

Marie

Marie sat at her desk nervously tapping her fingers, her notebook unusually blank. Wishing Betty was sitting opposite her, reassuring her that everything was going to work out. To make matters worse today Michael was out of town all day, supervising an audit for a large company and was only able to send her comforting positive texts.

Before Butterflies she had been used to being alone but the new energised Marie was missing company. Desperate for the phone to ring. The morning dragged meaning Marie drank more coffee than was good for her nerves, she did manage to attend to some of the outstanding Butterflies business. After lunch, which was a couple of bites from an apple and yet more coffee, she found herself checking her mobile once again for messages. As she placed it carefully down onto the desk it rang, it was Brian at last.

'Hi Marie, I'm outside a coffee shop in the High St, are you free to come and meet me?'

Taking a deep breath, she said softly, 'Sure I can be there in ten minutes you do mean Gracie's, don't you?'

'Yes, I'm sat outside.' With that he ended the call and Marie checked her hair and make-up and

putting the answer machine on, locked the office
and walked briskly towards the High St.
 Brian was engrossed in a newspaper as she
approached, he was the only male sat outside the
little café. She tapped him on the shoulder, and he
jumped up awkwardly and stammering slightly he
said, 'You must be Marie,' and he held out his hand
to help her into his chair. She sat down a little lost
for words, for both of them this was a hugely
momentous meeting. Recovering her composure,
she said 'could I have a pot of Earl Grey please.'
 Brian went inside and ordered for them both and
almost immediately the waitress brought the tray
out to them. Marie poured the tea into the bone
china cups and began to speak.
'I want you to know my side of this sorry story
Brian. Once you have heard me out it will be up to
you to decide what direction you want our lives to
go in going forward. What I will say at this point is
that I will respect any decision you make.'
 Marie took a sip of her tea and starting at the
beginning of her story. Explaining without being
too graphic how at fourteen she had been raped by
her uncle at his house, while her mother had gone
away for the weekend. No more than a child at the
time. While she had known it wasn't right her uncle
had made her promise to keep it a secret. Bribing

406

her by giving her money to buy an expensive tape recorder that she had coveted at the time. She had kept the secret until it had become obvious to her mother that there was something wrong. It was never right that a teenager was being sick every morning for no apparent reason. It was only when the Doctor suggested she could be pregnant, that Marie tearfully told her mother what had happened. Subsequent test results confirmed the Doctor's suspicions and Marie was sent away where she wasn't known, to a special home for unmarried mothers to have the baby. An abortion had not been an option and Marie explained she had been left there with no contact with her mother until the birth was imminent.

Once having given birth, Marie said all she could remember was being told that the baby had sadly been still born, because of her age they had never let her see the baby. Until her mother's recent revelations, she wasn't aware if she had given birth to a girl or a boy. Nor did she know that it had lived. She had been allowed a few days to recuperate and then her mother had taken her home and eventually sending her back to school as if nothing had happened. The subject had never been mentioned again. She had been for counselling, she paused at this point and reached into her bag for a tissue 'I'm sorry Brian, this is difficult and truthfully only the second time I have told anyone the whole story.'

'When did you finally find out I hadn't died at birth?' he asked.

'Only when Mother died and left the letter with a solicitor, she didn't even have the decency to tell me herself. When did you find out about me? Was that my mother too?'

Taking a deep breath Brian said, 'Yes but as my adoptive mum had always been honest with me, I decided with her blessing to try and trace my birth mother. That's where it began. Unbeknown to me she contacted your mother to let her know I'd started looking for you and your mother wrote directly to me to save me getting involved in a lengthy search.'

'Your mum knew the story too?'

'I'm not sure how much she knew, she died around the same time as your mum she had cancer and knew for some time that she hadn't got much time left.'

'Gosh I am sorry seems like they were both trying to clear their consciences before they died.' Said Marie bitterly.

Brian looked at his watch and said, 'I don't have a lot of time left as I promised to be home for my daughter's school play tonight and I have another meeting before I set off home. I'm sorry but I had the urge to meet you sooner rather than later.'

'I understand, l am so happy to have met you I don't have any other family as such, I would love to meet yours.'

'Before I came today I had more or less made my mind up that this meeting would be a one off, hearing your story today I don't know how I feel now.' He paused and went on 'So you never married and had children, I thought I might have half brothers and sisters to contend with.'

Marie glanced at her hands and grimaced, 'I was married for a short while, but it didn't last, he wanted children, but I refused I was too scared that I would have another baby die on me.'

'That's a tough lie to have lived with. I have to go, I'm sure we still have questions for each other. It's time to think about how we move forward.

As for me I'm in shock, knowing I'm a product of a rape needs coming to terms with but give me a little time. I do want you to come and meet my family or should l say our family.'

He stood up and leant down and kissed Marie on the top of her head and walked away.

Marie sat for a while deep in thought. The meeting with her long-lost son had gone far better than she had dared hope for. In just less than an hour she had revealed her innermost secrets to him and although he had been visibly shocked, he hadn't walked away. It was with a feeling of real optimism that she walked back to the office. Looking forward to talking through everything with Michael.

Zack

It didn't take Zack long to get bored, he found himself pacing up and down the cottage missing the hustle and bustle of his touring days. He had given up trying to persuade Chrissie to spend more time with him, after all he could see her point of view. He had left her alone for months, even years and she had never complained. He loved her too much to rock the boat at this stage of their lives, if he was honest, he hadn't thought too much about what he would do after quitting touring and ultimately leaving the band. The rest of the band had also been keen to have a break. After all they had been together for forty years and now were all keen to slow down. He resolved to organise a reunion just to see how all the other guys were coping with this supposed retirement. Meanwhile he too had a plan forming he had begun to think that it was time to put his money to work.

After dialling his accountant's number, he made an appointment to see him the next day and then realising that it would be hours before Chrissie would be free, he decided to take a stroll into the village. Walking further than he had intended or to be honest the longest distance he had walked on his own for years. He turned to go back, with the thought of a pie and a pint in the pub in his mind, but then he saw John Mason's factory. It wasn't the slightest bit pre planned, without thinking he went into the reception. He asked if John Mason was available, as he spoke the blonde whose badge said she was Maggie blushed realising immediately who was standing in front of her.

Good manners overtook her, and she cleared her throat and said, 'Who shall I say wants him.'

Zack hesitated for a moment and replied, 'Barry Reynolds, it's a business matter.'

Maggie turned away and spoke into the Tannoy 'calling John Mason to reception'.

He sat down still not quite sure what had prompted him to come into the factory, but as he waited to meet John, he decided to feign an interest in buying the business. That way he reasoned he could give a measured opinion to Chrissie, should she ask for his advice.

John Mason walked into the reception area, once an imposing figure now weighed down with troubles. Zack introduced himself by his real name which was Barry Reynolds. His middle name being Zachariah, named after his great Grandad. He had been known as Zack ever since his teenage years, it felt strange being Barry again after all this time. John walked in and shook Zack's hand at the same time asking what he could do for him.

'My partner is looking for premises and she heard your business was up for sale.' He responded without naming Chrissie; he went on 'To be honest I came in on impulse as I was taking a walk.'

John looked surprised, 'I haven't actually put it up for sale yet,'

Zack apologised Really sorry about this John, but I know I should have told you that I'm Chrissie Matthews's partner. She doesn't know I'm here. I just came in on impulse as she is so keen for Butterflies to buy this place.'

'Well, you had better have a look around, I'm due out in half an hour so we had better make a start.' He led Zack out of the small reception area and out on to the factory floor. Zack was surprised at the noise that hit them as the doors swung open. Pop music blared out, not quite overpowering the whir and hum of the lines of machines. They walked through the centre aisle as all fifty heads turned to look at the visitor to their territory. John was pointing out different lines and areas. At the end of the long room, they turned round to face the machinists. Zack began to feel uncomfortable and realised this had been a mistake, there was no way that he would get out of there now without being recognised, what had he been thinking? Chrissie was not going to be happy about this.

John not realising his discomfort indicated a door to
the side, but before they could walk through into the
stockroom one of the supervisors approached John
to ask a question but looking directly at Zack, she
dropped the bundle of work and yelled 'oh my god
its Zack, in our factory!!'
John looked confused and said, 'The girls seem to
think they know you, who are you?'
Zack had the decency to blush and said, 'I'm sorry,
Barry is my real name, I really didn't think I would
be recognised here.'
'Obviously that didn't work I guess you had better
pacify this lot and sign a few autographs, or else
they won't ever get back to work and this order
needs to be finished by tonight.'
"That all makes sense now, let me go and see if I
can reschedule my appointment then we can
perhaps go and talk where there is none of this
disruption.' He walked away grinning leaving Zack
signing autographs. Writing on just about anything
the girls could get their hands, some real fans had
their tabards signed to be embroidered later. After a
fifteen-minute scramble for signatures the Tannoy
interrupted the music, the receptionist called Zack
to the office and then said, 'Time to get back to
work girls.'

Slowly the machines started to hum as the workforce turned their concentration away from an aging pop star and back to the order that had to be finished. Work that would give them their piece work bonus at the end of the month. Obviously at this point no one was aware that the factory was up for sale, or that their jobs could possibly be at risk, as they were always so busy.

To them Zack was simply an unexpected visitor, and visitors usually came in search for somewhere to get their designs into production.

Back in John's office Zack sat down and said, 'Impressive set up you've got here mate I can see why Chrissie is so keen.'

'First things first, can I call you Zack as everyone else round here seems to know you as that.' John said as he waved his hand in the direction of the production floor.

Zack grinned, 'Sorry it was impulsive of me, and since I retired to live here, I do sometimes forget I was a rock star. When I saw the factory, I just felt I should check it out for Chrissie, we've been together for over forty years, she has put up with me being away and all the other crap that goes with being famous. '

'Chrissie and her team are well thought of here and it would seem to be the obvious move, we have full order books plus the space for her team and their commitments. Did you see the prospectus that we gave to Butterflies?'

'Yes, briefly but would appreciate a copy so as I can take it to my accountant. I don't have a problem with your price it's going to get the team to agree to me financing this. Chrissie especially she is so fiercely independent.'

'I understand, will you want to be involved?'

'Absolutely not, I don't want to be included in any shape or form. I have my own plans but first I just want to see Chrissie happy. All these years coping with me have been tough on her and she is so uncomplaining I owe her big time.'

John smiled, 'Butterflies have first refusal, and it is not public knowledge yet that I am selling but would appreciate a definite answer within a week.' he handed Zack a copy of the prospectus.

'That sounds fair to me I will see what progress the Butterflies Team have come up with and take it from there.' Standing up he shook John's hand and John showed him out.

Zack walked down the road and went into the pub which he now thought of his local and ordered a pint. Sitting in the corner, he was comfortable there, he had sung the other night with the local group, but he was comfortable everyone spoke to him, but he wasn't pestered. Today all he wanted to do was think over his plans which involved helping to get Chrissie out of the garden room. Which years ago, he had had built with the intention of having his own music room. But touring had put an end to that, now Chrissie had used it for her endless hobbies. This was a perfect opportunity, but he knew that he had to tread very carefully he couldn't afford to upset Marie.

Marie

It was six o'clock and Marie was sat at her desk not really doing anything constructive, too many thoughts whirling around her head. Michael was late he had promised to be back to talk over John Masons proposal and more importantly she wanted to talk about her meeting with Brian. Where was Michael? She realised that she just wanted a hug and a strong shoulder to lean on. He walked through the door at 6.30 beaming from ear to ear. 'You can stop drumming your fingers I'm late I know; I've bought wine and a takeaway.'

Marie stood up and threw her arms around his neck. 'Wow that's some welcome I'm glad to see you too.' He said unravelling himself away from her and went on 'So your place or mine?'

'Let's go to yours its Saturday tomorrow and grinning seductively she said, 'I've got my toothbrush!'

'Come on then, move your car into my space and I'll lock up.'

Marie moved her car into Michaels secure space and almost hopped into his car and as he approached her, he laughed as he watched her poking around in the bag on the back seat, trying to find out what food he had bought.

'Well, well Marie don't tell me you are hungry?'

'I'm starving I kind of forgot to eat today.'
'It's a Chinese a feast for my lady!'
Marie giggled 'Don't remember being called a Lady
before, wait till later I can promise you won't be
calling me a lady'
 Without making any further comment Michael
reversed his car into the road and drove the short
way to his house in companiable silence. Once
inside he uncorked the bottle and quickly dished up
the food and they carried the dishes into the dining
room. Marie poured the wine and said, 'We need to
talk but I would rather eat now and then we can curl
up on the sofa and chat.' Michael watched as she
loaded her plate and began to taste the feast in front
of her, 'such a treat to see you actually eager to eat
rather than just pushing your food round your
plate.'
'I never did!' she replied taking another mouthful of
her Chicken chow Mein
 Michael laughed and said, 'Oh yes you did.' Wiping
his mouth with apiece of kitchen roll he went to
speak when Marie yelled 'kitchen roll don't you
have serviettes?'
Huffily he responded by saying 'Serviettes madam
with a takeaway eaten out of foil containers don't
be ridiculous.'

They were both laughing now, and Michael said gently, 'What do you want to talk about first business or Brian.'

Marie thought for a moment. 'Brian first,' she paused, taking a sip of her wine went on, 'I met him at the coffee shop in the village and once I got over my initial nerves I decided to take control of the situation.'

'Why am I not surprised at that?'

Marie slapped his knee playfully, 'I decided it would be easier to tell him everything I knew at the outset rather than let him find out in dribs and drabs. It was a little drastic, I know, but I wanted him to know that it was also a huge shock to me. I understood that it was going to be difficult for him when I told him he was the product of rape.'

'That indeed would unsettle anyone, how did he take it?' Asked Michael.

'Calmly, but he did say he needed time to think but does want me to meet his family even clarified it by saying our family.'

'That sounds positive, after all he could have just walked away, give him a little time and see what happens.'

'I feel much better now, I know it won't be easy but meeting him was a huge step for me, so hopefully

all secrets are out there, I just hope his wife is
supportive.'

'My thoughts are that she can't be much of a wife if
she doesn't encourage and support him in this.'

Michael cleared away the dishes and Marie curled
up on the sofa cuddling a cushion deep in her own
thoughts, quite oblivious to Michael loading the
dishwasher. Hearing him open the kitchen door and
banging a spoon on his beloved cat's dish. She
grinned to herself knowing that Benjie would now
be tucking into the remains of the Chinese food, he
certainly was a spoilt cat. Personally, Marie didn't
really like cats she had tried hard to pretend to like
this one, but it was his eyes. He stared at her and
made her feel as if she shouldn't be there. Cat and
master obviously were not used having a female
around the house. She stood up and was about to go
and find Michael when he came back in carrying a
tray of coffee and brandy.

He carefully placed the tray down on to the coffee
table and said, 'Now time to talk business.'

He went out of the room again and came back
holding his briefcase. Marie said, 'I'm not sure what
I want to hear about this, I have got mixed feelings.'
Michael got out a sheaf of papers and handed a
copy to Marie who merely glanced at them. 'Tell me

honestly can Butterflies afford to buy John Mason out?'

'The figures say no. That's with my accountants' hat on, you could borrow some money, but it would be a large commitment, and you would be taking on the debt for a long time.'

'To be honest that was more or less what I expected you to say. I do have some money, plus there is the money from my mother's estate which I could put to good use, but I don't know how long before that will be finalised,' she tailed off.

'You asked for my advice; the figures are worst case scenario. What we really need to establish is how much the other two want to be involved, as I see it Chrissie is the only one behind the manufacturing side of the business.'

'If I'm honest I have left that side of everything to her, Betty hasn't shown any interest only when she thought that Derek was spending too much time at Chrissies.' Said Marie.

'Do you really think he fancied her?'

'I really haven't a clue but Betty was very anti Derek keep going round to Honeysuckle Cottage, but she has it has all quietened down since Zack has permanently moved in.' answered Marie.

'I think we should all sit down on Monday and talk it through.' Said Michael thoughtfully.

'Good idea, but at my age don't want to take on a large loan so let's do a brainstorming session and take it from there. I'll organise a breakfast meeting for early on Monday morning.'

Quickly she turned her attention to sending of emails and after writing a few hasty notes she snuggled up beside Michael and said, 'I'm exhausted it's been quite a day; can I go and soak in your lovely bath?'

Michael smiled and said, 'Only if I can come up and scrub your back.'

'I was rather hoping you would say that' she answered giggling softly.

Betty

Betty woke from a deep sleep and seeing an empty space beside her she sat up and saw Derek standing fully dressed staring out of the hotel bedroom. 'I'm so sorry Derek I really felt rough.' She said quietly. He turned to look at her and answered quickly, 'At last sleepy head how can you sleep so long with all this going on? Are you feeling any better now?' Betty looked at her watch, 'Oh my goodness its nine o'clock, I don't remember the last time I slept this long why didn't you wake me?'

Derek sat down on the bed beside her and took her hand and stroked it gently, 'I left you because I needed time just to think, I went with old Crabtree and then when I came back you were still asleep so I went for a walk along the shore and just blew away a few cobwebs.'

Betty sat up and stretching said 'I'm fine now but I am hungry can we go and eat?'

'Good idea anyway come on get showered, I'm starving. I'll meet you downstairs in reception in twenty minutes will that be, okay?'

Betty got out of the bed and walked over to the window where Derek had been standing, the view was magnificent, there certainly was something to be said for waking up and looking at the ocean.

After a quick shower she dressed, went down to meet Derek, for the first time in a long time Betty actually felt nervous, Derek was expecting her to make her mind up. He wanted to know what she wanted to do about the contents of his uncle's will. The biggest problem was that deep down she knew that Derek had already decided, but for her this was going to be life changing, just as she also had to decide what direction she wanted to go with Butterflies.

Forcing herself to smile she caught the lift down to the reception and Derek stood up and said, 'I thought we would walk down to the seafront, we're too late to get dinner in here so I thought we could try that little café on the front.'

Betty agreed though she was aware that this was intended to encourage her to persuade her that this area was really going to be a desirable place for their retirement. Biggest problem was for Betty was not working she knew that she wouldn't be happy not being employed the memory of how bored and miserable she had been between taking early retirement and starting up Butterflies had been such a miserable time for her.

They sat in the window, Derek ordered coffee, for him pie and mash, for Betty fish and chips. Both ate and drank in relative silence after the waitress cleared away their plates Betty asked for more coffee. Derek took out a sheaf of papers from his rucksack and said, 'I think we need to go through this together tonight. Earlier I phoned the solicitor because I have questions, we are going to go in to see him again in the morning before we set off home.'

Betty reached into her handbag and produced a notebook and grinning she said 'As you can see, I have questions as well, but just so I can fully understand exactly what is at stake here can you go through it for me. I was so expecting just a cracked teapot, this legacy is a lot to absorb in such a short space of time. Now you have actually seen the property you must have a clearer idea of what it entails.'

'That's why we are going back tomorrow, there will be stuff to clarify.' He took a deep breath and went on, 'Uncle has left me or should I say us.' Betty winced at this knowing her name wasn't in the will anywhere. The old man didn't like her and to be fair she had only met him a handful of times and that was mainly at funerals and other family gatherings to which she had felt obliged to attend.

Ignoring his wife's expression Derek ploughed on, 'The small holding which includes the main house and several outbuildings and.' he hesitated at this

426

point, 'It seems there is a couple of fields across the road which are currently a caravan park.'

'Great so if and I guess if we move there, we look out at travellers is that what you're saying?'

'No, you misunderstand Bett the whole site now belongs to me|?'

'What caravans and all?'

'Yes, and it provides a very good income look at this.' He pushed a sheet of paper across the table for Betty to look at.

'Blimey and you will have to run, it what about the small holding?'

'We Betty we, there is a manager on the caravan site at the moment, but he wants to retire this year. The small holding is neglected, it used to be a market garden, but Uncle has let it go over the last few years.' He paused, 'It could be re- instated certainly has possibilities.'

'This is mind boggling how would we be financially?' Gasped Betty.

'There is a very healthy bank account and a vast number of investments which have still to be completely unravelled. I honestly think it's an opportunity we can't afford to turn down.'

'I'm not sure, don't you think it's a bit late in life to make such a big move?'

'Probably, but think about it, we've never done anything impulsive before and we could do this and still keep our bungalow. Rent it out perhaps.'

'Whoa, steady on Derek I can't just walk away from Butterflies I have invested too much money in it.' She reddened at this point she had never told Derek about the money she had put in to help the start-up of the business.'

'Now you tell me, I thought we didn't keep secrets from each other, what else should I know?'

'Nothing Derek, it was just part of my retirement money I didn't tell you because well you were just not interested in me or anything I was doing at the time.'

'All the same it's a bit late to tell me now.' He glanced at his watch and said 'we have to go back and sign some papers in the morning, and before we drive back, we will have the keys and we can go and look over the place. We have to come back after the funeral next week anyway plenty of time to think about it, I know you don't make rash decisions anyway.'

They left the café, the evening was still warm despite the lateness of the hour. They walked along the cliff path; all the while Derek was enthusing about the possibilities and plans; he had for this inheritance. Betty kept quiet but listening to his enthusiasm felt decidedly anti the move. It felt very much like he had decided what direction he was going to take , regardless of her feelings.

The next morning, they dressed and packed their few bits into the car and after mutually deciding to skip breakfast they drove to the solicitor's office.

Once the meeting was over. during which Derek did most of the talking, Betty sat only half listening as Crabtree handed him the deeds and keys saying, 'when you come back next week I will be able to release all the funds to you, I just need confirmation of your bank account details But I warn you it would be advisable for you to take copies of the will and those financial statements into your bank beforehand, We don't want the money to be frozen and you accused of money laundering do we?'

'I hadn't thought of that, I'll ring you when that's sorted.' Said Derek as he stood up to leave. Betty followed him and as they got back in the car she asked quietly 'Exactly how much money is involved here Derek?'

'I knew you weren't listening Betty what is wrong with you?'

'I'm fine this is just a lot for me to take in. How much?'

'There is around £700,000 in bank accounts and investments which have still to be fully assessed.

Plus, the properties of course.'

'Oh my God I didn't realise, where are we going now?'

'We are going to have a good look around and take a few photos before we drive home, I don't want you being negative about this at this stage. There's plenty of time for discussion and decisions to be made later.'

'Okay,' Betty answered meekly, 'you're right.' As they pulled up outside the house Betty said, 'It's huge Derek I had no idea.'

'The land all round belongs to it plus the site over the road.'

'So many caravans how many?'

'Currently about two hundred but only one hundred and fifty belong to the property the rest are privately owned and pay rent.'

 Seeing that Betty was overwhelmed Derek stepped out of the car, taking out the keys from his pocket he led her up the neglected garden path to a solid front door which Betty noted could do with a coat of paint and the beautiful brass knocker was crying out for a rub over with polish. Once inside Derek stood back and let Betty wander from room to room, she knew that if she checked he would be standing in front of a window with his fingers crossed praying for her to be charmed with the building that he was determined to move to.

Each room was full of old furniture and Uncle seemed to have been a bit of a hoarder for every surface was covered with china ornaments and some ghastly old lamps which may well have been attractive at one time. She went into the bathroom upstairs and was horrified to see a pampas green bathroom suite with revolting dark green tiles, shuddering she shut the door and went back downstairs and after checking out the gloomy reception rooms she braced herself for the kitchen. Gasping she called out to Derek 'I can't believe this, how can anyone put a beautiful kitchen in like this when the rest of the house is a dump.'

'Apparently Uncle had it replaced a couple of years ago when he had a lady friend come to live with him.'

'She certainly had good taste this is a fabulous kitchen, such a shame about the rest of the house. Can we just go out into the garden please?'

'It needs a lot of work I warn you.' Said Derek as he unlocked the back door, they stepped out and he sighed as he saw her face drop even further.

'That's an understatement Derek it's nothing short of an overgrown field, just a massive amount of work.' He pretended to ignore her and proceeded to take photos, they went back inside and while Betty sat in the kitchen, he went around taking more pictures.

 When he had finished, he asked Betty if she wanted to go over to the caravan site to take a look, but she declined saying she had seen enough, With that they decided to close the house and set off for home.

 They were both subdued during the long drive, Betty was desperately trying to keep her feelings in check, she knew that Derek really wanted this move and she didn't want to dampen his spirits too much so she tried just to accentuate the positive points which were not many. Her main thought was they should sell the whole estate and enjoy the money, this thought she kept to herself, deciding that she could download the photos once they got home then perhaps Derek would realise what a thankless task, he wanted them to take on.

Chrissie

Chrissie was calling for Zack, she had woken up
late but he was nowhere to be found but his car was
still outside. Pulling on a shawl she ventured out
and went down the garden as she got to the
workshop she could hear music.

'Zack what are you doing down here?' she walked in
and he was sitting at the desk in the corner a sheaf
of papers in front of him. Before he could hide
them, she grabbed one a page and after scanning it
she screwed it up and threw it at him. 'How dare
you this is my workshop; you have no right to even
think about changing it find somewhere else for a
bloody music studio.'

Zack picked up the crumpled page, smoothing it out
he said, 'Calm down why don't you, you're jumping
to conclusions as usual.'

'Really what else am I supposed to think? You're
sitting here listening to music drawing up plans
anyone would think you own the place.'

Zack sighed 'That's just it Chrissie. I do but before
you throw anything else this is just part of a bigger
plan I have.'

'Where exactly do I fit into this plan?'

'Come on let's go back inside and have a coffee and
I'll tell you where exactly you fit.'

With that he went out and left Chrissie standing

looking at her precious machine room, with a feeling of panic almost overwhelming her. Truth be told this was precisely what she had dreaded when Zack had announced he was coming to live in Honeysuckle cottage permanently. Heart sinking, she closed and locked the door and went in to face him preparing to have blazing row with him, he was sitting at the kitchen table two glasses and a bottle of vodka in front of him. Chrissie looked at her watch, 'It's only eleven o'clock bit early for this isn't it?'

'Never stopped you before, you used to wash down your toast with it, now sit down, let me talk, don't interrupt for once.'

She did as she was told, taking a large gulp from the glass, sat back and folded her arms waiting for him to speak, trying to quell the feelings that were threatening to overwhelm her.

'I don't know exactly where to start so just let me explain, you can ask questions later.'

Looking directly at her he took a sip and then refilled her glass.

'These last few months although I love being here, I'm bored, I miss making music.' he held his hand up as Chrissie opened her mouth to object but he went on. 'I always wanted to spend some time writing songs, but my first love is music. I've

When she was satisfied the room was ready
Chrissie sat down and tried to piece together all that
she had heard before the phone call. This
unexpected generous offer from Zack was almost
definitely going to upset Betty and possibly Marie.
She decided to talk to her daughter before she made
a decision.

In less than hour she heard Zack's car pull up
outside with his usual screech of brakes, a quick
slam of the door and Summer ran up the path into
Chrissies waiting arms, leaving Zack to bring in her
rucksack.

'Mum, I can't believe it you haven't changed a bit;
doesn't she look wonderful Dad?'

'Zack laughed 'I reckon it's all down to the vodka.'
Chrissie scowled at him and retorted 'Well it's
certainly not the stress-free life you think I've been
living!' with that she threw a cushion at him and he
ducked, just missing a hastily picked vase of roses
from the garden.

'How long are you staying?' she asked 'Your room
is ready as always.'

'Just tonight, I need to go back to the embassy
tomorrow to pick up my visa, I really wanted to
come home and see you both. I have to admit I was
curious as to how long you would cope with

actually living together properly. I quite expected you might have killed one another by now.'

Zack replied before Chrissie could respond he said, 'I think we're doing well; I've settled better than I thought must be getting old, I do miss the band but not the touring.'

'He even goes to the pub and the locals are so used to him they treat him as one of them now.' Said Chrissie butting in.

Zack went into the kitchen and produced a chilled bottle of champagne and three glasses and raised a toast, 'To family life possibly forty years too late but all together today.' Chrissie grabbed her camera and took photos for she knew that it could well be another seven years before her daughter came home again.

'Do you fancy going to the pub for lunch Summer? As usual there is no food in the fridge, just plenty of vodka!'

'Ah could be difficult I am vegan now, what's the menu like?'

Chrissie produced a crumpled menu from the drawer and once they established that there were a couple of options available for Summer. Zack phoned and booked a table. An hour later they were seated waiting for their food and Chrissie took the moment to put Zack's proposed purchase of the

local factory to his daughter. At first Summer
giggled thinking her father was actually going to
work in it, but when Chrissie filled her in on how
well the manufacturing / sewing side of Butterflies
was going. Along with the fact that her famous dad
was still going to be making music of some kind she
said, 'I think it's a brilliant idea, it's about time you
spent some of your money Dad.'
 He had the grace to laugh but said. 'Seriously that's
another thing you are going to need somewhere to
live when you finish doing good works all over the
world.'
'I don't plan on coming back for a few years yet.'
She replied.
'You will still need somewhere to live,' he paused
for a moment to judge her reaction. 'I've bought you
a house, it's in the next village, I've had it done up,
I'll rent it out for you and the rent will go into an
account towards your pension.'
'I don't know what to say, you know I don't even
think about tomorrow but thank you I really
appreciate it, Dad. Such a special thing to do'
'Summer it's the least I can do for you.'
'I'll drive you over there tomorrow morning but
there is an alternative motive.'
'What's that?'

'You'll be able to look after us two when we can't look after ourselves.'

At this Chrissie nearly choked on her drink all she said was, 'God I hope that's a long way off.'

She sat back and was only half listening to her daughter telling Zack all about the children she was teaching in the orphanage, her thoughts were firmly fixed on Zack and how his actions of the last couple of weeks had delighted and surprised her, there was just one little loose end they still had not got round to getting married. That would be the icing on the cake, if only she had said yes when asked.

'Dad, have you managed to find my half-brother Joe yet?' asked Summer. Zack sighed, 'No Summer, I haven't after I divorced his mother, I have tried tracing both of them, but the years have gone by and nothing, the way I look at it now is that he is old enough to come to me if he wants anything. I have the strongest feeling that they are both dead. I was able to divorce because they had disappeared for so long, I left a settlement for both of them, but it is still in an account waiting for one of them to claim. To be honest I need to put it behind me, except for Joe it was a horrible mistake, I still miss him but there comes a time when you have to let things go. I'm sure he will find me if he decides to look.'

Chrissie looked bemused and said, 'I didn't know you knew about Joe?'

Summer answered, 'Dad told me after he told you, he felt I should know.'

'I see, I'm pleased, after all we are a bit of a disjointed family but at least we are all talking.'

'Why didn't you and Mum ever marry? Not many married couples get to be together as long as you two.'

'You forget we have spent a lot of that time apart; I'm your wild rocker dad remember was always on the road.' He paused for a moment to fill their glasses he looked at Chrissie and said impulsively 'Chrissie Mathews will you marry me?'

Without hesitating Chrissie said, 'Yes Zack I will.'

Summer jumped up kissed them both saying, 'about bloody time' and went to the bar and ordered a bottle of champagne.

Chrissie took Zack's hand and said, 'Today feels like my birthday and Christmas all rolled into one.'

Zack told her later that he had been going to ask Chrissie to formalise their long-term haphazard arrangement ever since he had retired but was worried that she would turn him down yet again, so when Summer turned up out of the blue, he knew he had to take advantage of them all being together.

Lunch over, the three of them took a slow arm in arm walk home and Summer took control of the situation by offering to postpone her return to India. She hadn't taken any holiday for the last couple of years and this seemed the ideal moment to stay, that way she could make sure her mum and dad finally walked down the aisle, Chrissie insisted this was not going to be a rock and roll wedding, just a small affair in the village. Zack was more than happy to go along with this but made one stipulation of his own and if he could get his band to come down then he would get a marquee erected in the garden of the pub and he would sing with the band one last time. The time scale for all this was extremely daunting, Chrissie now had so much going round her head that when they got back to Honeysuckle cottage, she began the first of many lists. Silently thanking Marie for showing her how important lists were. First, she had to decide how to approach the meeting the next morning once she had that out of the way then she could think about the wedding with the help of her daughter.

Marie

Marie was ready for the office early; she had crept away from Michael's house as the sun was coming up at five o'clock. Driving herself the short way back to her apartment, leaving Michael fast asleep. He had opted to work from home on a Monday. There was just enough time to read through John Mason's proposal again and make her notes, even though she had asked advice on the figures her gut feeling was that this was not the right time for her to take on such a big project. The weekend had been special, finally she felt that she had found a life other than work. Michael had arrived late in her life, but he was everything she had ever wanted, and she was determined that from now on he would come first. She loved the fact that he had analysed the figures, merely giving her the bald facts. Any decision would be up to her once she had spoken to Betty and Chrissie.

She wasn't worried about Betty, all she would be interested in was whether her stake in the business would be safe, the sewing side was completely down to Chrissie. This could be difficult as she knew Chrissie was going to be pushing to take over the factory.

Marie put her papers into her briefcase and before leaving she called Michael to tell him she would meet him in the wine bar after she finished work. Betty was already in the office and Marie could smell the coffee and guessed that knowing Betty as she did there would be doughnuts and cupcakes to sweeten the meeting. There was a time before Butterflies that she would have turned her nose up and this food but now in her new relaxed state she looked forward to a chocolate cupcake occasionally.

'Good morning, Betty, how was your weekend, did you collect the cracked teapot?'

'Hi, yes weekend was, well different and there is no teapot, I will tell you all about it after the meeting. Before that I have a couple of frantic messages from Jenny, she needs more work if we can as she has hit a few financial problems.'

'We'll worry about Jenny later, now are all the temps in place for this week?'

'Yes, all sorted need to go through next week as well as there are some new urgent requests, they can wait till later today, one of them is a request for me for a two-week stint and I have already tentatively agreed that one that's if I am not needed for anything else.'

With that Chrissie burst through the door, cheeks glowing, hair piled on top of her head, Marie sat her

down and looked at her as she sipped her coffee,
thinking she had never seen her looking so happy,
she hoped fervently that her anticipated outcome of
the meeting was not going to upset her too much.
 Marie opened the meeting formally and Betty took
minutes, first on the agenda was to go through John
Masons figures and discuss the possibilities. At the
same time, she took the time to try and give
Michael's view of the figures without seeming to
actively discourage the purchase. Betty was first to
speak, her opinion was very much that that side of
the business was making a good profit where it was.
She didn't think Butterflies could sustain such a
huge investment. Chrissie had decided prior to the
meeting to keep her offer until the end but as it was
looking like it was going to be her against the other
two. When it was her turn to speak, she said, 'It will
come as no surprise to either of you how I feel
about this I think the two business will merge
perfectly.' She paused and said, 'I was expecting
your response and would like to say that I will
invest in the factory and amalgamate the Butterflies
business into it.'
 Marie gaped at her saying, 'It's a big investment
please don't borrow any money for this, I don't
want your heart ruling your head.' Betty kept quiet

445

thinking this unexpected turn of events meant she
might have to reveal her future plans.
'I've given this a lot of thought, last week Zack
went to look over the factory with the result that he
has offered to buy John out and the funds are ready
to transfer. I don't know how this will work for
Butterflies as such, but I am determined to take up
this offer, the rest is up to you.'
 Marie looked thoughtful and said, 'Oh wow, I
wasn't expecting this what about you Betty?'
'No not something I had even considered; however,
I am going to confuse this whole issue even more. I
wasn't going to say anything yet, but this rather
changes things as far as Butterflies is concerned, I
will be moving away in the next six months.'
 This second bombshell was met with complete
silence. After a minute Marie said, 'I think we
abandon the agenda now and keep this as a general
meeting. Come on spill Betty, what is going on?'
Betty went on to explain about Uncles legacy, the
estate would be settled next week, and Derek was
going to move up there almost immediately. Only
coming home every other weekend. Once all the
renovations were done Betty was as she said,
reluctantly going to move up with him. She had
hoped that this would give her time to pass over her
part of the business to Marie. Marie was quiet for a

moment while trying to digest all this information, the morning had taken a completely different direction to what she had expected so she said 'Chrissie I am really pleased for you, it is well deserved, how we fit this into Butterflies as such I don't know at the moment, but I for one am behind you all the way. Will Zack be working with you?'

'Oh god no, he wants the workroom for a music room.'

'Bloody expensive way of getting a music room.' said Betty.

'Quite.' Said Marie, 'but it's great for you Chrissie now are there any other bombshells before we get on with our Monday jobs in hand.'

'No' said Betty.

Chrissie hesitated and then said quietly, 'Well actually I'm getting married in the next month as Summer is home!'

'Hang on are you getting married to Zack after all these years? When did Summer get home?' Asked Marie.

'Summer came home yesterday, she is going to stay for a month, I think she just wants to make sure we actually do it at last.' Answered Chrissie.'

'So exciting, no wonder you are glowing this morning. Tell you what you go ahead with the factory purchase. I think that is best for all of us. I will talk to Michael and decide how we start to split the business and sort out all the detail, but don't get me wrong Chrissie I think this is all good positive news. Chrissie stood up and said, 'I really appreciate your good wishes, now I have to go and push my busy bees they have a large order of curtains to get out by tomorrow.'

She left the office and unchaining her bicycle form the lamppost she cycled off down the road singing at the top of her voice.

Betty said, 'I have to go, I'm due at the estate agents in town I'm doing holiday cover for two weeks.'

Marie looked at her diary and said, 'might be a good idea to meet after work tomorrow, so we can talk through everything.'

'Good idea I'll ring you tomorrow.'

After Betty left Marie sat deep in thought, this morning's revelations changed everything and right now she wasn't sure how she felt about it. Her ten o'clock appointment arrived just as Jenny rang say she needed information for one of her orders. Marie took down all the details and the day just flew by. Leaving her very little time to think about the future of Butterflies she looked at her watch and was shocked to see it was five thirty. She stood up and stretched, she was stiff from sitting for so long and now felt the need to talk over the day's events with

Michael. Her mind was a complete turmoil, the day had gone off at a completely different tangent to her expectations. The proposed purchase of John Mason's factory had been a worry, mainly because her instincts and Michael's advice had convinced her that Butterflies as a business could not afford to take the risk of such a large investment. She had not wanted to upset Chrissie. Zack's very generous offer had removed that worry but losing the lucrative sewing side if the business would leave the business light of work. But as Michael had already pointed out it was only making a good profit because the overheads were so low because of Chrissie's generosity. Had Butterflies put in an offer for the factory it would have been a completely different story.

She stood up and stretched trying to relieve the tension in her aching shoulders, her mind still in turmoil she walked through to find Michael. Who was back in the office after working from home in the morning. Looking around she saw Michael deep in conversation with his new business partner. The door firmly closed

Back in her own office she poured the last of the coffee into her personalised bone china mug and sat idly doodling on her pad.

Michael came in half an hour later and said 'Are you finished for the day? I need to talk to you.'
'Yes, I'm finished in more ways than one.' She replied despondently.
'So not a good day then?'
'Not bad, just a very surprising one.'
'In that case close up and we can go to the wine bar, it's quieter than the Dolphin we can have a booth before it gets too busy.'
Agreeing that Michaels idea was good Marie shut down the computers and applying a spritzer of perfume and her lipstick she hauled her briefcase off the side, then changing her mind she pushed it under the desk and mentally gave herself a night off.
 The wine bar was quiet, and they found a booth in the corner, as Michael went to order the drinks her phone rang and seeing a number, she didn't recognise she let it go to voicemail and then switched it off and slipped into her bag. Whoever it was could wait until tomorrow.
Michael sat down heavily opposite Marie and pouring out the wine said, 'Before you say anything I know it's a school night, but your face and my news tell me we are going to need this and probably more.' Marie managed to smile and said, 'It

certainly turned out to be a very different day and
right now I'm not really sure how I feel about it.'
'Tell me and I will see if I can help.' Said Michael
clasping her hand and giving it a comforting
squeeze.
Marie explained that she had been reluctant to move
on with the factory purchase mainly on Michael's
advice, but her gut instinct was telling her it was
wrong. Then completely unexpectedly Chrissie had
said Zack had offered to finance the project for her.
Michael looked surprised and said, 'Well I didn't
see that coming how do you feel about it, will it still
be Butterflies?'
'Truth, is I haven't a clue, I didn't know how to
react, I suppose it was such a bolt from the blue I
didn't even have time to question it.'
'But Zack I don't get that is he going to be
involved?'
'No, I did at least ask that much.' She went on to
explain that Zack had retired and was bored
especially since Chrissie was working and using the
garden room as a workshop meaning he had
nowhere to write and play his music. He had made
the decision to move back to the village
permanently. While he was walking through the
village, he had gone in to see John Mason on
impulse and made him an offer he couldn't refuse

apparently. Thus, freeing up the workshop for him
keeping Chrissie happy at the same time.
'All I can say he must have plenty of money to
throw around, he won't make a fortune out of
manufacturing.' Said Michael with his accountant's
head on.
'To be honest he seems to have more money than he
could ever spend and that's without all the
properties he owns, he has been with Chrissie for
forty years all be it most of that time touring and
now he wants to make up for lost time.' said Marie
and then went on to say, 'Then to top that they are
getting married.'
'Oh, good heavens when?' asked Michael.
'Well, it has to be soon as their daughter is over
from India for a visit and she apparently helped
push them in to finally tying the knot. Chrissie is so
excited she all but floated in and out of the office.'
'I bet she is, but that decision will leave you with
more problems?'
'Yes, but before we go into that there's more.' She
paused and taking a deep breath, explained that
Betty had been away for the weekend to visit a
solicitor who had a legacy to tell Derek about from
his uncle. Betty was expecting a very little windfall,
but it turned to be out much more than either of
them were expecting. The long and the short of it is

that it is a massive business and property opportunity, that they can't possibly ignore. Meaning Betty is going to be moving away eventually.

'Talk about a bolt from the blue.' Said Michael thoughtfully.

'More like a thunderbolt, not sure at all how I feel or what to do next, everything is moving so fast and in completely different ways to how I anticipated,' she paused as her mobile beeped, she fished it out of her bag and mouthed an apology to Michael who watched closely as Marie paled.

So as not to impose Michael stood up and went to the bar to get another drink and a menu for dinner, he hung back until he saw Marie switch of her phone and slide it back into her bag.

'You alright Marie you look a bit upset,'

'No not upset just a bit overwhelmed so much to think about.'

'What now?'

'Brian, oh don't worry its good news we are invited to meet the family on Sunday for lunch.'

'What both of us?'

'Yes, both of us, as its quite a drive just for lunch Brian has booked us into a guest house.'

'That sounds promising how do you feel about it?'

453

'Nervous, excited I don't know really, will you come?'

'Of course, after all we are a couple, aren't we?'

'I hope so I just worry that I'm leaning too much on you, my life has become so complicated lately.'

'l will help you as much as l can Marie, though it's not a good time but I have to tell you anyway as it will affect us both at some point.'

Marie shifted in her seat and a worried expression crossed her face and she said, 'You mean there is more to worry about?'

Michael took a deep breath and said, 'before you say anything this is not something I have just decided on the plans were in place before you moved into my office and my life.'

'I am actually scared of what you are going to say.' Said Marie tentatively.

'Don't be it's a big step for me but it might eventually help you reach some decisions.' He paused to take a breath and went on, 'I've sold the business and I'm only working for another three months, just in an advisory capacity.'

'Phew that is a big move, but we will be okay, won't we?'

'Of course, I wasn't going to tell you yet but listening to everything you have going on I think

454

it's important that you have the complete picture. We both have massive changes ahead.'

Marie sat back in her chair and said, 'I think we had better eat and you can tell me about it I'm starving I could eat a horse.'

'I fancy fish and chips you going to join me?'

Marie agreed and while Michael was ordering she got out her notebook and started to write one of her lists. Laughing Michael took away her pen and pad and told her that he wanted to tell her why he had sold his business. Marie listened intently as he explained that he had always promised himself that if he could afford it, he wanted to retire at sixty, but it had taken a couple of years longer than he had anticipated. Finding a buyer hadn't been as easy as he had thought but his new partner had come in temporarily and they had agreed a sale last week. He assured Marie that if Butterflies wanted to carry on using the office that had been agreed.

'What do you propose to do with all this free time? You must have a plan,'

'Had a plan, you mean.'

Marie looked puzzled 'I'm confused what was your plan? Why have you changed it, surely if it is something you always wanted to do you must do it.'

'There's a complication, an unexpected complication.' Said Michael quietly.

The waitress brought over their fish and chip
supper and Marie let the subject drop while they ate
the meal. With so much to talk about once the food
was finished, they decided to take their drinks
outside and sit and enjoy the warm evening sun.
Marie determined that while she needed to discuss
her problems, she was disconcerted that Michael's
dilemma was going to affect her as well. She leant
on the solid wooden garden table and looking
directly at him she said, 'come on Michael tell me
what has happened to your plans, you listen to me
all the time, now it's time to for you to talk to me,'
 Michael looked uncomfortable and blushing
slightly said 'It's you, you've changed everything.'
Marie went quiet for once she was almost at a total
loss for words, it was the sudden realisation that she
was important to Michael, and she knew that
whatever she said next could not only affect their
relationship but any decisions she was to make
about the future.
'Me how can I? What have I done?' Marie looked
upset and confused and waited for him to explain.
He took her hand and quietly explained for many
years he had been alone; the plan had formed over
time. Only now had it come together.
 Eventually she spoke quietly and taking his hand,
she said, 'Wow that is a lot to take in. I had no idea

456

that you were thinking of retiring early, or that you had made plans to travel.'

 At this point she was careful not talk about feelings and avoiding this she asked him where he was planning on travelling, Michael explained that for the first year he had planned to fly to America. Once there he was going to hire a RV and travel to all the places he had always meant to visit, go off the beaten track and avoid most of the top tourist spots. For this he reckoned he would be away for about a year and then he would come home and plan phase two which was to be Asia or Australia. Marie interrupted him and admitted that not only had she not been to any of those places she was ashamed to admit that her passport had expired years ago, and she had never bothered to renew it. 'I'm amazed, have you never wanted to travel, explore the world? Asked Michael.

'To be absolutely honest l have never thought about, I suppose I never really had any friends or family to travel with. So apart from a week in Majorca with my mother twenty years ago, which was an unmitigated disaster, that's the only time I used my passport. Who will you be travelling with?'

'Oh, just me, I learnt a long time ago that I like my own company and up until now there hasn't been anyone I could even contemplate spending time with.'

This last comment was met with silence from Marie, she eventually plucked up courage to say, 'I think I understand but I don't think we have been altogether honest with each other and so much has happened today I am feeling confused.' She reached into her bag and Michael laughed as she put her pad and pen on to the table in front of her, and he took the pad and wrote No,1 Michael loves Marie with a little heart beside it. With a fluttering heart Marie responded by saying, 'I don't think I have ever said this to anyone before, but I do love you too, I didn't realise it until you said you were going to be away for a year.'

Michael stood up and taking her arm, he suggested they take a long walk home or rather back to his house and now everything was out in the open they could consider all the options but all he was insisting on was that they plan the future together.

Chrissie

Chrissie left the meeting in the Butterflies office in a state of confusion and trepidation, the future was now looking far different for her now, unlike six months ago. So much to think about. Secretly she was surprised that Marie hadn't pushed for the factory to remain under the Butterflies banner, plus the shock that Betty was moving away just added to the confusion.

Once back home Zack's car was missing so she went down to her workshop to talk to Sue and the girls, she wanted to tell them of her plans personally, not hear it from gossip, she owed them that much. It was important that she show them how much she appreciated all their hard work and support. There were jobs for all of them in the factory. At the same time, she was anxious to speak to Derek, Betty had been a little vague about when he was actually going just saying she was going to follow him at a later date, she would miss him he had been a terrific support she was more than a little worried that she wouldn't be able manage the move without him.

Walking through the garden to the workshop where the windows were all open and she could hear the radio above the hum of conversation and the machines. Sue was at her desk and stood up saying,

459

'So glad you called in Derek has been looking for you he seemed agitated that you weren't here he said to ring him when you have minute.'
 Chrissie agreed that she would, then taking Sue to one side, she explained that the sewing operation was moving lock stock and barrel to John Mason's factory. Sue was pleased as although it had worked well in the workshop, space was becoming short as the workloads were increasing plus it was hot in the summer and cold in the winter. It was as far as she was concerned a perfect solution as the machinists all knew each other, all in all it was a brilliant prospect. Chrissie wanted Sue to tell the team rather than herself. Promising to keep them informed of moving plans and anything else that would affect them. But right now, it was more important that they complete the orders on time.
 Satisfied that she could safely leave Sue to sell the move to the girls, Chrissie went out into the garden and sat on the bench and tried to gather her thoughts, the side gate opened, and Derek poked his head round, the one person she wanted to talk to. Knowing he would have already been told about the move all she could say was 'Oh Derek how am I going to move all this without you?'
'It is all a bit sudden, the last thing I was expecting but this move is an amazing opportunity.'

'When have you got to go?' asked Chrissie.

'It is flexible at the moment so I know Betty will want me to help you out, mind you between you and me, she doesn't seem to keen on going.'

'I'm sure she will be ok after all it is an amazing windfall.' Said Chrissie.

'I worry that she won't leave Butterflies at the last minute, I really need her skills not just in the bookkeeping of the caravan park, but the management of the garden centre.'

'Oh, I didn't realise it was that big.'

'Neither did I at first but luckily there are a couple of managers in place who have been with my uncle for years. Once I put them under new contracts, I can relax a bit so yes if you want, I will be here for the move.'

Chrissie was so relieved she threw her arms round Derek's neck just as Zack and Summer came round the side of the cottage. 'I don't know you ask a girl to marry you and the very next day I find her in the arms of another man!'

Derek laughed and said, 'Zack good to see you mate, this must be your daughter?'

'Yes, this is the elusive Summer home from the darkest depths of India.' Summer stopped him there turning to Derek she said she had heard everything about him and went on to explain that she was home to renew her visa, not for money. Her father always teased her that she only came home when she was broke. Now she was staying on for the wedding, that's where they had been, to organise the pub for the reception. Zack had got a special licence that morning. Chrissie yelled 'OMG when are we getting married? How much time have we got?'

'Precisely a week,' said Zack.

'A week I can't be ready in a week.' Said Chrissie 'what about invitations and everything?'

'Come on mum, you never wanted any of that stuff, Dads booked the pub now Derek you and Betty will be there won't you? Go and ask Sue and the sewing team just give them the time and place, I'll sort everyone else just give me a list.'

Derek went off to talk to Sue, Chrissie followed Zack into the kitchen where Zack had put a bottle of champagne to chill. Just as he was opening it Sue knocked on the door, without waiting burst in and said, 'fantastic news Chrissie can we make your dress please!'

'Mum that's a great idea you don't want anything too bride- ish do you?'

 Before she could answer Zack said, 'I just ask one thing, your flowers must come from the garden and pin them in your hair.'

They looked at each other and Chrissie grinned knowing full well Zack was being sentimental remembering the Isle of Wight festival all those years ago and she said, 'This time I will be wearing clothes!' Turning to Sue, she told her she would be thrilled for them to make her dress. As she was going to the factory with Zack the following morning to finalise the purchase, she asked Sue to go with them to pick out some fabric. She suggested Derek could take Sue then they could start to plan the move at the same time.

Summer borrowed Zack's car and went off with the list to let everyone know the time and date as she left Zack quietly reminded her to insist, that there were to be no presents. This was to be a celebration and more than anything he wanted a party to remember.

 Once they were alone Zack said, 'I'm so pleased we've finally agreed to this,' and he put his hand in his pocket and pulled out a little box 'I thought you deserved this, Summer helped me choose it,' he handed the box to Chrissie, as she opened it she started to cry 'it's perfect emerald my favourite.' As he slipped onto her finger he said, 'I wanted to buy you a big diamond solitaire, but Summer said you would never wear anything flashy, this matches your eyes.'

'Oh, Zack I don't know what to say it's too much.'
'Nothing is too much for you Chrissie, you put up
with me all these years it's payback time.'
 Chrissie twisted the ring round her finger and
looking at the kitchen clock told Zack that she had
to go down to the workshop to help pack the order
that was due out the next day. Zack let her go and
went into the small room he was using as an office
to make a few calls. Anxious to make it a
memorable day for Chrissie and Summer he phoned
round and persuaded his old band members to come
out of retirement to play at the wedding, but at the
same time asking them not to speak to the press,
there was no way would Chrissie want this day
turned into a media frenzy, he had managed to
shield her all these years and didn't want to spoil
things now.

Betty

Betty had left the office feeling, disappointed. Marie had not been as upset at the prospect of her leaving the business as she had anticipated. This left her feeling below par all day. Derek was unsympathetic; he couldn't understand why she couldn't concentrate on their future together and simply walk away from Butterflies.

'I can't explain it Derek, it has all happened so quickly, I feel confused.'

'Everything happens for a reason and this is perfect, in front of us we have the chance of a lifetime, if we keep the bungalow we can always come back in a couple of years. There is always the chance that it will be too much for us to handle. If it does, we can sell up and then will be financially secure.'

'I know, but it's not about money now it's just seeing Marie's reaction she seemed pleased that I will be leaving eventually.' Said Betty wistfully.

'I honestly think Marie doesn't feel like that at all, after all you and Chrissie dropped the bombshell at the same time you didn't really give her time to react. Giving up the manufacturing part of the company is a big issue. You know that it's the most lucrative part. Without it Butterflies is only a small business. '

Betty didn't respond but walked into the kitchen and poured them both a glass of wine, she stood looking out of the window. Derek was right, her problem was more that she had always felt Marie couldn't cope without her. She shook herself and took a sip of her wine, time to go to talk positively to Derek, and best of all plan for the weekend in Venice.

Back in the lounge Derek was sitting by the coffee table with all the new property information spread out. Betty smiled at him and sitting down beside him she handed him his drink and said, 'I think you need to talk me through all of this, I'll make notes so I can work out exactly what you want from me.' Derek reached for his note pad, handing it over to her said, 'I was hoping you would say that.'

He went on going through all aspects slowly, but the priority was the renovations of the house, the plan was for him to go up and supervise the work, leaving Betty to finish up with Butterflies and to move up as soon as there were a couple of rooms habitable, giving her time to pack up the bungalow. Luckily, the kitchen was reasonably new and didn't need any work. As Derek wasn't brilliant on the computer, so Betty agreed to organise food deliveries to be delivered direct. The caravan park was a worry but a conversation with the existing

manager was comforting he agreed to stay on for
three months and he would hand over the books to
Derek when he went up next time so that Betty
could go through them and transfer everything on to
their laptop.

The Garden Centre was a bit more of a worry as it
had been closed for three months and the plant and
tree stock was by now dead. There didn't appear to
be an inventory of the stock in the shop which in
itself was a problem. Derek said, 'What are your
thoughts on the Garden Centre Bet?'

'Not sure but I know it is going to need a lot of
sorting out. Would it be a good idea to keep it
closed for the foreseeable future and then rename it
and re-open when we have had time to start again
with it?'

'Yes, that's pretty much what I was thinking, if I'm
honest that's the bit I'm looking forward to the
most, what about you.'

'Certainly, I fancy the shop part that would suit me
best.' Said Betty brightening up a bit.

'Exactly, that's what I thought.' Answered Derek.

Derek went out of the room leaving Betty studying
the paperwork and came back with a bowl of crisps
and a fresh bottle of wine. They decided that as they
were going to Venice at the weekend, they needed
to check out the major tourist attractions and think

about packing. This resulted in more lists after Betty googled the city and added places to her wish list. They sat in relative silence for a while each thinking their own thoughts. Betty was concentrating on what she was going to pack when she suddenly laughed saying, 'Is there any reason now why I can't go out and buy some new clothes, I've got rainy day savings which technically I'm not going to need now.'

Derek hesitated and then said, 'Good idea, better get something for Chrissies wedding while you're shopping.'

'Gosh that's only next week, will your suit still fit or is that wishful thinking?'

'It will have to fit; I'm not going to need a suit for anything else.'

'Derek, I insist you try it on now, you can't go out in a suit that doesn't fit properly.' Said Betty.

'Besides, you remember what old Crabtree said you must go and see the bank manager.'

'Crumbs, thanks Betty I had forgotten about that, there is so much going on. Tell you what why don't we take the time tomorrow to go shopping and visit the bank? Do you think Marie can spare you for the day?'

'I'm supposed to be at the estate agents but its only minding the phones. I'll put someone else in. I'll send Marie a message now, while I do that go and try on your suit.'

While Derek went through to the bedroom Betty sent a text to Marie, merely apologising that they had urgent financial business to deal with. Derek came back ten minutes later, and Betty laughed it was very tight, with a very shiny seat, when he turned round. They agreed that it was only fit for the bin not even good enough for a charity shop. That decided that, shopping was first on the agenda in the morning.

Betty

'Hurry up Bet, stop dithering around, you know I
have to be at the bank by ten.' Said Derek as he
paced up and down jangling keys nervously.
'Coming just had to speak to Marie, just had some
messages come in that I needed to pass over.'
'Surely she can manage on her own for one day.'
Betty chose to ignore that last remark and picking
up her handbag walked past him out to the car.
 It was only a short drive into town and Derek
parked the car and as Betty wasn't needed in the
bank, she arranged to meet him in Marks and
Spencer coffee shop in a couple of hours' time. First
Betty had a plan, Derek's suit could wait for the
first time in years she was going to shop for herself
without worrying about the cost. There was a little
boutique just of the high street and for once instead
of gazing in the window, wishing she could afford
to buy. Today she was going to shop seriously,
fulfilling a fantasy that she had had for some years,
to be able to walk down the street carrying one of
the boutiques fancy bags. First, she had to walk
through the door instead of drooling at the window.
Today was different, Derek would no longer be able
to complain about her spending, besides she had
been saving for a rainy day in a separate bank
account. Now it looked very much as if the rainy

day was a real long way off or maybe it had passed by. Betty peered in the window, her heart racing the outfits in the window were a little too formal for Chrissies wedding. Gingerly she pushed open the door and looked around. There at the side was a rail of dresses the sign above them saying 'Just Arrived.' The only assistant in the shop was busy with another customer so Betty took advantage and browsed, without even glancing at the price tags. Picking out three dresses she held them up in front of her and the assistant left the other lady for a moment and led Betty to one of the plush changing rooms at the back. The dresses slipped on easily and Betty realised that she had lost weight without even trying, it must have been since working with Marie they had frequently missed lunch. Quickly she discarded the pink spotted dress and was then stuck on deciding between a cornflower blue wrap dress and pale grey and white striped one with a matching white bolero. Both completely different to her usual style, in reckless moment she handed them both over to the eager assistant without checking the price tags. Nevertheless, she did flinch when she glanced at the receipt.

Looking at her watch she realised there was still time to buy shoes and of course a handbag before meeting up with Derek for coffee. Finding exactly what she wanted and feeling extremely pleased with herself she walked to Marks and Spencer.

Derek was waiting in the coffee shop, beaming all over his face. Standing up he put his arm around her shoulder he took her bags from her and as they sat down, he said 'That was the first time in my life that I have had a Bank Manager practically kissing my feet.'

'It went well then,' asked Betty. Before he could answer she said I could murder a coffee before you fill me in with all the details.'

Derek grinned and went to the counter; he came back with two coffees and two slices of cake.

Sitting down he said, 'thought we should celebrate with cake.'

'We should celebrate with more than cake but first what happened at the bank? Where are we really with all this money?'

'It was quite straightforward really first he contacted Crabtree who went through the finances in detail and arrange transfer of all the funds into one account by the end of the week.'

'Is that wise putting all our eggs in one basket?' asked Betty.

'It's only temporary, we are going to have a business account, and new joint account and we have to decide on what kind of investments we need. I have all the paperwork for you to look at. He wants to see us together in ten days' time to sign everything. '

'Sounds alright to me more to the point are you happy with it?'

'Yes, I think so, we need to go over all the figures, but there is more money than Crabtree told us but that's nothing to worry about.'

'It is a huge amount, just feels unreal, a bit like winning the lottery at the moment.' Said Betty.

'I suppose it does but even so we have a lot of hard work ahead of us if we are going to make it work for us.'

'I know that, but it is an exciting prospect.'

'You've changed your tune a bit what's convinced you?'

Betty didn't answer immediately unsure whether to admit that shopping had excited her instead she told him that as Butterflies was changing and everyone seemed to be going in new directions. Now she was looking forward to a new challenge.

'Now do you want another coffee, or shall we go and get me a posh suit, looking at all your bags it seems Marks and Spencer's isn't good enough for you anymore.'

Betty had the grace to blush and said, 'I just wanted a change, but do you know what, I don't feel the slightest bit guilty.'

Finishing their coffee, they went through the store to the menswear dept. Betty was looking forward seeing Derek in a suit again. He soon picked out a smart navy suit and for once didn't need encouraging to buy shirts, shoes and ties to match. Normally he would insist that his old wardrobe was good enough. They left the store both laden with bags. Betty did have to make a detour to the lingerie department, after all something a little sexy was in order after all this could be a weekend to remember.

Once outside it was just a short walk back to the car, and Derek suggested they stop at the pub and have a late lunch.

Betty readily agreed saying 'saves me cooking tonight and I can pack ready for our trip tomorrow.'

'I had almost forgotten that, I was just thinking how that one phone call from the solicitor has completely changed our lives.' Derek said thoughtfully.

'I'm sure it's for the better.' Replied Betty as she leant over and squeezed his hand.

Chrissie

Chrissie was sitting alone in looking fondly around the workshop. Anticipating that when Derek was back from Venice on Tuesday, they would begin the move to the new premises. Until then this was still Chrissies special space, she was going to be sad to turn it over to Zack.

A knock on the door brought her out of her reverie, she called out 'Come in Sue you really don't have to knock.'

Sue walked in holding a dress covered with a sheet. 'Oh, my goodness Sue have you finished it already? OOH let me see!'

Sue hesitated and said 'we followed your instructions Chrissie; just hope it's what you were expecting.' Carefully removing the protective sheet Sue revealed the dress.

It was exactly as Chrissie had sketched. Plunging neckline to show off her boobs that Zack so loved. The skirt was tiered, finished at ankle length. Each layer of the skirt was trimmed with pale cream satin roses exactly matching the cream embossed satin that Sue had found in the warehouse of their new factory.

Taking off her jeans and tee shirt she held the dress up to the mirror and ran her fingers down the laced back. Chrissie slipped it over her head, Sue zipped up the side. Chrissie spun round to show the movement of the tiered skirt. Looking at herself in the mirror she said, 'Sue it's perfect I love it.' Then she went quiet. Sue asked her what was wrong. Chrissie answered that there wasn't anything wrong, and the dress was exactly what she had pictured herself wearing at her wedding and it feels strange the fact that after forty years together they were finally getting married.

'Never a cross word eh Chrissie?' laughed Sue.

'Cross words? Truth is if we added it up, we have probably been apart far longer than we have been together

'I'm so glad, I wasn't sure but seeing it on you I can see its perfect for you. Now what about flowers and something for your hair, I know you don't want a veil

'I will pick some roses from the garden for my bouquet and for Zack, I will just pin them in my hair.'

Sue looked at her quizzically and laughing Chrissie explained that she had pinned flowers in her hair at the Isle of Wight festival where she had first met Zack. Omitting the fact that she had stripped naked and run into the sea with her hippy friends.

'Before you take it off, I ran up a muslin slip to wear underneath, in case you wanted to protect your

modesty.' She paused then laughing went on
'Though looking at that neckline I think it may be
too late for that.'
'Cheeky,' said Chrissie 'my boobs have always been
my best feature, I'm not about to hide them now.'
'Joking apart do you like it really?'
'Yes, it's perfect, I love the shade of cream and the
edging round the tiers is exactly the right size and
colour, where on earth did you find it at such short
notice?'
'I was over at the factory and John gave me free rein
to pick anything I want. This trim was ordered in
error, so I put it to good use. There is plenty more
over there in that box if you need it for anything.'
'I may use some instead of ribbon with my bouquet.'
Said Chrissie.
 Chrissie slipped off the dress and handed it back to
Sue to hang up and said, 'Now down to business
what do I owe you?'
Sue hesitated and looking embarrassed said.
'Nothing, call it a labour of love.'
'I insist, how much'
'I promised not to tell you, but Zack paid for it, very
well I must add, also he gave us all a bonus!' Sue
said sheepishly
'Typical Zack he can't keep his nose out of
anything.' said Chrissie grinning.

'Just as well' said Sue 'If he hadn't done just that we wouldn't be moving to the factory.'

'Very true,' replied Chrissie, 'leads us nicely into where are we with the move?'

'I think we have everything under control, Derek's away this weekend but he has organised a van and help for shifting the machines when he's back. Then the factory shuts down for annual holidays and everything will be set up before you get back from your honeymoon.'

Chrissie giggled, 'Hardly a honeymoon we are just going to one of Zack's country houses to sort out some equipment and organise putting the house on the market. Somehow Zack needs to clear the house and talk to the staff.'

'Goodness he's got staff?'

'He has several houses, that are all permanently staffed, they will have to be told what is happening, but I know Zack will pay them off.' She paused, 'So what with the factory move there is no way we could even think of going away. We will later, but the wedding has to be soon as Summer has to be back in India by the end of the month.'

Sue covered the dress carefully with the sheet and as she hung it up Chrissie told her to get off home and with a quick hug, she left Chrissie to close up arranging to meet up and go over the plans in detail.

She was delighted that Chrissie loved her dress, extremely pleased that she had admitted to her that that Zack had paid the team a large amount of money, knowing that they would pull out all the stops to give Chrissie the dress she wanted. Seeing her so happy with the final result made everything worthwhile.

After Sue left Chrissie sat at her desk in the corner of the now quite crowded workshop and following in the style of Marie began to make a list. Zack had taken Summer to check out the house he had bought her while it was still empty before the tenants moved in. He had with no expense spared had it completely renovated and wanted Summer's opinion before he rented it out. He was still uncertain as to whether the place should be furnished or not. He could of course furnish it from one of the houses he was selling but he would let his daughter decide on that one. Cunningly he had told Chrissie that they were going to his house to go over the contents, but the reality was with the help of Summer he was planning a surprise honeymoon.

Marie

The alarm had gone off at 6.30 am but Marie was up and pacing around long before that, leaving Michael asleep in her bed. Last night she had wanted him to be near her, but illogically this morning she wanted to be alone with her thoughts for a while.

These past few weeks felt very much as if her life was going into freefall. Not for the first time, she was almost unable to put her thoughts into any kind of logical order. Life had become a huge challenge. There was Butterflies, the business she loved and cherished but the changes ahead were happening fast and along with her turbulent personal life she was struggling to prioritise anything.

Today was momentous in itself Michael was driving her to meet with her son Brian and his family. A son and family she hadn't known existed until very recently.

Sensing her apprehension, Michael was up and showered and sat Marie down and made her some toast and sat with her while she ate it. Then leaving her to get ready he sat at his laptop and sent of messages to clients in preparation for meetings planned for the next week.

'I'm ready Michael,' said Marie. Michael looked up approvingly, 'You look great, I'll put the bags in the car, while you lock up.'

He took the bags to the car and waited; Marie slid into the seat next to him. Struggling with shaking hands she tried to fasten her seat belt. Seeing her dilemma and taking charge Michael leant over and fastened the belt for her. Without saying a word he drove off, Marie relaxed slightly and sat back and closed her eyes while listening to Michael's favourite Four Seasons CD. It wasn't until they came to a stop in a traffic jam on the motorway that she spoke. 'I know I keep asking this Michael, but do you really think I'm doing the right thing? What if they all hate me, I don't know how to deal with teenagers, it's scary enough having a son after all these years but a whole family, it's just not real.'

'I will say it again Marie, just be yourself and take everything as it comes, if it doesn't work out then it wasn't meant to be and we will move on together.'

'I know but I'm just terrified, it has been so much to take in and I really have no idea what to expect or even how to behave.'

'It is a big thing I admit but they know as little about you as you do them so just take this visit as it comes. After all, you can at least walk away, knowing you have tried if you feel uncomfortable.'

481

Marie merely nodded and turned away to look out
of the window. Deep in thought, it didn't matter
how much Michael had tried to placate her the
prospect of meeting her new family was quite
frankly terrifying. The rest of the journey was spent
in relative silence as Michael had put on another
soothing CD.
 Pulling up outside the address Brian had texted
over to Marie, she was pleasantly surprised to see
the house was larger than she had visualised. The
drive curved round making parking easy. Michael
parked behind a brand-new BMW and smiled to
himself, knowing the car would get Marie's
immediate approval, knowing her son had the same
taste in cars as she had. Taking her hand, he told her
not to worry, the bed and breakfast that Brian had
booked for the night was on the seafront, he
promised they could walk on the beach and blow
away any cobwebs and chat about everything later.
 Marie took a quick peek in the mirror, after
checking her lipstick satisfied that she looked okay
she stepped out of the car squared her shoulders
said, 'let's do this before I lose my nerve.'
Michael rang the doorbell, while Marie stood
admiring the beautifully manicured garden. The
polished oak door opened quickly by Brian who
kissed Marie on the cheek and putting out his hand

to Michael he said 'you must be Michael; Marie has told me all about you.'

'All good I hope,' laughed Michael.

Brian stood back and invited them in, ushering them into the front room he said, 'Meet Alice.' Alice walked towards them and kissed them both warmly on the cheek. Although at that moment Marie was convinced her eyes were cold and wary and she was embarrassed to feel her palms sweating and discreetly wiped them on her black jeans, grateful for her choice of wearing a dark colour.

Alice spoke, 'Somewhere we have two daughters who are more than likely glued to their phones and haven't even heard the doorbell.'

Marie laughed nervously and followed Brian through the house and out into the back garden, where Alice had set a table ready for lunch on the patio. She walked over to one of the chairs and carefully pushed a sleepy shiatzu off the floral cushion. 'Oh, he's so cute what is his name? Asked Marie.'

'We call him Rocket, why Rocket I have no idea why that was the girl's choice, but a rocket he is not. Cute he is but he's greedy and spoilt, why in fact sometimes I think he is running this house.' Said Alice smiling but Marie noticed that her smile didn't reach her eyes. Lunch was to be served on the terrace and Alice poured home-made lemonade into tall glasses. Michael stepped in and led the conversation carefully avoiding who Marie actually was. This suited Marie as talking about her business was a neutral subject and Michael was keen to talk about his early retirement and plans to travel. They were interrupted by the two missing daughters appeared, Marie gasped standing in front of her were twins, not only was she not expecting this a shiver went over her as all she could see were two teenage girls who looked uncannily similar to how she had been at that age. Alice quickly said 'This is Poppy and Millie, 'hesitating she said 'Girls meet Marie.'

Marie smiled and as she said hello the girls sat down and proceeded to dish up their lunch. Marie was grateful at this moment she hadn't been introduced as grandma that would have certainly been a step too far at this point. Lunch was a delicious home-made quiche with salad, with fruit salad to finish. Once the meal was over Poppy began to question Marie about Butterflies, Millie didn't pretend to listen just plugged in her earphones and ignored everyone. Poppy's questions became personal when she asked Marie how she knew her, Dad. At this point Alice intervened and aske Poppy to take Rocket for a walk and she started to clear the table. Seizing the moment Marie gathered up some dishes and followed Alice through to the kitchen. It was here that Marie plucked up courage to have a heart to heart with her by saying, 'Thank you for inviting Michael and myself today, I do appreciate that it is a difficult situation for all of you, but I want you to hear the truth from me. I'm not sure how much Brian told you.'

'Brian obviously told me what he knew but you know men they don't go into detail so yes sit down and let's chat, do have a coffee.' She poured out two mugs of coffee and sat down at the table opposite Marie, who took a deep breath and began.

'I'll try not to get too emotional, but you must understand this is difficult to relive what was a very painful part of my life. Made more painful by meeting your daughters today, I thought for some reason that they would be younger. How old are they I didn't like to ask them.'

'They are fourteen, fifteen in two months.' Answered Alice.

'That's when it all started for me, I was fourteen, and I was raped by my uncle. I was scared to tell my mother as she was very close to her brother, but she found out when I was taken to the doctor because I kept being sick. When the doctor finally

realised, I was pregnant he told my mother who
promptly sent me away. The fact that I had been
raped was never discussed or addressed in any way.
I missed almost a whole school year and spent
seven months in a grim unmarried mother's hostel.
When my baby was born, I wasn't allowed to see it,
it was taken away.' She hesitated and went on, 'I
still say it because that was how I always thought
about the baby, I was told it had died, they thought
it best that I never saw it, as it would have been to
upsetting for me.'
'Oh, my goodness how awful, what happened next?'
asked Alice.
 Marie went on to tell Alice how she had been taken
home and sent back to school and the subject was
never mentioned again for all intents and purposes
she had never been raped or given birth.
 Alice was horrified and seeing Marie's obvious
distress she went over to Marie and giving her a
hug, 'Brian did give me a brief outline, but hearing
the story from you has put it in more perspective.'
Marie continued, 'Seeing your girls has thrown me a
bit, all through lunch I kept seeing myself at that
age and comparing my life with theirs. I so wish my
mother had protected me more. '
'It is a really sad story Marie, I find it hard to

believe that your mother could give away your baby, her grandchild.' Said Alice.

'It is hard on so many levels, I got married and quickly divorced because my husband was desperate for a family, but I couldn't let myself get pregnant again because I was terrified of having a stillborn baby, plus I never told him about the pregnancy.'

'Marie did you have counselling?'

'I did but I was too young to benefit from it, unfortunately the trauma of it shaped my life. I did marry,' she paused, 'looking back I think it was to get away from my mother more than love.'

Alice asked quietly, 'you and Michael is this a permanent relationship or are you just friends?'

'I want it to be permanent, but it is complicated we have to sort a few things out, it's a relief he has been with me all through this difficult time and he is very caring,'

With that Brian came back into the room and said that he had spoken to Michael and he had agreed to that they should stay and Brian began to open bottles of wine. He looked at Maries doubting face and said 'I'm going to light the barbecue and you're staying for supper, later you can get a taxi back to the hotel,'

He walked over to Marie and took her hand and grinning he said 'come on Mum, time to relax and get to know us with a few glasses of wine.' Marie although taken aback with the use of the word mum. The first time she had ever been called that, it brought a tear to her eye.

She smiled and stood up and followed her son into the garden where Michael was having an animated conversation with the two teenagers, Michael looked over at her and winked, it was in that instance that Marie knew everything was going to work out well. All the weeks of stressing about meeting her extended family vanished. She looked round the table at the group all happily chatting. It all came to head when Poppy stood up and said 'grandma, will you sit with dad I want a photo of you both together' this nearly broke Marie and a huge tear rolled down her cheek as Brian came and stood behind her with one hand on her shoulder.

It was late when Brian called a taxi, they said their goodbyes, both were really quiet in the back of the car until they got back to the hotel.

Michael opened the door for Marie and led her towards the bar saying 'I think we should sit and have a nightcap before we go to bed. I know I promised you a walk along the beach, but I think it's a bit late.'

Marie merely nodded and sank down into one of
the comfortable armchairs, once their drinks were
served Michael took Marie's hand and said, 'l don't
want to ruin what l think has been a fabulous day, I
can see how elated you are but there is something l
need to ask you Marie.'
Marie smiled and said, 'it's fine ask away.' her heart
was beating fast knowing that she loved Michael
but crossed her fingers the last thing she wanted
was a proposal.
 Michael said, 'l was going to leave this until
another day but to be honest l'm bursting to ask
you,' he hesitated then went on 'will you come
travelling with me?'
Without pausing to think Marie replied, 'yes, yes l
will.'
Michael leant over and kissed her and then asked
the other question that was bothering him, 'what
about Butterflies? Will you be able to walk away
from it, after all it is your baby.'
'I have thought a lot about all of this and to be
honest so much has happened to me this past year
l've realised that it's time for me to follow my
heart, l've followed my head for too long and l 've
missed so much.' she paused and took a sip of her
drink and said, 'l know exactly what l want and
today has just underlined what is missing from my

life. Butterflies will carry on without me, I have planned for that so yes I'm coming with you.'
 Michael sighed with relief and they sat quietly finishing their drinks and Michael said, 'there is a lot to talk about but now we need to get a good night's sleep as we have to drive home in the morning and we both have a busy day to make up for being away.

Betty

The sun was shining when Betty and Derek landed
in Venice by ten o'clock in the morning. Once
through the security they stood outside the airport
and Derek surprised Betty by saying 'I think we
should take the water bus to the hotel. It takes a bit
longer, but we get to see more, give us a chance to
soak up the atmosphere.'

Betty agreed and they walked in the direction of the
waterbus, dragging their cases behind them. The
water bus stopped close to their hotel, which Betty
had upgraded as soon as their financial future had
changed so dramatically. The hotel did not
disappoint it was opulent, typically Italian decor.
They were greeted as if they were royalty. Betty
was delighted when they got into the room, it was
overlooking the canal and the large doors opened
inwards to reveal an ornate Juliet balcony. Betty
stood there just drinking in the view, Derek came up
behind her and put his arm round her shoulder and
whispered, 'thank you Bet this was a really good
idea, just what we needed but I'm so pleased we are
here but right now I'm starving,'

Betty laughed and agreed she was starving too;
they decided to take a stroll alongside the canal and
have a late lunch. The lunch was superb and sitting
in the sunshine and drinking a delicious Italian

sparkling wine just the tonic that they both needed.
The meal lasted for longer than they had anticipated
and Betty suggested they take a slow stroll back to
the hotel and sit on the patio outside and plan the
next day. Unused to both of them feeling so relaxed,
Derek took the initiative and order a bottle of wine
to be drunk while they deliberated on the next day's
activities. Once they had reached an amicable
agreement to Dereks delight and possibly with the
help of the wine, Betty began to talk animatedly
about their future and as darkness fell, they decided
to have an early night. Betty walked up the stairs
with her fingers crossed behind her back. Saying a
silent prayer thankful that she was wearing new
almost sexy underwear and for the first time in a
very long time not only would they be sharing a
room but a queen-sized bed. All she asked was that
the Venetian air would work its magic and finally
bring back the spark in their marriage.
 The next morning, they set off early, just having
coffee both feeling full of the meal they ate
yesterday. Before they went out unknown to Betty,
Derek who was feeling completely renewed from
the night before, went to reception and ordered
champagne and special dinner on the terrace, for
when they got back from their day exploring
Venice.

Derek was desperate to go for a gondola ride and up until now Betty had strongly disapproved of spending so much money. Somehow the magic of Venice or the newly ignited spark between completely changed her mind and didn't even complain when Derek splashed out extra to have a gondolier who would serenade them.

After the trip Betty declared it was one of the most special experiences she had experienced, while Derek smugly counted his brownie points and secretly rejoiced his late god father's generosity, at last Betty was smiling.

After a break for coffee, Betty said 'I have decided that maybe we should change our plans for this afternoon, there is a lot of walking involved and it's warmer than l thought it would be.'

'l don't mind at all Betty, what do you fancy doing?'

'l really would like to go to the Murano glass factory, as we need to buy a wedding present for Chrissie and Zac.'

Derek googled the factory, to reach the island they had to catch the vaporetto where they were able to watch a glass blowing display. Followed by a visit to the shop, where Betty was in her element and wandered around wishing they could buy far more than they could carry. Delighted to find the assistant

spoke perfect English, Betty managed to get details
of their wholesale section. While Derek waited
patiently outside and Betty bought three beautiful,
coloured glass butterflies.

By this time, they were both exhausted and made
their way back to the hotel for a nap before dinner.
Derek was pleased and more than a little surprised
when Betty showed him her purchases and the
business card for future bulk purchasing. Betty was
quick to explain that she was mentally making plans
for the garden centre shop she was planning on
developing and running when they finally made the
move to Norfolk.

At last, they were both moving in the same
direction in complete harmony and after a well-
deserved nap they dressed and went down for three
course meal, that could only be described as five
stars.

After the most romantic evening, either of them
could remember spending in years. The trip having
worked its magic and reenergised them both. They
held hands as they went up to bed and fell asleep in
one another's arms.

Unfortunately, the next morning they had to leave
after breakfast to catch their plane home, both
happier and more optimistic than they had been for
a very long time.

494

Chrissie

Chrissie almost bounced down the stairs causing Summer to scream 'slow down mum everything is organised nothing for you to be rushing around like that.'

As she said that Zack came in carrying a pile of presents and cards. 'Where on earth have you been? Asked Chrissie,

Zack laughed and said 'I thought you would be flapping so I went down to the factory, just to check all is ready.'

'Well, is it?'

'Absolutely Sue is organised all ready to go next week, they had all these parcels for us and they are going home now to get ready.'

'That's good but I'm not sure we should be going away there's still stuff to do.'

'We are going and everything will be fine just go and get dressed. Summer help your crazy mother get ready,

Summer led Chrissie upstairs while Zack paced up and down the lounge, his nerves were jangling, unusual for a man who had been used to getting on stage and performing in front of thousands of people. Today was different, he was marrying his first and if he was being totally honest his only love, with his daughter as matron of honour. A big moment which he had thought would never happen.

When Chrissie came downstairs, she looked so beautiful and Zack immediately remembered the day they met, to him Chrissie was smiling as broadly as she did while running naked into the sea after the Isle of Wight festival all those forty years ago.

The three of them walked the very short distance to the local church, Chrissie had insisted on walking, as a car would be a waste of money as it was only about a hundred and fifty yards and the pub was practically next door where the reception was going to be held. Zack had been in to check out that everything was ready.

The little church was packed and there were a few mutterings as Zack and Chrissie walked hand in hand down the aisle, breaking tradition, with Summer following closely behind.

After the short service, the wedding party walked to the pub to have their photos taken in the garden which was decorated with flowers. The sun shone all afternoon, the buffet was declared as superb. In true Zack style the champagne flowed, but Chrissie truly thought the highlight of the day was when Zack's band set up in the huge marquee, she could see that Zack was itching to sing with them for one last gig, she gave him a gentle shove, without hesitating he was soon on the small stage singing his heart out, Dedicating his performance to his beautiful wife and daughter.

Chrissie took the time to mingle searching out Marie and Michael who were standing arm in arm moving gently to the music. Marie said, 'what a perfect day Chrissie, we are so happy for you.'

'Thank you, I still can't believe all this is actually happening. Zack still won't tell me where we are going, he's even had Summer pack my case.'

Marie laughed, 'just enjoy yourself you have a lot to do when you come back. Betty and I would like to make a short speech when the band have an interval, please.'

Chrissie looked a little bemused but said 'of course I'll tell them.' she moved on to find Betty who gave her a big hug, along with a beaming Derek gave her a kiss on the cheek.

'How was Venice, I hope it lived up to your expectations, 'asked Chrissie.

Before Betty could respond Derek answered, 'Chrissie it was a fantastic break, just wish we had gone for longer, we will definitely go back one day. Betty laughed and said, 'It did us both the world of good.'

'I hear you are giving a speech with Marie later.'

'Yes, it will be short we just had few things to say before we all go our separate ways.'
Chrissie looked surprised but before she could comment Summer called her away Zack had finished singing and it was time to cut the cake. While the cake was being distributed Marie and Betty were preparing their speech.

They walked on to the stage and Marie grabbed the microphone, 'testing testing.' This silenced the chatter in the marquee she went on to say, 'l would like to thank Zack for all he has done for Butterflies and for Chrissie especially, and to formally welcome him to our village, such a shame he has been in hiding from us for forty years,' she paused for laughter and then said 'come up here with us please Chrissie.

Chrissie looked a little bemused but obeyed, Betty took the microphone and said, 'l will keep this brief as l know you are all desperate for the band to come back and replace us.' she paused and looked at Marie and said, 'On behalf of all the butterflies here.' a cheer went up. 'l heard yesterday that Marie is moving on, off travelling with Michael, meaning a huge change for the business.' she stopped for a moment and pulled a parcel out of a bag and handed it to Marie. 'This is for you as a small thank you for the fun we have had with the Butterflies business

and to thank you for involving me in what has been
a fun adventure.' She turned to Chrissie and said
'this is for you Chrissie and to thank you for all the
fun and inspiration you have brought to the business
and wish good luck with the newly named factory
'Butterflies Lingerie.' both Marie and Chrissie
opened their parcels and inside were the stunning
Murano glass butterflies that Betty had carefully
brought back from Venice.

Chrissie was openly crying and Marie took the
microphone saying 'oh my goodness so much
emotion for one day, l've one more thing to say l
promise it won't take long, Betty here is also off on
an exciting new venture in Norfolk so l can honestly
say we butterflies are spreading our wings and
about to experience huge changes again in our lives.
The Butterflies name will live on as we are handing
over the reins of the office to Jenny,' she paused
while everyone clapped. 'Thank you all for your
support,'

As they went to leave the stage a container was
opened, hundreds of butterflies were let loose.
Causing everyone to cheer and clap. Zack stood
grinning at the side of the stage, aware for the first
time he had done as much as he could to give
everyone a day to remember,

499

Printed in Dunstable, United Kingdom